Zelo's Daughters

Ann Neely

Parson's Porch

Book Publishing

Zelo's Daughters
ISBN: Softcover 978-1-951472-28-3
Copyright © 2017 by Ann Neely

Cover art: Original watercolor by Judy Ford.

Bible verses and quotations are from the New American Standard Bible, The Open Bible edition. Thomas Nelson Publishing

To order additional copies of this book, contact:
Parson's Porch Books
1-423-475-7308
www.parsonsporch.com

Parson's Porch Books is an imprint of **Parson's Porch & Book Publishers** in Cleveland, Tennessee, which has double focus. We focus on the needs of creative writers who need a professional publisher to get their work to market, & we also focus on the needs of others by sharing our profits with those who struggle in poverty to meet their basic needs of food, clothing, shelter and safety.

With Gratitude

On a sticky note attached to the top of my computer I printed: DON'T FORGET YAHWEH. Then beneath a line running across, the words, THE HOLY SPIRIT. Below that I drew a cross and below that, JESUS. When I open my computer that note flutters and reminds me to pray. There were times I would be so excited to start writing, I would get a cup of coffee and begin cranking out words. Dead words. Whatever life this book contains did not come from me. So, thank you, Yahweh, for giving me permission to write our book. And thank you for all your help—even the times you woke me in the wee hours to point out a redundancy or a cliché.

A special thank you to my husband, Bob, my own computer guru, for all your support and computer help. I tried your patience daily, for I am a digital dunce. A huge thank you to our son, Scott. You cheered for me from the beginning, and you said the nicest thing: "After the first fifty pages, Mom, I forgot you wrote it." And this: "It doesn't sound girly." To our son, Rob, and daughter, Michele, time and circumstance precluded your involvement, but you were always on my mind.

Deedie Scaife, my Best Friend Forever and *Forever*, there must be better words than "I love you."

Cece Warner, sister-in-law, sister: Your constancy and love mean so much to me.

Pat Jewell, you set my mind at rest from the beginning and encouraged me. Johnnie Lu Stephens, church librarian, you allowed me to keep stacks of reference books at my home for a year. What a blessing that was. Thank you for your love and support, my sweet neglected friends, Midge Stewart, and Faye Varady.

Mary Webb, Concord, CA, I will never forget your Creative Writing Class, your encouragement, and the open mic reading you took us to in Berkeley. What a trip!

Perry Ritchie, you are a foundation stone in my spiritual journey.

Last, I want to thank David Russell Tullock of Parson's Porch & Company. You are an answer to a specific prayer: Yahweh, please go before this book, and find just the right publisher.

Book One

Chapter 1

IN LATE SUMMER THE NILE RIVER floods its banks and replenishes the land with rich volcanic silt scoured from the southern mountains of Ethiopia. When the waters recede, the Egyptians plant their seeds and rejoice in that great annual blessing sent by Sothis, god of the Nile.

Yahweh, God of the Hebrew people, sent a man named Moses with a different kind of blessing, a different kind of flood. Its waters rose on a swell of slavery and crested on ten plagues. It overflowed the land when Hebrew slaves threw down their tools and abandoned the quarries, the jade mines, the dredging barges, the brickyards, the dying vats, and Pharaoh's building projects.

At the behest of Moses, the descendants of Abraham, Isaac, and Jacob asked their former masters for gifts: silver, gold, and clothing. They stripped the coffers of Egypt. Then the Hebrew people, in a swirling mass of over a million souls, drained from every corner of their captivity. They left Cairo and Memphis and Ramses. They flowed north and returned to the land of Goshen, the rich delta Joseph had given his brothers 430 years before. From there Moses led the twelve tribes into the wilderness toward the Promised Land.

The flood of Yahweh, God of Israel, did not replenish. The flood of Yahweh, known as The Exodus, stripped away the nation of Israel and decimated the land of the Pharaohs.

Enoch and Rachel, Hebrews of the tribe, Manasseh, buffeted by surging crowds escaping the city of Ramses, made their way toward Goshen. At dawn they had left the paved streets and prosperous neighborhoods of Pharaoh's officials and the vizier's villa where Rachel lived as a house slave. Now, with the early sun peeking over thatched roofs of mud brick hovels, Enoch led his sister through a maze of narrow passages and shadowed alleyways. Swept along like two fig leaves caught in a swirling eddy, they struggled through every crossing. People merged from all sides, their possessions distributed among family members, or if they were fortunate, piled on wagons and carts loaded with old people, children, dogs, and baby goats and lambs. Animal dung slicked into mud and added to the stench of sweat and stale beer on clothes and, it seemed to Rachel, the foul breath of everyone who passed. Din and babble drowned conversation.

Anyone who noticed would have seen the strong resemblance in the two young Hebrews: square jaw, broad forehead, expressive eyebrows arched over brown, almond-shaped eyes. And the hair—a mass of kinky, black curls. As much to steady her as to keep her from bolting, Enoch kept a firm grip on Rachel's arm. She had not wanted to leave her mistress. At fifteen Rachel was tall and fit; if she decided to bolt, he would have a chase. Enoch pulled his sister close and shouted in her ear, "Can you walk faster? We have to get home by sunset."

Stymied by a cart with a broken wheel, the crowd pushed forward and then surged around the cart, forcing Rachel against the rough wood. "Enoch, stop!" She wrenched her arm free, struggled against the tide of bodies, and turning into a dim alley, inched along the wall. *Hopi would never bring the carriage this way,* she thought. Keeping a tight grip on her bags, she pressed her back against the wall. The pouch her mistress had tied around her waist earlier that morning gouged. She reached around to shift the metal objects it held.

Before sunrise, Rachel had heard her mistress coming down the long hall from the kitchen stairs, her sandals slapping the marble floor, light from her lamp playing on the walls. Dressed in an ankle-length white tunic, her black hair smooth and shiny with oil, the young woman entered the sleeping room the two had shared for five years. "What did Hopi want this early?" Rachel asked. Asmath did not answer. She stopped and knelt at the corner shrine before a variety of gods of wood, stone, gold, and jade. After a few moments she rose, wiping tears from her pock-marked cheeks. Even in low light, Rachel could see the aftermath of the worst of the nine plagues the family had experienced—the plague of boils brought by that strange man, Moses. Rachel watched as Asmath moved around the room and lighted three more lamps.

The walls, painted with murals from ceiling to floor, seemed to come alive and dance in the flickering light. Blessed by Ra in the fan-shaped rays of the sun, brown Egyptian women in white tunics, their hair braided, happy in their work, cut papyrus, poured water, bathed in the blue water of the Nile. Babies and children, depicted as tiny adults, nursed and frolicked. How many times over the last five years had the two girls sat upon their bed and made up stories about the women. There was Marwat, kneeling with her jar among the reeds at the water's edge. If she filled six jars her father would give her a gift. What would it be? And Hepsut. Her baby fell in the river and drowned. But wait. She prayed to Ma'at, the goddess of harmony, who restored the baby to life.

"Your brother has come for you," said Asmath. She sat on the end of the bed.

"Come for me?"

"To take you home."

"Take me *home*?"

"Stop repeating everything I say, please, and get dressed. Put on the blue linen.

"But this is my home. Which brother?"

"Enoch. He has a gap in his teeth, like yours. Other than that, he is well-favored. Maybe I'll go with you."

"Enoch...he is my oldest brother. He must be twenty-eight or thirty by now."

"He says we have to hurry." Asmath pulled the night dress over Rachel's head and slipped on the blue dress. "Sit down. I'm going to put your hair in one plait; that's the quickest. Who is going to oil and care for this pile of hair?" She wrenched Rachel's woolly, black hair into a single, thick braid, reaching to mid-back, and fastened a gold and mother-of-pearl clamp on the end.

"But I am not going anywhere. I'm staying here. This is my home."

"Come with me." Asmath threw a cloak over Rachel's shoulders and then covered her own with a shawl of white wool. She took Rachel's hand and led her from their sleeping room to the dark porch. The recent plague of hail had destroyed the lush vines and overhead lath that had housed hundreds of tiny, green tree frogs. Now, their cacophony silenced, the few survivors clung to the stucco walls, peeping pitifully. Below, in the destroyed garden, at the base of a split tree, doves cooed, their sad murmur seeming to mourn their lost nest of eggs.

The young women stood at the once-ornate banister, now splintered, overlooking a wide plain dotted with barely visible villas, homes of Pharaoh's court and officials. Beyond the walled garden, beyond the dark strip of the Nile, a pale lavender horizon promised a clear dawn. That secluded porch had always been their special place. There, under the vine-covered lath, the mistress and her slave-companion learned to weave. There, on hot afternoons, Hopi, their bodyguard, a eunuch trusted to sleep outside their door, pulled the cord that swung the reed ceiling fan. Had they not laughed and watched him doze while his huge arm pumped up and down? "Listen," said Asmath. "Do you hear it? Look out there. Do you see it?"

In the distance, on the edge of the desert, far from the mosquitoes of the humid Goshen delta, Rachel saw the lights of Pharaoh's palace. She saw torch lights, as ephemeral as fireflies, approaching from the distant darkness into the outskirts of Ramses. The still air carried a buzzing sound, almost like a swarm of locusts. "People. Coming this way."

"Those are your people. The Hebrew people."

"Pharaoh finally granted Moses' request, I suppose," said Rachel. "They will worship in the desert three days. Then they will come back. But why must I go?"

"At first that was Moses' request. Now Pharaoh has said he will kill Moses if he sees his face again. Everything has changed. Mother told me about it. Moses has called all the Hebrews to Goshen."

"For what purpose?"

"Enoch says he is gathering the Hebrews. They are leaving Egypt forever, every last one."

"That cannot be..."

"Mother hoped you would be able to stay with us, but with the plagues and all that has happened, that will not be possible." Asmath pulled Rachel down onto the settee. "Enoch said we have to hurry." Rachel sat on the edge of the Nile-blue lounge as if she feared the embroidered water lilies would entangle her and pull her under. Asmath sighed and laid on Rachel's lap a red linen tube sewn with scale-like mother-of-pearl disks. A cord of twisted gold and red drew the pouch closed at one end. "This is a good-bye gift from Mother. Open it."

"No." Rachel shrank back. *Good bye? What do Pharaoh and Moses have to do with me?*

Asmath smiled—a sad smile that hardly tilted the corners of her mouth. She loosened one end of the tube and shook out the contents, rattling the disks. A tangled wad of gold objects landed in Rachel's lap with a metallic clunk: toe rings, finger rings, gold chains, amulets, earrings, pins, a sewing kit. A handful of loose pearls played a plinking tune upon the gold. "Look at these," said Asmath. She reached into the pile and held up a pair of palm-sized gold hair combs inlaid with lapis lazuli. "And this is from me." She handed Rachel a small, round mirror backed with gold, worn to a fine patina.

"I cannot take your mirror."

The sad smile reappeared. "Since the plague of boils scarred my face, I take no pleasure in mirrors. You are still comely. Take it with my blessing. And now the last thing." Asmath went to the shrine and returned with a pale, green jade goddess, the length of a hand span, finely carved in every detail, down to the ridged feather on her head. "Ma'at, goddess of truth, justice and harmony. She will do battle against Apep. He has manifested greatly these last months."

"The god of chaos..." *Apep—he must be at work now,* thought Rachel. Asmath closed her slave companion's hand firmly over the cool jade. She gathered the gold objects from Rachel's lap, scooped up the pearls, and dropped everything into the tube. Then taking the now-warm goddess, she added it to the tube and drew the end closed.

"Stand up." She lifted Rachel's dress and tied the pouch around her slender waist. She lowered the dress and patted the waistline. "It hardly shows. Come on, we have to pack a bag."

☙

Now on the streets of Ramses, Enoch fought through the crowd and joined Rachel against the wall. She adjusted the veil Enoch had insisted she wear and shouted over the noise, "I'm not used to wearing one of these things. I don't like it." They drew their feet back when a man leading two donkeys brushed past. They watched the passing crowd. Leaning toward her brother's ear, she said, "These people look like a caravan of ants carrying beetle parts. Where did it all come from?"

"Moses spread the word and told the people to ask their masters for whatever they wanted or needed. The Egyptians want to be rid of us, so they gave whatever anyone asked."

"Moses! Now we must leave because of him. He is the one who brought all those plagues."

"That is the reason they want to be rid of us. They are afraid of Moses and his plagues."

With a side glance at her brother, Rachel tied the veil around her waist. She thought about the pouch and the gold Asmath's mother had given her. *I did not have to ask for things like a groveling slave.*

Enoch studied his sister. With her polished skin, the expensive blue linen dress, her eyes, kohl-lined in the style of Egyptian women, she could be one of them. Except for the hair. He could not help smiling. Rachel's thick, unruly hair had escaped the braid, and the clasp hung to one side. He lifted a hank of hair and waggled the clasp before her eyes. "You might want this." He laughed. Without warning, Rachel darted into the crowd and hid herself in a group of women balancing bundles of black wool on their heads. The distress on Enoch's face when she jumped into his path—*yah!*—took away all joy in the trick. The crowd flowed around them while he bent, hands on his knees.

Chagrined, she said, "I know a short cut to the market. We can cut across there." With twisted lips and dead eyes, he motioned, *lead on.*

Within minutes Enoch realized Rachel did not know a short cut. He asked directions from a man balancing a yoke heavy with casks of beer. With a braying laugh, the man shouted, "You are here, man. Stick your nose in the air!" It was true; wonderful aromas warred with the stench of the streets and

11

led them toward the increasing racket of honking and squawking fowl. They entered the south side of a large market square. Sun beams struggled through smoke from cook fires, revealing shops with awnings lining the west side, while buildings to the east remained obscured in deep shade. Spreading across the square, thatched roofs of kiosks seemed to float above a sea of hungry Hebrews made ravenous by the smell of smoked Tilapia and roast duck, commodities least affected by the recent plagues.

The scourge of locusts and hail had reduced the amount of produce for sale: olive trees, fig trees, and date palms had been stripped; vegetable crops had been beaten beyond repair; flax had been decimated. But wheat, not yet ripe, had been spared. The plague on the livestock had devastated the cattlemen, indiscriminately killing vast herds, not sparing the lone ox tilling a small patch. Yahweh had shown neither preference for the rich nor pity for the poor.

Instead of raising prices, vendors asked no payment for what little they had. Once the market opened, they pressed meat pies and fried cakes and the last remaining jars of olive oil upon astonished Hebrews. They stuffed ducks and geese, raw, smoked and living, into baskets. Onetime slaves ransacked Ramses' market with the consent of their former masters, who appeared to be saying, *take it with our blessing and be gone forever.*

Enoch had no interest in food, free or otherwise. He craned his neck but could not see beyond the milling crowd. "Which way from here?"

"I do not know. This is as far as Hopi brings us."

His sister's love for the eunuch had been apparent in their tearful farewell. "Hopi brought you here?"

"Of course. He is our bodyguard. We never go anywhere without Hopi. We come in the carriage with four bearers, and Hopi walks alongside. They stop, and we get out, and Hopi follows us, and then we get back in and—"

"All right. We will go straight across from where we came in. If we keep the sun to our right we should be going north toward Goshen. Let's go." They elbowed through the crowd to the other side where several streets left the square, none more promising than another. While Enoch speculated with two men, as lost as he, on the proper course, an old woman handed a loaf of bread to Rachel. A small female child held out two boiled goose eggs. Rachel pulled the clip from her hair and pressed it into the woman's wrinkled hands. Asmath would never take anything without paying, nor would she. She hurried after Enoch.

They fell in behind a man and his dog, herding several dozen sheered sheep. Unable to pass, they followed the sheep until Enoch began to growl deep in his throat. When the shepherd turned his flock to the right at a cross street, Rachel followed Enoch to the left. After more turns, Enoch stopped. "I know we've come this way before. See that sheep dung?" Rachel produced a bland smile, but decided not to mention Enoch's disgust when she failed to find the market. Narrow alleys widened. They found themselves in a prosperous area of white, limestone walls where, instead of leather flaps, wooden doors gave entrance. The evenly-spaced doors ended abruptly at a shadowed dead end. Boxed in on three sides, Enoch let out a curse, threw down Rachel's bags, and hit his head with both fists.

A heavy door creaked open a crack. A fat hand with rings on every finger opened the door wider, and a bald man with a neatly trimmed black beard peered out. He studied the roughly dressed Hebrew and the almost Egyptian woman. "What is the matter?" He raised his eyebrows.

"My sister and I are trying to get out of this city." When the man drew back, Enoch lowered his voice. "Please—we are lost. Can you help us?"

"Without hesitation, the man, who looked to Rachel about Enoch's age, said, "I can. You may come through our house. It opens onto the main street." He opened the door all the way and with a smile, beckoned. "Come. Come." Holding his lamp high, he stood aside, a short, fat man with lively, black eyes, dressed in a fine, white linen tunic. "I am Phinehas. This is my master's house."

Enoch and Rachel stepped over a high, black marble threshold. The little man set about lighting lamps in niches, illuminating a room unlike any Enoch had ever seen. Vases carved from precious stone stood on high and low pedestals around the room. On two walls, rugs rich with red and yellow yarn, hung heavy on ranks of dowels; masterfully painted murals covered the two remaining walls. Highlighted with gold paint and hieroglyphics to describe the miracles they wrought, life-size gods paraded in a solemn file: with human bodies clothed in traditional tunic or loin cloth, they had fantastical heads of hippopotamus, bull, crocodile, jackal. Enoch could not tell if they had they entered a dream or a nightmare. He realized his mouth hung open and shut it.

As the room brightened, they spied, laid upon an alabaster bench, covered only in a white cloth across his loins, the body of a dead man, his skin as white and leached of life as the bench. A black and brown spotted cat leaped from the carpeted floor and curled itself into a tight ball upon the white cloth. "Please excuse my master," said their host, "he cannot rise to greet you." Rachel turned away. The sun god Ra loomed with his hawk head and piercing eyes. She fainted.

&

Earlier that dawn morning, Ra, tallest of Asmath's household gods, had seemed to watch from his corner as Asmath packed a large, woven bag. Rachel had few duties, but from the time she had begun her new life as hand maid to the young mistress, she had been charged with keeping the ever-burning shrine lamp filled with oil. Largest of the household gods, and standing eye to eye with the ten-year-old girl, Ra's presence filled her with dread. She tried to avoid his penetrating stare, but his eyes seemed to follow her, and when she turned away, her shoulders hunched under his fierce gaze. As time passed she came to terms with his visage and built a mental wall against him. *Was he not just a statue made of painted wood? Had she not grown taller than he?*

Asmath packed Rachel's clothes and folded in her own best shawl, woven of the softest white wool, made by the woman whom Asmath's mother had hired to teach them to weave. The vizier's wife had always been kind to her daughter's companion. As the girls grew and became inseparable, she had treated them as equals. Never to the lady's face, only to Asmath, Rachel referred to the vizier's wife with affection. "May I say goodbye to our mother?"

"No. She has a headache. You know how excitable she is, and she has been crying." Asmath lowered her pearl-studded veil. Only the family could look upon her scars. "Let's go down to your brother." She took Rachel's hand, and they descended the stairs to the kitchen where Hopi blocked their way. "It's all right, Hopi," said Asmath. The eunuch shifted his bulk to the side and stood with arms crossed, scowling at the sleeping man slumped against the wall.

"Enoch," murmured Rachel. Her brother, bearded chin on his chest, hair so like hers, snored softly, a half-eaten meat pie in his lap.

"Let him rest a while," said Asmath. "He has come a long way. And you should eat." She motioned to the cook who wrapped two pieces of flat bread around chunks of duck breast and laid them on the table. The woman scooped up two bowls of goat's milk, still warm from milking, and set them before the two young women.

"I cannot eat," said Rachel.

"Clio, fill a water bag and make four more of these and wrap them in papyrus," said Asmath.

Enoch raised his head. "What?" He eyed the huge black man who had pushed him against the wall with orders to stay there. Keeping his back to the wall, Enoch stood. Asmath motioned with an open hand for the eunuch to stand down. Enoch laid the pie on the table and walked to his sister. He enfolded Rachel in his arms; she did not return his embrace. "How you've grown." He rested his hands on her shoulders and looked her up and down. "You're a woman now."

Under the weight of his hands, Rachel squared her shoulders, scaffolding to strengthen her resolve. She did not allow her gaze to waver but had the odd feeling of looking into her own eyes. "I am a woman now, Brother, and I am staying here." *Asmath will not listen,* she thought, *surely my brother will. He is the one who sent me here.* Tears spilled over but she did not wipe her face.

"Rachel, Sister, you cannot stay here. It is not safe. Outside of Goshen, no Hebrew is safe." Keeping eye contact with her brother, Rachel pulled away and slowly backed toward Hopi. Enoch turned to Asmath. "Mistress, please speak to her."

Asmath took Rachel's limp hands in her own and looked deeply into the almond-shaped eyes. "Sister of my childhood, I hoped I would not have to say these sad things to you, but I must. My father does not want you anymore." Rachel's shoulders slumped; the scaffolding had fallen away. "You have to understand, it is because of what your God did to our people." Breathlessness, a preamble to tears, tightened Asmath's voice. "The plague of boils—my father relives it every time he looks at me." She pressed the veil against her tears. "And when he looks at you."

Rachel covered her face with her hands. "I am so sorry. Would that I had scars too..."

Asmath coaxed Rachel's hands from her face and held them tightly. "Look at me. I know. I know how you have cried for me. But there is more: my father has decided to send you to the slave market."

"The market!" They had passed the market one day. Hopi had closed the carriage curtain with such vehemence there had been no question of peeking.

"Mother told me. If Enoch had not come today, Hopi and I were planning to take you to Goshen ourselves. Mother made up a story for Father. We were to say we went to the market and you ran away. Why do you think Mother had the pouch ready? She did not gather those things this morning."

"I had nothing to do with those plagues. Why must I suffer?"

"That argument is over," said Asmath. "If you are sold as a concubine, someday, when your looks are gone, you will end up in a brothel. You will never see your family again. I cannot protect you. Hopi cannot protect you. You must go now. The Hebrews are leaving Ramses. My father will be back from the palace today."

Enoch put the food into Rachel's bag and hung the straps over his shoulder. He removed a length of tightly folded fabric from his girdle, shook out the dust, and placed a wrinkled veil on Rachel's head. "I don't wear a veil. I have never worn one."

"All Hebrew women cover their hair. This veil belonged to our mother." He fiddled with the veil's balance, dragging Rachel's hair back and forth until Asmath took the rough fabric, and framing Rachel's face, placed it properly.

Rachel embraced the cook and her three helpers. She and Asmath had spent many hours in the kitchen pestering Clio while she taught them to make bread. She moved to Hopi who made no effort to hide his tears. She laid her head on his massive chest and spread her arms across his belly. Awkward, with spread fingers, he patted her back. She remembered the first and only time he had touched her. During the plague of darkness, the two had left the hysterical family upstairs and had stumbled down the stairs to the kitchen. In the thick darkness, they had sat against the wall, his arm tight around her shoulders.

At last Asmath and Rachel embraced. Enoch grasped his sister's elbow and gently pulled her away. "Time to go. Mistress, you and your family have been kind to my sister. May the one true God, Yahweh, bless you and keep you." A shadow passed over his countenance. He knew that unspeakable tragedy would strike her family that night. He turned to the cook and her staff. "If any of you are Hebrew you need to get to Goshen as fast as you can. The God of Israel is rescuing his people tonight." With a last, long look, Rachel allowed her brother to lead her out the door. Dew chilled their feet as they crossed the ruined garden and passed through a shattered wooden gate. They joined the throngs of Hebrews heading for freedom.

❧

Now, Enoch sat on the rug merchant's floor with their new friend and wiped a wet cloth over Rachel's face. He said, "She's not waking up."

"She will." Phinehas patted Rachel's hand vigorously. "She keeps saying, Hopi. Who is that?"

"A kind man. He was going to risk his life to save my sister. Phinehas, have you heard of a man named Moses?"

"Another man who risked his life."

"I do not think he was ever in danger. Yahweh has a plan to deal with Pharaoh. Why have you not left for Goshen?"

"My Master never recovered from the plague of boils. I had to stay and nurse him. Now I am waiting for the embalmers to come for him."

"You cannot wait any longer. Here she comes. Rachel, sit up."

By mid morning Enoch had lost hope of reaching Goshen by dark. *I am in Sheol,* he thought, *dragging a spoiled girl, accustomed to riding in a carriage, and a fat man, carrying a cat, fourteen bags, and a rug.*

Phinehas, of the tribe, Manasseh, trusted house slave of Barak, a trader of fine objects and rugs, had bidden his master a one-sided farewell, dropped their cat into a basket, and loaded his new friends with whatever they would agree to carry. Before closing his master's door, he surveyed the parade of gods one last time, made a rude Egyptian hand gesture, and then, with a smile, he followed Enoch and Rachel into a wide street, streaming with hurrying people.

A small craft, tossed by turbulent waves of humanity, Phinehas clutched his cat basket like an anchor. Unaccustomed to being jostled by men in loincloths and women herding goats and children, Phinehas' bravado dissolved into bewilderment. Wearing his wide, tooled leather girdle tight around his waist, his master's turban (*he will not need it*), and his expensive blue and white striped coat, his face glistened with grease and sweat. In his travels with his master, his one complaint had been his designation as the person to ride backwards. He lamented to himself that with a little notice he could have hired a carriage and bearers. And for once he could have ridden frontwards...His master's bag of gold bumped against his thigh. *With a little notice, I could even have hired a caravan.*

Whenever they stopped, Enoch paced. Rachel avoided looking at the sour downturn his mouth had developed and carried on an animated conversation with Phinehas. She pitied the little fat man. Rachel expected her brother to dump his bags in a pile and leave him and his cat by the side of the road. She believed Phinehas feared the same. His eyebrows had pushed a deep wrinkle into his forehead.

The Goshen delta had always been known as the black land because of the fertile, dark soil. At Heliopolis, to the north, the wide Nile River divided into a hundred creeks and streams, shattering the rich farmland, like a broken plate, into odd-shaped wedges connected by foot bridges. Yahweh had spared the land of Goshen from plague, but most of the crops had wilted and died. When slaves abandoned the foot pumps, the neglected irrigation ditches dried up. The escaping Hebrews fanned out over dry fields. They crossed narrow bridges and turned down almost forgotten paths toward home.

At last, Enoch, Rachel, and Phinehas left the confining streets of Ramses and turned onto a hard-packed levee road. They seemed to enter a different world. The air cooled. Verdant plants and the chirrup of insects muffled human sound. The air smelled of fish, alive and dead, and fecund mud. Creek water, low, and slow, eased along each side of the levee where thick clumps of reeds hid the nests of waterfowl. Disgruntled, voiceless storks clacked their yellow bills; cranes and herons shrieked their own displeasure. The heavy birds, legs pumping, beating wings half opened, lifted and settled, and lifted again over clumps of reeds and papyrus. Smaller birds fussed and flitted on low branches. Spring hatching had come to the delta.

"I remember this smell," said Phinehas. "When I was small, some boys and I used to fish in a stream like this." At the last moment, he had rolled up his master's best rug and thrown it over his shoulder. Now collapsed, the rug bumped the ground, before and behind, with every step. "Tilapia, if I recall." He shifted the rug. "My mother would cook it for us. Fried it whole. And we would sit under the tree and eat it. Then my mother died."

"Phinehas," said Rachel, "I know you were a lovely little boy."

"I was always small for my age," he said, "but I was never fat. As a child."

Crowds thinned as people turned down paths leading to tribal villages. The three passed sour piles of cut papyrus. In the slow current, an abandoned dredging barge, spades jutting from a pile of dried mud, swung back and forth on its rope. They walked all afternoon, down one path and onto the next, led by Enoch, who found it easier to walk ahead and wait, grim-faced, rather than check his pace. Rachel and Phinehas would lose sight of him, only to find him around the bend, waiting, fists on his hips.

The sun had reached two hand-spans above the horizon when, once again, they came upon Enoch. This time he shielded his eyes against the setting sun and peered across the creek toward a half-plowed field. "That's not right. Wait here," he said. Happy for the respite, Rachel and Phinehas moved to the side of the path. Phinehas threw down the rug, and groaning, sat heavily, legs outstretched, ankles crossed. Rachel perched on the roll and unwrapped Clio's meat pies. Content to rest and watch Enoch, they ate and slapped mosquitoes.

Enoch removed his sandals and girded his tunic. He waded waist-deep into the creek and climbed the far bank. Hundreds of white ibis farmed the field. Tinted rose by the low sun, their oval bodies seemed to float above the surface of the rutted ground, their black legs lost against the black earth. Three pairs of yoked oxen, with crowds of ibis perched on their backs, stood in the field, plows still attached. Enoch approached two of the pairs and threw off the yokes and plows. He took a fist full of straw and wiped bird dung off the broad backs. A hard slap sent the animals toward the creek. He released the plow from the third pair and led them across the field and down the bank, into the water. He positioned their heads upstream, and while they drank, he washed them. Last, he washed himself, and with Phinehas pulling from the front, managed to coax the beasts up the bank.

"Would they have died?" asked Rachel.

"Oh, yes," said Enoch "They've been led to water all their lives. They have forgotten how to think for themselves. They've been standing out there a long time. They may yet die."

"Where are we?" asked Phinehas. "This seems familiar but it has been a long time..."

"You are in Manasseh, my man. We're almost home. You will stay with us tonight."

"Are you sure we'll be welcome?" Phinehas eyed the cat basket. The beloved Sekhmet, named for the goddess of war (Phinehas could not remember why) had been found in a rolled up carpet after a buying trip to Tyre. It had been a long trip and the tiny kitten had been near death when his master heard a faint peeping. "I thought it was a bird!" He had said. Phinehas smiled when he thought of it. His master would not touch the kitten but sat at Phinehas' elbow while he dripped boiled goats milk into its mouth. Sekhmet became queen of the house; the two men bantered in mock jealousy over whose lap she deigned to grace.

"You and Sekhmet will be welcome. But be careful. We have dogs."

Chapter 2

WEST OF GOSHEN, WITH NO MOUNTAIN to hide behind, nothing but the yellow sands of the desert, the Egyptian sun god, Ra, must travel to the flat horizon before his day is done. There the goddess of the sky, Nut, swallows Ra and night falls. In the morning, Nut gives birth to Ra and a new day begins. How many times had Rachel heard that story? It was time to get those myths out of her head forever. *The sun will set,* she thought; *nobody is going to swallow anybody.*

Like an apparition, Enoch, Rachel, and Phinehas walked into the family compound through thick blue smoke. Seventeen-year-old twins, Perez and Hazer, called the Uncle Twins by the family, looked up with streaming eyes from the fire pit. In unison they yelled "Enoch's here!" and ran to meet their older brother. "Rachel!" they shouted upon seeing their sister and veered instead to give her a raucous greeting. Rachel found herself lifted off her feet by strong arms and swung around by identical, laughing brothers. They reeked of smoke. When they set her down and stood back to look at her, she saw two younger versions of Enoch: wild, black kinky hair, promising beards, thick expressive eyebrows, and a gap in the large, very white front teeth—a family trait without exception.

"Stand still," she ordered the two. "Let me see you." They stood at attention, elbow tucked at waist, each holding an imaginary spear in an encircling hand. She remembered them as nine-year-olds, chasing her with a beetle, doing everything in unison, one finishing the sentences of the other; she remembered them as ten-year-olds, tied by the neck in a line with other boys, carried off by night down the very path she had just traveled. How she had cried. Two years later, when she was ten, she had been taken down that same path and through the streets of Ramses to Asmath's house—not tied by the neck to other children, but in a carriage with a huge black man running alongside. Why had her fate been so different from theirs? She pointed to first one and then the other. "You are Hazor. You are Perez." They grinned and shook their heads, no. She laughed. "You can't get by with that. Did you think I would forget?" She was one of the few who could tell them apart, but they had never learned her secret. *It's all in the gap,* she thought. "What are you holding in your hands? A spear?"

Before they could answer, three women, a dozen children, and several dogs swarmed from the yard and four hovels rimming the goat paddock. Rachel stood astonished at their exuberance as the family embraced their beloved Enoch. One woman, great with child, clung to him and then stood aside and watched as her six small children—three girls and three boys—climbed their father like a tree. With children hanging on like monkeys, Enoch called to the twins, "Bring her here, boys." The two hooked their elbows with Rachel's and marched her to the family. Enoch took her hands in his, and looking deeply into her eyes, said to her, "This is our baby sister, come home." He smiled through tears, dropped her hands and stood aside, beaming, while the sisters-in-law embraced her.

Enoch's wife, Sarah, her beauty battered by fatigue, leaned over her pregnant belly and hugged Rachel. "What is this?" she asked, fingering through the bunched veil to the pouch at Rachel's waist.

"Some gifts from my mistress."

"You know," said Sarah, rubbing her belly, "my Enoch loves you so much, he would not trust anyone but himself to go for you."

A fully veiled woman with large sad eyes hugged Rachel tightly, revealing a frail body beneath folds of black fabric. Rachel thought she detected a slight tremble in her reedy muscles. "I am your brother Jabus' wife." As an afterthought she added, "My name is Adah. Zelophehad and Reuel are my sons."

A third sister-in-law came forward. "I am Hannah. Your brother Jorham is my husband." Tears filled the woman's eyes. She added with a husky voice, "He has not come home yet." She pointed to several children playing. "That one is mine. That one over there. One over there." She gave up. "Five in all. I'm sure Jorham will be here soon..."

"I have not been around many children," said Rachel, "but I like them."

Phinehas stayed back, holding the oxen, content to watch. A family like this could smother a person. His mind wandered as he watched the greeting ceremony unfold. Long ago he had a brother—just one—an older brother. He remembered beatings. He remembered a pretty little red-haired girl named Abigail. *Rachel will have to watch that wife of Enoch's. And who is this coming last out of the house? Another brother, older than those delightful twins. An unhappy brother...*

Phinehas speculated. But he was not to be ignored; Enoch put his arm around his new friend. "This," he said with a flourish, "is Phinehas. We learned on the way that he is the second son of Great Uncle Hershon's third wife. We could not have made the trip without him. And this—here in this basket—is Sekhmet the cat, Phinehas' owner." In keeping with the spirit of Enoch's introduction, the short, fat man in his turban and rich striped coat, bowed deeply to the family. He accepted a bowl of water from a small female-child.

Jabus, the "unhappy brother," nodded toward Phinehas and joined Rachel, who basked in the lingering happiness of her brother's antics. Enoch had been so driven all day, it was good to see a lighter side of him. Jabus hugged Rachel, then took her by the elbow and led her a short distance from the women. "Welcome home, Sister." Before Rachel could speak, her second oldest brother, one year younger than Enoch, lowered his voice and spoke in her ear. "My sons are here. I will not have them look upon your shame. You will cover your hair immediately." He released her, stood back, and crossed his arms.

Had Jabus struck her in the chest, Rachel could not have felt more pain. She blinked, stunned, and felt her lips grow numb. She leveled her tone: "Of course, Brother. I would never want to lead children astray." She set her bowl of water on the ground and untied the veil from her waist. A screaming child captured their attention. "You need to do something," said Rachel, as she settled the veil on her head. "I believe your boy is hurting his little cousin." She and Jabus watched as Enoch pulled his son from beneath the older boy. "I have only been here a short time. Who did he learn such behavior from?"

"Zelo is twelve. He has been the oldest male here; he thinks he is the head." Jabus walked away and called to his son, "Zelo, come in the house."

Rachel rejoined the group and stood by Phinehas. Barely moving his lips, he said, "I saw. Are you all right?"

Rachel turned away from her relatives and pressed tears from her eyes. Her eyebrows took on a bleak slant. "I think I have been brought to a foreign land." Shouts of joy, equal to that for her, greeted a new arrival, a laborer of some kind, pushing a cart.

"Mordecai's here," shouted the twins. A stocky, muscular young man, muddy to his bowlegged knees, pushed a large, two-wheeled cart into the compound. Enoch and his brothers greeted the newcomer with whacks to his back and ruffled his stringy hair. Hazer and Perez held him in a headlock until he threw both of them to the ground, thrilling all the little boys who jumped on the Uncle Twins for a wrestle.

Enoch pulled Mordecai away from the scuffle and said in a low voice, "Are you ready, Cousin? I have not yet told Rachel." Mordecai did not answer. "Everybody, Rachel, do you remember cousin Mordecai?" Without waiting for her to answer, Enoch began to question his cousin. "Why are you so late Mo? I have been worried."

Overtaken by shyness, Mordecai could hardly speak. His tongue had cleaved to the roof of his mouth. He hung his head and swallowed hard. "Well...Moses said to ask for things. I decided I had to have the carving tools. So I went to the wood shop. For three years those were my tools. When I got there I decided I needed the cart." Mordecai wrung his hands, noticed his mud-encrusted nails, and hid his hands behind his back.

"You got the woodworkers tools? And the cart too?" said Enoch. It was more a statement of astonishment than a question.

"He gave them to me." His tone said, *I did not steal them.*

"Well, of course he gave them to you, Mo." Enoch laughed. "Yahweh bent their hearts to give us anything we asked. He would have given you his daughter if he had one—if you asked for her."

"He *does* have one." With a look of horror, Mordecai swung his head toward the path. Everyone laughed and slapped their knees—had he accidentally asked for the daughter? Had she followed him, just out of sight, the whole way?

When the laughter died, Phinehas and Rachel exchanged looks of pity for the shy, skewered man. She said, "I do remember you, Cousin. When I was a little girl playing in the yard, you were always so kind to me. I think I've seen you since..."

Enoch took Rachel's hand. "Sister, do you not remember? Mordecai is your betrothed." Rachel jerked her hand away. "When you were eight years old and Mo was thirteen, our parents planned it. But they died, and then Mordecai was conscripted, and you went to Ramses to live with the vizier's family. You will be married tonight..."

What? Rachel searched the faces of her relatives. *Why is everyone smiling and nodding? Married? Who was this man? This dolt with his cart? I do not know him, not really. What could any of their plans have meant to an eight-year-old girl?* Her gaze shifted to Phinehas. His eyes, stretched wide, his eyebrows, arched to their zeniths, confirmed what she was thinking: *this is wrong, wrong, wrong.* Rachel tried to take in what Enoch had said: their parents died; she went to Ramses; Mordecai was conscripted. Rachel felt her knees buckle. She clutched the veil under her chin. *Jabus said it would be a sin if it comes off my head...*

"Catch her!" shouted Enoch. "That's the second time today!" he bellowed.

When Rachel roused, Sarah and the sisters-in-law helped her stand. "Come," said Sarah, "we have things to do." Like a gaggle of geese with one wobbly chick, they ushered Rachel into the nearest house.

At twenty-five, having neither father nor uncle, Enoch, the eldest son, had taken his place as head of the family. Conscripted, slaving, and starving, with no one left to care for his sister, he had made the decision to place the ten-year-old Rachel with an Egyptian family, the man, a vizier in Pharaoh's court. Now, five years later, he knew he must take full responsibility for that decision and the effect it had on his young sister. He needed to gain her trust, and not only hers; he needed the respect and trust of his brothers who had come back under his wing. He knew if he had their trust he could gain their obedience. He had learned at meetings with the tribal elders that a great undertaking lay before the Hebrew people. They would be led by Moses into an uncharted future. Invoking the name of Moses would not be enough; they did not know Moses. Enoch must be strong. He had begun with the announcement that Rachel would marry Mordecai that night. The whole thing had not gone well. Disgusted with his performance, he thought, *I should have prepared her. How can she ever trust me now that I betrayed her?* If the truth be known, she had not trusted him from the time she first laid eyes on him in

Asmath's kitchen. She trusted Hopi more, and now Phinehas. *I will have to do better*, he thought.

While the sisters-in-law readied Rachel for marriage, Enoch and his brothers slew a young goat for the special meal Moses had decreed all Israel must eat that night. The little boys grabbed their necks and threw themselves to the ground, frolicking with morbid glee as Enoch caught the blood in a bowl. Enoch did not understand it all, but as family head, he decided to show his obedience by following Moses' instructions exactly: the goat was to be roasted whole with the head and entrails; no bone was to be broken; any that remained must be consumed in the fire. Moses had called the meal *Passover*. He had said the Hebrew people would remember that night, that meal, forever, for it would become a rite to be celebrated throughout every generation.

Enoch set the bowl of blood aside and laid the carcass on the fire. Soon the smoke took on an aroma to starve by. Enoch explained to his brothers and Phinehas what Moses had said about the meal: "We will prepare it this way every year in the Promised Land."

"But why?" Hazer and Perez asked.

"That is what a rite is," said Enoch. "It is to remind people of an important event that has happened before." His twin brothers had served at the palace under the very eyes of Pharaoh. "Did they not have rites in the palace and were they not done the same way every year?"

"The Promised Land," said Jabus. "How are we going to get to this magic place?" He spit.

"Moses will lead us," said Enoch.

"You have been saying this until I am sick of hearing it. All he does is bring plagues upon the Egyptians and make them hate us. And can you blame them? I keep expecting to hear the sound of marching feet when Pharaoh's army comes to kill us."

Phinehas took in everything Enoch and Jabus said. He had known Enoch only a short time, but he believed his new friend to be a good man— a little impulsive, not as wise as he would be someday, but a man with good instincts. What did it all mean? A Promised Land... Phinehas himself had heard about that place. Did a priest from the tribe of Levi not come to his street and gather all the Hebrews and tell them? Did his heart not swell with hope? Was he a gullible fool? Was Enoch? He had nursed his master and watched the hurrying Hebrew nation pass by his window, leaving him behind. Did he not despair when his shrewd master could not negotiate with the gods a speedier death?

Phinehas did not miss the irony as the men prepared the goat for sacrifice and the women prepared Rachel for what she must view as her own sacrifice. Why did this man, Moses, this God, Yahweh, demand such sacrifice, such obedience? A poor goat. A poor young woman. *Surely He has a plan?*

Rachel, discretely veiled, emerged from the house alone. She walked to the side of the house and sat on a fallen log. Enoch left the menfolk at the fire and sat beside her. "I am sorry," he said, "I should have told you on the way. To prepare you…"

"And where is my husband?"

"He has gone to the creek to wash."

"And none too soon."

"He came from the brickyards," said Enoch. "But Mordecai is a master carver. He was falsely accused of theft and sent to the brickyards. When he went back to the wood shop to get his tools, he found an old friend there, an old man who could not walk. Mordecai asked the master for the cart and pushed the old man to his own village. Miles away."

Rachel ignored Enoch's story and asked, "Why must I be wed tonight? What is the hurry?" She knew she must obey her brother; he was a law unto her. Maybe she could change his mind. He would never change hers.

"We are leaving Goshen." Enoch laced his fingers and began to squeeze his hands together. "Yahweh is sending one last plague."

"Oh, Asmath, my sister…I will not be there. You may think me young and useless, Brother, but during the plagues, I was a help to the vizier's family."

"This plague will be so terrible, no one will be able to help. Pharaoh will want to kill us. For all I know he will kill some of us." More vigorous squeezing turned Enoch's knuckles white. "If you are married and I am killed, you will be safe. Well, *safer.*" He relaxed his hands and rested his forearms on his knees. "Mordecai is a good man."

For a brief moment Rachel felt sorry for her brother, burdened with the cares of the family and clearly exhausted. Had he not run all night to come for her? "But, Enoch, he is so…rough." *And bowlegged,* she thought, *and he smells.* But she held her peace. Her brothers and cousin were not wealthy like the vizier and his son, Asaph, with access to the bath house and oils and scents.

"Mordecai is a good man." Enoch repeated. "He will be a good husband to you. Can you not trust me? Would I ask you to marry a bad man? Can you not trust our parents? Would they ask it?"

"You are not *asking,*" said Rachel, "and we were children then. Who knew how we would turn out?" Sarah came around the corner and spied them talking. She motioned for Enoch to come.

"Now what," he mumbled. "We will talk some more later." He joined his wife who threw a backward look at Rachel.

Sarah, supporting her unborn baby with both hands, led her husband to the opposite side of the house. "What? Sarah, I have to see to the meat." Enoch loved his wife. Every time he could manage it, usually when his master fell into a week-long drunken stupor, he had slipped away from the granary where he kept the tally sheets. Did they not have six children with number seven coming soon? His face tensed with worry; this was not a good time to be pregnant. But his master had given him the wagon and ox. Yesterday the worn-out ox had dropped dead; today Yahweh had provided two more. Maybe everything would be all right.

Enoch believed Yahweh did reach down to his creation and provide. He believed the stories his father and uncles had taught him: that Yahweh called Abraham to leave the land of Ur and settle in the land of Canaan; that over 400 years ago, Joseph, son of Jacob, rescued his eleven brothers from a terrible famine; that the Hebrews came to Egypt to dwell in the black land of Goshen. Those were stories taught to Hebrew children in every generation. More recently a king arose who did not know Joseph nor respect his descendants; he enslaved the Hebrew people. But did Yahweh not send Moses to lead them to freedom? Moses had not told the elders where they were going, but wherever they traveled, the wagon would be the best thing he could imagine for their journey.

Sarah let go of the baby and grasped her husband's arm. "Your sister," she hissed, "has a pouch of gold tied around her waist."

Enoch suppressed a smile and decided to whisper, too. He had felt the pouch when he first embraced Rachel in Asmath's kitchen. Feigning surprise, he said, "How do you know?" He peered at his wife—two conspirators, they were.

"I saw it when I cleaned that fancy dress of hers. It bulges with gold." The baby pushed a knee against her own rough tunic, causing her to wince.

"Where is it?"

"What?"

"The pouch."

Sarah looked at her husband as if to say, *you dullard*, and spoke slowly: "*Around-her-waist. She refused to take it off.*"

"Then how do you know what's in it?"

"She told me. Now listen, Enoch," she forgot to whisper, "as her older brother and head of the family, you should take the gold and give some to Mordecai so he can pay the bride price." She nodded, agreeing with herself.

Enoch looked into his wife's hopeful brown eyes. They said, *we are going to be rich*. He did indeed have a right to do exactly as Sarah said. He paced around a bit, bringing a slow smile to his wife's full lips. He wanted to kiss her; instead he stroked his beard. He pursed his lips and squinted his eyes in consideration. This went on until she thrust her head forward and said, "Well?"

"No."

"No?" She dropped her chin and peered from the tops of her eyes. Enoch felt a twinge of shame for teasing his wife, but the expression on her face cheered him beyond reason. If he had known of her grasping nature, would he have married her? Probably. Betrothed to him since childhood, she had been a most comely child, arbiter of the rules over the other girls. Betrothals were almost impossible to negate; it would be easier to change her mean-spirited ways—or so he had thought.

"Sarah, first, Rachel is not your child. She does not have to mind you. Second," he grasped his wife by the shoulders and gave her a gentle shake, "I sold her into slavery when she was ten years old. What more would you have me do to her? She will bring her own dowry into her marriage." He leaned over the baby and kissed his wife soundly. "Now be nice to Rachel. She's practically an Egyptian; she needs our help."

&

The women prepared the flatbread and herbs for the special meal. The goat was roasting. Mordecai walked the short distance to the creek, pulling up a clump of hyssop on the way. He stripped off his short, hemp tunic and filthy loin cloth. He stank. He saw himself through Rachel's eyes: dirty, an ignorant hulk among her handsome brothers; unworthy. He submerged his body under the cool water and considered drowning himself. Instead, he scrubbed his clothes. He rubbed the hyssop over his grime-encrusted body, flinching as the rough weed scraped across tender scars on his back. He worked his fingers into his long tangled hair and beard and allowed the current to carry away the caked mud. He wanted to lie on his back and float to the great sea, but all the waters of the sea could not wash away the horrors of Pharaoh's brickyard.

The vast brickworks lay at the edge of the encroaching desert northeast of the city of Ramses. Under a brutal sun, and taskmasters no less cruel, the Hebrew slaves made bricks. They hauled water to mud pits, mixed in straw with a hoe to the right consistency, and loaded the mixture into wheel barrows. They carted the mud to stations where wooden forms stretched in long lines across the yard. As one man pushed the barrow along, another scooped the mud with his hands into the form. The bricks baked dry in a constantly rotating system: by the time wet bricks were laid in one section, another section would be dry and the bricks carried off to Pharaoh's never-ending building projects. The crack of the lash punctuated the low drone of groaning men, the grinding of the cart wheels, and the plopping sound of wet mud.

Mordecai made bricks in his sleep. All night he mixed the clay and straw until it came together in a perfect blend. With crusted hands, he dropped the exact amount into the wooden frame, using just the right amount of force to push the mud into every corner. Pat it down. Screed the top smooth. No straw sticking out. Not enough mud, and more could not be added—that would cause a horizontal crack and the brick would be inferior—it had to be reformed. In his dreams he writhed from the lash.

He learned to scoop out just the right amount of mud. He learned sooner than some poor boys. He remembered a time when an overseer, smelling of beer, gave a boy one more chance to make a perfect brick. Work stopped. Maybe if we had kept working, Mordecai had since thought, the overseer would not have made an example of the boy. Slaves had watched in horror as the overseer grabbed the boy by his thin arms and thrust his head and shoulders deep into a barrow of mud. The boy struggled and kicked and then his body stiffened and quivered. The overseer pointed his lash toward a stunned Mordecai and another boy. "You. You. Take him to the trench." Neither made a sound as they pulled the lifeless boy from the mud and laid his body face up in a cart. They pushed across the wide yard. The sun crusted the surface of the mud. Moving as quickly as they could, they laid the small figure, seemingly half statue, half flesh, in the dead trench with other men and boys who had been sacrificed to Pharaoh. Flies and stench drove the boys back to their station.

Mordecai made no friends. Who needed the sorrow? He saw Jorham from time to time, and Enoch checked on him once in a while, but his fellow slaves kept to themselves and spoke little. What was there to talk about? Who wanted to hear about someone else's misery or their past life? Or their hopes for a future that would never come. That would be worse than silence. Like a giant grindstone, the brick works pulverized the Hebrews' bodies, but they enslaved their own emotions.

Makeshift outbuildings with thatched roofs and open sides stood at intervals around the yard. At noon the overseers allowed the slaves to rest in the shade for an hour. Mordecai usually slept to escape the stink of the nearby latrine. One day he thrust his hands deep down into a wheelbarrow where the mud was still cool and pliable. He fashioned a bird the size of a woman's fist and staked it on a twig to dry in the sun. He made another. And another, each one better than the last. Soon he had a row of birds. To Mordecai it seemed only moments until the work gong sounded. Men and boys groaned and shuffled into the sun dreading the long, hot afternoon. At the end of the day, Mordecai was again surprised by the sound of the gong. All day, oblivious of his misery and the sun, the thought excited him that maybe he could make a fish, a frog. He could almost feel the cool clay in his hands as he imagined how he would shape a fin or the knobby joints of a frog's foot. He joined the crew as they trudged to the shelter for the night.

An unfamiliar overseer dressed in a clean, white tunic stood at the corner of the shed. He held up one of the birds by the stick. "Who did this?" No one answered. Mordecai stopped breathing. He felt the blood rushing in his neck. The overseer tapped his whip twice on the corner post: He raised his eyebrows and sighed deeply. "Who?"

Mordecai spoke from the rear. "I did, master."

"Come with me." Holding the bird by the stick, the overseer struck out across the yard. Mordecai followed. He had been beaten but never tied to the post and lashed. He could almost feel the leather cutting into his back, and then they walked past the whipping post. He had never skipped in his life, but he wanted to. He wanted to frolic in circles, stiff-legged, like the lambs. They left Pharaoh's brick yard and entered the darkening streets of Ramses. After twists and turns too numerous for Mordecai to memorize, the overseer stopped at a low, rose-colored, stucco building with ranks of tall windows on each side of a wide door. After a brief foray into the building, he returned with parting words, "Stay here."

Mordecai stood alone in the doorway. How would he get back to the brick yard? The sun's last golden beams struck his back; sawdust motes carried his shadow far into the room. He could see everything but the deepest corners. The huge wood shop, supported by wood columns, stretched away fifty or more cubits. At least forty men labored with bent backs, kneeling, carving gods and lintels and parts of statues. Wood shavings, and scraps littered the floor. A large man, tall and broad, lumbered from the back of the room, kicking sawdust, bringing Mordecai's shadow into focus. As he drew closer, the boy noticed his red face and worn leather apron. His gray beard smelled of stale beer.

"Who are you?"

Mordecai stammered, "I—I don't know, Master."

"You don't know your *name?*"

"Oh." No one had ever asked his name. As surprised as if he had lifted a brick and found his name there, he said, "Mordecai. My name is Mordecai."

"The master held up the clay bird by its twig. "Did you make this?"

"Yes, Master."

"Can you carve?"

"I never have."

"Come in." He followed the master inside. "Sit here." He sat against the wall near the door. The master handed him a fist-size block of wood and a small sharp knife. "Carve this bird." The man laid the clay bird on the ground and walked away. Mordecai turned the block of wood in his hand. *There is a bird in here,* he thought, *all I have to do is find it.* He tested the knife against his thumb. Sharp. He had never held a sharp knife. It seemed to fit his hand. He began to carve. Within an hour he had carved a perfect sparrow with a cocked head, open beak and delineated feathers. Someone had set a lamp beside him. He had not noticed. By the light of the lamp, he bored a hole in the underside of the bird. He twirled the bird by the twig and waited.

He surveyed an empty room save an old man and a carver at the far back corner. *When did everyone leave?* he thought. He had missed the evening meal of bread and fish at the brickyard. He would never find his way back in the dark. Hungry and worried, he dozed.

The master joined the nodding boy and took the bird from his hand. He turned it, held it low into the lamplight. "Come with me." Mordecai followed the master to the far back corner where a carver waited with a man-sized bust of Ra. The master said to the carver, "Bring it all." He marched the astonished carver, with his tools and the half-carved bust, to the spot by the door and left him there. He walked back to Mordecai and jabbed his finger in various directions. "This is your corner now; you sleep here; there is the grind wheel. Keep your knives sharp. Keep your space clean. Do not spit on the floor." He walked away and soon returned with a leather apron and a box of chisels and knives. He left through a curtain-covered doorway on the back wall and did not return, so Mordecai found a broom and swept up Ra-Carver's mess. He shook out the sleeping mat. He gazed out the window. *Have I died?* he thought. *A window. A breeze. This must be the best corner in the shop and I don't even know how to carve.* His mind churned.

One old man, with the last lighted lamp, remained, leaning against a center column. The master stood in the curtained doorway and said, "Those other men are paid labor. You are on loan from the brick yard. Do good work and you will never go back there. Do not leave without permission. My daughter will feed you." The curtain closed.

Mordecai smelled food. Lentil stew? He was starving. After what seemed hours, a sour looking woman in a sour smelling dress pushed through the curtain and plunked down a bowl of congealed lentil stew with a piece of moldy bread teetering on top. In the three years he stayed at Pharaoh's wood shop, the food never improved, and the master's daughter never spoke.

The hunch-backed old man removed his apron, and carrying his bowl and the lamp, hobbled over to Mordecai's new home. "May I join you?" Without waiting for an answer he groaned and settled his thin haunches on the ground. Like a weaver-bird nest, his long black beard housed sawdust, wood shavings and other bits. He cleared phlegm from his throat and said with a wry twist of his lips, "Abandon hope. The food never gets better. Most of the time I cannot tell what it is. I am Elias, tribe of Levi."

The walls of the room receded into deep darkness. Their faces glowed, seeming to float in the meager amber light. Mordecai looked into faded, kind eyes, topped by wild, thick, black eyebrows. Deep wrinkles started at the outer corners of Elias' eyes and crisscrossed downward to disappear into his beard. There had been no old men at the brickyards.

"You know," said Elias, with a sweet smile, "you are an answer to prayer. I have been praying for someone to talk to."

There was something about the old man's voice…Mordecai did not expect it, did not understand it: his tense body, his mind, ever alert, even in sleep, relaxed. A surprising flood of tears streamed down his face. He laid his head on his arms and sobbed. Elias placed his hand on the boy's neck and blessed him.

&

At the creek, the shriek of a hawk caught Mordecai's attention and wrenched his thoughts back to Goshen. The sun had almost set, and cool air had settled over the water, dragging down smoke from thousands of cook fires. The smell of roasted meat hung heavy in the smoke. Tonight every Hebrew family across Goshen would eat the special meal Moses had decreed. Tonight his new life would begin. No more brick works. No more wood shop. He would marry Rachel. She had fainted at the thought of becoming his wife. *Will marriage to me be a kind of slavery to her? What if she never accepts me? What will I do?* Mordecai climbed up the bank and wrung out his clothes as tightly as he could. He gave them a good shake and put them back on. Shivering now, he thought how good the fire would feel. His sandals lay where he had left them, but now a small black puppy no larger than his fist slept curled upon one of them. "Where did you come from?" He picked up the puppy, held it to his face, and breathed in the sweet puppy smell. *Some things you never forget,* he thought. A hawk sat on a willow branch not six feet above. It spread its wings briefly, settled and turned its head sideways, looking every bit, a miniature of Ra. Mordecai tucked the puppy into the crook of his arm and headed home.

The meat sizzled, almost done. Enoch, his brothers, Phinehas, and all the little boys stood around the fire. Mordecai joined them, turning periodically to dry his clothes. The smell of cooking meat had set the dogs to whining. Jabus reached to tear off a piece to throw to them. "No," said Enoch, blocking his brother's arm. "Moses said this meat is holy to Yahweh. Whatever we do not eat must be completely burned up."

Jabus knocked his brother's arm away. "Now this Moses tells us what to cook and how to cook it—and what we can and cannot feed the dogs! This is too much. I hope I never meet the man."

"Moses will be the salvation of our people," said Mordecai. *Salvation*—he had never said that word out loud. It was a big word. He was more comfortable with little words. His tunic had begun to steam. He turned his back to the fire.

"And what do you know about this man Moses, Cousin?" said Jabus.

"I worked at the wood shop with Moses' cousin. Just today on the way to Goshen, Elias told me all about Yahweh's plan for Moses and the Hebrew people."

&

By day the young man and the old had carved for Pharaoh. But by night, by the light of the single lamp, they had discussed and debated, and Elias had taught him the old stories about Abraham, Isaac, and Jacob and his twelve sons. Joseph, sold into bondage by his brothers, had become trusted in Pharaoh's court, and during a seven-year famine, proved to be the great savior of Egypt and the surrounding nations. Because of Joseph, Pharaoh had given the land of Goshen, the best land in Egypt, to the starving Hebrews. There they had raised their flocks and multiplied into a great nation.

Mordecai remembered the teaching from childhood when his uncle and father had taught him and his cousins about Yahweh, the one true God, creator of all that exists. But when Elias talked about praying to Yahweh—the God who made the sun, and the stars, and the moon—Mordecai could not get his imagination around it.

"But Mo," Elias had said, "if Yahweh made everything, who made you?"

"Well, he did," Mordecai admitted. "I know he did. But he does not want me to speak to him. What would I say? What would *he* say?"

Elias pointed out that in days of old, men called upon the name of Yahweh. "Did Yahweh not tell Noah to build the Ark? Did he not tell Abraham to pick up and go to the land of Canaan?"

Now, standing at Enoch's fire, emboldened by the memory of Elias' words, Mordecai looked squarely at his cousin, Jabus. "Elias says Moses was sent by Yahweh to lead us to the Promised Land, just like he told Abraham to go to Canaan."

"You are only repeating what you hear," said Jabus. "You are nothing but a talking bird." All eyes followed Jabus as he stalked into his house. Zelo followed his father, imitating his posture and demeanor, but seven-year-old Reuel, Jabus' younger son, so different from their volatile father, stayed behind. Enoch had taken a liking to the quiet, gentle boy who always seemed to be by his side. He draped an arm over his nephew's shoulder and pulled the boy close.

The molten sun passed beyond silhouetted date palms, and twilight turned the sky lavender and orange with long streaks of gray clouds. Broken strips of distant streams and canals glowed silver against the darkening land,

and cook fires dotted the flat delta. Night sounds overtook the chortle of roosting birds, until the chatter of creepers and the croaking and peeping of frogs filled the evening to bursting.

Time had come for the marriage ceremony. With his back to the fire, Enoch spread his arms wide, and circling his hands in the air, coaxed his family to join him; counting himself they numbered twenty-two souls. Rachel's fainting spell and Mordecai's glum face quashed any excitement that might bubble up. Sarah, clearly unhappy and angry with Enoch, and not above tweaking an ear, kept her six children close; Jabus, disgruntled, and his wife, Adah trying to make herself invisible, stood with Zelo and Reuel; the Uncle Twins, Hazer and Perez, stood together, arms interlaced across their shoulders; Jorham's wife, Hannah, worried for her absent husband, forced her five unruly children into submission; Phinehas stood with the cat basket at his feet. He had put his elegant striped coat on Mordecai, partly because the young man shivered, and partly to show Rachel her bridegroom had possibilities. Rachel, who had exchanged her mother's veil for Asmath's best shawl, waited next to Sarah.

Exhaustion drew lines and shadows on Enoch's face; he had left Goshen the night before and walked to Ramses. He had managed a short nap in Asmath's kitchen under Hopi's watchful eye. Now he surveyed his family and tried to summon the energy to sound hopeful.

"Rachel, Mordecai," he said, "come here." Sarah prodded Rachel forward. The bride and bridegroom stood before Enoch a distance apart. He pushed them together, placed Rachel's hand in Mordecai's rough paw, and spoke: "This is a special night. Yahweh will do a new thing. So we will not celebrate this marriage as we normally would, with dancing and the tambourines. But we are joyful to bring Rachel and Mordecai together in marriage. When Rachel was seven years old and Mordecai was twelve, our mothers decided they would make the perfect match. Tonight we honor that contract on behalf of our parents who died. Even when Mordecai was taken to the brickyards, our dear mothers spoke of a night like this and never gave up hope that the two of you would be wed."

Suddenly Rachel threw down Mordecai's hand. "Wait!" she shouted. Groans and gasps followed her as she ran from the circle and disappeared into Enoch's house.

"Ra-chel!" Enoch called after her in disgust. His shoulders sagged. The children disbanded; their defeated mothers, shaking their heads, watched them go. Mordecai nuzzled the puppy for comfort. Phinehas, deciding he needed more comfort than a puppy could give, went forward and put his arm around the piteous bridegroom.

Moments later, Rachel ran out the door and resumed her place in front of Enoch. Once again she wore her mother's veil. She smoothed the veil and placed her hand in Mordecai's. "Now I am ready."

Enoch nodded quiet approval to his sister and continued, "May Yahweh bless this union with many children, and may you be happy and prosperous in our new land, wherever it may be." An awkward silence followed. "You two, go sit on the log and get acquainted. We will call you when the meal is ready." Clapping followed Rachel and Mordecai. Little girls giggled and peeked around the corner of the house.

The couple sat, backs straight, and watched the goings on at the fire. "It's cold," said Mordecai. He slipped out of Phinehas' coat and draped it across Rachel's shoulders.

"Now you will be cold."

"I never had a coat at the brickyards." Rachel assessed her husband. His shining, black hair had dried into curls, and his beard, while not yet thick, held promise and framed his sun-baked, square face. His deep-set, kind eyes seemed to understand her anger and fear. He handed her the puppy. "His name is Morsel."

She laughed. He remembered the first time he had heard her laugh. It had been at the rich man's house. But now was not the time for memories. Now was the time to make memories. "Why that name?" she asked.

"When I first saw him, a hawk was just about to swoop down and grab him up—a morsel. She laughed again. "I could not leave him," he said.

"No. I love him already." She tucked the puppy under her chin. "Asmath and I never had a puppy. Our family always had cats. My master had his favorite mummified. She sat with the gods in our room."

Mordecai leaned toward Rachel and drank in her scent. Sandalwood. She and her mistress had smelled of it. Had it been two years? The first time he had heard her laugh, she had laughed at him. He and Elias had come to the vizier's house to replace a balustrade.

&

Mordecai's carving skill had surpassed anything the master had hoped, and his trust in the young slave grew. By Mordecai's third year in Pharaoh's wood shop, the master allowed the pride of his shop to go alone to measure for special jobs. One day Mordecai and Elias gathered their tools and pushed their cart to a rich man's house to measure the second-floor porch for new balusters. They had carried their tools up the stairs and passed through a bedroom with mural-painted walls. Elias' rolling eyes pointed toward the corner shrine. Mordecai had no idea people lived in such splendor. He wanted to whisper, and he did, until Elias, who was somewhat deaf, kept saying, *What? What?*

They had toiled through the morning, ripping out the termite-ridden wood, throwing it off into their cart. By afternoon they had plied their measuring rods and string, marking a damp clay slab with careful notes. Two girls, maybe thirteen years old, watched from the bedroom window. A mountainous, bald Ethiopian with gold earrings, bare chest, and a long, batik skirt, stood, arms crossed, in the doorway. Mordecai knew better than to make eye-contact with the giggling young women, even though he had the uncomfortable feeling they were laughing at him. He kept to his work, head down, but stolen glances revealed that the short one had the straight hair of an Egyptian and the tall one had wild curly black hair. The aroma of sandalwood drifted out the window and wrapped around his imagination.

"Come on Rachel," said the straight-haired girl, "let's go." They disappeared down the stairs, chattering nonsense. Mordecai straightened. *Rachel. Could it be?*

Mordecai woke before dawn the next morning, his mind spinning with thoughts of the tall, beautiful girl. He convinced himself that he had indeed seen his cousin, Rachel, betrothed to him when they were children. Did she not have the square jaw of his cousins and the beauty of his mother and aunt? *And that hair...*

For four days Mordecai and Elias hauled the balustrades up the stairs, hammered in the balusters and corner posts, fitted in the notches, and tapped in the locking dowels. Every night he left frustrated and disappointed, haunted by thoughts of the girl. *Where was she?* Finally, the master and mistress of the house came to inspect the work. His own master came to inspect. At last they left him alone to sweep and clean up. He wanted to shout her name and search the house.

And then, there she stood at the window, she and the other girl. Watching. He looked full into her face. *It has to be her,* he thought—the almond eyes, the features of his family so evident, and the hair, oiled, tamed, smelling of sandalwood. The broom hung slack in his hands. He felt like a block of wood, his shape unrealized. She smiled, and there it was, the gap in her front teeth. And then they were gone, down the stairs giggling and screaming— shocking behavior to a young man who knew nothing of young girls. But she had smiled at him and removed any doubt that he was betrothed to the girl who lived in the rich man's house. The scowling eunuch appeared at the door. Mordacai swept up the last of the trash and followed the slave and the scent of his betrothed down the stairs. He turned to face the huge man, and tilting his head back, spread his lips, revealing his own gap. He tapped a fingernail against his teeth and watched as a grin, by stages, captured Hopi's face. Before it was over, his eyes disappeared, and his cheeks nestled under his ears. "I will be back," said Mordecai. He loaded his tools, waved at the mound of flesh, filling the doorway, and left. He never made it back to the vizier's house. But the girl who had smiled at him that day had become his wife.

&

Night descended upon the black land, but thousands of fires in thousands of family compounds tamed the dark and domed it with an amber glow. Moths and night hoppers swarmed in a mindless swirl and beat against Enoch and his brothers as they cut the edible portions from the roasted kid and took the pieces into the house. They left the remains to burn on the fire as Moses had directed. Enoch took a handful of hyssop (Moses had even specified the weed to use) and dipped it into the rough wooden bowl holding the kid's blood. Jabus watched, fists on his hips, as Enoch brushed the blood on the lintel and on each side the door.

"What is all this?" demanded Jabus "Do not break a bone of the goat. Do not eat it outside the house. And wasting what we could give to the dogs. Now you are smearing blood on your house." With each accusation, he waved his arms in ever-widening circles. He began to curse.

"Jabus. Stop. I will explain it all once we get inside." Enoch stepped past the leather skin and held it aside, waiting for his brother. Jabus brushed past, and Enoch wedged the locking pegs through holes in the leather and into their slots. "No one goes out from here on," he said with a stern look at Jabus. He held up his hand to stop his brother from speaking. "Eat, everyone, and then I will tell you what this is all about. Trust me."

The women spread mats across the floor and laid out four large platters of meat, unleavened bread, and bitter herbs—parsley, lettuce, and root greens—just as Moses had decreed. The hungry family sat on the floor, wall to wall, in the small house. They wrapped bread around the meat and ate. The women fed the sleepy children and laid them in a corner like a litter of puppies. Now the adults sat with their backs to the walls and waited for Enoch to speak. Sarah absently rubbed her belly. Mordecai and Rachel sat together, playing with their puppy, full to bursting with curds. Phinehas leaned his back against the door frame, the cat basket beside him. He tied and twisted a strip of goat hide, fashioning a tether for Sekhmet.

Enoch, shoulders rounded by fatigue, stood in the center of the room. He contemplated each member of his family; he knew how each would react to the things he had to say: things fearful, things that would tax their imaginations, things unheard of. He began: "If you trust me, you must trust what I am telling you now. Moses was sent by Yahweh to rescue us from Egypt." Enoch held up his hand to still the stirring and shifting among his family. "At first," he continued, "Moses asked Pharaoh to allow us to go three days into the wilderness to worship Yahweh, but Pharaoh refused. Then Moses and Aaron, his brother, warned Pharaoh that if he did not let us go, Yahweh would punish Egypt. When Pharaoh continued to refuse, Yahweh sent nine plagues to scourge the land of Egypt."

"Nine!" said Sarah. "I do not remember that many."

"Because you were in Goshen," said Enoch. "The plagues were meant for the Egyptians."

"But the blood came here," said Hannah.

"It did, but by the time it washed down this far, it was diluted," said Enoch. "The same for the frogs and lice. Mordecai, you were in the middle of them all."

"I was," said Mordecai, "but an amazing thing happened. When the hail fell and the lightning bolts rained down, we stood under our shelter and none fell on us. Our overseers could not say the same; we filled the dead trench with their bodies." He grinned. "The whipping post was shattered to pieces."

"Perez, Hazer, you were at the palace," said Enoch. "You saw the plagues."

"We saw everything," said Hazor. Pharaoh preferred twins to stand guard at his palace doors. Handsome and without blemish, the twins were taken from a fishing boat and carried to the palace where they were groomed and bedecked in linen, given spears to hold, and assigned to flank the throne room door. Day after day for four years they witnessed everything that transpired at the palace. The first time they saw Moses, they saw Aaron turn his staff into a serpent; they saw the palace magicians turn their own rods into serpents. When they saw Aaron's serpent swallow the others, they wanted to dance and leap, but they also wanted to live. They spoke to one another with the secret language they had developed; they spoke with their eyes, a raised eyebrow, a blink. No smile crossed their lips.

Perez spoke: "Pharaoh would wait for Moses and Aaron to leave— we opened the door for them—then he would stomp around and flail his arms in the air. We saw the officials, begging him to let the Hebrew nation go. He would order all his advisers to get out. We could not get the doors open fast enough. Then another plague would come, and they would all be back, begging Pharaoh to end it."

Hazor said, "After the plague of boils we were sure Pharaoh would give in. Everyone in his court suffered with that one. Even his family."

"My family suffered terribly from all the plagues. Especially the boils," said Rachel.

"They were not your family, Rachel," said Sarah.

"Well, yes, but—"

"Never mind," said Enoch. "Nine plagues. Sent by Yahweh. Tonight will be number ten."

Ten! Shocked voices battered Enoch. A child woke and cried. "Tonight," Enoch spoke over the babble, "Yahweh will send the worst plague anyone could imagine: the first-born of every living creature in Egypt will die at the hand of Yahweh." At Enoch's insistence, his oldest dog had been brought in. Now it twitched in its sleep, scraping. "From Pharaoh's first-born son, to the priest's first-born, to the servant girl's child, to the cattle and all the other livestock—all the first-born of all flesh will die. *Then*, Pharaoh will let our people go."

"But why *that?*" said Rachel. She thought of Asmath's older brother, Asaph. So handsome. He had never hurt anyone. Asmath's mother would never survive this horror. Another thought filled her with dread: what if she or the master were first-born children? Asmath would be left alone. Rachel pulled her knees up tight, pulled down her veil, and sobbed into Morsel's warm body.

Jabus sat against the wall, lips pursed. Enoch addressed his brother; he had said he would explain everything. "Jabus, you asked about the blood on the door posts—"

As if his brother's voice had awakened him, Jabus leaped to his feet and shouted, "There will be blood on the floor when Pharaoh gets through with us." He grabbed the front of Enoch's tunic and pushed him hard against the wall.

"The blood will protect us," Enoch shouted into his brother's distorted face. Mordecai rushed to Jabus, wrapped his powerful arms around him and pulled him away from Enoch. The sisters-in-law, on their feet now, stood over the sleeping children. Jabus shook off Mordecai and rushed to the door with balled fists. "Move, man," he said with gritted teeth to Phinehas.

"I think not," said the fat man. "Enoch said we have to wait inside," He closed his eyes and waited for the blow. Jabus planted his feet and drew back his fist. Once again, Mordecai, now joined by Hazer and Perez, held Jabus' arms.

Twelve-year-old Zelophehad pulled at his uncles, screaming, "Papa. Papa." At last, Jabus, his face red and dripping sweat, relaxed his arms and flung himself into a corner where he sat, eyes darting. Zelo sat by his father. Adah, holding Reuel's hand, joined her husband and Zelo in the corner, but Jabus did not acknowledge them. He drew up his knees and laid his head on his arms. Dust from the dirt floor and sleeping mats filled the air. One by one family members reclaimed their places against the wall.

"The blood," Enoch continued, "will protect us. When Yahweh sees the blood, he will pass over us. All the family heads in all the houses in Goshen have applied the blood."

Jabus lifted his head. He was not finished. "This is outlandish. Who told you all this? No—do not tell me—*Moses*."

"Moses does not work on his own. He is directed by Yahweh," said Mordecai.

"And once again the talking bird speaks," said Jabus. Rachel, still tented under her veil, slipped a hand out and laid it on her husband's arm. She wanted to explore the mat of thick hair but kept her hand still.

Now listen to me everyone," said Enoch. "We must be ready to leave tonight." He had dreaded telling them this, had put it off until after the meal.

Hannah said, "Leave tonight? What about Jorham?" Enoch knelt before his younger sister-in-law. She clutched his extended hand and began to cry.

He had delayed going for Rachel while he searched for Jorham, his younger brother by three year. He knew where to find his sister, but his brother, conscripted from a Goshen wheat field three months before, had been shipped across the Red Sea to the Sinai copper mines. Starved and worked to death, few returned from the mines, located along the eastern coast where the Sinai desert meets the Gulf of Suez—the worst place for a Hebrew slave to end up. Two weeks before this night, Enoch had caught a fishing boat across the sea. Heading south along the coast, he had searched for many days, hiding during the day, slipping into the slave barracks at night to question the miners. His description, containing only six words, had become a desperate plea: *he looks like me only taller*. Distraught and dispirited, without a single lead, he caught a boat heading north and returned to Goshen. "He may show up yet. If he does not, I will take care of you and the children. You know that." Enoch patted Hannah's hand and turned back to the room. He said again, "Yahweh is rescuing his people tonight."

"But where are we going, Enoch?" said Sarah. "You never tell us that. Are we going south to where the black Ethiopians live?"

"Yahweh has promised Moses we are going to a land flowing with milk and honey. A rich land. Moses calls it The Promised Land. That is all I know. We have to trust Yahweh."

"And do not forget Moses," Jabus snorted.

When no one had anything else to add, Enoch said, "But for now we will just rest a while." He put his back to the wall and inched down to sit with Sarah. He snored so soon and so loudly, Reuel thought he must be teasing and laughed.

Sleep eluded Phinehas. As the spring evening cooled, the dying embers in the fire pit gave little heat or light. He could hardly remember when he had lived in such a humble house as this—dirt floor, rough plastered walls, thatched roof. But he had. Of the tribe of Manasseh, a direct descendant of Joseph, he, too, had lived in a village located on one of the many branches of the Nile in the land of Goshen. Not far north of Enoch's compound, his family, with aunts, uncles and cousins, had kept a paddock of goats and farmed flax for making linen cloth and wheat to fill Pharaoh's granaries.

Although they had once been allowed to live free, no living Hebrew remembered that happy state. The elders did remember the days when Pharaoh tightened his grip on the twelve Hebrew tribes. They told stories of their anguish when boy babies had been thrown into the Nile. Like his cousins, curled in sleep on the floor around him, they lived in bondage and served

Pharaoh. And like his cousins, in spite of their own poor state, Phinehas, and his older brother, Shemida, had learned about Yahweh, the one true God. The glow of the coals, the smell of close people, pungent and sweet, the snoring dog sounding human, carried him back to nights when he had felt safe, and the voices of his father and uncles had discussed and debated the stories of creation, the tower of Babel, Noah and the flood.

And then his father and mother died, and Shemida, unchecked, began to torment his younger brother. Phinehas remembered having his head slammed against the wall more than once. He remembered being battered, tripped and shoved. Then a smile played at the corners of his mouth and he remembered a bright summer day when a little boy with knobby knees named Phinehas played in the yard with his cousin, Abigail. Her red hair flamed in the sun. Sheol opened its jaws that day and swallowed up the boy. He never saw his home again. *Tomorrow I will see it*, he thought. *Maybe I will see her.*

The dog howled. Phinehas realized he had fallen asleep. Enoch threw a small log on the fire. He watched the sparks for a moment, then raised his voice over the howling, "It's time to go. Everybody up. Yahweh is rescuing his people tonight."

While his family stirred, Enoch peered out the small narrow window. What was that strange light? He could plainly see the goats and oxen. Everyone wanted to know, "Is it morning?" Sleepy people shuffled to the door and stood in a shaft of light. Neither moonlight nor early morning sun, a light, plenteous and pure as white fire, shined from a high pillar in the eastern sky and rained down upon Goshen. Only Yahweh could send such a light; the wonder of it reflected in their faces.

&

Phinehas, Enoch, and Rachel walked to the edge of the path. The men faced each other. "Thank you for everything," said Phinehas. "I need to find my family." He turned to Rachel, and saw her worried brow. "It's not that far. I'm sure I can make it before they leave."

"We will meet again," she said, then sang to the basket, "Goodbye, Sekhmet." She stood with Enoch in the path and watched her new friend and distant cousin walk away. The basket under Phinehas' arm and the dragging carpet roll threw his gait off, making his striped coat swing oddly. "We could have put the carpet in Mordecai's cart," she said, as he walked into the strange light and disappeared around the bend. There was something about him that made her want to call him back.

The women fed the children yogurt and cheese and dressed them warmly. They rolled sleeping mats and gathered things that would go into making a new home: cooking utensils, grinding stones, looms, churns. They packed unleavened bread in pouches and filled water bags at the well. The women loaded everything into Enoch's wagon and atop it all they securely tied children too young to walk and bleating newborn kids.

The men set the dogs to herding the goats while they dismantled the paddock and loaded the posts and troughs. They gathered flints and kindling and tools. Enoch yoked the oxen. Thank you, Yahweh, he thought; apparently neither of the massive creatures was first-born. He hooked them to the wagon. A worm of worry entered his mind: *what am I going to feed the oxen?* They were not like goats or sheep which could live off the land. Zelo and Reuel sat astride the oxen, kings of the caravan. And then, standing in the light of Yahweh, ready, they waited their turn to leave. And waited.

"Why do we not leave, Husband?" said Sarah.

Enoch raised his voice and spoke to his waiting family: "I think Manasseh is the seventh or eighth tribe to leave. Moses has set a fixed order; we are supposed to go in that order. Every tribe has a banner to follow." He spread his arms, palms up, in apology. "Judah is first. Then Issachar or Zebulun—I cannot remember; then Reuben, and Gad..." His voice trailed off. *Some leader I turned out to be,* he thought, adding this failure to all the others. He looked at Jabus, expecting a blistering comment, but satisfied that he was part of a disgusted consensus, Jabus said nothing.

Finally Sarah and Hanna let the children loose to play. Reuel and Zelo grew weary of straddling the oxen and dismounted. Everyone decided he was hungry, so the women fed them flat bread and soft cheese.

Like the sound of the Nile when it roils in late summer, the clamor of many people, approaching with wagons and herds, grew from a low rumble to a roar. They were the first of a multitude. Excited, noisy Hebrews passed by Enoch's compound, a few at first, then more and more, until a parade of wagons and carts creaked and rattled their way past the watching family. Wagons as loaded as their own crowded the path; children cavorted among the goats and sheep and dogs. Down the hundreds of paths and footbridges that made up the maze of Goshen, they headed toward the strange light with directions to regroup east of the city of Ramses.

Enoch repeatedly stopped passersby and asked, "What tribe are you?" *Judah; Issachar; Zebulun; Simeon; Reuben; Gad.* Enoch never saw a banner—their path was far from a main route—but without fail when one tribe petered out, another began. The elders had taken to heart the importance Moses had placed on an ordered leave-taking. When a runner finally brought word that Manasseh's turn had come, the sun languished in the afternoon sky, and the cool, spring morning had become a bitter accusation from Sarah. The mysterious column of white fire had long since changed into an equally mysterious pillar of cloud. The children had to be regathered, water pouches refilled, and a last trip to the latrine accomplished.

Enoch's family joined the flow of Manasseh's thousands. Enoch took hold of the lead ox's ring and Zelo and his younger brother, Reuel, looking as proud as any of Pharaoh's horsemen, finally kicked the oxen into motion. Mordecai, with Rachel by his side, grasped the handles of his two-wheel push cart and fell in behind the dogs and goat herd. They left their home by the stream of the Nile River in the land of Goshen. No one looked back.

Chapter 3

AT LAST, ENOCH THOUGHT, *WE ARE on our way to the Promised Land.* His burden had increased a hundred-fold, but he determined to concentrate on the path before him and trust Yahweh to get them through. The warm brass ring and the hot breath of the plodding ox comforted him. His family's elation quickly died. The once-familiar path stretched before them, muddy and acrid with goat, oxen, and ass droppings and deeply rutted now from wagon wheels and carts that had gone before. The smell did not bother anyone—they lived next to a goat paddock—but the ruts... Enoch looked ahead to the next wagon and the next, to Manasseh, his tribe, his people: some dressed in rough clothing; some in finery given by their Egyptian masters; some bent from years of hard labor; some young and vigorous; all toiling and pulling their way through the mire. He marveled that every path, every road, every footbridge in Goshen would carry thousands upon thousands of Hebrews to freedom that day. *My footprints and my tracks will mingle with theirs on this road.*

Freedom. What would it feel like? His heart seemed to beat faster; his mind expanded at the thought of it. His own plot of land. He pictured himself standing with his sons on a wide plain, his dogs herding hundreds of goats into a corral for sheering; or maybe he would be standing on a hillside looking down into a green valley with his own goats grazing. His children would never be taken away to serve a cruel king. He looked over his shoulder past the loaded wagon. There were his brothers' wives trudging through the rank mud, and Sarah, working to keep her balance, supporting the unborn baby in her hands, as was her habit. There were his little daughters, holding up their skirts, stepping high, and his sons, more precious than gold, now stomping through the mud. They would be free. His brothers followed behind with the dogs, working the goats, and last, Mordecai and Rachel with their cart. They would all be together in the Promised Land. He looked east toward the pillar of cloud standing high in the sky, visible above the willows lining the path. His lips moved silently. *Thank you, Yahweh. Help us.*

A small brown bird hung from a low twig and fussed, pulling Enoch's thoughts away from life's larger wonderment. He noticed that the heavy birds, the storks and cranes, no longer displayed their anger at the intrusion. They wearily stood at the water's edge and cocked their heads, staring at the passersby with piercing eyes, waiting for the hubbub to stop. They would have a while to wait, thought Enoch; Manasseh was the eighth tribe to depart. Four to go. He hated to think how deep the muck would be when the last Hebrew crossed the last bridge.

At times Enoch watched with envy as those without wagons passed. Their herds and flocks mingled with slower groups and would have carried some of their goats away if not for the vigilance of Perez, Hazor, Jabus, and the dogs. With no room to pass, whenever one wagon stalled, the line of wagons halted. Wheels came off or mired, and time after time men rallied to help their fellow neighbors. Anyone could be next.

The women welcomed the stops. A stop meant rest for them and the children. By late afternoon all the children had climbed onto the wagon. When Enoch heard Sarah calling his name, he hurried back to his wife, knowing she could go into labor at any time. She stood stalled, mired in mud, overtaken by bleating goats and barking dogs. Her face wet with tears, she supported the baby with laced fingers. *Shame on me*, he thought, *this is my wife, my love.* He carried her to the wagon. She laid her head on his shoulder. "Can we go back home?"

"We'll be off this path soon, I think. Girls, pile some of those mats up for your mama."

"Oh, look," said Sarah. Slats from a wagon floated slowly by. "Someone has lost their wagon. What will they do? What if our wagon gives out?"

"They will walk like all these other people passing by. They will make it. With Yahweh's help, we will all make it—even if we have to walk."

"I do not want to live with the Ethiopians."

Enoch pointed south. "That's south—Ethiopia." He pointed to the cloud of Yahweh. "That is east, the way we are going." He kissed his wife, and raising one finger, leveled his eyes upon his six children. Once he had their attention, he said, "Take good care of your mama." By the time he returned to the oxen, the girls had gathered to pat and caress their mother, and the boys had poured a bowl of water.

Hannah and Adah, calf-deep in the muck, sighed in unison, having watched the scene. "Sarah is a lucky woman," said Hannah. "If only Jorham were here... He is sweet like Enoch. Oh, Adah, will I ever see my husband again?"

"Come on," said Adah, "we're starting." She kept her disappointment in her husband, Jabus, and his son, Zelo, to herself. *Would that Jabus go off to the mines and never return,* she thought. *And I would re-marry and—*

"Mama." Adah looked up. Reuel, worn out from riding the ox, now rode on the wagon with his cousins. He held out a bowl of water for his mother. She took the water and shared it with Hannah. "You are a good son, Reuel," she said. The wagon eased forward. The women resigned themselves to the mud and their churning thoughts.

Late in the afternoon they crossed the last bridge south of Ramses. Enoch breathed a thank you to Yahweh and pulled the wagon to a stop in the deep shade of a large willow tree. "Everybody out!" he shouted.

The women and girls, along with neighbors and new friends, found a secluded spot to bathe. Rachel swirled and scrubbed the hem of her dress in the slow-moving water, then she raised her dress and splashed water onto her arms and legs. "I have never been this dirty in my life," she said to no one in particular.

"Do you think we have?" said Sarah.

Rachel pretended not to hear. Sarah plainly had not forgiven her for keeping the gifts from Asmath's mother. Rachel had tried not to think of her mistress now that the woman's only son lay dead. She had always been kind to Rachel, treating her like a daughter. *Today she must be pulling out her hair,* she thought. *Or she may be dead and Asmath is left alone to mourn.* Rachel fingered the goddess in her pouch. Among the sharp angles and shapes of the gold items, the jade goddess, Ma'at, was easy to find. *I could ease her out of the pouch and sink her in the creek,* she thought. *But what if I should need her? She is not evil like some of the gods. Not scary like...* Enoch whistled loudly, his signal for the family to gather.

The women climbed up the bank, Rachel and the sisters-in-law pushing and pulling Sarah. They wrung out the hems of their dresses, re-dressed the girls, and returned to the wagon.

The boys and men had stripped and swum and, pulling the dogs from the herd one by one, had allowed them to swim and cool off. The boys watered the oxen and goats while the women assembled flat bread and cheese. The children, fed and watered, climbed onto the wagon for naps. Sarah settled herself in a corner nest and instantly fell asleep. Enoch cleared a place at the rear for his oldest dog.

Before pulling the oxen into motion, Enoch sent Perez up the willow tree. "Ramses is to the left. As far as I can see—there is no end to them—people are moving to the right of the city. Follow the tracks, Brother." In the company of neighbors, Enoch's band joined the throngs of Hebrews heading south of Ramses, eastward, toward the town of Succoth. Within an hour they left the influence of the Nile—the black land—and headed into the red land, a barren waste of rose-colored sand and rock.

⁊

Mordecai, elated to leave the sucking mud of Goshen, now struggled to push his two-wheeled cart through coarse sand and the ruts of a thousand wagons. And the rocks—head-sized and fist-sized stones littered the ground; but

45

worse were those hidden beneath the sand, throwing the cart sideways or stopping it with a jolt. He thanked Yahweh that his hands, rough from the brickyards, could take the punishment. His feet, however, were not faring as well; with each step his sandals slipped and shifted, and the sand scoured blisters. Abandoned wagons and carts with broken wheels or axles littered the way. Mordecai prayed their fate would be different.

Rachel helped when she needed to, pushing, shoving the cart along with him, but he knew her heart was not in it; her heart remained at the vizier's villa with *her Egyptian family*. The thought of it made Mordecai's lip curl. He corrected himself. At Pharaoh's wood shop he had learned from Elias, his wise, spiritual father, that Yahweh would not bless a resentful heart; that a resentful heart fed on itself, until there was nothing left but bile and sickness. By an act of will, as Elias had taught him, he rearranged his thoughts and thanked Yahweh that his betrothed had lived with a kind family and had not known the hardship he had suffered. He felt better instantly and glanced back at his wife following close on his heels. Wife—he still surprised himself every time he thought of her in that way. Would she ever know, would he ever be able to tell her, that thoughts of her had carried him through the worst times of his life? How he had clung to the image of her, framed in the vizier's window. That smile. He wondered how it would be to kiss those lips.

"Mordecai," Rachel called. The perpetual noise of barking dogs, bleating sheep, baaing goats, shouting, and wheels crunching across the sand, had settled into an incessant drone. Like the roar of night sounds, all the notes blended, and no one noticed except for the occasional scream (there were many reasons to scream—snakes, injuries, scorpions), and now most of those, too, were ignored. "Mordecai," Rachel called again, "Morsel and I are dying of thirst." She dragged the last word into a loud whine. Mordecai stopped. He shook his hands to restore life into them and examined the bloody blister on top of his left big toe. Rachel stood by the cart, poured a bowl of water for the puppy, then took a long drink, dribbling water down her neck. She handed the water bag to Mordecai and sat on the back of the cart.

"You might want to be careful with the water." He finished the puppy's bowlful and said, "I do not know when we will see another well." Rachel started to answer when a man, riding a small donkey, shook his fist, cursed, and kicking the donkey, pulled his wagon around them. A woman and four dusty children looked down with disgust as they passed. "What did he say?" demanded Mordecai.

"I think he said, 'my donkey will soon be dead.'"

Mordecai laughed and coughed. He looked toward the cloud of Yahweh, diffused now by dust churned into the air. An afternoon wind seemed to be rising from the north. "Put Morsel under a mat. This dust is bad for him." Rachel broke open the last goose egg the old woman had given her at the market and fed the yolk to the puppy. She hemmed him into a corner and covered him.

"Where are Enoch and everyone?" she asked. She shielded her eyes with her hand and looked ahead. "I do not see them."

"I think we got separated." At the look of alarm on Rachel's face, Mordecai added, "Don't worry. We will catch up to them. Let's go." He took his place behind the cart, gripped the handles and pushed. Immediately his toe began to throb.

By late afternoon the suspended sand dust filled the air with a pink glow. Mordecai stopped. He had tied his head cloth over his mouth and nose. Dust filled his hair and mud rimmed his eyes. His toe was on fire and now the top of his right foot had developed a blister. "I don't care how many people have to go around, I am stopping." Rachel did not argue. She had wrapped her veil around her face. She removed it and shook out a cloud of rosy dust.

"I do wish we had caught up to Enoch," she said. To their surprise no one pushed around them. Everyone, it seemed, had stopped simultaneously. The vast Hebrew nation, wrapped in a desiccated pink shroud, spread around them as far as they could see.

"I have never seen so many people in my life," said Mordecai. "You know, I am starving. What do we have to eat?"

"Nothing but the white of a goose egg, and we must save that for the puppy." Rachel climbed onto the cart and searched the sea of people for Enoch's wagon. She thought she and Mordecai would be eating flat bread and cheese with the family. Was it her fault they had fallen behind? Was she supposed to pack food? She could not see far, but she saw a familiar figure. "I see Cursing Man up there," she said. "Why don't you go borrow some food from him?" Mordecai helped her down and felt the pouch around her waist.

"That has got to be uncomfortable. You could roll it in a mat and put it on the cart," he suggested.

She ignored him and began to break up the egg for Morsel. *We would be better off if you had wrapped some bread around your waist,* he thought.

"I have no idea where we are," said Mordecai, "but there are a lot of us here." Enoch had shared two sleeping mats with them. Mordecai pulled the mats from the cart and spread them out. He lay down, facing away from the second mat, and slept instantly. Rachel stood, watching her husband. Small cook fires began to spring to life as far as she could see. *Well,* she thought, *I may not have packed food, but he did not bring things to build a fire.* As night fell, the dust settled and the air began to cool. The pillar of cloud changed imperceptibly and began to glow, pouring light upon the encamped Hebrews. Rachel lay down with her back to her husband. She tethered the puppy to her wrist, tucked him between her breasts, and covered herself with Asmath's best wool shawl. She, too, slept instantly.

"Stop!" Mordecai's shout pierced Rachel's dream. She woke to the sounds of a struggle and the creak of the wagon swaying on its axle.

"What is it?" She stood, clutching the puppy and her shawl. The pillar of fire revealed the retreating figure of a running man, dodging between wagons and campfires.

Mordecai rummaged through the cart. "A thief. Trying to steal my tool box. He did not get anything." He unloaded the cart, and stashed his tool box and Rachel's bags underneath. "I was foolish to think I could leave our things in the open."

"Your nose is bleeding." Rachel reached deep into her bag and retrieved a square of cotton cloth. She poured water onto it and handed it to Mordecai. "*That*," she said, "is the reason I am keeping *this* right *here*." She patted the pouch.

Mordecai handed back the cloth. "No, sit down. We are going to do something about your feet. Do you have a knife?"

"Well, they hurt, but I don't want to cut them off," he grinned.

"Ha. Ha. Give me the knife." Rachel made a small cut in the cloth then ripped it in half. She unraveled long threads from her sleeping mat. "Hold still." She laid the pieces on his bare feet and wrapped the threads around many times. As she worked, he watched and marveled to himself, *this is my wife—what a wonderful word.* With his feet wrapped they lay down again, back to back. It seemed they had just closed their eyes when the shofar sounded—the call to awake and prepare to travel. No hint of light shown in the eastern sky. By the light of the column of fire, Mordecai and Rachel reloaded the cart. The puppy, listless now from lack of food, lay in Rachel's arms. "I do not think he is going to live." she said.

Mordecai took his place between the handles of the cart; when the throng inched to life, he pushed. "You did well with the wrappings," he told Rachel. Preoccupied with the puppy, she did not answer. "Rachel, listen— dung dries fast in this air, if you want a fire tonight you need to find the driest you can and pick it up." Without hesitation, Rachel cleared space and began to toss dung onto the cart. By mid-morning, Mordecai's strength waned, and Rachel's movements slowed. "Climb up and see if you see Enoch," he said. *Are we going to starve to death on the way to the Promised Land?*

Rachel peered over the trudging people. Was that Phinehas? She squinted. Who else had a blue striped coat like that? Who else carried a rug on his shoulder, a basket under his arm, and ten bags hanging everywhere? Rachel cupped her hands around her mouth and shouted, "Phinehas!" The short fat man plodded through the sand and ruts, his eyes down, his feet dragging. "He cannot hear me. I'm going to go get him. Cut over." Rachel waited for a flock of sheep to pass then jumped from the cart and threaded her way through wagons and walking groups, calling her friend's name, losing sight of him from time to time. Oblivious, Phinehas trudged on.

Phinehas, slave to a purveyor of fine objects and rugs, was not in the desert. He had gone home to his master. He and Sekhmet. He cut open a pale green melon, the color of his jade scarab amulet, and scooped out the seeds. Later he would separate the tan-colored seeds from the clinging tendrils and roast them. But for now he cut into the cool flesh, and taking a bite too large, let the juice drip down his chin. *Oh, Sekhmet, come sit on PaPa's lap. What is this? A bowl of figs? Yes, Master, I will have some, thank you.*

"Phinehas." Rachel stood in his path and thrust her palms against the dust-covered coat.

Phinehas stopped. He raised his eyes and blinked. Sweat and dust covered his face like pink plaster. Through startled tears he said, "Rachel. Is it you?"

"It's me." She smiled at his confusion, patting his arm. "Mordecai is bringing the cart over. We lost the rest of the family."

"Lost the family?"

"Not lost-lost. Just misplaced. They are somewhere up ahead. Where are your people? Your brother? Did they go off and leave you?"

He shrugged. "Let's just say they misplaced me." He wiped his eyes, dragging a thin slick of mud across his cheeks.

Rachel looked for Mordecai but did not see him. "Let's go find my husband. If you cut across, everyone gets upset. One man cursed us because we stopped." Rachel hung some of Phinehas' bags on her shoulders. They found Mordecai with the cart's axle stuck on a rock.

"You are a welcome sight, brother," said Mordecai. The men beat each other on the back, raising clouds of dust. Phinehas made a pile of his belongings and together the men freed the cart. Rachel uncovered the puppy. Cradling the lifeless body, she began to cry.

"What's the matter?" asked Phinehas.

"We don't have anything to feed him. We think he's dying," said Mordecai.

"I have food. Let's get some into the little fellow." Phinehas threw off the coat and dug deep into a woven bag. "We can all eat. They ignored irate travelers who flowed around them and unrolled the carpet behind the cart.

Rachel fed yogurt and bread to the puppy. They watched as he began to brighten. "Oh, Phinehas," she said, "I think you've saved his life." Phinehas dug into the bag again and after much rooting and sorting pulled out a linen-wrapped bundle the size of Mordecai's two fists. With a flourish he folded back one corner flap. He had their full attention; they leaned toward him; he turned back the opposite corner and laid bare a perfectly formed loaf of bread.

"Close your mouths," he chuckled, "I'm not finished." More rooting and he came up with a packet of smoked fish.

People slowed, looked their way. "We may cause a riot," whispered Mordeai as if anyone could hear him. Phinehas divided the loaf into thirds, made pockets, stuffed in smoked fish, and passed Rachel and Mordecai their share. They ate, talking with full mouths.

"I thought we would be with Enoch, so I did not pack any food, said Rachel.

"But I could not keep up," said Mordecai.

Phinheas looked from one to the other. "But no one is blaming anyone..."

Mordecai and Rachel smiled thinly at one another and shook their heads, no.

"You know," said Mordecai, "Elias taught me that Yahweh always provides if we trust him. But we were not trusting him, Phinehas, and yet here you came."

"Well, maybe you were trusting more than you thought."

They piled Phinehas' cat and his belongings onto the cart. "I don't know how you carried all that," said Rachel, and turning her back to the men, reached under her dress, and released the ties on the pouch. She opened one end and took out the mirror. She buffed the smooth polished brass on her dress and grinning, handed it to Phinehas.

"Maybe I was also trusting more than I thought. You came just in time." He looked in the mirror. His mouth gaped. Mordecai, trying not to laugh, had been trying not to laugh since first laying eyes on Phinehas; then he let out a loud guffaw. Rachel handed the mirror to Mordecai. He looked at his mud-rimmed eyes and sand-filled beard. He laughed so hard tears ran.

"I hate to look at myself," said Rachel. She held the mirror at arm's length. "This is not funny." She laughed. "Tonight we each get one bowl of wash water. May we, Husband?"

"I think we must."

By standing outside the handles, and with a little practice, the two men managed to coordinate their movements and push the cart together. The Hebrew nation passed southeast of Succoth and entered the wilderness.

By the second night the great congregation stretched from east of Succoth to the edge of the wilderness, a day's walk from Judah, the lead tribe, to Napthali, the last tribe to leave Goshen. Once again, as darkness fell over the hot sands and the air cooled, the pillar of cloud stopped moving forward and changed into a stationary column of fire.

As the dust settled, Phinehas unrolled his rug, and Mordecai and Rachel stashed all their belongings under the cart. Never again would they foolishly leave anything in the open. They washed their faces with as little water as possible and settled for the night. The three made a circle of stones and piled the dung Rachel had gathered into a neat pile. Rachel and Phinehas watched intently as Mordecai unsuccessfully struck flint until sweat poured down his face. He sat back on his haunches. "Do we really need a fire?"

"No. We're fine" said Rachel. "Tomorrow I will pick up some sticks if I see any. Phinehas, you should have seen Mordecai last night. I guess you wondered why we put everything under the cart? Well, we had a robber." She paused for effect. "Mordecai fought him off, and he ran away without getting a single thing."

Phinehas watched as Mordecai's shoulders relaxed, and the angst of failure washed from his weary eyes. Where had this young woman, spoiled and cossetted in a rich man's house, learned to express such sympathy? With a few words, a little story, she had covered her husband. *Oh, to get such a wife as that,* he thought. He had worried about the young couple. Maybe they would be all right after all... "I think we need a fire. A reward for chasing off the robber." He took the fire pan and surveyed the neighboring camps. Rachel and Mordecai watched as their friend rounded his shoulders, clutched his fire pan to his chest and shuffled to the chosen campsite where a large family sat around a roaring fire.

"He looks so pitiful, maybe you should go with him," said Rachel.

"I could never beg like that." At the brickyard and the wood shop Mordecai depended on no one, asked for nothing. Not even Elias could tear down that wall.

Phinehas returned with a pan of glowing embers. They built a fire, ate bread and fish, and finally lay down for the night. Mordecai covered his head against the chill and slept. He woke when Rachel said, "How could Enoch go off and leave us like that? We were all together and then they were just gone."

"We will catch up to them tomorrow. I'm sure he did not mean to." *Rachel needs to start trusting me... not that I am doing so well...* sleep overtook his worried thoughts.

The next morning Rachel woke alone under the cocoon of shawls and sleeping mats and supposed Mordecai had gone to the men's latrine. One of the greatest problems the travelers suffered—what to do about bodily functions—resolved when they devised a system: at the end of the day, several families worked together and dug latrines for the men and women. Makeshift fencing with mats provided a bit of privacy. Rachel dreaded the latrine and the line of women leading to it. She blushed at conversations of the most personal nature. When her turn came she thought, *if Asmath could see me now...*

Phinehas puttered at the cart. He had not seen Mordecai. He and Rachel repacked and waited. They dare not leave their campsite for fear of losing the man in the turmoil.

Mordecai had left his sleeping wife long before dawn. Enoch and the family could not be that far ahead; why should Rachel worry another day? By lining up on the constant and bright light of the pillar, he tried to keep from veering off the track of wagon wheels and roiled sand. He knew Enoch well enough to know that he would be worried about Rachel. Not that Enoch mistrusted Mordecai to take care of her. *If he had not trusted me,* he thought, *would he not have nullified the marriage?*

"Mo, stop man." Enoch's voice cut into Mordecai's ruminations. The cousins exchanged a Hebrew kiss: right cheek, left cheek, right hand resting on the left shoulder of the other. "We've been worried about you. Where is my baby sister? Did she run you off?"

"I don't run off that easy," said Mordecai, grinning. Although said in jest, and Enoch smiled to take the sting out of the question, he knew his brother-in-law had doubts about the marriage, as did he. "Your little sister is back a way with Phinehas."

"Phinehas?"

"It seems we've adopted him. Or maybe it's the other way around. We were starving when Rachel saw him. He has food."

"Let's go get them." Enoch struck out, threading through the snarl, meeting a herd of goats head on.

"How has the family been faring?" asked Mordecai, dodging goats.

"Sarah is in a bad way. We think she is carrying twins."

"I'm sorry you had to come back. With Phinehas to help me, we should make better time. But Rachel has been worried."

"One of the oxen fell dead." He pointed. "There they are." Rachel stood on top of the cart waving her arm in a wide arc. She jumped down, ran to meet them, and linking her arm in Enoch's, led them back to Phinehas.

Greetings over, Enoch and Mordecai took hold of the handles and pushed the cart toward the family's camp. They pulled up next to the wagon as Jabus, arms bloodied, pulled the dripping liver from the dead ox. He and Enoch turned the bloody slab over several times and examined it, pointing, saying, *there and there.* "Hold on to the dogs," Enoch said. "Come here, men, and all you boys." He waited for every male to gather around the carcass. "You all need to see this." He held out the liver. "See those worms? Those ridges? This is a bad disease that will make us sick if we eat it. Never, never eat meat when the liver looks like this. And do not let the dogs eat it either. Will you remember?" He looked at the boys. They all nodded solemnly. While Mordecai modified the yoke, the rest dug a hole, rolled the dead beast into it, and set it on fire. "In good conscience," said Enoch, over Jabus' protests, "we cannot leave it here to be eaten by some innocent man or beast."

"Enoch stood in front of the remaining ox, rested his forehead between the huge brown orbs, and said, "I beg you—please do not die."

Chapter 4

LIKE A CLOUD SHADOW, A SLOW-MOVING blot upon the land, the great Hebrew nation moved across the sands of the wilderness toward the Red Sea. The sons of Jacob, twelve tribes, separate but united, numbered 600,000, not counting women and children. They left in their wake a wide scar of tracks and ruts and the detritus of a vast population. Disasters befell them along the way. Wheels came off; axles broke; oxen died. They persevered. They loaded their possessions and their children on their backs and they walked. They moved within the borders of their tribes under their banners; they moved in martial array according to Moses' plan. Yahweh did not remove the pillar of cloud by day nor the pillar of fire by night.

Once reunited, Enoch's family traveled with confidence. Everyone had a job to do and they did it or they answered to Enoch. Every day they learned something new, like the importance of finding kindling and plenty of dung for their nightly fire. Phinehas had gained his walking legs; he and Mordecai kept pace with the cart. Rachel helped with the children. When they came to a well she hauled water for the flock. They grew lean and burned by the sun.

Late one afternoon, on the way to Etham, on the far edge of the wilderness, Mordecai spotted Cursing Man's abandoned wagon and his dead donkey. "Did I not tell you that donkey was half dead?" Rachel gloated. "Poor thing."

"Let's push over," Mordecai said. "I believe the fool has left the harness. We can use the leather for something." They pulled the cart alongside the wagon. "It looks like the axle broke and pulled the donkey down. They just unloaded and walked away." Mordecai lifted the donkey's head to loosen the harness; a large brown eye opened and rolled toward him. Mordecai sat back on his heels. "He's not dead!"

Phinehas peered at the prostrate donkey. "I guess we need to put him out of his misery. Mo, can you cut his throat?"

"This is awful," said Rachel. "What's wrong with him?" The donkey raised its head. Mordecai scratched it between the ears.

Phinehas prodded and manipulated the animal's legs. "I don't think anything's wrong with his legs. Maybe we can get him up."

"Undo him, Mordecai," Rachel ordered, "let's get him up. Maybe we can keep him."

"I don't know about this," said Mordecai. "How much water do donkeys drink?" Rachel straightened her mouth and leveled a flat stare at her husband.

"All right. All right. Come on Phinehas." Rachel crooned encouragements to the donkey while the three of them heaved the animal to its feet. Mordecai led the donkey to the cart. "Rachel, get him some water. Not too much. We have to ration. Would you look at this." He walked the donkey around the cart. He looked in the bowl. "Why are you being so stingy? This poor animal is dying of thirst."

Mordecai had never owned an animal. Morsel belonged to Rachel, but the donkey would be his. "What if Cursing Man sees him and wants him back," he worried.

"I'll take care of that," Rachel said. She took a rock from an abandoned fire pit and rubbed soot onto the donkey's face.

Mordecai stood back and admired his black-faced donkey. "You, Rachel, are a wife among wives."

"I can't wait to show him to Enoch," said Rachel, pouring more water. She squinted toward the east. "I think they've left us again."

Mordecai led the donkey in another circle. Over his shoulder he said, "This is the reason we fall behind. If it is not an orphan with a cat, it is a dead donkey. And I'm not going to take the blame anymore."

Phinehas grinned. "He is quite pleased with himself and his donkey."

"I would say so, yes." *A wife among wives*, she thought.

As if Yahweh knew they needed rest, the cloud stopped. Neighbors pilfered parts from the abandoned wagon then set it on fire. That night a man played jaunty tunes on his pan flute, and Mordecai, Rachel, and Phinehas rested among new friends. Mordecai had never danced, but when Rachel pulled him into the circle, he laced his arms shoulder to shoulder, threw off his sandals and stomped in the sand.

The next day, at their noon break, they drew up behind the family wagon. Sarah had doled out food but did not offer anything to Rachel and Mordecai. Phinehas called them aside and said, "Do not fret. I have food and mine is better than theirs." From the depths of one of his many bags he brought out more smoked fish, cheese and bread. Rachel saw Sarah standing on the back of the wagon, rubbing her belly, watching. Raising her bowl toward Sarah, Rachel nodded and smiled.

"Rachel," said Phinehas, "It is never wise to poke a beehive."

They camped at Etham on the edge of the wilderness. Mordecai turned his donkey into the shelter and led him to a pile of scrub the children had gathered. He tried to tell the story of the dead donkey to a distracted Enoch, who interrupted, "Moses has called a meeting of the elders. I am going, Cousin. Do you want to come?" At Mordicai's enthusiastic nod, he said, "Go get Phinehas and keep it quiet. I do not know if we will be welcome, but I have heard a disturbing rumor."

At a distance from the camps, Moses customarily set up a Tent of Meeting. From there he judged the people and issued decrees. The three walked for an hour through encamped Hebrews toward the farthermost camp of Judah and beyond. Enoch estimated 600 men assembled outside the Tent of Meeting. "There is our banner." He pointed out Manasseh's leaders who stood near the Tent of Meeting along with the other tribal heads.

Moses, an old man of eighty, his long beard blowing in the late afternoon wind, addressed the assembly. Flanked by his elder brother, Aaron, priests, and Joshua his young protege, he spoke the words Yahweh had given him:

"You are to turn back from Etham and camp before Pi-Hahiroth, between Migdol and the sea; you shall camp in front of Baal-Stephon, opposite it by the sea. Pharaoh will think the sons of Israel are wondering aimlessly and are trapped by the wilderness. Thus I will harden Pharaoh's heart and he will chase after you; and I will be honored through Pharaoh and all his army, and the Egyptians will know that I am Yahweh."

Enoch, Mordecai and Phinehas returned to their camp in silence. Enoch's heart churned. He was wearied of second-hand news, but now he wished he had not gone. He would surely get blamed for this news. He waited until the children slept, then he gathered the adults around the fire. He wanted to run out into the desert and cut his own throat—save Jabus the trouble.

His eyes moved from face to face around the circle. On his left, the Uncle Twins, Perez and Hazer, burnt now from the sun, stood shoulder to shoulder, their unlined faces open and trusting. Sarah: her huge belly bucked with the unborn child. She leveled her eyes toward Enoch as if to say, *what now?* Jabus, scowling—nothing new there—stood next to the black-veiled Adah who gazed into the fire. Hannah, her face a bleak mask of worry for her missing husband, wrung her hands absently. Phinehas next; his eyes also moved around the circle. Mordecai sat on a rock and peeled back the rag to check his blisters. He must have told Rachel; she pressed her lips into a straight line and gazed toward the pillar of fire.

Without preamble, Enoch said, "We are turning back toward Migdol. It seems Pharaoh has decided to come after us with his army." He braced himself.

Like a swarm of bees, questions filled the cold night air and stung Enoch from every side. *What? Turning back? Pharaoh is coming? Should we not go forward?*

"These are Yahweh's orders," he said. "We will do as Moses says."

"*Moses,*" said Jabus. "Always Moses." He kicked a rock into the fire, sending embers awhirl.

"That's right," said Enoch. "Always Moses. Yahweh has made Moses our leader. Has he not brought us this far?"

"Where are we going back to?" asked Perez

"We are going to a place called Pi-Hahiroth—*between two gorges*. We will follow the wadi to that place. It is between Migdol and the sea."

"The sea. Not a stream or a river... the sea? We will be trapped at the sea..." said Hazor.

"We would be better off if we had stayed in Egypt," said Sarah. She covered her face with her hands. "Oh my little children. My baby." She began to cry. Adah and Hannah sobbed.

"I told you I wanted to stay with Asmath," said Rachel. "You should have allowed me to save my life." Mordecai looked sharply at his wife but said nothing. "But surely," added Rachel, "there will be boats to carry us across the water..."

Jabus spoke with finality: "We will die here in this wilderness. Moses cannot save us from Pharaoh's army. This is our end."

"We will trust Moses and see," said Enoch.

"Oh, all right," said Jabus with false jollity, "we will just wait and see."

Enoch held his palms up in supplication. "Please, my family. Please trust Moses and Yahweh. Would Yahweh have brought us this far only to kill us? Why would the one who created all that exists do a thing like that? Is he some double-minded evil god like the gods of Egypt?" Enoch rested his gaze on each member of his family. "Is he?"

Phinehas spoke. "I do not know Yahweh very well," he said. "But when I was a small boy, my father and uncles taught me that Yahweh has compassion for his people. Did he not protect Noah and his family from the flood?"

"I just thought of something," said Mordecai.

"Here comes the talking bird," said Jabus.

"No, listen. Are we not carrying the bones of Joseph with us to the Promised Land? Joseph was a prophet. He knew that someday we would be going to a land of milk and honey and he wanted to be buried there. Surely Yahweh would not leave Joseph's bones in this wilderness. Or at the bottom of the sea." No one spoke. Peace seemed to settle over the gathering as they took in Mordecai's words. Like a rope to grasp, they held onto the logic of that one thought.

Enoch grinned. He wanted to hug Mordecai's neck. "So there, we will be the family that trusts Yahweh." He held out his arms. "Let's hold hands and make a pact." Jabus allowed Sarah and Adah to grasp his hands. Enoch said, "We will trust Yahweh, no matter what." Every voice repeated the promise, some with more conviction than others.

Enoch told them, "Get some rest. And," he held up a finger, "keep the children close tomorrow. We do not want them to be afraid."

Mordecai led the donkey and walked silently with Rachel and Phinehas to the cart. He built a small fire and sat in deep thought beside it. By now every soul had heard the news that Pharaoh would be coming with his army. The cold night air carried frenzied conversations and troubled voices from other camps. Bundled against the cold, Rachel joined him by the fire. "Phinehas already sleeps. You said just the right thing tonight—about Joseph's bones...

"Everybody had something to say." He stood. "I am tired, too. Good night." Mordecai abruptly left. Rachel sat alone by the fire. She fingered the pouch and sought Ma'at among the gold objects.

⅋

The next morning, at the sound of the shofar, they reversed direction into a cold, dense fog unlike any seen before. Under the pillar of fire, every droplet danced in rainbow colors. Few noticed. Loose sand at Etham and the previous day's ruts made the going hard. The blisters on Mordecai's feet bled. *I am a dung beetle,* he thought. *Nothing but a dung beetle.* To Rachel he was nothing but a slave. She would rather be in Ramses, a slave herself, than married to him. Did she not say as much last night? In front of the whole family? And boats, she had said. How many boats would it take to carry all of them across the sea? Hundreds. It would take hundreds of boats. It would take hundreds of boats months to get them all across. His thoughts shifted back to dung beetles. In truth they were hard working little creatures. They shaped the dung and once begun they never quit. Uphill. Downhill. Pushing, rolling balls of dung much heavier than themselves. And dung beetles were beautiful. He smiled. Did the jewelry makers not call them scarabs and fashion them into amulets and pendants? *Well,* he thought, *if I have to be a dung beetle, I will be the best one I can.* He shoved the cart with a jolt, wrenching the other handle from Phinehas' hand.

By mid-morning Mordecai, Rachel, and Phinehas lagged, but Enoch rigged a pole and rag to his wagon and Rachel kept the family in sight. The din of travel noise made conversation almost impossible. A flock of sheep had come up behind them. Or they had fallen back into it—no one knew. "How far is it to Migdol?" Rachel shouted toward Phinehas. He struggled to keep up with Mordecai on the other handle. If the little man bogged down, she helped him push out, but as the days passed, Phinehas grew stronger and leaner.

"My master and I came this way once to buy rugs at Elim. That's a seaport, behind us now. If we had not turned back, we would have ended up there. I think Migdol is a full day's travel away. Maybe two."

"So we have a little time before we die."

"You mustn't say that."

"I know. Joseph's bones."

"It's a good argument."

"I know. I was proud of Mordecai for coming up with it."

"What?" Mordecai heard his name.

"Nothing," she shouted.

"I hope you told him you were proud?"

"I did." Rachel ran her tongue over her teeth. Grit. She squinted at the sky. The lovely fog had dissipated. Not a single cloud except for the pillar. Just blue, blue. They had followed what seemed to be a wide sandy trail into a funnel of crags and low, rose-colored mountains. By midafternoon high cliffs rose on each side of the winding trail. Every foot fall, every word, every grind of wheel, echoed off the cliff walls, intermingling into a roar. No breeze found its way to the floor of the narrow canyon. Mordecai and Phinehas stripped to their loin cloths and pushed on. A bed of rocks replaced the deep sand and conquered more wagons. They stopped at a broken cart, along with other travelers, and pulled off bits for the evening fire. But the cloud kept leading them onward.

They came upon a man adrift with two goats, three small, dusty children, and his possessions, his body undecided on a stance: shoulders slumped in defeat, fists defiantly wadded on his hips, he stared at the pillar sadly, shouting angrily, "Is he ever going to stop? We cannot take much more of this."

Mordecai and Phinehas stopped the cart. Mordecai threw a mat on the donkey's back. "Was that your cart back there, Brother? Here, put your children on the donkey. My wife will lead him and you can walk beside." Mordecai loaded the man's goods onto the cart.

Rachel hugged each of the children and the men settled them onto the donkey. Rachel took hold of the harness. The man put his hands together and bowed. "May Yahweh bless you forever. My name is Simon, tribe of Ephraim These are Chuza, Gad and Anna."

"Are you alone?" asked Phinehas.

"No. We fell behind. My wife died in childbirth. I told my brothers my wife would have no trouble, and we would quickly catch up. Sad to say, I was wrong. We had to bury them." As he spoke, the children wailed. "Then my cart fell apart. These rocks are terrible." Rachel poured water for the children and showed them the puppy. When the crying stopped, she wiped the children's faces with a wet rag, and the little band started up.

Rocks covered the floor of the gorge, deepening at every bend. Goose, the name they had given the donkey because of his strange bray, picked his way, proving himself to be not only humorous but also sure-footed. Deep shade crawled down the crags, and cool air settled in the gorge. Surely the cloud would stop soon.

"Look, Rachel." Anna, Simon's daughter, pointed. Phinehas dropped his handle and ran ahead. Everyone peered into the gloom. In moments Phinehas returned, carrying a curly-headed baby at arm's length. He stood the child on the back of the cart, removed his hands from the child's armpits, and backed away with a grimace.

"Phinehas, for shame. That is no way to carry a baby," said Rachel. She rushed to the child and cupped the dirty, tear-streaked face in her hands. Snubbing hiccoughs shook the small body. "Hello, baby. Where's Mama? Where's Nana?" Fresh tears flowed, but the child did not make a sound. Rachel held out her arms, "Come here." The baby fell into her embrace. Rachel peeked under the dress. "She is smelly." The men and boys stood with pained expressions; the girl cheerfully watched as Rachel cleaned the child. *Is that not always the way of it,* Rachel thought.

"My baby sister died," said Anna. "I love babies."

Look, the shade has gone." said Phinehas. The cloud had turned to fire, lighting the gorge from side to side, illuminating the flood of humanity, its animals, and its portage, in its journey to the sea. "We should eat, and then I think we need to keep going. I think Yahweh wants us to make haste," he said. They shared what little food they had.

"We need to keep a watch for whoever is looking for the baby," said Mordecai. Rachel made no comment as he and Simon grasped the handles of the cart and pushed. From time to time they rested. Rachel often raised the shawl and peered at the sleeping baby. Near morning they passed from the gorges onto a broad stretch of sand. Endless camps stretched as far as they could see. To the east the early morning sun glinted on a wide stretch of water: the dreaded sea. Dusky blue mountains guarded the far shore. Men stood at the mouth of the gorges shouting, waving new arrivals on. For hours they had been directing the tribe of Manasseh. "Move on. Do not stop here. Find your tribe." One guide pointed north. "Manasseh is that way."

"I am from Ephraim" shouted Simon.

"Also north," shouted the guide.

"It looks like we will be together a little longer," said Phinehas.

They pushed north but had not gone far when Rachel said, "Look what I see." She pointed toward a white flag, whipping in the brisk sea breeze. Enoch, had been watching for them. He brought his three sons and his nephew, Reuel, to meet them. "Enoch, look who we found on the way." Rachel turned the baby in her arms so he could get a good look. "Is she not beautiful?"

"Who does she belong to?" asked Enoch. "Is she Arab?"

"We do not know," she said, "does she look Arab to you?"

"Rachel," Simon interrupted, "we want to take the baby. Anna is missing the girl-baby we lost, and one more child will not make a difference to me."

"That sounds like a good idea," said Mordecai.

Rachel felt her lips go numb. *I cannot faint*, she thought. *When I wake the baby will be gone. I will not faint.* "No," she managed to say. "I will keep the baby until we find her mother."

Mordecai said, "Now, Rachel..."

Phinehas saw the color drain from Rachel's face. He lifted the baby from her arms. "I will help Rachel look for the mother," he said. "I am good at finding people. Anna, child, we are sorry about your baby sister, but the baby will stay with Rachel." With that he walked away and headed for Enoch's wagon. When he looked back Rachel had gone to her knees, and Simon had led his bawling daughter away.

Late that afternoon the pillar of cloud stood over the vast, pale-pink sand beach at the edge of the Sea of Reeds. Thousands of people from the last three tribes—Dan, Asher and Napthlai—had emerged from the gorges and settled on the wide beach. A damp breeze, smelling of ocean, blew across the camps from the eastern sea.

One of Enoch's nanny goats stood tethered to Mordecai's cart where Rachel sat under a wind-blown tent Phinehas had rigged with his voluminous coat. Morsel frolicked and made the baby laugh, while Mordecai and Phinehas sat nearby, speculating.

"Do you suppose she wandered off?" said Mordecai.

"Maybe her mother died and there was no one else around," said Phinehas.

"This baby was abandoned," said Rachel with finality. She had heard enough of their nonsense.

"You do not know that, Rachel," said Mordecai.

"Do you want to know how I know it? I know it because she is a female. No one would leave a male baby behind. No one. And," she added, "if she had been a male, someone would have already picked him up." The men thought about that.

"That is cold." said Phinehas. "Are you saying people would have left her to die because she is female?"

"Not exactly. Maybe everyone thought someone else would take her."

"Maybe no one saw her," said Mordecai.

"You cannot always think the best of people." she said.

"I will think the best until they prove me wrong." said Mordecai.

"I have a question for you, Husband."

Phinehas stood and said, "I think I'll go for a walk." They watched their friend until he was out of earshot.

"Why were you so willing to let Simon take her?"

"Not because she is a female," he said.

"Then why?"

"Well, you have to understand it was not a planned thought on my part."

"Yes?" Rachel arched her eyebrows.

"She is not a puppy or a donkey we can just take... Maybe we should go to Moses."

"What! Why?"

"I know that baby's mother is out there somewhere. We could be accused of kidnapping."

"If her mother is out there, we will find her. But if we do not, then what?"

Mordecai chewed on the inside of his jaw. Finally he said, "If Moses agrees, then we will keep her."

"I have named her Kore—*partridge*—was she not a like a baby bird lost from its covey?"

"Rachel. You are only setting yourself up to be hurt. We are not naming that baby. Surely you realize—

Phinehas suddenly stood over them. "Something is happening. Listen. Mordecai jumped to his feet and pulled Rachel up. She held the baby in one arm, the puppy in the other. A shout started in the west, from the tribes camped nearest the mouth of the gorge, and grew louder and louder until it became a shrill scream, rolled across the beach, and shook every person in every tribe with panic. "Pharaoh is coming!" they shrieked. "He is here with his army! The Egyptians are here! Pharaoh and a thousand chariots!" Wave after wave of anguish overtook the people. Women screamed and tore their hair; children cried and clung to their mothers. Some people threw sand onto their heads and ripped their clothes. Some ran in circles, unable to think.

Her eyes wild with fear, Rachel screamed, "Let's get under the cart." Phinehas had the cat basket under his arm, ready to run, he knew not where.

Mordecai found himself on top of his cart. "Stop!" he yelled, his words harried by the force of the rising wind. "Pray! Pray! Everybody, pray to Yahweh. He will save us. Get on your knees. Get on your faces before Yahweh." A few people fell to their knees. Then more. And more. From one end of the vast beach to the other, Hebrews knelt, fell on their faces, and lifted their voices to Yahweh. "Help us. Do not forsake us," they cried.

Eyes remained fixed on the mouth of the gorges, but the panic slowly subsided. Rachel watched as men, friends and strangers, thanked her husband for his great deed in calming the people. Enoch rested his hand on Mordecai's shoulder. "Brother, you were heroic." Not since Elias had befriended him that first night in Pharaoh's wood shop, had Mordecai felt so blessed. *I am but a dung beetle,* he thought, *yet Yahweh used my voice.*

Still the east wind grew in strength. Whatever was not tied down blew away. The flag on Enoch's wagon sailed off across the camps. Dogs, their tongues hanging, worked the restless goats and sheep. Children hunkered under mats.

Moses, in the midst of the camps, made his way through the throngs, assaulted by accusations: "Is it because there were no graves in Egypt, that you have taken us away to die in this wilderness? Why have you dealt with us this way, bringing us out of Egypt? It would have been better for us to serve the Egyptians than to die in this wilderness."

Moving toward the sea, Moses said, "Do not fear! Stand by and see the salvation of Yahweh, which he will accomplish for you today, for the Egyptians whom you have seen today, you will never see again forever. Yahweh will fight for you while you keep silent."

Shouts arose, "Look at the cloud!" As one would trace a storm in its course across the horizon, so fingers pointed, and all eyes followed the pillar of cloud when it shifted from before the people and moved behind them to the mouth of the gorge. Then the Glory of Yahweh, his fire, filled the opening from side to side. The consuming terror slowly abated as the people realized that no one, not even Pharaoh and his army, could breach the pillar of Yahweh. The east wind grew stronger still; the sun set behind distant hills; night fell.

Light from the pillar of Yahweh pushed back the dark and revealed the plight of the people: Pharaoh behind them, the dark sea before. Moses motioned the Hebrews forward, and they gathered on the banks of the sea. His hair, beard, and clothes whirling wildly in the wind, he lifted his staff, stretched out his hand over the dark water, and stood steadfast. Then Yahweh swept the sea back by the strong east wind and turned the sea floor into dry land. Thus he divided the waters. By the light of the pillar, the first of Yahweh's chosen people, the tribe of Judah—75,000 men, their wives and children, and their flocks—moved across dry land toward the far shore. At a distance, they saw a wall of water standing high to their right and another to their left. As with Judah, so all the Hebrew nation filed in their tribes, in their ranks, behind their banners across the sea on dry land.

Somewhere in the tribe of Manasseh, a tribe of 32,000 men, with their families and herds, Enoch, followed closely by Mordecai and his cart, led his ox-drawn wagon, his herd of goats, and all his family, to the western shoreline and started across the wide expanse. To the east the hazy blue mountains of early afternoon seemed dark and menacing. And what of Pharaoh and his army? What other horrors lay between this sea and the Promised Land? Enoch scooped up a handful of sand, and marveling, allowed the wind to blow it away and with it his fears. *Is anything too difficult for Yahweh?* He thought. He laughed and kissed his ox squarely between the eyes.

"Hurry, Enoch," urged Sarah from the bed of the wagon. "What if that water breaks?"

Stooped and veiled to her eyes against the wind, Rachel carried the baby on her hip. "Mordecai, Phinehas, look." She stopped to pick up a clam shell and held it up. "I am going to save this shell forever to prove this was not a dream."

Before dawn the sea bed rose gently to meet the last tribe at the eastern shore. The shadowed mountains still ranged far to the east, allowing the arrivals a wide beach. Enoch had set up camp to the south, not far from their crossing. He jumped down from the wagon bed and announced to the family, "That's it. That's the last of them. I saw the last dog chase up the last goat. Poor old Moses is still standing there."

"But what of Pharaoh?" asked Rachel. "What happened to him and his army?"

"I suppose the pillar of fire killed them in the gorge," said Phinehas.

At daybreak joy turned to sorrow. A groan went up from the people. Enoch and his brothers stood on the wagon bed and watched with dread as Pharaoh's army advanced between the walls of water and started across the same path the Hebrews had just traveled. Jabus shouted, "Here they come. Surely we die."

From one end of the beach to the other the congregation began to wail and gather their belongings in haste. "To the mountains!" they cried.

Enoch had re-yoked the ox, when suddenly, Hazor and Perez shouted, "Come up, Enoch. Look at that!" No one could take it in; Moses stood on the eastern shore watching as Pharaoh's 600 chariots began to swerve and careen. Mayhem overtook the army of Pharaoh. Only then did Moses hold up his hand and raise his staff. As the Hebrew nation watched, the waters broke and crashed upon the horses and chariots, and the sea returned to its normal state. The people watched for many minutes, but not one Egyptian came out of the water alive.

"And I thought there would be boats..." said Rachel. She felt tears on her cheeks and dried them on the baby's hair. She leaned into his chest, as Mordecai put his arm around his wife for the first time.

And so the people of Yahweh saw the great power of their God, for he had saved them from death by the hand of Pharaoh. They revered Yahweh and believed in him and in his servant, Moses. Joy and awe for Yahweh filled the hearts of the Hebrew people. And the twelve tribes of Jacob camped by the sea under their banners in their tribes.

&

And Moses and the men sang a song of exaltation and praise to Yahweh for the mighty deed he had performed for Israel at the sea:

"I will sing to the LORD for He is highly exalted; The horse and its rider He has hurled into the sea.

"The LORD is my strength and song, And He has become my salvation; This is my God, and I will praise Him; My father's God, and I will extol Him.

"The LORD is a warrior; The LORD is His name.

"Pharaoh's chariots and his army He has cast into the sea; And the choicest of his officers are drowned in the Red Sea.

"The deeps cover them; They went down into the depths like a stone.

"Your right hand, O LORD, is majestic in power, Your right hand, O LORD, shatters the enemy.

"And in the greatness of Your excellence You overthrow those who rise up against You; You send forth Your burning anger, and it consumes them as chaff.

"At the blast of Your nostrils the waters were piled up, The flowing waters stood up like a heap; The deeps were congealed in the heart of the sea.

"The enemy said, 'I will pursue, I will overtake, I will divide the spoil; My desire shall be gratified against them; I will draw out my sword, my hand will destroy them.'

"You blew with Your wind, the sea covered them; They sank like lead in the mighty waters.

"Who is like You among the gods, O LORD? Who is like You, majestic in holiness, Awesome in praises, working wonders?

"You stretched out Your right hand, The earth swallowed them.

"In Your loving kindness You have led the people whom You have redeemed; In Your strength You have guided them to Your holy habitation.

"The peoples have heard, they tremble; Anguish has gripped the inhabitants of Philistia.

"Then the chiefs of Edom were dismayed; The leaders of Moab, trembling grips them; All the inhabitants of Canaan have melted away.

*"Terror and dread fall upon them; By the greatness of Your arm they
are motionless as stone; Until Your people pass over, O LORD, Until
the people pass over whom You have purchased.*

*"You will bring them and plant them in the mountain of Your inher-
itance, The place, O LORD, which You have made for Your dwelling,
The sanctuary, O Lord, which Your hands have established.*

"The LORD shall reign forever and ever."

Miriam, Moses' sister, took up her timbrel, and other women took
up theirs, and the women danced and sang:

*"Sing to Yahweh for He is highly exalted;
The horse and rider He has hurled into the sea."*

The sun sank across a silver sea behind jagged western mountains,
turning the clouds first gold, then orange. Tired and subdued after a day of
dancing and merriment, Enoch and his family huddled around the coals of a
driftwood fire provided by the children who had played on the beach all the
long day. Salt in the wood made sparks and an eastern breeze carried them
into the air. Phinehas had bought fresh fish from a local fisherman; the
women had baked flatbread and milked the goats. Sated now, the family
stared into the fire. Conversation lapsed into long silences, then someone
would burst out with another astounding act Yahweh had performed.

"What I cannot take in," said Hazor "is the dry sand. How does a
seabed become dry?" That thought settled in.

"Or how about the way the water piled up on each side...like a wall..."
said Sarah. "I was so afraid it was going to come crashing down." Heads
nodded in agreement.

"It did," said Perez, "on the Egyptians. What must it be like to have
such power?"

Rachel held the dozing baby and leaned against Mordecai. He tossed
a small shell into the fire, stroked the puppy, and said, "Elias says his cousin
is shy and humble."

"I wonder what he's doing right now. He's old; he must be exhausted,"
said Rachel. "I'm exhausted."

Enoch caught Jabus' eye. Surely the man had changed his mind about
Moses. He waited for his brother to speak. *I must not challenge him,* thought
Enoch. *I will give him a chance to dig himself out of his ditch.*

Hazor said, "So, Jabus, what do you think about Moses, *now?*"

"Speak up, big brother." said Perez.

The twins learned to keep their mouths shut in Pharaoh's court, thought
Enoch. *Where is this coming from?* He wanted to knock their heads together.

Jabus stood. "Why would Yahweh choose a shy, humble, exhausted, old man? We will see how he holds up to this kind of power." He motioned for Adah, Zelo, and Reuel to follow and left the campfire.

Morning of the second day on the beach dawned clear and cool. The army of dead Egyptians had washed ashore and lay naked along the water line. Like crabs and gulls, picking and tearing the flesh of the dead, human scavengers now moved relentlessly over the bodies and stripped them of their clothes, shoes, belts and helmets. They made piles of shields and spears. And like the rearing crabs and screeching seabirds, in their greed and frenzy, they sparred and fought one another. At last they left the corpses to the marauding armies of the sea. They took their booty among the disgusted people.

Rachel left the baby with Hannah and walked toward the beach. The east wind whipped her blue linen dress around her ankles and threatened to blow her veil away so she wrapped the ends around her neck and tied it in the back. She had become accustomed to the veil and wearing it somehow comforted her. Enoch disapproved of women leaving the camp so she must hurry. She stopped a man carrying his goods threaded on a spear across his shoulders. She pointed to her choice and offered a toe ring in her palm. The man sneered. She reached into the bottom of her bag and added a pair of gold earrings. He turned his mouth down and shook his head, no. She fished out a thumb ring and added it to her palm. No. She turned to walk away.

"Wait." A gruff acquiescence and the deal was struck. *Hopi would have done better,* she thought, *but still, not too bad.* She stuffed her prize into her bag and headed back to camp.

The people of Yahweh, rescued from the Egyptians and free at last, rested a second night on the eastern shore of the sea. Every family had stories to share, stories to tell their grandchildren and their grandchildren's children forever. They told momentous stories of Moses and his power, from Pharaoh's court to the crossing of the sea. They told intimate tales of when little Eli fell off the wagon, or Naomi had the baby in the back of the cart. Great joy and awe filled the Hebrews. They could not praise Moses enough. Was he not Yahweh's man? And Yahweh was their God. Had he not delivered them from bondage?

Word moved through the camps that Yahweh would lead them away from the beach on the third morning. The people had pulled up every scrap of wheat grass and beach vine. If they stayed any longer, the livestock would suffer. Enoch had bought salt from a caravan, and the family had spent the afternoon packing bags with salted fish. Phinehas dug out a bag of barley flour and Sarah made it into patties. They ate. They gathered around the fire for a last night of rest.

The children had been put to bed in the wagon. The adults gazed into the coals of the fire, each lost in thought and reverie. "Mo," said Hazor, rattling the peace. Heads snapped to attention. "Here's what I want to know, Cousin: how can a man get so bogged down so fast?"

Mordecai raised his eyebrows and at a loss, looked around the circle into the faces of his curious family. Enoch shrugged. They clearly did not know what Hazor was getting at. "Bogged down?" said Mordecai. *What is this all about?* he thought.

Perez spoke up, revealing himself to be a part of this twin-show. He ticked off on his fingers: "A wife. A dog. A donkey. A baby. And a goat. In that order. What's next, Mo? A monkey?" This brought chuckles all around.

Mordecai threw the last driftwood stick onto the dying fire. "We have two monkeys already." More chuckles. Everyone nodded their approval.

"Mordecai," said Rachel, piercing her brothers with narrowed eyes, "I bought you a present." All eyes focused on Rachel. "I was going to give it to you later, but since you must be feeling *bogged down,* this is a good time." She reached into her bag and pulled out a pair of soldier's shoes. She held them high for all to see, receiving the desired reaction: complements for herself for such an astute gift. Made of fine leather with shin guard and enclosed toe and heel, they were hardly worn. The long laces twisted in the breeze. She pulled out a small vial of olive oil and a wad of wool. "They need to be oiled." She piled the shoes, the oil and the wool onto her stunned husband's lap.

"Oh my. Oh my." Mordecai caressed the shoes tenderly. "Oh my."

"Here, you take the baby. I will oil the shoes," said Rachel. She laid the sleeping baby on Mordecai's shoulder, took the shoes and began to rub oil into the stiff leather. The family watched, mesmerized, as the warmth from her hands and the fire relaxed the leather and burnished it to a mellow glow.

Enoch broke the silence. "Tomorrow we leave this beach. We need to get some rest."

"This beach has chilled my bones. I think I will sleep by the fire tonight," said Phinehas. He left and returned shortly with his sleeping mat. When Rachel and Mordecai arrived at the cart, they found Phinehas' rug draped over the handles and their mats laid out underneath. They made beds for the baby and the puppy under the cart, then sat shoulder to shoulder under the rug. Mordecai examined the shoes.

"No one ever gave me a present before."

"Never?"

"No.

"Well, that makes me sad."

"I gave you a present once."

"When I was small? What was it?"

"Not so small. What is that around your neck?" Rachel's hand flew to her neck. She pulled out a leather thong holding a carved bird. Designed to lie flat on the chest, its wings spanned the width of her palm.

She frowned. "You. That carpenter boy was you. You left the birds hanging on the banister. Asmath threw hers in a box. I put mine on and never took it off." Rachel held the bird tightly, remembering the shy boy who worked on the terrace banisters. "I thought it was the prettiest little thing I had ever seen."

I thought you were the prettiest thing I had ever seen."

"Did you recognize me?"

Mordecai lifted the veil from Rachel's head. He stroked her wild curls. He had dreamed of such a moment since the day she had smiled at him. "Asmath called you 'Rachel.' I thought it might be you. Then I remembered your hair. But when you smiled I knew for sure."

"My father's hair. We all have it. The gap came from our mothers, yours and mine."

Rachel twined Mordecai's beard in her fingers. "You had no beard then. No wonder I did not recognize you..." She stroked the mat of hair on his arm, something she had wanted to do since the first night, then she took his rough hands in hers and kissed them. She looked deeply into her husband's eyes and saw there all she would ever need or want.

The last morning on the beach, Rachel and Mordecai woke to the sound of sea birds screeching on the shore. Phinehas peered around the rump of the goat he was milking and said, "We are moving. Some of the tribes have already left."

Rachel headed off to the women's latrine with the baby. She walked along the line and asked of the women she met, "Do you recognize this child? We found her in the gorges before we crossed. Do you know this child?" She met with shaking heads, and sad eyes, and hands reaching out to caress the beautiful little girl. No one knew the child nor had anyone heard a rumor of someone abandoning a child. Rachel realized just asking the questions had weakened her knees. But she had done her duty. She could tell Mordecai so.

At the cart, Phinehas had poured bowls of warm milk for Rachel and the baby. She sat with the child on her lap and tried to control the trembling in her hand as she held the cup to the child's lips. Phinehas gave her a keen look and handed them a piece of flat bread. The cat bawled pitifully. With an eye on Rachel, Phinehas opened the basket and put in a bowl of milk. "I am going to let Sekhmet go. I cannot keep her in this basket any longer."

"Will she not run away?" said Rachel. Her throat felt tight but her hand steadied. *What if one of those women had said, yes, I know this child?*

"She will surely run away. But it is cruel to keep her in this basket. Sometimes doing the right thing hurts. Sometimes it breaks your heart."

Mordecai perched on the back of the cart and laced up his new shoes. Fists on his hips, he marched up and down before Rachel and Phinehas. "How do I look?"

Phinehas grinned and almost said, *bogged down*, but decided not to tease his friend. Instead, he pointed east toward the distant mountains and said, "You look like you are ready to do battle against the sands of the desert."

"What a wife I have gotten." Mordecai regarded his feet one last time and exchanged a long look with Rachel. Then he broke the spell and began to load the cart.

Chapter 5

THE HEBREW NATION, AN IMMENSE SPRAWLING animal, crawled southeastward. Like a tick on its back, a two-wheeled pushcart kept apace. Rachel looked back toward the west, beyond the raucous birds, beyond the sea and the distant mountains, beyond the past and into the future. *Good bye, Asmath, my sister. May the blessings of the one true God, Yahweh, bless you and keep you.* She turned, kissed the baby's head and fell into step behind her well-shod husband.

They followed the cloud of Yahweh into the wilderness of Shur, a barren expanse without any sign of water. The wind blew in a steady westerly direction, a withering, hot wind that dried their sweat and brought insatiable thirst. High thin clouds diffused the sun and bleached the blue as pale as the shell Rachel had placed in her pouch.

By mid-day the sullen sun had yet to burn off the clouds. The sand grasped the heat and threw it back into the air. The pillar stopped. Like lizards the people dived under their carts and wagons or made shelter with their cloaks. Rachel wasted no time settling herself, the baby, and the puppy between the wheels of the cart. Mordecai and Phinehas, worried about the water, shook all the water jugs. "Not much left," said Phinehas. "We will have to ration it."

"Yahweh will provide," said Mordecai. He had begun to think about Yahweh with a logic he did not fully understand. It had started when he made the connection about Yahweh's purposes for the bones of Joseph. The idea had come into his mind as fully formed and pure as the light from the pillar: *would he leave the bones of Joseph in the bottom of the sea? Would he bring us this far only to have us die of thirst?*

"He did provide," said Phinehas with a grin. He sent us beer."

"Beer? What beer?"

Phinehas threw back a pile of sleeping mats to reveal four pottery jugs. "This beer." He smothered his hoot to keep from waking the baby.

Mordecai stood speechless, transfixed by the sight: not just any jars—large jars. How had he missed them?

Phinehas grinned. "I guess you're wondering where I got them? I thought so...They washed up on shore last night. Enoch got some." Mordecai stroked the jars and sniffed one of the corks. The only good thing about the brickyard had been the daily ration of beer. A beating was bad enough, but the slave who had his arm marked for beer reduction, or worse, who had his ration cut entirely, would suffer greatly from hunger and dehydration. Beer and bread formed the greatest part of the worker's diet, whether slave or free.

Deprivation meant death from malnutrition; some, facing a bleak future without beer, had committed suicide.

Phinehas believed that part of the rebellion fomenting in the camps of the Hebrews was rooted in withdrawal from beer addiction. They said they longed for the onions and melons, but what they really pined for was the beer. "It must have been on a wagon for the soldiers," he said. "They were going to celebrate after we were all dead. Let's have a bowl." He gouged off the wax, freeing the cork on one of the jugs, and poured two bowls of the dark amber substance, more a thin gruel than a liquid. Foam coated their mustaches as the nectar oozed down their dry throats. "One more." He poured into Mordecai's bowl then his own. They savored the second bowl.

"I just do not believe it," said Mordecai wiping foam from his beard. "Is Yahweh not a great and good God?"

"I've got to let Sekhmet out," said Phinehas. He pulled the basket from under the cart and took out the cat. He held the limp creature to his chest—a last farewell. He set the cat atop her basket, stroked her gently, and watched with slumped shoulders as she bolted and dashed off into the tangle of wagons, carts, and makeshift tents. "She's gone."

Mordecai poured another bowl for Phinehas and patted his shoulder. "I'm sorry, my friend. Let's get some rest." They draped Phinehas coat over the handles of the cart and lay down side by side. Phinehas tried in vain to hold back his sobs. "The last thing my master said was, 'Take care of Sekhmet.' I tried, Mo. I really did." He slept, snoring loudly, his mind fermenting elaborate, angst-filled dreams.

Mordecai, afraid to move, kicked to the side, connecting with Phinehas' foot. "Phinehas, look. Look, man."

Phinehas opened his eyes a slit and focused on his round belly where Sekhmet crouched guarding a half-eaten lizard. "No more smoked fish for you." He stroked the purring cat. "I should have trusted you sooner."

"I smell beer," said Rachel, throwing back the coat. "You've been drinking beer!" Fear flamed her eyes.

"It's all right, Rachel." Mordecai sat up. "What is the matter?"

"Asmath's father drank beer. When he drank too much, he would beat our mother." Her eyes darted as she remembered the nights when Asaph would come to their room, and the three would cower until the beating and the crying ended.

"We are almost out of water," said Mordecai. "Yahweh has sent this beer. It washed up on the shore and Phinehas and Enoch managed to get enough to keep us alive."

"Don't worry," said Phinehas. "I have known men who could not drink beer without becoming violent. We are not like that. We will mix what water we have with the beer and even the goat and donkey can drink it." It will be good for the baby. Beer makes them round and happy."

"The goat gets a double portion," said Mordecai. "If we run out, we can drink goat milk until she quits giving."

For three days they traveled farther into the wilderness. The people hoped for water, prayed for water, but they found none—neither well, nor stream; neither river nor lake, nor oasis. Though demoralized, thirsty and hungry, the tribes kept to their ranks. Finally, in the afternoon of the third day, word spread from the leading tribes that water had been found. In their excitement the throngs lost their discipline, pushed forward and packed together. No sooner had relief and joy spread among the weary people, than word came that the water proved to be bitter and undrinkable. Arguments arose among the people, and condemnation of Moses stirred the tribes into a frenzy of anger.

"Well, I want to see this water for myself," said Rachel. Maybe it is good water, and they do not want to share it."

"I do not believe the people would do that," said Mordecai.

"But Mordecai, some of the people among us are rabble and hangers on," said Rachel.

"I cannot push the cart through this crowd."

"You go," said Phinehas, "I'll stay here with the baby and the animals."

"We should take the baby," said Mordecai. "Maybe someone will recognize her." Rachel packed a bag with food; they slung the empty water skins on their shoulders. To Rachel's surprise Mordecai carried the baby, and they set off for the pools of water. They walked steadily for two hours threading their way through the tribes. At last they arrived at the pools where hundreds of people, bitter as the waters, milled about with glum faces and curled lips.

Rachel wrinkled her nose. "It stinks of sulfur here," she said.

"What are they waiting for? Let's go back," said Mordecai.

Grumbling, "What shall we drink?" the crowd shifted and parted then closed behind Moses as he passed through its fringes.

"I could have reached out and touched him." Mordecai whispered. He had never seen Yahweh's man up close. *He looks like Elias,* he thought. A memory brought tears to his eyes—something Elias had said about his cousin: "Of all men Moses is the most humble." After seeing the man Mordecai believed it: he had exhibited no measure of bravado or expectation of recognition.

"Why can they not trust him?" he said to Rachel. "Has he not proved himself trustworthy? It has only been five days since Moses brought us through the midst of the sea. Why can they not remember from one thing to the next?"

"Shush. People are looking."

"I may shout."

Moses did not answer the people nor take much notice of them. As they watched, he cried out to Yahweh. Those standing near the waters of Marah—for *bitter* would be the name of that place—would forever tell what they had seen with their own eyes: Moses threw a tree into the cloudy water and it cleared and became sweet.

Then Moses spoke the words of Yahweh to the people: *"Here Yahweh made a statute and regulation, and here He tested you. If you will give earnest heed to the voice of Yahweh, your God, and do what is right in His sight, and give ear to His commandments, and keep all His statutes, He will put none of the diseases on you which He put on the Egyptians; for He, Yahweh, is your healer."*

Moses left the water's edge as humbly as he had arrived. Awed and subdued, the Hebrews filled their containers and assisted the old and infirm. Mordecai and Rachel filled their bags and headed back to Phinehas. They met people from the farthermost camps who had heard of Moses and the tree. "Is it true?" they asked, "is the water unlike any other?" They passed camps of laughing, dancing people, revived not only with water but also in spirit.

"Why can they not feel this happy just to be free?" Mordecai groaned. "Why do they not trust Yahweh?"

"Well, they did not all find beer."

"That is no excuse." Mordecai's anger dissipated when Rachel stopped and poured sweet water into an old man's bowl.

"May Yahweh bless you, my child."

"And you, Grandfather." She smiled in answer to his toothless grin.

They walked on. "You are a good person, Rachel."

"Who did you think you took to wife?" She bumped him, knocking him sideways.

Mordecai made a show of stumbling, shaking the baby into laughter. "No one seemed to recognize her," he said. "She is a pretty baby, is she not?"

"She is comely. So, may I name her?"

"No. Not yet. I really think we should go before Moses. We do not want to be accused."

They stopped at Enoch's wagon with the good news of the water and then walked on to the cart. Rachel said, "Sarah thinks she is having twins. She is huge. You know we have twins in every generation of our family."

"Yes, I know two—your wild brothers."

Rachel laughed. "Will you ever get over that 'bogged down' jest? You mustn't pay Perez and Hazor any attention. As children they were always playing the fool. They are jealous."

"Of what?"

"The donkey." It was Mordecai's turn to bump Rachel, and when the baby chortled, Mordecai kissed her head. *Oh my*, Rachel thought, *there is a Papa in there. Her name will be Kore. My little partridge.*

The cold night air captured the blue smoke of a million dung fires and draped heavily over the camps. Phinehas had his own fire going and had laid out salted fish to bake on the stone. The baby fell into his arms. He no longer thought of her as the stinky baby he found in the gorges and tickled her soundly. The cat peeked from her open basket while Morsel frolicked at their feet. The goat and donkey drank their water noisily. Rachel and Mordicai exchanged satisfied smiles; it was good to be home.

"Now wait. Stop." Phinehas held his palms toward them. "You're telling me, Moses threw a tree in the water, and the water became sweet. That is what you are saying?"

Rachel poured a bowl of water and handed it to Phinehas. "Taste it."

He took a sip and joy spread over his face. "I never tasted such good water." He downed the rest of the bowl. "It's better than the beer. How did he do it?"

"Yahweh did it," said Mordecai. "Moses held up his arms and prayed. Then he threw in the tree."

"What did he say?" Phinehas had wondered how a person might talk to the creator of all that exists.

Mordecai and Rachel exchanged a look and shook their heads. "We did not actually *hear* it," said Rachel. "We were at the back of the crowd."

Phinehas looked askance at his friends. "Who told you all this?"

"Everyone," the two said in unison.

"But if you did not actually hear it..."

"Phinehas, must you lay eyes on a thing to believe it? Must you hear the words?"

"No… but it helps."

"Did you hear Moses ask Yahweh to part the sea?" asked Rachel. "Did you see Yahweh create these mountains? Yet there they are, before your eyes."

Mordecai spoke. "He promised the people that if we would obey the commandments of Yahweh, he would not put on us the illnesses he has put on Egypt. I did hear that with my own ears." He looked puzzled. "Rachel, now I think about it, how did we hear that? We were at the back." She shrugged.

"Does that mean that if we do not obey he will put those illnesses on us?" asked Phinehas.

"That must be what he meant," said Mordecai.

The two men began to discuss the ways of Yahweh over their nightly campfire. Soon Enoch, the Uncle Twins, the boy, Reuel, and several neighbors joined them. "I never knew how starved I was," said Phinehas. "To sit as brothers with men who know the one true God and talk about the wonderful deeds of Yahweh…it is my greatest happiness. Do you know, Mo, how blessed you were to have Elias, Moses' own cousin for a friend?"

"I believe Yahweh brought me to the wood shop so Elias could teach me. But remember, I did not know about his cousin, Moses. Would you like me to tell you the time I first heard about Moses?" All heads nodded.

Content on her mat, warm in Asmath's best shawl, Rachel leaned against a cart wheel and listened. The low drone of men's voices sometimes lulled her to sleep—she determined this would not be one of those nights—and she would wake when Mordecai shook her for bed. Most of the time she listened intently to ancient stories and precepts she had never heard or had forgotten. Sometimes she served up her opinions with their morning mush.

Mordecai began: "We had been working on a huge sarcophagus of Pharaoh's brother-in-law. His body had been at the embalmers for several months, and his tomb was ready, so we had to get it finished soon. It was six cubits long and two wide and it rested on the center blocks so we could all work around it. I will never forget, Elias was on his knees, carving the middle toe on the right foot." Reuel laughed. "And I was at the other end working on the headdress. I look out the window by my corner, and there stands Elias. He leans into the window; his beard is mopping up sawdust as usual. Only it is not Elias. I am thinking it has to be his twin. The man motions for me to come over, so I go. Without saying a word, he points to Elias and disappears below the window. I look around to see if the master is watching. He is not, so I walk to the foot of the coffin and whisper real quiet, 'Your brother is here.' Now Elias is deaf, so he says real loud (Mordecai used his rendition of an ancient crone): 'My brother! Here? Where?'" Reuel clamped his hands over his mouth.

Mordecai continued his story: "Everyone looks up, and just then the master comes in. So I say, without moving my lips, 'Outside.' And point to the window."

"Elias puts down his chisel and walks straight up to the master. Now he's a little old bent man, and he says, (speaking to Reuel, Mordecai used his toothless, shaky voice) 'Master, I have worked here for twenty years. I have never even put you to the trouble of beating me. Now my brother is here, and I am going outside to talk to him.' The master turns red but does not say a word, so Elias goes out the front door and does not come back for a long time. Then without a word, he comes in, picks up his chisel, and finishes the toe." Reuel slapped Enoch's knee.

"That night Elias tells me all about it: his twin brother came to tell him important news: their cousin, Moses, has returned after forty years. He had been living across the Sea of Reeds in the land of Midian. One night he was near a mountain, shepherding his father-in-law's flock—a man named Jethro—when he saw a bush on fire, but not burning up. It just kept burning. Then the voice of Yahweh speaks to him from the bush and says, 'Take off your shoes; you are on hallowed ground.' So he takes off his shoes, and then Yahweh tells him what he wants him to do."

Mordecai paused for a drink of water. "Go on, Mo," said Enoch.

"I could finish tomorrow night if you are tired." Mordecai looked into the faces of his audience.

"What!"

"No."

"Go on, man."

"Yahweh tells Moses that he must go back to Egypt and rescue the Hebrew people from Pharaoh. But Moses says, 'Rescue the people! Why me? I am not brave. I cannot speak to people. Get somebody else.' But Yahweh says that Aaron, Moses' brother, will speak for him and help him. So Moses travels back to Egypt and meets with all the elders and tells them Yahweh's plan: Moses will ask Pharaoh if the people can travel for three days into the wilderness to honor their God. But Yahweh will harden Pharaoh's heart, and Pharaoh will say to Moses, (for Reuel's sake, Mordecai curled his lip and deepened his voice into a brutal rasp), 'No, you cannot go!'" The boy leaned against Enoch and covered his ears. Smiling, Mordecai continued: "Then, according to the plan, Yahweh will send the plagues and punish Egypt, and then Pharaoh will let us go free. And that is what happened. Elias knew exactly what would happen."

"And so did you," said Phinehas.

"Not all of it," said Mordecai. "If Elias said it, I knew it would happen. But I did not know how soon it would happen or what it would be like. When the blood came upon the waters, I was as shocked as everyone else. By then I had been taken away from the wood shop, back to the brick yard..." His eyes drifted into the distance as he remembered the day his life at the wood shop had come to an end. He hardly noticed when his cousins and friends left.

Rachel joined Mordecai and Phinehas at the fire. "Husband, are you too tired to tell us why they sent you back to the brickyards?"

"I can tell you." Lowering his head, he stared into the coals and sighed deeply. "The last day at the villa, I went back to the wood shop. I was so happy. All I could think about was you. I had found you. I could not wait to tell Elias that I had seen you again. When I got there, everyone was standing around my corner. They had dug up the ground under my sleeping mat."

"You slept on the ground?"

"Rachel, my own mat, out of the cold? It became my home. Anyway, all the carvers and the master stood there. Tools were strewn around. They had been buried one by one in oiled papyrus. I tried to tell the master that I did not do it. I had no oiled papyrus. Where would I get it? But he would not believe me. Elias told him maybe an enemy or a jealous worker had done it. He would not listen. An overseer came and took me back to the brickyards. It was as if I had never left—all those twisting alleys. I was there for a year—

during the time of the plagues. When the plague of blood filled the streams, we had to make bricks with it. Some people thought they were beautiful. Baked in the sun, the bricks turned black."

"One night Enoch sneaked into my hut. He told me to hold on, to do whatever I had to do to stay alive. The last plague would drive Pharaoh to let us go. We would be leaving Goshen soon. He told me that he was going to the copper mines to look for Jorham and then he would go to the villa to get you, and that we would be wed. Something you were not told, it seems..."

"And the stripes?"

"The first day back at the yard. Twenty lashes. Two things kept me alive last year. The memory of you standing in that window and Elias' promise that *Yahweh had sent Moses to set us free.*"

&

Sarah walked to the cart one evening with Enoch and joined Rachel. Heavily pregnant, she eased herself onto Phinehas' rug, and extending her legs, took the baby onto her knees. She chuckled. "This is as close to a lap as I can get."

"Do you think it's twins?" Rachel hoped for peace between her and Sarah. She poured a bowl of water for her sister-in-law.

"Oh yes. It's twins. Listen. I've been asking people about this girl-baby." Sarah twisted the baby's hair around her finger, observing the curl as one might examine a fuzzy caterpillar. Rachel reclaimed the child and settling her on her lap, rocked with her.

"There may be a woman I've heard of... She travels outside the camps with a goat herder. It is said she's a prostitute."

Rachel wanted to pull her veil down and hide. She leveled her gaze at Sarah. "We found the baby abandoned in the middle of the camps, not on the outskirts."

"It is said the woman brought the child into the camps, hoping someone would take her."

"Then her hopes have been fulfilled."

"A prostitute's child..."

"What do you want, Sarah?" *What must I do to satisfy this woman,* she thought.

"You can buy whatever you want, Rachel. I do not know if the family will agree to let you buy a prostitute's baby. None of my sons would ever be allowed to marry her. Not Hannah's nor Adah's boys either. But do not worry. I have not told our sisters. Here comes my husband." She held up her hand, and Enoch pulled her to her feet.

Mordecai and Rachel watched as Enoch and Sarah walked away. "What is wrong? You look sick. Are you going to faint?"

"No, but I am going to vomit." Rachel thrust the baby into Mordecai's arms and dashed behind the cart.

Chapter 6

Daylight at Marah. The pillar of Yahweh had completed its subtle change from fire to cloud. No one could say, now it is fire; now it is cloud, but the cloud stood white and bright against the lingering stars in the early lavender sky. The Hebrew people enjoyed these glories every morning, for Yahweh did not remove the pillar, nor did he waver in his plans.

Dew had fallen during the night wetting the animals' hair and all the Hebrews' goods, yet it seemed rain never fell. They had left the coast and the territory of the osprey and moved into the desert where hawk, kite, and eagle circled high above, diving with a variety of distinctive shrieks upon their prey of lizards, scorpions and horny toads. Occasionally the travelers saw a herd of gazelles or the occasional ostrich in the shimmering distance.

Rachel had been sick again that morning. Now she watched her husband lace up his sandals. She marveled that a new pair of shoes could make such a difference in a man's outlook. He faced each day with anticipation, expecting milk and honey around the next rock. She had no idea that the dung beetle had become a soldier on a quest for the land of promise. As for herself, she longed for a house, and the promise of a new land could not come too soon. She would do what Mordecai had said and trust Yahweh for those things. After all she had seen for herself His power. Had he not rescued the people from Egypt, parted the sea, made the water pure? *But I am small*, she thought. *How can I expect Yahweh to care about me? About Sarah and her hateful schemes? About the baby?* She fingered the pouch and felt a surge of relief when she found Ma'at's small hard shape. The little goddess would do battle for her against Apep, the god of chaos. *She will help me*, thought Rachel; *did Asmath not say so?*

The people moved past the waters of Marah and filled every container to brimming. Who knew when they would find water again? The sun flogged the slow-moving tribes. After Marah they did not camp at night, but traveled by the light of the pillar. After two days an oasis appeared in the distance. They argued. It is a trick of the desert, many said. No, said others, it is real. See—trees. They had seen many mirages along the way: lakes, trees, herds of cattle floating just above the surface of the sands. The oasis of Elim proved to be real.

The Hebrews arrived at Elim in the wilderness of Sin. The people exclaimed, "Are we back in Egypt?" Seventy palm trees and shade and twelve wells spread before the weary travelers. The wells gave plenty of water for everyone, but the first tribes to arrive claimed the best shade and proximity to the wells.

"Why do we always eat the dust of the first tribes," Jabus complained to Enoch. "Judah and Simeon in their thousands are first to the water, first to the shade. Even you cannot think this is fair, Brother."

"Well, I do not think it is fair. But if we switched around, can you imagine the confusion?" Jabus had to concede the impossibility of shifting the order of the tribes. So Enoch's family constructed a pen of gathered stones and hauled water from the nearest well.

Phinehas walked the length of the oasis. He returned to the family with news that a caravan route ran through Elim. "We need to be ready when a caravan comes through," he said. "We need to think about what we need."

"I need a spindle and a loom," said Rachel, "and some wool. It is time we had a tent. And a bag for churning and making butter. And a grind stone."

"We need tent poles and pegs," said Mordecai. "I need wood so I can make a loom and spindle."

"I need a bag for churning butter and making cheese and yogurt," said Rachel.

"Butter," said Phinehas, drawing out the word. "You know how to make butter?"

"Asmath and I spent a lot of time in the kitchen."

"I'll buy you three bags."

On the second day at Elim, a jubilant outcry of *caravan! caravan!* spread over the camps. A sixty-camel caravan had entered the oasis. Enoch, the Uncle Twins, and Jabus joined Mordecai, Rachel, and Phinehas in the rush to get to the caravan. Within minutes excited crowds churned into a noisy, jostling mob. Frail people fell underfoot. The five men anchored themselves with linked arms and surrounded Rachel. They pulled desperate women and children into the protective circle. An island in the whirl of chaos, they stood firm until the brawling crowd moved on.

Mordecai held his arm tight around Rachel. "This is the last time you are going to a caravan." Rachel did not argue.

The next day, disgruntled with the caravan fiasco, Mordecai and Phinehas left for a trading foray into the camps. Not everyone had come up short; trade goods from the caravan should have dispersed throughout the people.

Phinehas had transferred his rings to leather thongs around his neck. He had lost so much weight the rings fell off his fingers. Now he could pull out one ring at a time without revealing his wealth. Mordecai had done the same with some of Rachel's rings. They worked their way through Manasseh and into the adjoining tribe of Ephraim with no luck. Phinehas took the lead; Mordecai knew nothing about trading. Caravan items were abundant but even Phinehas could not make a deal. They found themselves on the outskirts of the camps where shepherds kept their flocks.

Black tents spread in groups of two or three across the sands. Made of black goat hair mats sewn together, the tents stretched over several tent poles and could be enlarged by simply setting up more poles and sewing on more mats. Once they had been soaked in water, the wool mats became waterproof. The sides could be rolled up to permit a breeze or lowered and banked for warmth. The women had their own tent, well-stocked with cushions and rugs, and usually larger than the men's to accommodate a small central fire pit. All tents had a wide awning stretched over the door flap with rugs and mats beneath for shady afternoon naps and entertaining guests.

"I agree with Rachel. We need tents," said Phinehas. "If we had some wool, Rachel could weave the mats."

"And tent poles. We have got to get some tent poles," said Mordecai.

The sun had reached its zenith when the two stopped at a prosperous looking group of four tents. Herds of black goats grazed among clumps of gray-green bushes. At the second largest tent, three men sat smoking a communal pipe in the deep shade of a wide awning. Phinehas poked Mordecai. Bundles of goat hair flanked the sides of the tent. From his travels, Phinehas knew the protocol for visiting tent-dwellers. The two stood humbly at a distance, waiting to be summoned. A darkly tanned man with the longest, blackest beard Mordecai had ever seen motioned them to come into the shade. Phinehas and Mordecai unlaced their sandals and stepped onto the rug. They sat cross legged, relieved to be out of the broiling sun. The men exchanged greetings, while a woman poured bowls of water. Mordicai downed his water thirstily, but Phinehas held his bowl and after a few moments took a sip. Two old men lay down and immediately began to snore. The head man inquired about news of the camps and passed the pipe. Phinehas took a puff. With a penetrating look into Mordecai's eyes, he held tight to the pipe but let go when Mordecai tugged it out of his hand. They discussed the caravan, the sea crossing, and the bitter waters of Marah.

Nobah, the head man, exhaled a cloud of pungent smoke and motioned toward the bundles. "This wool is the highest quality. Long. Soft." The trading had begun.

Nobah passed the pipe. Phinehas took a long puff and handed the pipe to Mordicai, who by now looked pale and greenish. He managed to squeak, "I need a nanny goat," before he jumped up and disappeared around the side of the tent. Guffaws followed him, but he was too sick to care.

"I can sell him a freshened nanny," said the head man. He motioned for a young boy to go cut one from the herd. "Do you need wool?"

"I need tent poles," said Phinehas.

The head man shook his head, no. "Wool."

"I need a skin for making butter."

"Wool." The pipe passed between Phinehas and Nobah.

After two hours Mordecai and Phinehas laced up their sandals and bade the grinning head man good-bye. They led a pregnant nanny goat loaded with two bundles of wool, and each carried five tent poles on his shoulder. Mordecai patted the flat butter churn made from a goat skin. "How did you do that?"

"I told you I used to go with my master to buy rugs." Phinehas looked sideways at his young friend. "I've smoked the pipe with Bedouins. It does not get any worse than that."

"Don't tell Rachel."

"I would never."

Thrilled with the goat, Rachel rubbed her hands over its bulging belly. She buried her hands in the bundles of wool and marveled at the tent poles. "One, two, three… ten poles. It will take me a year to weave enough mats to cover these." She hugged the churn to her chest.

That night the baby lay sucking her thumb in Rachel's lap, while the dung fire burned weakly. No one had the energy to stoke it. "You should have seen the rug merchant," said Mordecai. "That poor herdsman had no chance."

"You did not cheat him, did you Phinehas?" She asked.

"Two rings. One with a stone. No, the trade was fair, but I am sure Nobah—that is his name—thinks he got the best of me. I believe he is a good man, but he is wily and used to winning."

The next morning dawned cold, almost bitter, but Mordecai knew the sun would soon bake away the chill. He crawled from under the sleeping mats, leaving the warmth of Rachel, the baby, and Morsel. It would be a good day to make the spindle and loom. Soon they would have plenty of warm shawls and covers and even a tent.

Phinehas moved quietly about the camp, gathering supplies. Since his success at Nobah's camp, trading fever had come over the man. He raised a finger to Mordecai and pointed north. By the light of the pillar of fire, he led the donkey from the camp.

Mordecai contemplated the wooden box that had been his at Pharaoh's wood shop. *I used to be a wood carver,* he thought. *Then I became a dung beetle. But now I have Rachel, and my wife needs a loom.* Enjoying the solitude, one by one he laid out his tools; his rough hands caressed each lovely shape: the chisels, the planes, the awl. He tested the knife against his thumb. It had become dull from lack of use.

&

Early on the day now known as the first Passover, Mordecai had left forever the brick yard he had renamed *Sheol*. No one had stopped him or his fellow slaves. The overseers stood with slack arms and watched their workforce file past the shattered whipping post. The plague of hail did massive damage. Egyptians died, huddled in their bunkhouses. Word had gone out that the Egyptians would give whatever goods the Hebrews asked. But how long would this generosity last? Surely they would lash out at Yahweh's people. Mordecai decided it would be safer not to ask for anything but to go straight to Enoch and the home-place in Goshen; he joined the noisy throngs heading north. But the tools...the tools had become extensions of his hands and had unlocked his imagination. His heart ached to hold them again, to own them. He turned back through the tangled alleys of Ramses, weaving his way back to Pharaoh's wood shop.

At last he stood in the wide doorway. He looked down the length of the long room at the bent backs of the paid laborers and there, near the back, Elias crouched, carving a bust of Anubis, a god with the body of a man and the head of a jackal. Mordecai drank in the aroma of fresh carved sandalwood and acacia, and tears burned for the year he had lost. He walked boldly to Elias, knelt and put his arm around his friend's thin shoulders.

"Why are you still here?"

At the sound of Mordecai's voice, Elias threw down his chisel and swiveled to lay his head on Mordecai's chest. He hugged his friend as if he would never let him go. Mordecai kissed Elias' head and repeated, "Why are you still here, Elias?"

The old man sat heavily and extended his legs, displaying red swollen ankles. "Would you look at that? I would be gone if I could walk."

The master's voice boomed from the rear of the room. "Who is this back from the dead?" He lumbered past the motionless carvers. Still smelling of stale beer, he pounded Mordecai on the back like a long-lost son. "Have you come back to us?"

Elias' rheumy eyes bulged.

"No, Master. I have come to ask you for my tools."

"Your tools, eh?" He scratched his armpit. "I always planned to get you back, boy. Never could get around to it. I still have your box. Somewhere." He thought a moment and pointed vaguely toward the curtained doorway. "Go look in there."

This a trap, thought Mordecai, but he went to the doorway and pushed the curtain aside. The master's daughter turned briefly from the pot she stirred, recognized him, and pointed her wooden spoon. Tools had been added to the box: a plumb line, a hammer, an ax. Nodding to the woman, he carried the box out of the kitchen. "Master, I need the cart to carry Elias." With his bulging eyes and now his gaping mouth, Elias looked every bit like a frog. Mordecai almost laughed. The master did laugh—a sound no one in the wood shop had ever heard.

Mordecai had pushed Elias through the streets of Ramses and the levees of Goshen and delivered him to his twin brother—what a trip that had been—and that night he had married Rachel. Now as he laid out his tools on the back of the cart, he chuckled. Now he had his own tools and Rachel for his wife. He found his marble stone, spit on it, and began to hone his knife.

By mid-morning, Mordecai had carved a narrow spindle measuring three hand widths long. He cut an angled notch in one end for starting the wool and tapered the other. He shaped a small wooden bowl designed to hold the tapered end as it spun. He set Rachel to sanding the spindle and taught her to follow the grain and smooth any nibs and rough places. He showed her how to strain the sand to remove any rocks and debris that would scratch the wood. The wool would seek and snag the smallest imperfection. While Rachel busied herself with the sanding, he chose the straightest pole and cut it into two equal lengths. He rounded the edges for the top and bottom of the loom. He cut another into two equal lengths with squared edges for the sides. He drilled holes and made pegs to join the corners and tapped them into place. He sanded the loom.

Rachel pulled a handful of oily black wool from the bundle. She fluffed the wool, hooked a bit into the notch, twisted and stretched it, and pulled the tension against the turning spindle. The first thread stretched out. "This spindle is so balanced," she said. "I have never used one this good. We could sell them. Nothing is as peaceful as spinning," she added, but soon her peace turned into a turmoil of memories.

Her mind drifted into a forbidden world—forbidden by her own will—for remembering brought only sadness. In her mind she saw two girls weaving on a shady porch. Cool Nile breezes, smelling faintly of fish, rustled the leaves on overhead vines. Asmath begged a story from Hopi. They could never get enough of the eunuch's childhood in Africa: did he have sisters? how did they braid their hair? had he ever seen a lion? Hopi would pull the fan cord, and rolling his eyes up toward the lath, spin a new story or add to an old one. He had been a happy little black boy, chasing his friends around the yard, when a neighboring tribe had raided his village. In the midst of the killing, he had been stolen away and sold into slavery in Egypt. Asmath's father had purchased him at the slave market.

Unbidden words escaped her reverie. "We could have saved Hopi."

"What? Hopi? Who is that?" asked Mordecai. He propped up the loom and admired his work.

"Someone I used to know." Rachel laid down the spindle. "Would you watch the baby? I need to go talk to Enoch." Rachel found her brother on his knees in the goat paddock. He and Reuel had just pulled a newborn kid free of its mother. Rachel watched the tiny kid, its cord hanging, search for the teat and prod its mother's bag to stimulate the flow of milk. Reuel poured water over his uncle's bloody hands. "Enoch," posed Rachel, "Why did we not take Asmath and her family to your house until the next day after that passover? They would all still be alive."

"What? What are you saying?"

"Did you not hear me, Brother? You let Asmath's family die." She began to pace, kneeing goats from her path. "You knew the first-born would die. Asaph was their first-born son. Their only son. Who knows who else? Maybe Hopi was first-born. Asmath could be completely alone now."

"Rachel." Enoch dried his hands and reached for Rachel's arm. She drew back. "This was Yahweh's plan, not mine. How can you blame me?"

"You knew it was going to happen. It was a cruel thing." She stopped pacing and faced her brother "If you do not at least admit it was cruel, I will never forgive you."

"Reuel, go on to your mother now," Enoch told the boy. "Thank you for your help." They watched the boy work his way through the goats. "Any father would think it cruel to lose such a son," said Enoch.

"Then why would Yahweh demand it of the Egyptians?"

"They enslaved our people. They drowned Hebrew boy babies in the Nile. Who knows how many boys died?"

"Is that the reason? Was it a punishment? A boy for a boy? Asaph was not even born then."

"Rachel, I do not know Yahweh's reasons." The kid was having no luck finding the teat. Enoch squatted and held it under its mother's belly until it began to suck loudly. "It is not wise to blame Yahweh." He wiped his hands in the nanny goat's hair. "We cannot know his reasons. Think about his incredible power. You have seen it. Do you really think you are worthy to question him? Do you think he would do anything without a plan?"

Rachel's head began to ache. She was weary trying to make sense of everything. She had said goodbye to Asmath and the past after the sea crossing. The spinning had brought back too many memories. She hung her head. "No. I am not worthy to question Yahweh. I saw what Moses did at the bitter lakes. I heard what he said. We are to obey Yahweh, and do right. He did not say we are to understand. But sometimes I think about my old life and the people..."

Rachel allowed Enoch to grasp her hands. Blood had dried around his fingernails. "I know you loved them. And that is not a bad thing. Some of us, like you and Phinehas, had good masters; some did not. Mordecai is lucky to be alive. Has he told you about the brick yard?

"Some of it."

"When the time is right he will tell you all of it."

"Maybe he is trying to forget. I am trying to forget my life in Ramses."

"You cannot forget five years," he said. "Enjoy your memories, and be thankful for them. But remember this one thing: the vizier had plans to sell you to the highest bidder."

"And now you must say cruel things to me." She pulled her hands away.

"I want you to realize, even though they were kind to you, *you were a slave.*"

"I was more than a slave, no matter what you say." She pushed through the milling goats and came face to face with Sarah.

Without a greeting, Sarah said in a low voice, "There is a prostitute who had a child. I heard about it at the well yesterday."

"The *well?* Since when do you go to the well? You are as big as a buffalo." Rachel regretted her words immediately. Did Asmath's mother not say honey is sweeter to the fly than vinegar? "I am sorry, Sarah. That was mean. If I can help you now that you are so big, I will."

Sarah seemed neither troubled by the harsh words nor mollified by the apology. She had information to impart. "I go to the well to talk and hear things. So far I just listen. I still have not told anyone about the child."

"This is all just gossip." Rachel left her sister-in-law and headed back to Mordecai. Her mouth twitched. *Big as a buffalo...*

Enoch watched his sister walk away. He turned back to the goats, but he could not forget the look in Rachel's eyes. Not a hint of tears. He needed to deal with this cold anger, for it was much more dangerous than Jabus and all his complaints.

Rachel returned to her spinning. Fresh worries displaced any thoughts of the past.

Cold night air descended upon the oasis at Elim. Mordecai and Rachel huddled by the fire and waited for Phinehas to return. "I don't think he should have gone off by himself," she said.

"From now on we will go together."

"Maybe it would be better to stay in camp. A woman at the latrine said robbers are in the desert."

Before Mordecai could comment, Phinehas pulled up behind them. "Lazy people. What am I going to do with you?" He tethered the donkey and warmed his hands at the fire.

"What did you bring us?" said Mordecai. "We have been sitting around here all day just waiting."

Phinehas picked up the loom and held it high. "So I see. This is masterful work." He pulled a mat from the donkey's back, untied his treasure and laid it on the ground.

"Meat!" his friends exclaimed. Mordicai and Rachel stroked the smooth, tan hide of a gazelle haunch.

"There should be enough for Enoch's crowd, too," said Phinehas with a grin.

Mordecai jostled his friend's shoulder. "Where did you get it?"

"Three Bedouin boys. I met them outside the camps. The oldest one was about twelve. One about ten and the little one was eight or nine. Mordecai, you should see them—all of them—with a sling. They can hit anything they aim at."

"Where do they live?" asked Mordecai.

"They are Bedouin—orphans. They live off the land. They said the Amalek raided their village."

"Amalek?" asked Mordecai.

"A tribe of marauders. According to those boys they are the ones who are picking off our stragglers."

&

Caravans traveled along established trade routes between the land of Midian, east of the Sea of Reeds, north through Edom, all the way to Damascus and then south through Canaan and westward to Egypt. At the Oasis of Elim near Midian, they came to trade and water their camels. When they drove their camels into the midst of the Hebrews, they had to trade from their saddles. Only after the mob, starved for goods, had departed with all the caravan had to offer, could the traders dismount.

The next morning, frustrated with their lack of access to the caravans, Phinehas suggested he and Mordicai camp outside the fringes and intercept the next caravan before it pulled into Elim. "They come from the north. We will wait outside the camps and be first for a change. There is nothing stopping us; we could leave today."

"Well, there is something stopping us," said Mordecai. "Rachel is not going to like this."

"I'll pack while you talk to her."

As expected, Rachel objected from start to finish. "I do not want to go stay with Enoch and Sarah. Sarah hates me. Jabus thinks I am wanton."

"Then Reuel can come stay with you."

There are robbers out there," said Rachel. "Did that woman not say so? I heard what Phinehas said about those Amalek. Nothing is worth getting killed for. Can we not trade within the camps?"

"Rachel, no one is going to trade olive oil or barley. Wouldn't you like some olive oil for your hair?"

"Yes, Mordecai. Go get killed so I can oil my hair. I think you should go now." She picked up the baby and walked away. She could think of nowhere to go, and by the time she returned, the men had made a pile of sleeping mats and water bags. She rebuffed Mordecai's hug and avoided Phinehas' eyes. She buried her face in the baby's hair and rocked her back and forth. Silently, she watched the men gather their supplies and walk away. Rachel called after them, "Get me a grind stone!" Mordecai raised his arm and kept walking. "Be careful!" Again Mordecai raised his arm. "I am with child," she said softly to her husband's retreating back.

The mournful notes of a distant flute followed Phinehas and Mordecai as they followed the camel route into the desert. A cold wind whipped their beards and worried the indistinct outlines of the tracks. They came to a ravine and stood on the rim. The dim limits of Yahweh's pillar barely illuminated the trail angling across the smooth bottom. "This is where they cross," said Mordecai. "A few more hours of this wind and the tracks will be gone."

"Let's go down and camp against that boulder," said Phinehas. They slid down the steep bank and stood on a smooth sandy bottom. "At least it's not as windy down here," he said. "Let's build a fire." They searched in vain for stones to ring a fire. Finally, Phinehas took his staff and dug a shallow hollow into the bank near the ground. They had debated about carrying the extra weight but finally decided to bring a bag of dry dung, enough for three nights. Mordecai had become a master fire-builder. He arranged a wad of dry weeds and piled the dung just so. A few strikes of the flint and the fire caught. They sat against the gully wall, legs extended, comforted by the fire. The plaintive notes of a flute came and went on the wind. "I wonder who that is," said Phinehas.

"Look," said Mordecai, "the pillar is so dim out here you can see the stars. I miss the stars." But Phinehas had rolled onto his side and with his feet toward the fire, pulled his striped coat over his head. Far to the north Mordecai saw flashes of lightening low on the horizon. Phinehas snored and soon so did he.

Daylight and the distant roll of thunder woke Phinehas. He unwound himself from his coat and stood stiffly. He prodded Mordecai with his foot. "Wake up. Look at that." He pointed north to the horizon where bolts of lightning flashed against a bank of black cloud. "I guess it does rain here sometimes."

"I saw that cloud last night," said Mordecai. "It's not coming any closer." The sun had not yet burned off the desert chill. They stoked the fire, hunkering near it. They ate salted fish and watched the distant lightening.

"What is that?" Mordecai cocked his head. A roaring sound. A vibration. Phinehas leaped to his feet and saw three figures on the rim of the gully, jumping, yelling, waving their arms, pointing north. "What? What are they yelling? I know them. It's those Bedouin boys."

A wall of water hit first Mordecai and then Phinehas they were thrown down and rolled along the ground, scoured by sand and rocks, pummeled and twisted by the rushing, churning water, carried along like two twigs. No sooner did they fight their way to the surface for a breath than the roiling water pulled them back under. Small trees and uprooted bushes ripped at their skin and stripped off their clothes. *My shoes,* thought Mordecai. His mind darkened and wandered. His last thoughts were of Rachel and his wonderful shoes. He would never see either of them again.

Phinehas came to, flat on his back. After a moment, his eyes focused on four bearded faces staring down at him. His hands crawled to his neck. No cords. No rings. One of the four twirled the cords around his finger and displayed yellow teeth in a wide grin. Slowly Phinehas sat up and looked himself over. No clothes. No shoes. Scratched and bloody. His soggy beard lay on his chest heavy with sand and gravel. A great sadness came over him. *Here I am in the middle of the desert,* he thought, *naked and dead.* "Mordecai!" *Where is Mordecai?* He looked around frantically and patted the ground as if his friend were under the sand.

"Go down," the one with the rings ordered the others.

Three of the men scrambled down the bank and stood over Mordecai. When one called, "He is alive," Phinehas felt a new wave of sadness. Better for his friend to have been killed than to suffer torture at the hands of these thieves. They hauled Mordecai up the bank and dropped him next to Phinehas. One of them bent to unlace the unconscious man's shoes. "No!" said the leader. "How can he carry his naked friend who has no shoes, if he himself has no shoes?"

Relief washed over Phinehas. They were not going to be tortured or killed. He watched in disbelief as the four men mounted their camels and prodded them up. Three turned their animals, whipped them into a trot and headed east. The leader stayed behind for a parting word. He stabbed his finger at the gully and shouted, "This is a wadi. No rain—dry. Rain—watch out." He turned his camel and followed his friends. Phinehas watched them until they disappeared into the morning sun. He turned his attention to his unconscious friend.

"Mordecai, wake up. Mo." He patted Mordecai's face, at first gently, then more forcefully.

Mordecai opened his eyes. "My shoes."

"They are on your feet, my friend. How, I do not know." Phinehas helped him sit up.

"You're naked," said Mordecai.

"So are you."

"What happened?"

Phinehas pointed. "This is a wadi. No rain—dry. Rain—watch out. That is what I was told."

"Told?"

"You missed all the excitement."

"I don't think so. Ohh, my head." A steady trickle of blood oozed through sand and matted hair and ran down Mordecai's back.

"You're bleeding. Let me press on it." Phinehas pressed the heel of his hand to the back of Mordecai's head. "We have been robbed."

"They stole our clothes?"

"I'll explain it all, but right now we need to find our clothes. Can you walk?" They followed the wadi until they came to a tangle of rocks and brush. "This must be where the water ran out," said Phinehas. "There's my coat." They spent the next hour pulling their torn clothes from the pile. At last they climbed out and laid their clothes on the hot sand to dry. "I wish I had found my shoes." Mordecai wrapped linen turban strips around Phinehas' feet.

Phinehas hobbled in a circle. "That works." Within the hour the hot sun and desert air dried the clothes. They dressed in their tattered garments and headed south for home.

"I dread this," said Mordecai. "What am I going to tell Rachel? At least I found the bags. She loves her bags."

Phinehas began to laugh. "A bag of melted dung. Yes, let's take that to Rachel."

"I can wash it."

Phinehas chuckled and glanced over his shoulder. "They're back!" Four camels approached slowly from the east. The sun blinded him, but he knew it was them. "They've come back to kill us. Run!" He hobbled a few feet and stopped. "Come on."

"I cannot outrun a camel. Keep walking."

"You did not see them. I thought we were dead." Phinehas had rolled his coat into a ball. "Maybe I can give them my coat. They already have my rings."

"Look straight ahead," said Mordecai. They linked elbows. Now they heard the camels, their padded feet soft in the sand, following closer and closer. The sound of creaking saddles and tinkling bells brought them closer still. Now the rank odor of camel filled their nostrils; the hot stench of camel's breath caressed the backs of their necks. Mordecai hunched his shoulders. *And so I die,* he thought. *Will I feel the scimitar as it slices off my head?* Sorrow almost brought him to his knees. Rachel would never know what happened to him. He would never see the land of milk and honey. One of the beasts bellowed and spewed foul spittle over their necks.

Phinehas and Mordecai, Hebrews of the tribe, Manasseh, stopped. They were not brave. They were not heroes. But they had had enough. Each man looked deeply into the other's eyes—a sad, silent goodbye. They turned, elbows still linked, to face their tormentors.

Laughter erupted from three boys perched on the saddles. They laid back, kicked their legs in the air and screamed with mirth. They banged their heels on the saddles and hollered, causing the camels to grunt and shift. Their glee could not be contained. The smallest boy almost fell off his saddle. Still they laughed.

Mordecai blinked. He could not take it in: three curly-headed boys, in three sizes, the whitest teeth, the whites of their eyes bright against dark unblemished skin, rough tunics. "Are these the robbers?"

"I saw you," shouted Phinehas in a language unknown to Mordecai. He pointed north. "I saw you back there. Mordecai, these are the three Bedouin boys. The boys with the hindquarters." The camels knelt and the boys jumped off. They ran to Phinehas and danced around him, babbling in their language. They patted him. They cavorted like lost dogs greeting their master. Then one boy pointed to Phinehas' wrapped feet, and paroxysms of laughter overtook them.

Phinehas looked at his feet and began to chuckle. He threw his balled coat into the air and hooted. He was going to live.

We are not going to die, thought Mordecai. *I am going to see the land of milk and honey after all. I am going home to Rachel.* Infectious joy overtook him. He jumped into the air—something he had not done since childhood—came down clumsily, and twisted his ankle. The boys shifted their ridicule to him. From the ground he watched them point and laugh and slap their knees. In spite of the pain he grinned and shook his head.

Phineas stood over his friend, fists on his hips. "Bowlegged people should refrain from jumping." Mordecai shielded his eyes against the noon sun and said, "We should go. Those bandits may catch up." Phinehas translated. The oldest boy grinned, took out his sling, and displayed it flat on his hand. He spoke to Phinehas.

"He says they will never catch up." The boys ran to the camels and started throwing goods onto the ground: robes, turbans, sleeping mats, tent rolls, cooking pots, shoes. "Those are my shoes," shouted Phinehas. "I thought the water...they stole my shoes..."

Mordecai frowned. "Whose camels are these?"

"Did I not say you missed the excitement? These camels belong to the bandits. Or they used to..." The oldest boy led Phinehas on a tour through the piles of goods. He held up a bone-handled scimitar.

"We have nothing to trade." Phinehas held out his empty hands.

"Yes you do!" shouted the boy. "When we traded for the hindquarter you gave me one of these." He reached inside his tunic, pulled out half a dozen cords and rings, and tossed them to Phinehas including the one he had given for the hindquarter. The rug merchant, taking pity on the orphans, had paid ten times its worth.

"Mordecai, come over here," called Phinehas.

"I cannot walk." The two younger boys disappeared into the wadi and soon brought a forked stick to Mordecai. They helped him to his feet. After an hour of trading, they hoisted him up to join Phinehas on the fourth camel. The oldest boy pulled out his flute and headed their little caravan toward Elim. They left the two Hebrews on the outskirts of the oasis and turned their camels into the wind. Phinehas and Mordecai watched them go until the last notes drifted away.

Rude jests and mockery followed the adventurers as they limped past neighboring camps. The soggy dung bag proclaimed their coming; the pillar of fire shown brightly on their scrapes and ravaged clothes.

"Ignore them," said Phineas. "We have procured bags for Rachel." He chuckled.

"I am going to wash the dung bag. Wait till she sees her new skin for making cheese. Butter and cheese bags. She is a rich woman. Remind me never to go anywhere with you again."

"Those boys followed us out there. It was their flute we heard last night," said Phinehas.

"You know they are killers," said Mordecai. "I'm beginning to think we were the bait."

"I have been trying to work it out."

"Me, too."

Rachel ran to meet them. Her first question, "What happened?" was followed by, "What's that smell?"

Later Rachel and Mordecai sat near the fire. She parted his hair and dabbed at the dried blood.

"How big is it?" he asked.

"As long as my finger. But not too deep. I have been so worried. What is a wadi?"

"It's a dry gully. But if it rains far away, the water rushes down it. In a flood. We were camping at the bottom."

Rachel hugged her cheese bag. "I can make cheese now. And the griddle. And the barley meal. I can fry cakes. Tell me again about the caravan."

"Well, it was not a long caravan. The Bedouins Phinehas got the hindquarters from came along and we did some trading. They brought us home on their camels."

"What a kind thing to do."

"Yes." On the opposite side of the cart, Phinehas snored loudly.

By morning, Mordecai's ankle had swollen, and sunburn added to their woes. Phinehas groaned with every move, walking as bowlegged as

Mordecai. Rachel left the men with the baby and their pain and led the nanny goats to graze.

Asmath's white shawl did not capture the sun's rays. She shivered in the morning breeze, but she was happy to be alone with her thoughts. *Soon I will weave a black shawl and the mornings will not be so cold.* A stumbling kid followed one of the goats and the belly of the other bulged in pregnancy. *Before long I will be as big as you,* she thought. *I will make the shawl big enough to cover me and the baby. The new baby. My own baby.* She felt a twinge of guilt. Was not Kore—her name, whether Mordecai agreed or not—her own baby now?" Today she planned to inquire among the shepherds about the prostitute. *Maybe Sarah made it all up just to torment me,* she thought.

&

After Mordecai and Phinehas had left to seek the caravan, she had resisted the urge to wring her hands. Instead she settled at her new loom and began to weave. Anger and worry drove the shuttle speedily through the threads. What if they were set upon by robbers and killed? Who would marry her? Mordecai had no brothers. Her husband was such a good man. Surely Yahweh would take care of him. She thought of all the kind things Mordecai had done for her. She had not been as sweet to him as she should have. What would she do without him? The shuttle fell between the threads, and she began to wring her hands. She became aware of someone standing behind her. Sarah. *You are a blister on my heel,* she thought.

"Where did Mordecai and that merchant go?"

"His name is Phinehas. He is a dear friend of ours."

"More like your second husband if you ask me."

What now? First the baby, now Phinehas. The Hebrew way declared that she offer her guest a cup of water and a polite reception. Rachel rose and poured a bowl for Sarah. "Have you found a midwife yet?"

"Could you add a little beer to that? It helps my backache. I do not need a midwife. My babies come easy. Twin boys this time. I am sure of it."

"I hope they are as wonderful as our brothers, Perez and Hazor," said Rachel, tipping the beer jug over the bowl.

"Who taught you to weave?"

"My mistress did not want her daughter and me to be ignorant. She hired a woman to teach us to weave. We learned to cook also."

"You still speak as if you were a daughter."

"But Sarah, I was treated like a daughter."

"While I was working in the wheat fields you were living a life of ease."

"I am sorry you had a hard life."

"But now I will have more sons, and you will have a prostitute's daughter." Sarah handed Rachel the empty bowl, turned, and walked placidly out of the camp.

&

Now on the outskirts of the camps, with the men recovering from their adventures, Rachel staked out the two goats, and making sure her veil covered her hair, approached a shepherd with a long black beard. "May I ask you a question, please?"

"I have no food to spare, young woman," he said kindly. "I wish I did."

"Oh no," she said. "If you are hungry, I have a new butter churn and a new cheese bag. I could bring you some of both."

He waved his hand toward his herd of goats. "I have all the butter I need. What do you want?"

"I have been told there is a prostitute who travels with a shepherd. A woman who gave away her female-child. Have you heard of this?"

The man thought a moment and said, "Bring your goats and come with me. We will go to my mother's tent. The pregnant goat followed on the shepherd's heels. Rachel tugged the other away from a scrub bush and followed the man toward a group of four black tents, the largest set apart. They approached the large tent where children played and four women sat in the early morning sun spinning and weaving black wool. They all stopped work and smiled, welcoming Rachel.

"Ma..." The shepherd addressed a small wizened woman. Rachel noticed her strong square hands at once. "This girl needs to speak to you." She gazed into the woman's eyes... kind, patient, and familiar as home. Rachel managed to whisper, *Jemimah*, before she collapsed at her teacher's feet.

Rachel woke with her head in Jemimah's lap. "When I saw that hair," said the old woman, "I knew it was you and no one else." The hands that had taught Rachel and Asmath to spin and weave now stroked Rachel's hair and wiped away tears that ran from the corners of her eyes. "I am glad to see you, too. Now stop crying and sit up." Rachel obeyed. "I remember the first time I saw you faint," said Jemimah. "A dog had killed a cat in the courtyard of your master's house." She spoke to her daughters, "You never saw such a screaming, jumping fit in your life, and then," Jemimah snapped her fingers, "she just went out. Pharaoh's physician came and said you would outgrow it. What did that bald-headed old goat know?"

Rachel pressed fresh tears from her eyes. "Jemimah, you were there. They did treat me like a daughter. They cared about me. They sent for Pharaoh's physician, did they not?"

"Of course they cared about you. What is this about, child? What is burdening you?"

Rachel dried her tears on the hem of her veil. "My brother's wife hates me. She is jealous of my family in Ramses. She says they did not care for me, that I was just a slave. My mistress gave me a pouch filled with gold objects. My brother's wife tried to take them from me. But my brother said no, the gifts should be my dowry. Now she wants to hurt me."

"And did you marry? Is your husband a good man?

Rachel did not realize she beamed until she saw Jemimah's three daughters nodding and smiling. Shelah, Jemimah's unmarried daughter said, "Yes, he must be."

"He will be your strength," said Jemimah, "but why are you here?"

Rachel told how they had found the baby, how Mordecai said they must go to Moses, how Sarah threatened to spread the word that the baby was a prostitute's child. She told what Sarah had said about the baby's future—that she would be called a bastard and no one would take her for a bride. "She torments me with this threat. I came to find out if anyone knows of such a prostitute. Sarah says she travels with a shepherd. Do you know of such a person?"

"Calm yourself, Rachel. Let me think." She sighed deeply and said, "There is such a woman, a prostitute. Rumor had it that she took her girl-child off." Rachel gasped. "Everyone thought she had sold the child or taken her into the hills and left her."

"I knew she had been abandoned. I told Mordecai so."

"The prostitute is dead. Some kind of wasting sickness. How much do you love this child?"

"Oh, Jemimah, you should see her. She is beautiful and sweet. I love her beyond telling."

"Will this Sarah stop?"

"Never. I am a bug under her foot."

"Then you must do what is best for the child." Jemimah held Rachel's hands in her own and said, "Since the woman is dead, I think we can leave Moses out of it. Here is my advice: bring the child to me. She will be my granddaughter, raised on my lap with all these." Jemimah waved her hand toward the children. "No one will ever know where she came from. She will make a good marriage. She will never know disgrace."

At camp, Mordecai played with the baby on Phinehas' rug. He had carved rattle toys for the child and the puppy. "She wants the puppy's toy and he wants hers," Mordecai laughed.

Rachel sat, pulled the child onto her lap, and buried her face in the sweet neck. How could she give up this baby? *So this is what heartbreak feels like,* she thought. Sarah would never stop; she knew it deep down where wisdom lay. Rachel saw the future like a scroll rolled out across the dry desert sands: word would spread, and when it came time to arrange her marriage, Kore would be as tainted as the waters of Marah. The stain would spread to their other children. *Brother of a bastard. Sister of a prostitute's child.* Rachel rocked the sleepy baby. *Oh, my little girl, how could I let that happen to you?*

"Mordecai, I have found a home for Kore. Please do not say that is not her name."

"No," said Mordecai. He took the baby back onto his lap. She reached up and patted his face. He kissed her hand.

"I knew you had come to love her, too." Through tears Rachel told Mordecai everything: Sarah, her threats, Jemimah's offer of a good life for Kore.

"Why have you not told me any of this? Did you not trust me?"

"I was afraid."

"But how do you know we can trust this woman?"

"Mordecai, I would trust Jemimah with my life. But I cannot do it alone. Will you help me be strong? Will you go with me?"

"What is the matter? You are a sad lot." Phinehas groaned and favored his sunburned parts as he sat down.

"Walk with me." said Mordecai.

"Do you mean I have to get up again? Look at your ankle. You can't walk."

"Hobble with me. Help me up."

Rachel settled the baby for her nap, and pushing the kid aside, began to milk the nanny goat. With every pull on the teat, her resolve grew. *I will be strong. I will do the best thing for Kore. I will never forgive Sarah. Never. Never. Never.* The goat bawled in pain.

And so Mordecai, Rachel and Phinehas, watchful for Sarah, took the baby by a circuitous route to Jemimah and her daughters. They sat in the shade under the awning, and Shelah brought bowls of water. Rachel laid the sleeping child in Jemimah's lap. "Her name is Kore—partridge. When we found her she was like a baby bird lost from its covey..."

Jemimah plucked at the baby's curls, extending them, allowing them to spring back. "Mordecai, you must be strong for your wife. She will suffer greatly. You must preserve her for your own child."

Chapter 7

THE DAYS AT THE OASIS OF ELIM came to an end as the people knew they inevitably would. The oasis, welcome as it had been to the thirsty Hebrews, surely was not the spacious land of milk and honey Yahweh promised. The pillar of cloud rose. They filled their water jugs and skins, packed their goods, and with the discipline of an army, fell into their ranks. The chosen people of Yahweh, supplied by the caravans, well-watered and rested, followed their God without complaint. They headed from Elim, eastward toward a mountain range in the land of Midian. Of that land they knew little. There, Moses had fled to escape Pharaoh's wrath and for forty years had tended the flocks of his father-in-law, Jethro, a priest of Midian. From Midian he had returned to lead the Hebrews out of Egypt.

Mordecai replaced the crude stick the Bedouin brothers had provided with an elaborately carved one of his own design. His ankle plagued him, so he asked Jabus for the loan of his sons, Reuel and Zelo, to help Phinehas push the cart. Jabus agreed on the condition that Mordecai feed the boys. Although he was proud to have sons, Jabus begrudged their every bite. "That's why Adah is so thin," whispered Rachel. "She gives her portion to the boys."

Reuel, everyone's favorite, proved to be a good-natured boy, happy to push the cart, gather stones and dung for the campfire, and help Rachel milk the goats. They had no sooner left Elim than Zelo threw a rock at Sekhmet. Phinehas grabbed the front of the boy's tunic, pulled him nose to nose and growled, "If you do that again, I will break your arm."

Looking every bit like his father, Zelo turned and stalked away. Over his shoulder he yelled, "My father says you are a worm."

Phinehas stood with his mouth open. "A worm?"

"Don't get too close to me" said Mordecai, "I'm a talking bird."

They were still laughing when Perez and Hazor strode into camp. The Uncle Twins tried in vain to keep straight faces. They had to hold each other up while Perez delivered his speech: "Enoch sent us. He said a crippled, talking bird and a worm are trying to push a cart here." The four men slapped their knees, bellowing with laughter. Tears streamed down their faces. They held their stomachs. Rachel watched, bemused, shaking her head. At last they organized themselves and started pushing the cart. All day they toiled across the burning sand. From time to time one of them spontaneously cackled.

At the evening campfire the Uncle Twins entertained them with stories of Pharaoh's court. Adding to the hilarity, neither ever finished his own sentence.

Hazor: Perez, do you remember the night the rat—

Perez: got under Pharaoh's throne? And everybody started chasing it—

Hazor: and it was a huge rat, and Pharaoh himself—

Perez: grabbed a torch and pushed it under the throne—

Hazor: and set the cushion on fire!

They beamed, loving the laughter. Everyone clapped.

Hazor: But that's not all. The rat ran across the room where we were standing guard—

Perez: and Hazor cut it in half with his sword!

Rachel screamed and covered Reuel's eyes with her hands.

And so they passed the days and the evenings. Rachel laughed with her brothers and Mordecai and Phinehas, but her heart longed for Kore. One moment she knew she had done the right thing; Kore would have a good life free from stigma. Then she would shake her head in disbelief that she had done such a thing. *I gave away my baby. Surely I could have thought of another way.*

Rachel had become watchful, but one evening, as she agitated the butter churn with unusual vigor, Sarah slipped up behind her. "I see you have now taken Adah's boy, Reuel, and the Uncle Twins. You are like a honey pot left uncovered. Where is that girl-child? I haven't seen her around for a while."

Rachel's eyes narrowed. *For a water buffalo you move quietly, Sarah.* Aloud she said, "The little girl is in a place where you can never hurt her. But listen: Mordecai thinks we should tell Enoch how you have treated me." She let that lie for a moment. "I told him, no, Enoch has enough worries... But if you do not stop this hatefulness, we will tell him. My brother will not be happy." Rachel watched, mesmerized, as Sarah stroked her belly, hands tracing circles under her breasts, moving down over her navel, then up her sides for another round. Rachel dragged her gaze away from Sarah's belly. "I may yet turn Mordecai loose. I am thinking about it."

"That will not be necessary, Sister—now that the child is gone." Rachel thought she saw a flicker of fear. "Still, I am thinking about it." Rachel arched her eyebrows. "After all I am Enoch's baby sister..." Sarah twisted her mouth, laced her fingers under her belly, and waddled away. *That will give her something to fret about,* thought Rachel. She shook the churn with fresh fury.

&

On the fifteenth day of the second month after leaving Egypt, the pillar led them to the Wilderness of Sin. The Hebrews found themselves in an inhospitable land, a vast, barren expanse without shade or water, lying between the oasis at Elim and the tallest mountain in a range running north and south. They camped.

Mordecai worried that Rachel would not be able to get over the loss of Kore. She talked to herself now, gesturing to no one with open, questioning hands, shaking her head, *no*. She paced. He considered going to get the baby. Surely they would give her back. Finally, he asked, "Do you want me to go get her?"

"Yes," she said, brightening, then, "No. This is for the best. Not for me. For Kore."

From the lead tribe, Judah, to the last tribe, Napthali, hundreds of thousands of black tents sprang up seemingly overnight and spread over the rose-colored sands. As slaves the Hebrews had lived on the grounds of Pharaoh's building projects or in the mud-brick hovels of Goshen. They had escaped Egypt with goods from their masters, but few, save the shepherds, owned tents. Frigid nights and blistering days had been incentive enough, and tent-making became an obsession. By the time they reached the Wilderness of Sin, most people slept under small shelters made of woven goat hair mats. Women frantically wove the waterproof, warm, and abundant goat hair into covers for their tents, bedding for warmth and clothing for their families.

Rachel spun and weaved with a fervor born of angst. At first, like a leaf tossed in the wind, her spirit suffered the loss of Kore. Then bitterness dried her tears and set her jaw. She had little to say and eschewed idle chatter. She enfolded herself and endured. She found focus in her loom and centered her energies, working until she had enough mats to cover the top and sides of four tent poles—the beginnings of a woman's tent—*her tent*; her anchor. Whenever they stopped she proudly piled her possessions inside and claimed sole domain of the diminutive fortress. By statute, upon pain of death, when she lowered the sides, no man but her husband was allowed to enter. During the day, with the sides rolled up, the tent became a canopy, and she might choose to invite Phinehas or her brothers to sit in the shade. She had planned for the good of her baby. She had stood up to Sarah. Once they settled in the wilderness of Sin, she began to weave mats for the men's tent.

In the shade of her awning, Rachel set Reuel to picking debris from raw goat hair. She sat cross legged before her loom and pushed the shuttle through the vertical threads. Back and forth; back and forth. Row by row. She wondered if Enoch and Mordecai had reached Moses and his Tent of Meeting. They had left at dawn along with other leaders and elders. The people thirsted and complained. Enoch seemed to find his role as a calming influence.

Phinehas, concerned about the mood in the camp of Manasseh, had stayed behind. Rachel watched as he approached from a neighboring camp. *He loses weight until I hardly know him*, she thought. *Where did the little fat man go? Now he even stands taller.* "There is a lot of unrest," he said as he sat and pulled

Sekhmet onto his lap. "Look at this cat. She's fat from lizards and birds. "Why do you not bring me something?" he addressed the purring cat. "Some leeks; some fish; some duck fat; anything would do." The cat leaped off his lap and jumped into her basket, abandoning him for her new kittens. Phinehas watched Rachel send the shuttlecock flying across the span of threads. He said, "Everyone is worried. There's no water here. Everyone has run out of barley and flour."

"Maybe Mordecai and Enoch will bring good news from Moses."

"That is part of the problem. The people are beginning to speak against Moses. I fear an uprising."

In the wilderness of Sin, the whole congregation of Israel grumbled against Moses and Aaron. Uninvited to the Tent of Meeting, Enoch and Mordecai stood apart and listened as the elders and head men assaulted Moses and Aaron with their same grumblings and complaints: "Would that we had died by Yahweh's hand in the land of Egypt, when we sat by the pots of meat and ate bread to the full. You have brought us to this wilderness to kill this whole assembly with hunger."

Then Moses said to the people, "What are we? Your grumblings are not against us, but against Yahweh. But Yahweh has heard your grumbling. At evening you will know that Yahweh has brought you out of the land of Egypt; and in the morning you will see His glory."

Aaron said, "Come near before Yahweh for he has heard your grumbling." Then the glory of Yahweh, his fire, flamed up in the pillar of cloud and a gasp rose up from the whole of Israel, to the uttermost ends of the congregation. Never had Yahweh's cloud flamed in the daytime.

At the camp in Manasseh, Rachel and Phinehas stood with their neighbors and gazed at the fiery pillar. "What do you suppose it means?" said Rachel.

"Who can know the intentions of Yahweh?" Phinehas poured himself the last dregs of beer.

The head men returned to their tribes. Without waiting for Gamaleil's runner to come with an announcement, Enoch gathered his family and neighbors, about a hundred people, and stood upon his wagon. He knew they would have questions. He held up his hand and the murmuring quieted. "You all know by now, Moses met with the elders and heads this morning. I am going to tell you things that will thrill you and seem very strange. Please understand this: Moses spoke the words of Yahweh who has heard our grumblings and discontentment. Moses said when we grumble, we are not complaining against him and Aaron but against Yahweh, Himself. We should remember that." His eyes drifted over the people.

A tall young man named Ishi raised his hand. "It is hard not to worry when we come to a place with no water in sight. I have three children."

Enoch spoke: "We also have seen what Yahweh can do. We have to trust him at every step along the way. We follow the pillar where it leads. That is trust. We walked through a wall of water at the sea. That took trust. Do we trust the sun to come up every morning? Do we say, during the night, what will we do if the sun does not come up?"

"These are Yahweh's words spoken by Moses: 'At twilight you shall eat meat, and in the morning, you shall be filled with bread.'" He held up his hand to quiet the joyful outburst. "The bread will rain from heaven..." The crowd exchanged incredulous looks. "After the morning dew dries, we will gather it. We will gather it up every day—one omer, or a large bowlful—for each person in the family." Again he held up his hand to still the babble. *Now I know how Moses feels,* he thought. "Do you understand what I said?" Enoch realized he was shouting. He lowered his voice. "Gather only the amount your family can eat in one day. No more. No less." The people nodded their assent. Enoch surveyed the crowd. He knew their thoughts, whether they understood. They did not. They were too excited to listen. "Ishi, you have five members in your family. You will gather two full portions and enough for the children, and the next day you will gather it again." Ishi returned a blank stare.

"Listen." He tried again. You must not try to save any until the next day. This is a test of obedience from Yahweh. Each day is a new day to trust Him for your bread. Will you obey?"

The people shouted, "We will obey." *No, you will not,* he thought.

"There is more." Again he held up his hand. "Moses reminded us that Yahweh created the heavens and the earth in six days. He rested on the seventh day. From now on, we will also have a day of rest—the seventh day. Every seven days will be a rest day, a gift from Yahweh to us. It will be called the Sabbath."

Jabus stood apart in a group of five men. "What does this Sabbath mean?" he shouted. "We all rest on the same day? Who can tell a man when to rest? That is outrageous." Arguments broke out.

"Wait!" Shouted Mordecai. "If Yahweh wants to give us a day of rest, is this not a good thing? Who would argue with Yahweh?"

Jabus narrowed his eyes at Mordecai and showed his teeth.

"There is more," said Enoch.

"More," bellowed Jabus, "I can take no more. Either we have bread or we do not. Moses asks too much." Followed by his friends, he pushed through the crowd and left. Others filled the empty spaces.

"Tell us, Enoch. We are listening," said Mordecai."

"For six days," Enoch sighed loudly," we will gather the bread. On the sixth day, we will gather a double portion. We will not gather any on the Sabbath—the seventh day. On the Sabbath, you will eat from the double portion gathered on the sixth day." He gave the people time to ponder this astounding instruction from the mouth of Yahweh. "Go to your tents. Wait and see what Yahweh will do." He watched the people leave, whispering among themselves. No one asked a question. They did not know what to ask.

The sun seemed truculent and slow, an anchor dragging time toward twilight and the promise of meat and full bellies. The people slept, and woke, and debated, and doubted what they had heard. Enoch asked Mordicai to join him to help explain to their neighbors face to face the test of obedience Yahweh demanded. "You must trust Yahweh to provide your daily bread. You cannot save it. On the sixth day you must gather a double portion. There will be no bread on the seventh day, the Sabbath." Thus they explained again Yahweh's instructions.

"What about the meat?" Jabus threw the question like a javelin. His friends elbowed one another "Will antelope fall from the sky?" Laughter and scoffing ensued.

"I do not know where the meat will come from," said Enoch. "But I know this, Brother: if Yahweh said he will do a thing, he will do it."

Ishi left Jabus and the mockers and followed closely behind Enoch and Mordicai. He spoke over their shoulders, "When I was a boy, minnows and tadpoles rained from a dark cloud. I saw it with my own eyes, yet when I tell it, no one believes me. Maybe it will be like that?" Enoch stopped, turned and studied the man. "You are on the way to trusting in Yahweh. But His ways are far beyond anything we can think up. Find better friends, Ishi."

Mordecai returned to his camp where Rachel and Phinehas suffered the absence of Perez and Hazor. Once Mordecai's ankle healed, the Uncle Twins took their raucous behavior and returned to Enoch's camp, but Reuel stayed with Rachel. Jabus did not seem to miss his younger son. Adah, however, sought him out for a kiss most every day. One day Phinehas and Rachel watched as Mordecai showed the boy how to hold the carving knife. "Adah knows he is better off with us," Rachel said. "Zelophehad torments him so."

"I had an older brother like Zelo," Phinehas said. "Reuel is better off with us." *And Rachel's empty arms need him,* he thought. *But one of these days, Jabus will decide to take him back. Better that she not get too attached. How many heartbreaks can she take?*

Reuel sat too close while she spun the wool into threads and wound them around the spindle. She worked around him, not having the heart to ask him to move over. His suntanned shoulder blades reminded her of a hatchling she had once found. Never mind the mites and Clio's screeching; it was a dear little thing. Rachel hugged her nephew. *If I had stayed with Asmath,* she thought, *I would never have known him.* "Aunt Rachel," said the little boy, "will we really have meat tonight?"

"Meat at twilight that is what Yahweh said."

"Will we kill the sheep and goats?"

"We cannot eat the sheep and goats. In a few days they would all be gone. Then we would have no wool, no milk, no butter, nothing left to sacrifice to Yahweh."

"No cheese."

"That's right, no cheese. Go in my tent and take a nap. It will make the time go faster."

Like a mirage, twilight and the promise of meat shimmered in the distance. Mordecai and Phinehas diverted themselves with a new idea: a plan to turn the cart around and yoke the donkey between the handles. They drew their plans in the sand and brushed them out and drew them again. They hardly noticed when the sun set beyond the darkening mountains and the sky purpled into twilight— "Look," Mordecai said, we need two notches on the …"

"But Mo, what if we..." Rachel milked the goats and listened absently to the men. Her thoughts, as always, turned to Kore. Why had Yahweh put the child in her path only to take her away? Would Ma'at do such a thing? She was the goddess of truth, justice and harmony, the enemy of that snake, Apep, god of chaos. Surely Yahweh is more powerful than Apep, she thought. Maybe Yahweh is allowing Apep to think he is in control only to crush him. She thought of Yahweh's heel smashing down on the snake and smiled.

Phinehas' gaze followed Mordecai's to Rachel and the goat. She had stopped milking, but held the teats in her hands and grinned. She wagged her head a few times, and still grinning, resumed her milking.

"At least she's stopped crying," Phinehas whispered.

"I think we're going to have to go get that baby back," Mordecai said under his breath. "I can't stand to see her like this."

"What if they will not give her back?"

"Jemimah loves Rachel. Maybe I should talk to Enoch."

A low-flying bird caught their attention. Sekhmet leaped from the cart and grabbed it in midair. She dashed under the cart and held the brown quivering body between her paws.

"Did you see that?" exclaimed Phinehas. "Look. There's another one. Here come some more. They're quail." The cat dropped the one she had and pounced on another. She left that one and ran to another.

A churning, mottled shadow spread beneath the pillar of fire and covered the Hebrew camps from one end of the wilderness to the other. A sea of birds, in a deafening roar of beating wings and frantic chirping, struggled against a stiffening wind and fluttered exhausted to the ground. Rachel picked one up and cupped it in her hands. It chortled pitifully. "Poor little thing... Phinehas, what are you doing?" she cried, her voice lost in the wind.

Phinehas clamped his hands around one bird and then another. And another. Whooping with joy, he twisted off their heads and threw his booty onto a growing pile.

Mordecai, hugged his wife and danced her in a circle. Rachel clutched the bird under her whipping veil. "He really did it," shouted Mordecai, "this is the meat Yahweh promised."

"Well, pick some up, man." Phinehas waved his arms. "Reuel, pick some up."

The camps roiled with flopping birds and raucous, laughing people, participants in a frenzied, wild game—a game with no bounds, no rules. The flock thickened, pushed back by the wind. The overjoyed Hebrews, jaded with the grounded quail, reached out and picked birds from the air like ripe fruit.

"That's enough, Phinehas. We should stop now," yelled Mordecai. Stop Reuel. We have enough."

"What?" said Phinehas. "Mo, we can eat quail for days. Look." He reached into the mass of beating brown wings and grasped a bird in each hand. "Look at that."

Mordecai shouted into his friend's ear, "We have no salt to preserve this meat. We should not gather more than we can eat."

"Did Moses say that? Did Yahweh?" Phinehas stood with fists on his hips, a bird dripping blood from each hand.

"No. But I think he hates greed. It shows lack of trust." Birds in hand, Phinehas shrugged and tossed his last headless victims onto the pile. They built a fire in disgruntled silence and set about pulling the breasts from the birds—seventy-three in all.

"We have a little salt left," said Rachel. "We can brine what we do not roast now." They laid the breasts on a rock in the midst of the blowing fire. What little aroma the wind spared them made them ravenous. Finally they ate, juice from the succulent breasts dripping down their chins. Sated and exhausted, they threw the remains and feathers on the fire.

"You were right, Mo," said Phinehas. He waved toward their neighbors, still lost in their frenzy of greed. "They haven't even started cleaning or cooking." Content to leave their neighbors to their folly the three tucked their mats snugly against the wind and slept.

The nation of Israel awoke at dawn to a layer of dew around the camp. When the dew evaporated, a layer of white, flake-like substance covered the ground. It was somewhat sticky and appeared as fine as frost. Rachel thought it tasted like a sweet cake Cleo made in her mistress's kitchen. To Phinehas it tasted like bread with honey. Some thought it tasted like wafers. Mordecai had long forgotten what any of those things tasted like; he declared it simply delicious. No one knew what it was, so they called it *manna - what is it?*

Jabus and Adah had set up a tent a short distance from Enoch. Adah gathered three omers of manna—three large bowls. "This is not enough," argued Jabus. "Where is Reuel's share?"

"He is eating with Rachel," said Adah.

"No one knows that. Go get more—some for Reuel. Extra for us."

Enoch and his family gathered eighteen omers—eighteen large bowls to accommodate thirteen children, his wives and the adults in his household.

Mordecai, Phinehas, Rachel and Reuel gathered four. Rachel filled the bowl four times and dumped it in the cook pot. "Does this look like enough?" She squinted into the pot and held it out for Mordecai to see.

"We will trust Yahweh. Take no more than that."

Rachel poked her finger into the sticky substance. "I have no idea how to cook it. Clio had nothing like this."

Mordecai thought a moment. "I remember something Moses said at the meeting: 'Bake what you will bake, and boil what you will boil.'" So Rachel placed her baking stone in the coals and shaped half the sweet stuff into cakes. She boiled the rest in goat's milk. They had cakes and gruel, and they had plenty to last until the next morning.

Many people missed the first manna gathering. Exhausted from a night of quail-madness, they slept until the manna melted in the morning sun. Their disappointment grew when they found their untended birds crawling with ants and scorpions. Rats scurried among the piles of dead birds. By nightfall, foxes, wolves, and hyenas skulked close to the camps and made furtive forays among the frightened people.

Rachel, Reuel, the baby goat and the puppy slept in the cart. Phinehas locked Sekhmet in her basket with the kittens and he and Mordecai took turns keeping watch. A woman's scream brought Mordicai to the fire. "I cannot sleep." He wrapped a shawl around his shoulders, sat, and tossed a handful of dung chips onto the coals.

"Talk to me," said Phinehas.

"About?"

"About trusting Yahweh." Phinehas rested his chin on his knees. He marveled to himself how obedient his body had become. "When we talk with Enoch and our friends at night, we talk about Noah, and Abraham, and Jacob, and how Adam came to name the hippopotamus. I have never seen a hippopotamus."

Mordecai chuckled. "I have not seen a lion or a giraffe. Maybe they are just stories."

"I want to know how to trust Yahweh. Not those things. How is it you have this great trust, while I am carried away by greed, like this rabble." He waved his hand at the surrounding camps "It shames me to say it, but if you had not stopped me, we would be sitting in a bed of ants."

"I am not sure how it happened." Mordecai's eyes misted with memories. "At the wood shop, Elias was my father, and my mother. He told me about the power of Yahweh. But I did not know that power. Then I saw it at the brick yard when Yahweh sent the plagues. And at the sea. I will never get over that."

"Nor will I." He surveyed the burning piles and scurrying rats. "Then I see all this mess we have made."

"But that is it. Yahweh gave us something good. We ruined it."

"By being greedy."

"Can you see it any other way?"

"It is a hard lesson."

"If you had a bad child, would you hold back the rod?"

On the second morning and the third, until the sixth, the great congregation, no less thrilled than they had been the first day, gathered the manna, one omer per person. By the end of the week, few people tried to save it, for it did indeed breed worms overnight and besides, Yahweh could be trusted to provide it the next morning. The women experimented with cooking methods: they fried it, baked it, roasted it, boiled it and mixed it with whatever condiments they had. They spread it with yogurt and mixed it with cheese. On the sixth morning, in obedience to Yahweh's plan, they gathered a double portion. They saved half of this portion until twilight for the Sabbath meal, and ate it all the seventh day. The bread of Yahweh stayed fresh and pure.

On the seventh morning, Enoch, and his large family, sat in a circle and watched Sarah and Hannah lay large trays of food in the center. Today they would eat the last of the manna they had prepared the day before. Jabus and Adah passed by with their bowls. "Where are you going, Brother?" called Enoch.

"To gather manna, where else?"

"There will not be any there. Did I not explain all this? You were supposed to take a double portion yesterday."

"We did. There is never enough to fill us. Every day we even take Reuel's share, and it still does not fill us."

Enoch sighed deeply. Would his younger brother ever learn? Enoch spoke clearly and slowly, "From now on, take only what you need for the number of people living with you. That would be three. You. Adah. Zelo. Three omers by measure. Three bowls. No more. If you do what Yahweh said to do, I promise your bellies will be full."

Jabus said, "How is taking less going to make us more full?" When Enoch did not answer, he shouted, "Are you not going to share? Must I eat a rotten bird?" Enoch rose, hugged his sister-in-law and emptied his bowl into hers. He rejoined his family. Sarah passed Enoch's bowl around the family circle; large hands and small filled it to overflowing.

Chapter 8

THE SONS OF JACOB SHOOK THE SAND from their sleeping mats, rolled their tents, and drove their flocks from the Wilderness of Sin without regret. They left behind the smoldering stench of feathers and the threat of predators large and small. The Hebrews wondered if Yahweh would continue to provide manna. He did. Each day, teased by one mirage after another, they wondered if they would come to an oasis, a well, a pool of water. They did not.

Compressed by narrow mountain gorges, the twelve tribes traveled by stages toward the highest mountain in the range. Scourged by unrelenting heat, they trudged deeper and deeper into the wilderness. At last the pillar came to rest at Rephidim, a wide, barren plain where foothills climbed to low mountains, stacked ridge upon ridge, rising higher and higher to the tallest mountain in Midian. At Rephidim the people ran out of water and patience.

Enoch felt real fear for the first time at Rephidim. He stood on the wagon bed with Mordecai and Phinehas and surveyed the angry crowds. They had watched as knots of three men or four merged and grew into twenty and swelled and began to move as one, as a mob. Raised fists and shouts of, "Water! Water! Where is Moses? Our children die of thirst. Have we been brought to this place to die? Our flocks need water!"

"I have never seen the men so enraged," said Enoch under his breath. "It would not take much for them to seize Moses and stone him. I fear it could happen."

"All they need is a leader, and they will be off," said Phinehas.

"They may have one," said Mordecai. "Look." Jabus and his friends pushed their way into the center of a noisy crowd of thirty or so men. Jabus raised his arms and yelled for quiet. The crowd settled.

Before his brother could form words, Enoch raised his own arms and shouted, "Men of Manasseh, listen to me!" Jabus' mouth fell open as Enoch's voice—was it carried on the wind or on the silence? —like a soothing balm, spread over the listening crowd: "I know you are thirsty. I am, too. So is my wife who is heavy with twins. And my six little children. And my goats. And my ox. And my brothers." He turned his hand toward Jabus. "I do not know where the water is. But I know the one who *does* know. His name is Yahweh. Moses is not a god. He is just a man like us. It is Yahweh's power in the cloud; Yahweh parted the sea and allowed you to walk on dry land; Yahweh sweetened the water at Marah. Moses is nothing but His instrument. Do you not know that by now? If you stone Moses, will Yahweh choose one of you to lead us to water?" Enoch gazed into the faces of Manasseh, his cousins and uncles, one by one. "Trust Yahweh. Trust his man, Moses. Trust in what you have seen with your own eyes. Every morning when you wake up and gather manna, say to yourself, today I will trust Yahweh. Did He not give me this bread? Go to your tents. Be the father your children need. Give them hope. Teach them to trust. Tell them that Yahweh will provide water."

Enoch, Phinehas and Mordecai climbed down from the wagon. Men milled about them and patted Enoch on the shoulder. He felt drained. What had he said? He could barely remember. Where had the words come from? A young priest whispered in his ear. "Moses is taking some of the elders to a source of water. Gamaleil has been watching you. He has sent me to get you."

"I cannot go." *What am I saying?* thought Enoch. He shook his head, *no.* "My wife is about to bear twins." Disbelief spread over the priest's face. "Take this man." Enoch placed his arm around Mordecai's shoulder. "Elias taught him for three years."

"You are Mordecai? The carver from Pharaoh's woodworking shop?" said the priest.

"I am."

"My great uncle will be so happy to see you." Joy spread over his face. He would not go back empty-handed.

"Elias. He is well?"

"You shall see."

Grinning, Mordecai said, "Phinehas, tell Rachel I have gone to get water." With that he and the priest left at a lope, headed for Moses and his meeting place.

Like two boys not chosen for the game, Enoch and Phinehas watched them go.

❦

Rachel sat weaving while Reuel played with the kittens. She had kept the boy close because of unrest in the camp. She noticed the shouting had stopped. *For now,* she thought. *But it's always something. Mordecai said the people should trust Yahweh more.* She thought about Yahweh. She remembered stories from her childhood about the one true God, stories about Abraham, Isaac, Jacob, and Jacob's wife, Rachel, her namesake.

Rachel—she had finally married Jacob. When they left her father, Laban's, house, she stole an idol and hid it in her camel's saddle. What a commotion that had caused. When Laban caught up with them, she sat on the saddle and watched as her father searched the tent. Jacob had promised Laban the thief would die. The woman must have been terrified. Rachel's heart twisted. She thought: *I have an idol! As surely as my namesake did, I have kept it hidden from my husband. But I do not worship Ma'at. I keep her as a remembrance of Asmath's love. Surely the God who created all that exists would not begrudge me this little thing? Would he?*

"Mordecai has gone for water." Phinehas' excited words shattered her reverie. He danced a jig with Reuel.

"Where to?" she said.

"I do not know. A priest came for Enoch, but Sarah is about to go into labor, so Mordecai went instead."

"With the new babies, maybe she will forget about you-know-who," she said.

"Would you like to go see Jemimah? And *everybody*?" Phinehas raised his eyebrows. "Reuel could keep the camp and we could go."

"Go get the Uncle Twins. Reuel's too young to stay by himself."

Like a welcome oasis emerging from a mirage, they spotted the four black tents, one larger than the rest, from a distance. Rachel ran, leaving Phinehas behind. Eyes roving, searching for Kore, she embraced Jemimah and her three daughters. Shelah, the youngest said, "She's playing over there." Kore fell into Rachel's arms, and for a happy hour they played.

Since they had brought Kore to Jemimah, Phinehas had not been able to get the youngest daughter out of his mind. Those eyes—the orbs of a gazelle. Her height—just right for a short man. He longed to see her hair; did it part in the center? Was it curly or straight? His hands briefly closed over Shelah's as he accepted a bowl of water. He talked with Jemimah and the older daughters, telling them news of the camps and the foray for water, but his attention rested on Shelah. He noticed the not-so-secret smiles passing between the sisters.

The old woman inquired about Rachel's state of mind. "I have never seen such grief," he said. "Sometimes she is almost sick. Mordecai wants to get the baby back for her." His eyebrows rose, questioning.

"Of course. I would never keep Kore against Rachel's will. She knows what is best. When it comes to the child she has shown wisdom."

"If we could just figure out what to do about Sarah. She is wicked," said Phinehas.

Shelah spoke up. "I think Mordecai should tell the brother all about it. Is he not head of the family?"

"Do you?" Phinehas had never heard the girl speak. Her voice, unlike some small women's, was soft and low.

"Yes," she said, frowning. "Sarah would obey him, would she not?"

"Not all women obey their husbands."

"I suppose he could beat her," said the oldest daughter.

"Enoch would never beat his wife," said Phinehas. "I would never beat my wife." He captured Shelah's gaze and held it.

"Then he must threaten to take away something she loves," said Shelah.

"Jemimah, may I speak with you alone?" asked Phinehas. The woman waved her daughters into the tent. He heard them giggling. He wanted to giggle himself.

"Jemimah." He did not know where to begin. He started again. "Jemimah..."

"Phinehas," she said with a toothless grin, "you would like to marry my youngest daughter?"

"Oh, yes. That is it exactly."

"I have no objections. Her betrothed died in Goshen. It is time she married. You seem like a good man. Kind. You are very short."

"I know."

"She is short. You will have short children. But you must ask my oldest son, Nobah. He is our head."

"Nobah?"

"You know him?"

"I have traded with him..."

"Nobah is our head. But," she tapped a gnarled finger on her chest. "Do not worry. I am the head's mother."

Leave-taking had been painful for Rachel. She had cried and rocked Kore until the child strained to be put down. Finally, Rachel embraced the women and walked away without looking back. "What did Jemimah say?"

"About what?"

"About whether you can marry Shelah, you slug."

"How did you know about that?"

"Well, let me see...you're talking to Jemimah alone and the sisters are laughing in the tent. And then there's the fact that you are bouncing instead of walking."

"I am not bouncing. Nobah is the head of the family."

"Nobah? That wily trader?"

"The very one."

"I wondered why my goat followed the man like a dog."

I will have to negotiate with him. Negotiating for a goat is different from bargaining for a wife."

❧

Mordecai trotted close on the heels of the young priest past the last campsites to the edge of the desert. The two approached a crowd of fifty or so bearded elders who suspended their spirited debates and murmured, shifting their shoulders, disdainful of the new arrivals. *What am I doing here? I cannot take Enoch's place,* thought Mordecai. A box carriage, painted red, simple in design, born by four young priests, parted the crowd.

"Mordecai, my son," Elias' voice boomed from his frail body. He opened his arms to receive Mordecai's embrace and kissed the young man's neck.

Elias waved to his bearers. "Put me down. Put me down." Mordecai, overcome with tears, knelt beside the carriage. Elias grasped his shoulders and searched his face. "You look well. He threw back his head, laughed, and rapped the side of the carriage. "This box is not nearly as exciting as the ride to Goshen you gave me in that cart." They laughed, remembering the day Mordecai rescued Elias from the wood shop.

"When I almost ran over that goose..."

"I knew we were going in the creek."

"You were going in the creek. The cart and I were staying on the path."

Elias' eyes sparkled. "How about that woman with the bundles on her head..." They laughed. Elias sobered. "You know, Mo, I still cannot believe the master gave you that cart. And he was happy to do it. That is the strangest part. Yahweh made him do it."

"And the tools. I made Rachel a loom with those tools."

"Ahh, the beautiful Rachel with the hair. And so you are married to her?" Mordecai frowned. "What? This is not a happy thing?"

"We have a problem. There is a baby..."

"Already?" Before Mordecai could explain, Moses and Aaron, their gray beards blowing in the afternoon breeze, walked through the crowd and unceremoniously led the assembly into the desert. Priests, elders, Elias in his carriage, then Mordecai, and last, the ox-drawn supply wagon followed Moses toward the great mountain.

Elias peered around and said, "We will talk tonight at the camp." The drone of Elias' snoring and the churning wagon wheels lulled the young man into a dreamlike state where he imagined Rachel, as she lay dying from grief. *"You should have done something. Are you not my husband?"* Maybe Elias would have a solution. The oxen grunted and drooled, their hot breath heavy and wet with the odor of hyssop.

Soon Mordecai noticed the wheels produced a crisper sound and the footing seemed firmer. The lay of the land changed perceptibly. Were they passing over a rock table? He looked into the distance. Did it form a wide basin? They approached the foothills, tumbled mounds of stacked boulders, rising to mountain ranges beyond. Atop one hill, a lone stone of immense proportions glowed in the setting sun like a gigantic nugget of gold and stood against a panorama of orange clouds. They passed below the monolith and turned south a short distance.

The company of weary old men, aided by young priests, set up camp. A purple twilight deepened to night. They ate and lay on their backs, marveling at stars shining with a brilliance not enjoyed since they left Goshen. "For all its blessings, the pillar overpowers the black night and the stars," said Elias. If I were one to negotiate with Yahweh, I would suggest one night a week it would be nice if we had stars..."

"Do you ever negotiate with him?" asked Mordecai. A bedroll and woolen covers had been given to him. Now he lay next to his old friend.

"In a negotiation, each opponent must have something the other side can use. Alms for the poor is a different story. I often hold out my empty hand. I want to hear about this baby."

So Mordecai told his mentor about finding Kore, and Rachel's love for the child, and Sarah's jealousy and her threats. He told Elias how they had taken the baby to Jemimah. "I do not think Rachel will ever get over this terrible sorrow. Short of killing Sarah, I cannot think of a solution." After many minutes, Mordecai asked, "Are you asleep?"

"I am thinking."

&

Morning dawned clear and cold. Never had Mordecai heard such groaning as fifty old men extricated themselves from sleep. The elders found Aaron in the shade of the hill. He pointed upward toward his brother, climbing steadily toward the prominent boulder. Someone said, "That is the staff he struck the Nile with." Moses climbed in the shade as the sun crept downward, until at last the sun and the man met at the boulder. The man chosen by Yahweh to rescue the Hebrew nation drew back his staff and struck the rock. The massive stone, as tall as eight men, split from top to bottom with a loud *crack!* and formed a fissure as wide as a date palm tree. A torrent of water gushed up from the bottom and poured down the hill, a silver flood in the sunlight, taking rocks and debris with it.

Some men fell to the ground at the clarion sound. Struck dumb, they stared open-mouthed at one another. As they watched, Moses started down the hill. He made no gesture of triumph. Was he not merely Yahweh's instrument?

Moses gave the place two names: Meribah, because there the people quarreled with Yahweh, and Massah, for there the people tested Yahweh, saying, *Is Yahweh among us or not?* The elders, a few young priests, and a young man named Mordecai, there by accident, witnessed what happened at the mountain called Horeb.

☙

"I wish you could have seen it." Mordecai relished the telling of his two days with Moses and the elders. He, Rachel and Phinehas sat with the family around Enoch's campfire. The glow did not come entirely from the firelight. Born the night before, now tightly swaddled, twin girls slept in first one lap and then another. Their mother, confined after childbirth, could not join them. Rachel did not miss Sarah; she rocked one of the babies in her arms and studied the tiny face. *I am going to have one of these.* She was having trouble concentrating on Mordecai's story.

"Moses struck the rock with his staff." Mordecai whacked the air. "And water poured out." He flung his arms into a wide circle. "And not just a little water. A river of water." He shook his head in disbelief. "Oh, you should have seen it."

"And where is this river of water?" asked Jabus. "Our goats cannot last much longer."

"It is coming. You will see. By this time tomorrow you will be watering your goats and filling your water bags. You may even bathe." The women gave a collective sigh.

"I want to swim," piped one of Enoch's small sons.

"Swim!" shouted Mordecai. He swept the boy up and swung him around to the calls of "me next" from clamoring children. Chaos ensued. Soon Enoch, Phinehas and the Uncle Twins, turned into alligators and the chase was on.

Later as the three started back to the cart, Reuel caught up with them and tucked himself under Rachel's arm. "Did your mother say you could come?" she asked.

"She doesn't mind."

Phinehas stoked the fire, took Sekhmet onto his lap and waited for more of the story. Rachel wrapped the end of her shawl around the boy and hugged him close. Morsel slept on her feet. "Tell us some more."

"You should have seen it." Mordecai said for the twentieth time. He gazed into the distance, remembering. "Fifty old men playing in the water. We got so wet we had to lay our clothes out in the sun to dry."

Later Rachel and Mordecai lay in her tent. *Soon we will have a proper tent,* she thought. *And another baby.* Her thoughts turned to Kore. She no longer said *a baby of our own*, for Kore was her own. The child seemed happy with Jemimah and her family. *But I want her back.*

As if he read her thoughts, Mordecai said, "I told Elias about Kore and Sarah's threats."

"What did he say?"

"He said we have to tell Enoch. He will have to reign her in."

"I do not think he can, or I would have already told him. One word from Sarah and Kore will be ruined. One word spread abroad."

"We will see. Elias made a good suggestion..."

"Mordecai...I am with child." She had hoped for more than a loud snore.

&

Mordecai's instincts had been correct: a rock table lay under the sands on the plain of Rephidim, and there the water from the rock of Horeb collected into pools. Yahweh blessed the people with water and they drank and watered their flocks. At Rephidim they trusted their God and his man, Moses. At Rephidim war came to Yahweh's chosen people.

Chapter 9

War with Amelek! On the broad plain of Rephidim, a horde, fierce and ruthless by reputation, amassed for war against Israel. "Tomorrow," Moses said, I will station myself on top of the hill with the staff of Yahweh in my hand." He charged Joshua: "choose men, go forth and fight Amalek."

Before dawn a call to war sounded, chasing Hebrews from their tents like ants from a kicked nest. Tribal heads, Enoch among them, hurried to the Tent of Meeting. Joshua, a true leader of men, outlined a plan and imbued them with courage and hope. They must do the same among the tribes and bring forth volunteers so Joshua could choose an army. In the presence of Joshua, Enoch's heart soared; with the help of Yahweh and Moses the army of Israel would be victorious the next day.

The next day! They would go to war the next day. Enoch's spirits plummeted. He made his way home. *This is reality,* he thought. *Those men gathering manna with their children—ordinary; those standing in line at the latrines— ordinary; that man milking his goat—where is his wife? Will his children be orphans? Where are these victorious soldiers to come from?*

By mid-morning under a bright blue sky, Enoch stood on his wagon and surveyed a restive crowd. What did Hebrew slaves know about war? Apart from a few shields and spears gleaned at the Red Sea, they had no weapons. Who would answer Moses' call? He knew his battle started right there, right then on the bed of that wagon. He had stationed trusted men throughout the crowd: Mordecai, Phinehas, the Uncle Twins, trusted neighbors, and the young man, Ishi, defector from Jabus' band. Enoch gave up trying to silence his brother and the rabble he collected. He waited for Jabus to speak.

"Who are these Amalekites? Why do we fight them?"

"They are killers of innocent Hebrews; they have been picking off our stragglers since we left Egypt. Now they are intent on killing us all. They have assembled for war. Do we have a choice?"

Jabus spoke. "About this Joshua: I have heard he stays at the Tent of Meeting with Moses. Now he snaps his fingers, and we are supposed to follow him into battle?"

A follower of Jabus spoke: "We cannot go against an army skilled with javelin and bow. We are shepherds." Assent rippled through the assembly.

"And woodcarvers." Jabus curled his lip at Mordecai.

Mordecai spoke. "Joshua will lead us into battle by the power of Yahweh. Remember what Yahweh did to Pharaoh's army."

Other men Enoch had sewn in the crowd began to speak up. "No one can stand against Yahweh." Many nodded in agreement.

"Listen, you Hebrews," said Enoch, "since the days of Abraham, Isaac, and Jacob, we have defended our flocks from lions, wild dogs and the likes of these jackals who sneak up and kill the weak on our fringes. We will kill them as we have from the beginning of time: with the sling. We are not defenseless. Our front line will hit them with the sling, and when they fall we will pick up their ax and their spear and their shield. We will arm ourselves from the Amalekites themselves." He had wondered whether such a plan would work, but the men seemed to believe in it. As tangible as a cool breeze on a hot day, one mite of Manasseh changed its mind. What of the other 30,000 or so Manassehites? Would anyone come?

"If you are able to use a sling, go gather perfect stones. If not, bring what you have—a hammer, a knife, an ax—to the north side of the camps. I will see you there at daybreak, and may Yahweh be with us all."

Throughout the afternoon, Mordecai pulled up his tent poles and sharpened the ends into points. He cut and smoothed hand holds in the opposite ends. The mats Rachel had woven and so proudly hung, now draped limply around the last center pole. "Let me get that last one for you," she said.

"No. Leave it. When I come home, I want to see it standing." Now he sat in a pile of shavings, staring at nothing. Rachel wondered if she should tell him about the baby. *No,* she decided, *I am enough to bring him home. He doesn't need anything else on his mind.*

Did they sleep? Neither was sure. Before dawn they emerged from their cocoon breathing steam into a cold morning. Subdued individuals formed lines at the latrines. Rachel vomited. Manna fell. Thousands of cook fires smoked the still air, burning noses and eyes. As usual the women patted the manna flat and made fried cakes or boiled it into mush. The men must not go hungry into war.

"Your javelins, my friend." Mordecai handed two tent poles to Phinehas and kept two. The friends exchanged deep looks. "You know," said Mordeai.

Phinehas nodded. "And you know."

Rachel watched the exchange. Her heart grew heaver by the moment. "Know what?"

Mordecai grasped Rachel's shoulders. *No one ever holds my shoulders unless something bad is going to happen,* she thought.

"If something happens to me, Phinehas will take care of you, and if something happens to me, I will take care of Sekhmet." Rachel chuckled or sobbed, she knew not which. Mordecai held Rachel's face in his hands. He wiped her tears with his thumb and anointed his own forehead. "They will keep me safe." He embraced Reuel and without looking back, shouldered his tent poles and started down the path. Phinehas hugged the woman and the boy and followed his friend.

Herds had been moved close to the camps or hidden high in the surrounding hills. The wide path leading to the grazing grounds teemed with goats, sheep and Hebrews: men heading for the battlefield and women and children migrating into the interior. Determined women shoved sons along the path—those too old to be with their mothers and too young to fight. Enoch had agreed to take seventeen-year-old Hazor and Perez with the promise they not leave his side. He and the twins waited for Mordecai and Phinehas. No one spoke as the five fell into step.

Jemimah and her daughters and a gaggle of children met the men on the path. The women carried sleeping mats, cook pots, water bags, baby goats. "Rachel is waiting for you," said Mordecai. He searched the faces of the children. "Where is Kore?" Jemimah drew a small shorn child from the folds of her dress. Kore, looking every inch a boy, toddled to Mordecai and held out her arms to be picked up. "Kore, baby." He lifted his daughter and like a bee starved for nectar, inhaled the sweetness of her neck. "You cut her hair."

"I thought it wise. It will help throw Sarah off the scent. You must come back so we can make everything right. Yes?"

Phinehas took Shelah's hand and led her a short distance off the path. "Have you inquired of your brother?"

"He agrees. For a price. You know my brother..." She skewed her mouth.

Phinehas longed to kiss straight those lovely lips. "Farewell, Shelah. With the help of Yahweh, I shall return soon."

He and Mordecai hurried to catch up with Enoch and the twins, finding them on the outer perimeter of the bivouac where Joshua staged the men for battle. Ragged lines of volunteers passed before a dozen commanders who barked: Too old. Too young. Too puny. Go left. Go right. Burly men, brooking no argument, yanked the rejects from line, confiscated their weapons, if they had any, and sent the men to the supply wagons. No one would be wasted.

Barren sands denuded of tents and flocks stretched westward where the Amalek camped. To the east rose a high hill, still in shadow, where someone had built a fire. Word spread that Moses would stand watch from the hill with the staff of Yahweh in his hand. Below the hill three figures emerged into the sunlight and strode steadily across the plain, digging their heels into the sand as they walked.

"I know them," said Phinehas. "It's those boys, those Bedouin boys...Mordecai, look..."

"I see them. What do you suppose they are up to?"

"Well, who are they?" said Enoch.

"Just the best slingers in the world, I imagine," said Phinehas. "Come on!" Phinehas dropped his tent poles at Hazor's feet and struck out across the sand. Mordecai and Enoch followed close behind. Phinehas raised his arm and hailed the boys.

Dressed in loin cloths, leather pouches tied at their waists, the boys approached Phinehas with unexpected decorum: gone, the joy; gone, the jumping glee; gone, the toothy grins. No whooping. No shouting. They stood in a row, bowed from the waist, and one by one stepped forward to kiss a stunned Phinehas on both cheeks. They moved to Mordecai, bowed, and one by one kissed him. They bowed before Enoch. The oldest boy, Zalmon, spoke to Phinehas in Arabic.

"He says they are here to fight the Amalek."

Surprised that Phinehas spoke Arabic, Enoch said, "They are too young. Joshua will not take them."

The middle boy fished a thumb-size stone from his pouch and placed it in his sling. He pointed toward a wheeling bat and whirled the sling until it became a blur. He released the sling, looked upward, waited. The bat fell dead at Enoch's feet. The boy walked a short distance and picked up the stone. He spoke to Phinehas.

"He says he does not like to waste a good rock."

"They cannot go." said Enoch. "No matter how good they are. That is final. Tell them to go home." Phinehas translated. The boys bowed to the three men, turned, and ran across the plain toward the first rank, the slingers.

"Oh, this is dreadful. They will be killed." Phinehas shouted after the boys. "Zelah, come back! Zalmon! Tek!"

❧

Rachel stood by the fire pit rocking her puppy. *Even Sekhmet looks sad,* she thought. *War. What does Mordecai know about war? He is a carver.* She pulled out the bird pendant he had fashioned so long ago and kissed it. She looked at her ruined tent, the mats hanging to the ground around the one pole. *Tent stakes. What weapons are those? Why did Yahweh not strike down those Amalekites and spare his people?*

A small crowd, Jemimah, her daughters and grandchildren approached Rachel's campsite. Thankful for the distraction, Rachel hugged the women and immediately looked for Kore. "Where is she?"

"Right here." Jemimah handed the shorn girl into Rachel's arms.

"You cut off her curls."

"That was the first thing Mordecai said, too. We saw your men on the way."

"I suppose you had to do it..." Rachel caressed the child's head.

"Sarah will not recognize her. She is just one more little boy running around. We will say he has been sick. We will get the matter of Sarah settled—somehow—and the curls will grow back. I promise." Jemimah patted Rachel's cheek, and then she set up her loom and soon became the center of calm. Who would think a battle raged where her tent stood the day before? Who would guess her sons may not come home? The women busied themselves at their looms. Occasionally someone laughed, then remembered and checked herself.

Toward the plain a blot of dust rose into the sky. "Reuel," said Rachel, "take Jemimah's grandson, Simeon, and go see what is happening. Stay at the edge of the camp. Go no farther." And thus the boys ran back and forth all the long day bringing reports of the battle.

Mid morning: "Moses is standing on the hill watching the battle. When he holds up his staff, we win. When he lets it down, we lose."

"Lose?" demanded Rachel. "Lose ground? Lose life?" The boys shrugged, exchanging bewildered glances.

Noon: "Moses is sitting on a rock. Aaron and another old man are holding up his arms."

"Why?" demanded Rachel.

"Someone said he got tired holding them up. They have to be up so we can win."

"That cannot be. Who has heard of such a thing," she said.

Mid Afternoon: "They are still holding up Moses' arms so we are winning."

"Have you seen your uncles? Your father?"

"My father did not go." The boy hung his head.

Rachel tilted his chin. *What sad eyes for a seven-year-old.* "Do not worry. Your uncles are brave soldiers. You can be proud of your family."

Late afternoon: "Those men are still holding Moses' arms up. We are still winning."

"I do not understand that." said Rachel. "What does that have to do with anything?"

"Aunt Rachel. Listen. When he lets his arms down, the Amalek wins. When he holds up his arms, we win. When he got tired holding up his arms, those men held them up. They are still holding them up." Reuel and Simeon rolled their eyes—a look that said, *women.* Soon they were off again with warnings not to set foot on the battlefield.

&

Joshua chose the men who fought the Amalek at Rephidim, men between the ages of twenty and forty, fit and willing to fight. Holding high the staff of Yahweh, Moses stood and watched from the eastern hill. On the plain below him, the army of Israel stood in their ranks. The sun at their backs cast long shadows toward the advancing enemy. No one broke.

The Amalek, in their thousands stretched from north to south across the wide, sandy plain, shouting taunts, thrusting their spears skyward. Their shouts became a roar when their infantry knelt and archers released a thousand arrows. While the arrows arched high overhead, Amalek surged forward.

The first rank of Hebrews waited in pairs, one holding spear and shield and one, a sling. Crouched like a lion in shade, stalking its prey, waiting... waiting... the slingers sheltered in the deep shadow of the shields. When the Amalek came into range, their arrows spent, the lion sprang. The slingers rose and whirled their slings sending lethal stones into the forward ranks of the enemy. Hundreds fell in the first volley. Wave after wave of stones made deep inroads into enemy lines, bashing heads, knocking out eyes and teeth. A spray of blood rose over the surprised Amalek. The lion laid low while the second rank of Hebrews raced into the fray, wrested weapons from the dead, dispatched the dying.

The Amalek surged forward with spears and axes cutting down men who had no knowledge of war. The slingers fell back then regrouped and another volley struck Amelek. By now the third rank of Hebrews ran forward and pushed into Amelek lines. The enemy adjusted to Israel's tactics. The fourth rank suffered.

"Stay together!" Enoch yelled over and over. He pushed forward, shoulder to shoulder with Mordecai and Phinehas, Perez and Hazor hugging his back. Back and forth the armies struggled until the lines became indistinct. Surrounded, Mordecai remembered the circle they had formed at the caravan riot. "Circle up!" he yelled. "Ishi! Get with us!" They made a tight circle and fought back to back, a churning rotating wheel. Four isolated men dashed to the circle, enlarging it, making it a force.

The sun dried the bloody sand, then the red dust churned into the air, clung to hair and beards, and dyed their skin blackish red. Sweat ran red from wounds and splatters. Their hands became slick with blood; they wiped them in the sand. Phinehas, facing an Amalekite with his eyeball hanging loose, vomited, but straightened in time to thrust his tent pole deep into the grotesque man's neck, receiving a fountain of blood in his own face. The stench of bowels loosened from fear, and entrails, and vomit, bred more vomit until there was nothing left for the body to give but its lifeblood.

Mordecai glimpsed the Bedouin brothers when one of them, the middle one, he guessed, leaped into the air. *He must have found his mark,* he thought, *the little killer.* Mordecai smiled briefly at the thought then, without compunction, thrust his pole into the belly of a burly Amalekite. Falling forward, the man crushed Mordecai's ankle. Brought to the ground, he dragged himself from under the man only to be fallen on by another dead Amelek. Perez and Hazor pulled him into the circle through Enoch's spread legs.

"We are done," shouted Enoch. "Work your way back. Back! To the rear!" Shoulder to shoulder, dragging Mordecai, the circle fought clear and staggered to the water wagons. At last they collapsed among hundreds of exhausted and wounded men. Old men and boys carrying water bags moved among the soldiers, for now they could be called *soldiers*. They had fought and they had killed. They lived. Others lived because they had been there. No tribe outfought the others. Valiant men, as they would forever be known, fought for Israel that day. They became a brotherhood, those who stood against the Amalek.

"It is over," said Phinehas. "I do believe it is over." He looked to the top of the hill where Moses sat on a rock, his arms supported by Aaron and Hur. For hours they had prevailed. Soon it became clear: the battle would be theirs. Israel chased the Amalek from the plain, pelting them with stones, killing hundreds as they retreated. At sunset Moses let down his arms.

&

By dusk the women had long since given up their stoic cheerfulness and waited for news. Reuel and Simeon had been gone for hours. "Here they come," shouted one of the little boys.

Their hair wet with sweat, stripped to their loin cloths, Reuel and Simeon plopped down beside the women. "The Amalek are running away." Rachel and Shelah embraced. "We went out to the water wagon and talked to Mordecai."

"Mordecai. Is he all right? You went onto the battlefield? You were not supposed to do that." Rachel said.

Reuel would not be scolded. Was he not a soldier now? "We went way around behind. Mordecai hurt his ankle. He can't walk."

"What about Phinehas?" asked Shelah.

"Mordecai said everyone we know is still alive."

Rachel thought about Kore and the children napping under the cart. *They will never know about this day unless we tell them. They will never know about the bravery of their fathers. We must tell them this story. Just as our fathers told us of Noah and Abraham and Joseph, we will tell them about Moses and Joshua and the day Israel defeated the Amalek.*

Rachel and Shelah, pushed forward by curious crowds, found themselves at the edge of the battlefield. They stood arm in arm overlooking tangled bodies, blood soaked sand, and mangled weapons. Cries and groans and the stench of battle filled their senses and drove Rachel to her knees. Men and women moved among the fallen, ministering with water and wads of wool until the wounded could be carried off the field. Hebrew soldiers carrying swords moved over writhing bodies, dispatching the enemy as they found them. Shelah vomited first, then Rachel. "We need to leave, Shelah, I am with child. I cannot faint."

Rachel cringed. A blood-covered wild man leaned over her. "It's me, Rachel. It's me." Mordecai lifted his wife's head. "Reuel came to fetch me. Enoch is alive. The twins are alive. Phinehas is standing right here." Rachel shifted her eyes to the other blood-soaked man.

"Oh, Mordecai, if I had known she was with child we would not have come." said Shelah.

❧

Hundreds of men made their way to the pools and streams of water that poured from the rock at Horeb. The Circle, as they now called themselves—Mordecai, Phinehas, Enoch, Hazor, Perez and Ishi—sat naked in a pool and scrubbed blood-grime from their bodies and loin cloths. Mordecai sank beneath the surface of the stained water and remembered the night he had washed in the Nile. It seemed so long ago...the night he had found Morsel and married Rachel. *Rachel. Why did she not tell me she was with child?*

"I do not think this stain will ever come out," said Phinehas. He swished his loin cloth with new vigor.

Enoch rose from the water and said, "Let's go home. We have a long day tomorrow." In the distance, people still passed among the dead and dying. The warbled trill of wailing drifted on the cold night air and grew louder as they neared the camp, until they seemed to enter a cave, echoing a single note of despair. The Circle turned into the wide path leading into the camps of Manasseh. They bade each other a solemn goodnight and went their separate ways. Leaning on Phinehas, Mordecai hobbled to their campfire where his crutch lay at the ready.

Rachel waited by the fire with Shelah and her sisters. Their husbands and brothers snored under mats spread about the cart. Phinehas ignored Shelah's outstretched hands and embraced his betrothed. She laid her head on his chest and said, "We lost no one."

Mordecai, with questioning eyes, pulled Rachel to her feet and led her away from the fire.

"I told you last night," she said, "but you had gone to sleep." He pulled her into his arms, pushed back her veil and buried his face in her hair.

"People will see."

"I do not care." Sometimes, like Elias, he wished Yahweh would give them dark, starry nights.

"Will the Amalek come back?"

"If they do, we will fight them. Where is our little boy?"

"Under the cart with Morsel and Reuel. She does look like a boy, doesn't she? Sarah came by today. She did not recognize Kore. She says, 'Whose little boy is that?' And I say, 'He is Jemimah's grandson.' Then she says, 'What happened to his hair?' And I say, 'He was sick and his hair fell out.'" Rachel smothered a laugh and snorted.

"Lies come too easy for you, Wife."

"Not really. When Jemimah makes up a story, it is easy to follow." They chuckled, two old married people, happy to be alive. "Maybe you'll have another little boy soon." They listened to the incessant wailing. "You're exhausted, Husband. Let's find a place to sleep. Half of Manasseh is around our camp."

Dawn had not yet broken over the pillar of fire. Cold air chilled Phinehas' arms and shoulders, waking him, rescuing him from a nightmare of blood-soaked sands. He tugged at his coat. He pushed his feet against a warm body. He sat up. The bottom half of his coat encased a small person with two sandal-clad feet protruding from one end and a mass of dark curls from the other. *Tek! You're alive!* Joy out of all proportion filled Phinehas' heart. He groaned as he crawled from under the coat. Every muscle in his body screamed. He found a pile of shavings from the tent poles, and threw them on the banked coals. The fire flickered. He sat hunched, contemplating the small boy whose feet darted and dodged through some dark dream. And his brothers... *Those wonderful little killers—that's what Mordecai calls them.* On the battlefield Phinehas had followed their movements until dust and turmoil blotted his view. They had killed more than their share of Amalekites, knocking out eyes and teeth, leaping with joy when their stones hit home. Later, after a heated skirmish he had looked for them, sighted them briefly, then watched in horror as arrows struck first Zelah and within seconds, Zalmun. Thinking Tek had perished with his brothers, he had searched for the boy's body. He thought about Tek, this youngest orphaned brother. Was he, what, eight? nine? He doubted the boy knew his own age.

Mordecai woke and limped to the fire. "I can hardly move." He pointed to the rolled coat. "Is that who I think it is?"

"It is. It seems he has attached himself to us."

"Do you think he will stay?"

"He is like a wild fox cub. The question is, can he be tamed?"

With Yahweh going before them and Moses standing behind them, Israel defeated the Amalek on the field of battle at Rephidim. When the sun set over the battlefield, Moses lowered the staff of Yahweh and came down from the hill. The echoes of battle subsided under the equally pervasive sound of the death wail. The Hebrews bore their dead to a cove in a hill where they laid the bodies in graves upon which they heaped heavy stones. Grieving women cut their hair and men, their beards. They tore their clothes and threw dust and ashes on their heads. The women wailed for three days.

Mordecai removed the arrows from the Bedouin brothers, and counting them dear friends, Rachel and Shelah washed their bodies. The men covered them with a mat and laid the boys in the same grave. Phinehas told Tek, "This way your brothers will be together for all time."

Tek laid his own pouch and sling on the mat. Parroting Phinehas, he said, "My brothers will fight over my sling *for all time*." Only Phinehas understood what the boy said or why this youngest brother laughed and clapped.

Chapter 10

WORD WENT OUT AMONG THE CAMPS at Rephidim that Jethro, Moses' father-in-law, a priest of Midian, had arrived with Zipporah, Moses' wife, and his two sons.

"At the latrines," said Rachel, "everyone gossips about this Zipporah. Why did she not go to Egypt with her husband? That is what they say."

"It is a hard journey," said Mordecai. "And then to come back across the desert..."

"That is exactly what I said. Why think ill of the woman or Moses? Can she help it if she is a Midianite?"

The news spread that Moses had taken the advice of his father-in-law and chosen judges from among the Hebrews. Once again Rachel heard gossip at the latrine: "A woman says her husband is going to be a judge. A judge! Think of that. Moses is our judge."

"Yes," said Mordecai, "but I have seen the crowds gathered around the Tent of Meeting. It is a lot for one man." He wondered who these judges would be. *What if Jabus becomes a judge*, he thought. A corrupt man could do damage. Or a man like Ishi who did not know his own mind...

That night when The Circle met, Enoch confirmed the news: "Moses has taken the advice of his father-in-law, Jethro. He has made judges from the tribes of Israel."

"Who is fit to sit as a judge?" asked Phinehas.

"How will it work?" asked Mordecai. "Will the people accept these new judges?"

"I hope so," said Enoch, "I am one." Silence came over The Circle. "It is all to help Moses. He is worn out from judging all the people. He trusts the advice of Jethro."

Phinehas broke the silence. "I cannot think of one better to be a judge than you."

"I agree," said Mordecai, "but how will it work?"

"The load will be divided. There will be judges—leaders are what they are—of tens, of fifties, of hundreds, and of thousands. If a judge of ten cannot decide the problem, the person will go to the judge of fifty. If he cannot decide, then to the judge of hundreds and so on."

"But you already lead our neighbors."

"That is why I was chosen. I am a judge of one thousand. Only now, if I judge, the person has to accept it."

Mordecai grinned. "Wait till Rachel gets to the latrine in the morning. She will say, 'My brother, the judge.'"

"One thousand," said Ishi. "You will be sitting under an awning all day. I could not stand it."

"We thought about that. We will judge one day a week. I have been with the other judges at the Tent of Meeting these last four days, learning the statutes and laws. There are many."

"Tell us some," said Phinehas.

"Well, most of it is common sense. For instance, if a man buys a slave and he sells the slave, the slave's wife goes with him. If a man kills another man, the murderer shall be put to death, but if a thief is killed while he is breaking in, the homeowner shall not be guilty."

When the men left, Mordecai asked Enoch to stay for a bit. "I need to ask you something as a judge, Cousin."

"I will do my best." Enoch rubbed his hands together.

Mordecai hesitated. *This is going to hurt Enoch... Maybe I should just wait... How to begin?* "If a person threatens to tell a secret that will damage an innocent person forever, what should be done?"

"Is the threat born of spite?"

"The one who threatens is jealous and has found a secret, a rod to beat with."

"Who is this innocent?"

"The baby we found in the gorges."

"Where is that baby? I have not seen her."

"You saw her. Jemimah cut her hair. To hide her. She looks like a boy now."

"But why all this, Cousin?"

"Because of the threat, Rachel had to find a safe home for her. We took her to Jemimah. But your sister is sick with longing for the child."

"What is this secret?"

"The child's mother was a prostitute; she has died."

"A child is not to blame for its parent."

"Someone has threatened to taint the baby's life with this knowledge. Even if we adopt the baby, no one in our family would be allowed to marry her. Our other children would bear the stain."

"Who has said these wicked things? This sounds like Jabus."

"Not Jabus...the person is your wife." Enoch's face seemed to melt. Alarmed, Mordecai moved to his side and gripped his shoulder, lest he fall forward into the coals.

Minutes passed. Elbows on his knees, Enoch hid his face in his hands. Finally he raised his head and said, "I am unworthy to be a judge. I cannot control my own house. Why did you and Rachel not tell me about this?"

"Rachel did not want to add to your burdens."

"The truth is, she does not think I can do anything about it." Mordecai did not answer. Enoch stood and paced. "One of the laws states that if a person steals an ox or a sheep, he must pay five oxen for the ox and four sheep for the sheep. What do you think the price for a stolen child would be?"

Mordecai watched his cousin go. He had laid a heavy burden on Enoch. Elias seemed to think it the only way. He thought about the statute: *Five oxen for one...*A grin played at the corners of his mouth. *Please, Cousin, do not bring us your eight children.*

Mordecai banked the fire and ducked into Rachel's tent. He could barely discern the stain of Amalek blood on the tent poles. Feeling as drained as if he had been to war, he sought comfort in Rachel's warmth. On the edge of sleep, a single agonized scream woke them. "What was that?" Rachel mumbled.

"The judge's wife. Go back to sleep."

The next morning Rachel sent Tek and Reuel to gather manna. She stoked the fire and placed the baking stone on the coals. "Mordecai, where is Phinehas?"

"He had business with Nobah this morning."

"He will come home with nothing. Nobah will strip him."

"But he will have She-lahhh." They laughed. "He left these with me." Mordecai pulled Phinehas' thongs and rings from the neck of his tunic. "Nobah is not the only wiley trader." He kissed Rachel. "I have news for you, Wife."

"Oh, wife, is it? What is this news?" She kissed him back.

"I do not know." He kissed her again.

"You have news, but you do not know what it is? No more kisses until you tell me."

"I do not know what it is, but be ready for something good." He bent to kiss her. She dodged and ran. He chased her around the cart with Morsel following close behind. They looked around to see Enoch and Sarah standing at the fire pit, each holding a newborn twin. Mordecai whispered, "Be wise." They joined the new arrivals.

"Oh, let me see," said Rachel, peering at the tightly swaddled babies. "They are so lovely." She noticed Sarah's face—red, splotchy, tear stained—and her eyes, swollen almost shut. Rachel threw her arms around Sarah and the baby. "Oh, my dear Sarah, what is the matter?"

"There, do you see, Sarah," said Enoch, "this is the person you have wronged. She loves you in spite of what you have done."

Tears ran down Sarah's face. "Oh Rachel, Rachel. What have I done?" Her chest heaved.

"It is the law, Rachel," said Enoch ignoring his wife. His voice could not have been colder. If someone steals an ox he must pay with five oxen. Sarah stole the baby from you. She must pay with her own babies." He handed his baby to a stunned Rachel. "Give me that one, Sarah."

Sarah fell to her knees with the baby. "Nooo," she moaned.

Enoch pried the baby loose and laid the tiny bundle in Mordecai's arms. "Now you know how Rachel feels. Get up. We are leaving." By now neighbors had gathered. Enoch waved his arm at them. "Go home," he shouted, "this is not your business." They wandered away, speculating about this harsh new judge who did not spare his own wife. Enoch half carried, half dragged his wife away.

"Enoch," Rachel called, "we do not know their names."

"Name them what you will," he said over his shoulder.

Rachel and Mordecai stood in shocked silence. "Surely he does not mean it," said Rachel.

"He cannot. He is teaching her a lesson. What should we do?"

"Wait until they get hungry, I think."

Tightly swaddled babies do not fuss. They sleep peacefully until they are hungry. So it was with Sarah's twins. They woke at mid-morning ready for the breast. Rachel had enjoyed holding them, now the time had come for the lesson to be over. Ignoring the neighbors, who followed at a short distance, Rachel and Mordecai carried the babies to Enoch's camp. Rachel and Enoch each carried a baby into the tent. The distraught woman, beyond tears or sound, lay on her mat. Enoch had forbidden Adah or Hannah to minister to her. She sat up and held out her arms. "They are hungry," she whispered. Enoch kissed the babies and laid them in Sarah's arms. "Thank you, Enoch." She sobbed, burying her face in the swaddling cloths.

"May I stay while you feed them?" Rachel asked. Unable to speak, Sarah nodded. Rachel helped her position the babies and watched as they nuzzled and suckled. "Sarah, I am with child."

"I will help you."

"I will need your help."

"What about the little girl? Enoch said you named her Kore. That is a pretty name."

"Yes. She is so sweet. I miss her so."

"Can you ever forgive me? Please say yes."

"I already forgave you. I know you are sorry."

"I was not sorry at first. I was defiant as I have been all my life. Taking what I wanted. Being mean to people to get my way. Enoch finally stopped trying to reason with me. That's when he said I had to give up the babies as payment for the wrong I had done you. It seemed so logical, the perfect punishment for a thief, which is what I am. I stole your happiness and your peace. Oh what have I done to your beautiful little girl?"

"It is over now, Sarah. She has been safe with Jemimah. We can get her back."

Later Rachel sat alone in her tent. She held the goddess Ma'at in her cupped palm. She turned the sculpture in the dim light. Ma'at had not seen daylight since Asmath had placed her in the pouch. Delicate carvings etched the feather and the features of the face. What tool had shaped those feet complete with toes, those hands crossed upon her breasts? Self-contained and mute she warmed in Rachel's hand. *If I thank you, will you hear?*

Mordecai threw open the tent flap causing Ma'at to glow green in a streak of sunlight. Rachel closed her hand. "Are you ready to go get Kore?" The excitement in her husband's voice brought Rachel to her feet.

"I am ready. I'll be there in a moment." She lifted her dress and returned Ma'at to the pouch. Leaving Tek and Reuel at the cart, Rachel and Mordecai threaded their way around unfamiliar camps and paddocks, following a new path to the grazing grounds. Nobah and Jemimah had re-established their tents north of the battlefield. "The blood," Jemimah had said, "it works its way to the surface. Sometimes at night I think I hear the cries of the men who died here."

Mordecai and Rachel passed near Nobah's tent where he and Phinehas sat under the awning, smoking the pipe. In a low voice, Mordecai said, "It seems the negotiations are still going on." A waft of smoke turned his stomach. They waved, walking on to Jemimah's tent, where Rachel spotted Kore peeking from behind the door flap.

"She's feeling shy today," said Jemimah. "Look who is here, Kore. It's Mama and Papa." Kore hid her face in Jemimah's lap.

Rachel brushed away tears. "She has forgotten me."

"We were at your camp four days ago. That is not possible." The old woman dislodged the baby and stood, motioning Nobah and Phinehas to come. She instructed her daughters, "Find your husbands. I have things to say." Soon a crowd huddled in the afternoon shade under Jemimah's awning. She addressed Nobah. "You have negotiated enough for Shelah. Where you are now is where it stays."

"But, Ma..." ventured the black-bearded Nobah. Mordecai and Phinehas, exchanging a look, bit their lips.

"Enough. Listen, my children. Rachel is my daughter. Mordecai is my son, and this," she lifted Kore onto Rachel's lap, "is my granddaughter. Phinehas and Shelah will be married in one week. Nobah, go cut out a pregnant goat for Kore. I want her to have plenty of milk. And get one with long hair. I am tired." She entered the tent and closed the flap.

Rachel carried Kore, Mordecai carried a bundle of clothes the children had outgrown, and Phinehas led the goat as they headed home. The sun had set behind the ridge, for they had stayed to enjoy a visit with their new-found brothers and sisters. "I suppose we know who is head of that family," said Phinehas. He laughed. "Did you see the expression on Nobah's face when his mother called a halt to our negotiations?"

"But, *Ma...*" whined Mordecai. They howled with laughter. "Where did you stand? Nobah did not seem happy."

"I happened to have the advantage at the moment. Nobah's not so bad."

At camp Reuel busied himself with the fire. "Where is Tek?" asked Phinehas.

"He left."

The three chorused, "Left?"

"He said doing nothing made his head ache."

"I was afraid of that," said Phinehas.

"It makes my head ache, too," said Reuel. "I am going with him next time."

"You must ask your father, Reuel," said Mordecai.

"I will not ask him."

"Then you cannot go."

"My father is a coward. He did not fight the Amalek. He is not my father."

"He will always be your father," said Phinehas. Reuel threw a dung chip into the fire and crawled under the cart with Morsel. Phinehas sat by the cart and leaned against the wheel. "It was not fair of us to leave you so long. I hope you will forgive us. It is good to have a person like you we can trust to look after the goats, and the puppy, and Sekhmet, and her kittens." Reuel did not answer. In spite of his stiff back, Phinehas stayed near the boy.

The fire had burned low when Tek entered the camp, and sang out, "Look what I found." Only Phinehas understood his excited babbling. He held a sling high over his head. "It is Zalmon's. I looked everywhere for Zelah's but I could not find it. I know it is there. Somewhere..." He sat on a rock by the fire.

"Let's take Reuel and search for it tomorrow," said Phinehas. "He has keen sight. Maybe you could teach him to sling."

"Come here, Reuel," called Tek. "You want to learn to sling?" Phinehas translated. Reuel sat on the rock by Tek and, with no common language, learned about the sling from a master.

&

Phinehas watched the boys and wished someone had taught his older brother to love him. The night they had left Goshen, he had said goodbye to Rachel and Enoch and followed the levee road to his family home. He had been gone twenty years, but he remembered everything: the goat paddock, the gate, the shape of the windows. The mud brick house sagged a little more than he remembered. *With my carpet roll across my shoulder, and Sekhmet's basket under my*

130

arm, in my huge striped coat and expensive turban, what a picture I must have presented, he thought. *But Abigail recognized me.*

Abigail had looked him over from turban to leather shoes. And she laughed and continued to laugh until he laughed. "Would you like to come see my cat?" He had felt like a small boy.

"I would." She crossed the ten feet separating them.

"I cannot open very wide. She might get out." He opened the basket a bit; she bent over and put her eye to the crack.

"That is a beautiful cat. Fit for a Pharaoh." She straightened to her full height, a head taller than Phinehas. I have missed you, Brother-in-law."

"When they took me away I was eight years old. You remember me?"

"Of course. You were my friend. I cried for a long time." She looked past him. He saw fear in her eyes. "Now I cry for different reasons..."

His brother strode toward them from the goat paddock. No wonder Abigail had recognized him—aside from the trimmed beard he looked like a short, fat Shemida. The man stopped five feet away and stood with his fists at his waist. "Well look who is here. Back from the dead and just in time to watch us leave. Go inside, Abigail."

"Shemida—" The woman hesitated. Two steps and Shemida landed a swift backhanded blow hard on Abigail's jaw, knocking her to her knees. Taken aback, with one eye on his brother, Phinehas grasped the woman's elbow and helped her up. He looked into her amber eyes and wanted to say, *run with me, we can hide like we did so long ago,* but three children watched and waited at the door.

"As you can see, I did not die." He watched Abigail and the children enter the house. "And you have not changed," he said, "You were cruel when we were children, and you are cruel now."

"You seem to have done well," said Shemida, massaging his hand. "There is nothing for you here." Phinehas watched his brother turn and walk away. He headed back down the road to Enoch's compound, but by the time he arrived, Manasseh had almost cleared, and the tribe of Benjamin had begun.

Now Phinehas contemplated his new family: Enoch's house with Rachel, Mordecai, and Kore. Soon Shelah would become his wife, and he would include himself in Jemimah's household. Shemida's rejection had turned into good, but worry for Abigail had become an itchy scab.

Mordecai interrupted his thoughts with a request: "I want you to translate for Rachel and me." He tapped Tek on the shoulder and pointed to Phinehas. "Tell him we want him to be our son."

The boy listened, then frowned and shook his head, no. He said only four words: "Phinehas is my father."

❧

Rachel wondered if the death wail would ever leave her dreams. For once, when word came to move camp and the cloud of Yahweh rose, she did not groan. She did not regret leaving that plain of sorrow and pain. She hastily fried patties of manna, shook sand from her sleeping mats, and helped pack the cart. She noticed most of the Amalek blood stayed behind when Mordecai pulled up the tent poles. The day he had re-establish the tent, neither had mentioned the bloodstains. Someday maybe he would tell her about the fearful dreams that rent his restless nights.

Phinehas, Reuel and Tek searched the battlefield one last time. They found slings Tek deemed inferior, but had not found Zelah's. "We will make a pattern from Zalmon's," Phinehas said. He had one goal: to shape two disparate boys into brothers. Tek needed Reuel because he had lost his brothers, his anchor, and Reuel needed Tek because of shame for his father and Zelo's indifference. The field of battle proved to be the perfect mold for the boys. They rooted in the sand until they had a basket of artifacts, and every night they pored over their treasures. Tek described the battle to Reuel in vivid detail. *Can it get any bloodier?* thought Phinehas. He cleaned the story up for the younger boy, but Tek learned more Aramaic every day.

"After today," said Phinehas, "we will leave this battlefield forever."

"Do not worry, Reuel. There will always be battles," said Tek. "We will practice until you, too, can knock a bat from the sky."

Chapter 11

THREE MONTHS TO THE DAY after the sons of Israel left Egypt, they came into the Wilderness of Sinai and spread their camps and their flocks before the mountain of Yahweh. According to their tribes, they arranged their camps. Enoch and his close family, with a view to joining with Jemimah and her family, pitched close by her, and Phinehas took Shelah for his wife.

Without ceremony, one day Moses went up the mountain to speak with Yahweh. On the same day, Tek killed a young antelope for the marriage feast. By the time Moses came down with messages from Yahweh to the people, Phinehas and Shelah had erected a tent and Phinehas had bought twenty sheep. "You have the goats, I will have the sheep," he told Mordecai." I was born to be a shepherd."

Mordecai had laughed at his friend. "I thought you were born to be a trader of fine goods." Three months in the desert had transformed Phinehas from a fat man to a man, lean and alert, darkened by the sun, ready for the challenges Yahweh might place before him. He had a wife and a son and it looked as if he would be rearing Jabus' son, Reuel. Now he had his flock of sheep. He went about with a contented look.

Moses called the elders and leaders, Enoch among them, and told them what Yahweh had said on the mountain. Enoch gathered those he judged, climbed upon his wagon, and raised his voice with authority. "Now hear what Yahweh has said: 'You have seen what I did to the Egyptians, how I brought you out on eagles' wings and brought you to Myself. You shall be a kingdom to Me, a holy nation.' Those are the words Moses heard from Yahweh." Enoch scanned the crowd. "Do you agree to be Yahweh's people?"

With one voice the people answered, "What Yahweh has said, we will do."

Enoch said, "Today and tomorrow you are to wash yourselves and your clothes, and on the third day Yahweh will appear to you in a thick cloud so you may hear him—his very voice. Furthermore, neither you nor your beast is to touch the mountain. You shall set bounds around the base of the mountain. Whoever touches the mountain will die. On the third day, when you hear the ram's horn give a long blast, you shall come up to the mountain."

Rachel sank to her neck in the mountain stream. How she missed the bath houses of Ramses and the times spent there with Asmath and her mistress. She closed her eyes and ducked beneath the water. The burbling laughter of Hebrew women could have been laughter echoing through the tiled chambers. She could almost hear the patting footsteps of female slaves moving among the bathers, pouring water, ministering to the needs of wealthy patrons. She stood and relished the hot sun on her shoulders as rivulets ran down her back. She and thousands of women and girls washed the desert sands from their bodies and laughed and played. Now that Sarah had made peace, she released her sisters-in-law to befriend Rachel. She relished the friendships of Adah and Hannah as well as Jemimah and Shelah and her sisters. Sarah washed Rachel's back. The rough wool seemed to scrub away the pain of separation, and for the first time since the day Enoch had taken her from the vizier's house, Rachel felt complete. She bathed Kore, crooning, "We shall be clean for Yahweh." They beat their clothes and laid them on the hot rocks to dry.

At camp Rachel handed Mordecai his clean tunic and undergarments. He draped his cloak over himself, and limped off with Phinehas, the boys and the other men to their bathing place. Shelah joined her to watch them go. "How suitable you are for Phinehas." said Rachel.

"He is the kindest man I have ever known. And my family loves him."

"Even Nobah?"

Shelah laughed, "Even Nobah. It is an odd friendship they have made. Have you ever seen men arm wrestle? That is the way of their friendship."

"Hopi taught Asaph to arm wrestle. Hopi always won."

"Who are they?"

"People in my household when I lived in Ramses."

"I met you and your mistress one day at the dying vats."

Rachel frowned, remembering. "You showed us a beetle they crush to make blue dye. That was you?" It had been hot and bright that day. Hopi had waited in the street while Asmath and Rachel threaded their way through a labyrinth of dying vats, rock-hewn basins filled with dyes of saffron, blue, and scarlet. Women stirred skeins of wool into the dye and lifted them out with sticks to dry on a network of hemp lines crisscrossing the yards. "We were covered in dye when we left. Oh, how Asmath's mother fussed."

"Your mistress gave me this ring." Shelah held out her hand. "She was very beautiful."

"Not anymore. The plague of boils scarred her face."

"We all have scars. Some are not visible. We had a hard life. One day my father came and just walked away with my mother. No one said a word to stop them."

"And then she became our teacher. She came to the villa to teach us to weave."

"And now we are together here in this desert. We are equal now," Shelah added without malice.

"We were equal then, we just lived in different circumstances. I was a slave, too. Sometimes I wonder if the past ever happened. Was it all a dream..."

&

On the third day after Moses came down the mountain, the people waited for the long blast of the shofar, the ram's horn that would summon them to the mountain. Today they would hear the voice of Yahweh. Who could believe such a thing? Mordecai whittled to pass the time. When a trumpet blast split the air his knife flew from his hand. People clamped their hands over their ears and trembled. Lightning flashes, loud thunder, and a thick cloud covered the mountain. The earth shook. The blast of the trumpet grew louder and louder until the people thought their ears would burst. Yahweh descended upon the mountain in fire, then thick smoke rose into the sky. The Hebrews, in spite of their terror, left their camps and gathered at a distance from the base of the mountain. They could not approach because of the sound and the furious tumult.

Rachel, ready to run if boulders tumbled from the mountain, wrapped her shawl around Kore. Mordecai's arms tightened around them. She became aware of a high-pitched moan at the back of her throat. Phinehas held onto Shelah and Reuel, who had dived under Shelah's shawl. Tek refused comfort and stood ready for battle, arms crossed, knees locked, heels planted in the sand.

From beyond the horn blast, the smoke, the fire, the thunder, and the lightening, the voice of Yahweh poured forth over the people with an enveloping power. Yahweh spoke all these words, saying:

"I am Yahweh, who brought you out of the land of Egypt, out of the house of slavery.

"You shall have no other gods before Me.

"You shall not make for yourselves an idol, or any likeness of what is in heaven above or on the earth beneath or in the water under the earth.

"You shall not worship them or serve them; for I, Yahweh, am a jealous God, visiting the iniquity of the fathers on the children, on the third and the fourth generations of those who hate Me, but showing lovingkindness to thousands, to those who love Me and keep My commandments.

"You shall not take the name of Yahweh in vain for Yahweh will not leave him unpunished who takes His name in vain.

"Remember the Sabbath day, to keep it holy.

"Six days you shall labor and do all your work but the seventh day is a Sabbath of Yahweh; in it you shall not do any work, you or your son or your daughter, your male or your female servant or your cattle or your sojourner who stays with you.

*"For in six days Yahweh made the heavens and the earth,
the sea and all that is in them, and rested on the seventh day; therefore,
Yahweh blessed the Sabbath day and made it holy.*

*"Honor your father and your mother, that your days may be
prolonged in the land which Yahweh gives you.*

"You shall not murder.

"You shall not commit adultery.

"You shall not steal.

"You shall not bear false witness against your neighbor.

*"You shall not covet your neighbor's wife or his male servant
or his female servant or his ox or his donkey or anything that belongs
to your neighbor."*

And so the Hebrews, the chosen people, heard the voice of Yahweh. But they could not bear the heaviness of it. They beseeched Moses to speak for Yahweh, for they feared His voice.

Mordecai said to Rachel as they sat under her canopy, "For the first time, I feel at peace. Now we know exactly what Yahweh expects of us. It is within our power to obey these commandments. We will disappoint neither ourselves nor Yahweh."

"I think we can keep them," she said, "but I am not brave enough to hear them face to face again."

From that time on, Moses relayed all the words of Yahweh. He wrote in a book the words of the covenant, and he taught the people the ordinances, laws and feast days of their God. Moses built an altar at the base of the mountain. There they sacrificed burnt offerings and Moses read all the words of Yahweh and consecrated the book of ordinances with sprinkled blood. He then dipped hyssop in the blood and sprinkled the people. Thus the covenant was established and all the people said, "What Yahweh has spoken we will do, and we will be obedient."

Then Moses walked among the people and said, "Do not be afraid, for Yahweh has come in order to test you, and in order that the fear of Him may remain with you so you may not sin." Then the people watched Moses and Joshua go up the mountain to be with Yahweh.

Enoch, Mordecai, Phinehas, and the Circle continued to meet around the campfire in the evenings to discuss the laws and ordinances. Enoch had begun to bring his boys and Reuel and Tek joined in. One evening Enoch unrolled a new scroll delivered that very day. Pressing out the heavy curl, he read thus: "If a person finds a donkey collapsed under its load, he should help the owner get the donkey up and return the donkey to the owner." Shocked at what he had read, he re-rolled the scroll and laid it in his lap. He looked around at no one.

"Well, I do not know about that," said Mordecai. "What if the donkey is left for dead like Goose?" Debate followed. Everyone knew about the animal Mordecai had found. Did they not make jest that only a fool would name a donkey? "I know that man to be a cruel man," said Mordecai. "He walked away from that poor donkey. I am not giving Goose back to him."

"But that is theft," said a neighbor.

"You should pay the man for the donkey," said Enoch. "When you blackened the donkey's face, that showed you knew keeping it was wrong."

"Well, why did you not say that at the time, Enoch?" Mordecai stood, stomped around the fire circle and returned to sit heavily on his rock.

"I did not know about the ordinance then," said Enoch. "This is a new law."

Phinehas spoke up. "I think these ordinances are going to be hard for us to keep."

Enoch picked up the scroll, advanced it, and read: "If what a man stole is found alive in his possession, he should pay double." Enoch shrugged. "That is what it says, Mo. Did I write it?"

"Well, I am no thief. I will pay the man. What is the price of a donkey?" No one knew.

"Now here is an interesting one," said Enoch, happy to move on. He read: "'If a man puts out another man's eye, he shall pay with his own eye. If he knocks out his tooth, he shall pay with his own tooth.' I hope none of you has knocked out any eyes or teeth lately?"

Chapter 12

BLACK TENTS AND FLOCKS OF SHEEP and goats spread for miles before the mountain of Yahweh. Manna fell like dew every morning, and peace settled over the people who embraced the words of Yahweh and his man, Moses. But discontent spread like a bitter root in the hearts of those who rebelled against the Living God.

The days of Moses' time on the mountain passed without serious incident. Twenty days. Thirty days. Forty. Where was the man? Rumors spread throughout the tribes that Moses would not be coming back. He was old, maybe he had died. Maybe he had been killed by wolves.

Enoch kept close watch over his human flock. Like hundreds of trusted men, he judged his people and taught them the ordinances of Yahweh. At every opportunity, he spoke with reason to the dissenters and tamped down seditious talk. "Who are you," he would ask, "that you question the Living God? Did you part the sea? Did you turn the water sweet at Marah? Did you spread manna over the earth for your little ones? We were slaves far from home. With Moses' help, Yahweh will lead us to the Promised Land. All we have to do is obey the covenant and trust Him."

One day Enoch stood in the wagon bed and read from the scroll of statutes. Jabus, supported by a group of malcontents, stood below and shouted over his brother: "We are nothing but ants for this Moses to play with...When we starve, we get bread. Fake bread! Bread that is not bread. When we thirst to the point of death, we get water. Where is this land of milk and honey? Where are the wheat fields? Where are the rivers teeming with fish? What must we do for Yahweh to get us these things?"

"Obey him!" shouted Mordecai who could be silent no longer. "You are a disgrace. You and these cowards. You allowed men to die at the hand of Amelek because you did not fight. Your own son is ashamed of you."

Jabus lunged toward Mordecai, but Enoch leaped from the wagon and pushed him back. "Jabus, Jabus. What are you doing, Brother?"

"I saw smoke and fire at the mountain," shouted a Jabus follower. "At least the gods of Egypt had a shape."

Phinehas, straightened himself to his full height. "A frog?" he shouted. "A crocodile? A goat? My master worshiped those foolish gods. They could not save him."

Turning his back on Jabus, Mordecai hoisted himself onto the wagon bed. He calmed himself, and lowered his voice. "I cannot believe your faith lies in a god fashioned from a block of wood—a block of wood carved by me. I was forced to carve those gods. In my ignorance, I, too, thought they had power. I would drill a hidden hole in every one of them to let the evil escape. If you think any dead thing has power—whether rock, or wood, or vain drawings, or carved images, or the sun, or moon, or the stars—Yahweh will punish you. He is a jealous God."

&

While the men argued, the women enlarged their tents, weaving panels of black goat hair, sewing them together. Rachel busied herself making warm cloaks and bedding and learned to make yogurt and different kinds of cheese. Kore played underfoot. Morsel grew to a gangling puppy.

Tek and Reuel hunted and supplied the family with meat and leather. For a time, Jabus took Reuel away. Tek hunted alone. Then Reuel learned to disappear from his father's house. Like a vapor, one moment he would be there, the next, gone, hunting with Tek, practicing the sling.

Phinehas and Shelah's brother, Joktar, tended their sheep beyond a narrow wadi west of the Mountain of Yahweh, a half day's walk from Manasseh. With their mats draped across the lower branches, they rested in the augmented shade of a stunted tamarind tree. "Why do you suppose Moses has not returned from the mountain?" Joktar asked, knowing Phinehas would have an opinion they could build an afternoon's discussion upon. Like a buzzing mosquito, a small intermittent sound worried their peace. Phinehas peered around his brother-in-law. He pointed toward a mirage where two figures emerged from the watery illusion. "It's the boys. Something has happened. Let's go meet them."

Reuel and Tek, muddy with sweat, babbled incoherently. "Stop. Slow down" said Phinehas, burying spread fingers in each sweaty mop of hair. "What? A calf?"

Tek took a deep breath and said, "Enoch sent us to get you. Aaron has built a Golden calf and set it up at the base of the mountain."

"What for?"

"They say it is a god."

"A god! Who said that?"

"People. They are worshiping it."

"Who is?"

"People." shouted the boys in unison.

Phinehas studied the agitated boys. "Enoch sent you?"

"He said come quick." Leaving Joktar with the sheep, Phinehas and the boys struck out for the mountain. "They are dancing and singing," said Tek.

"Is Moses coming back?" asked Reuel. Phinehas had no answer.

The peaceful camp Phinehas had left two days before had transformed into a noisy celebration. People streamed toward the mountain, singing, beating tambourines and drums. Disparate tunes played on flutes adding to the din. Dogs barked. Rachel and Shelah stood in stunned silence, watching Manasseh drain around them. "Rachel, Shelah, what is happening?" Both women gripped Phinehas' arms.

"This is what we know," said Shelah. "Aaron took gold jewelry from the people and melted it..."

"And made a Golden calf," added Rachel. "They set it upon an altar as a god."

Phinehas felt the hair rise on his neck. *A god.* "Keep the boys here. I am going to see if I can find Enoch." He looked around. "Where are the boys? Tek! Reuel! I'll be back with them. Stay here."

Before he reached the mountain, a cacophony of sound and the crush of twisting, whirling bodies engulfed the short man. Someone grabbed his arm and swung him around. He wrenched free, pushed on, and finally found Enoch and Mordecai in the thickest part of the crowd. "The boys found me." He craned his neck. "Where is this idol?"

Enoch pointed toward the mountain, but Phinehas could not see over the crowd. "We have to find everyone we know and get them to leave," shouted Enoch. "It is not safe here."

"Have you seen Reuel and Tek? They're here somewhere."

"No, we have to find them." Spotting his brother and sister-in-law, Enoch ran to them. "Jabus. Adah. What are you doing here?"

"Aaron told everyone to take off their jewelry, and we did." Jabus was hoarse from yelling and reeked of beer. "Aaron melted the gold and fashioned the calf. That is our god now. That is Yahweh. Look!" He pointed to an altar of large stones at the base of the mountain. A Golden calf about knee high gleamed in the late afternoon sun. "At last we can see God," shouted Jabus. The crowd parted, and Phinehas saw the idol for the first time. He stood aghast. Someone shoved him. He struck out with his fist and knocked a man down. The crowd shifted. People shoved.

"This is a desecration," shouted Enoch. "We have to leave here." He grasped Jabus by the arm, but he twisted away. "Adah, come with me." She gripped Enoch's extended hand. Jabus pulled her to his side and stepped between her and Enoch. "Adah stays with me," shouted Jabus with a doubled fist. "Join us, Enoch or leave us."

"Where is Zelo? He has to come with me," shouted Enoch.

"My son stays." said Jabus through gritted teeth. Suddenly a quiet settled over the noisy throng, leaving one last woman, eyes closed in ecstasy, twisting with her tambourine. Someone grabbed her arm.

"It is Moses." A whisper, a murmur, moved through the people, and all eyes focused on the mountain. Moses, carrying two stone tablets, and

Joshua threaded their way down. At last Moses stood near the camp, his face distorted with anger. He cast the tablets from him, shattering them on the rocks at the foot of the mountain.

Phinehas realized Tek had insinuated himself under one arm and Reuel under the other. Even his brave Tek feared the face of Moses. Grasping the boys by their arms, Phinehas turned, and pulled them through the crowd. "We are leaving here. This is not a safe place." Phinehas knew full well that Moses could call down fire upon the whole lot if he chose. He could bring down the mountain if he chose.

"What about my mother and father?" said Reuel, twisting his neck.

"I am sorry, son, they are not coming."

Enoch and Mordecai followed Phinehas away from the mountain. Tears blinded Enoch. "I tried so hard. Did I not explain it all? What will happen to my brother? My nephew? Poor Adah. She wanted to leave."

"Come on, Cousin," said Mordecai. He led Enoch away from the mountain of Yahweh.

That night the men enlarged Jemimah's fire pit and the families gathered around it. Enoch insisted they would be safer if they stayed together. He and Sarah, their children, Ada and her children, Mordecai, Rachel, Kore, Phinehas, Shelah, Tek, Reuel, the Uncle Twins, Perez and Hazor, and all Jemimah's daughters and sons huddled together. Enoch spoke: "We are in terrible danger. You have one hour to get what you need. No one will leave this place. Bring warm covers and sleeping mats, what food you can, your pets, and come back immediately. Yahweh is a jealous god."

Phinehas locked Sekhmet and her kittens in the basket and brought them to Jemimah's. Women tethered the milk goats nearby. Rachel carried Morsel and bedded him with Kore. Mordecai brought the donkey. It must be kept safe; he had not yet paid for it. They bedded the babies and children in the warm center of the women's tent. Once the children settled, the conversation turned to Yahweh.

"How long will we stay here?" asked Hazor.

"Until Yahweh reacts," said Enoch.

"So you think he will react." said Nobah.

"Do you remember the day we heard Yahweh speak?" said Enoch. "Then Moses walked among us and said Yahweh had showed his power so we would remember? He will react. His power is beyond our understanding. Can we endure it—that is the question."

Dread overtook the family. Mothers rose from fitful sleep to check the children throughout the night. Manna fell and the people stayed close by for the gathering. They ate and waited. By mid morning, stricken people began to filter back to the camps. Women set up the death wail, and a great moan spread over the multitude.

"Why are they wailing?" said Rachel.

"Something bad has happened," said Phinehas.

A man in priestly garb, gripping a bloody sword, suddenly stood in the midst of their camp. Splattered with blood from beard to foot, dripping blood from sleeves and hem, he calmly surveyed the family as they fell to their knees and covered their heads with their arms. Only Enoch stood and met the man's gaze. Never had Enoch seen a face so bereft of hope. He wanted to ask if he could help the man, but he dared not. The priest nodded to Enoch, turned and plodded toward the mountain. No one uttered a sound.

Within minutes, Zelophehad entered the camp. Covered in grime and blood, it entered Rachel's mind that he looked like the men after the war with Amalek. Enoch embraced his nephew and set him down. Zelo, his eyes fixed and unblinking, did not speak or cry. "Zelo, can you talk? Get him some water, someone." Everyone had a question. "Hush! Let him get his breath." After a few minutes, Enoch decided the boy had rested enough. He gripped his nephew's shoulder. "Tell us what happened Zelophehad."

Zelo looked hollowly into the distance and finally spoke. "Moses and Joshua ground the golden calf to dust. He mixed the dust with water, and made the people drink it. And they did. They drank the water. Then he said, 'Whoever is for Yahweh, come to me!' And a lot of the priests went to him. I was hiding under a cart. I heard what he said. He told the priests to take their swords and kill their brothers, friends and neighbors. I told my father what Moses had said. I told them all. But no one believed me." The boy shook his head in disbelief. "The priests left and came back with swords. Should the people not have run away? Why did they not run? Then the priests started swinging their swords." The boy buried his face in his knees. His family strained to hear his muffled voice. "Then the people started to run, but it was too late. My father..."

"They killed Jabus?" said Enoch. "What about Adah? Zelo, where is your mother?"

"She is dead." Zelo raised his head. "Everyone started to run away from the priests, but they chased down the men and cut them. My mother fell and hit her head on a stone."

Jemimah moved to the boy's side, and wrapping her veil around his head, she hid him in her bosom. "That is enough." She rocked the boy. At last he began to wail.

Reuel leaped up. "My father. My Mother." Before he could bolt, Rachel pulled him into her arms.

"I have to go see," said Enoch. All the men headed for the mountain. Hundreds of bloody bodies lay from one end of the camp to the other, slaughtered indiscriminately. Some lay where they had stood, while others had been chased into tents and goat paddocks. Wailing women and children hovered over the bodies.

They came to a man throwing ashes on his head. "Moses has gone back up the mountain," he said. "I hope he can persuade Yahweh to have mercy on us."

The closer they came to the mountain, the more bodies sprawled in pools of blood. "Spread out," said Enoch, "Jabus and Adah must be here somewhere." They moved from body to body and found Ada lying face down in the sand, unmarked, save a bruised forehead. After an hour's searching Enoch spied Jabus' body under a cart. The men exchanged knowing looks: Jabus had left Adah to fend for herself. Enoch examined his brother's body. "Run clean through. I do not believe he suffered long." Priests sent carts and wagons to take the bodies to a burial trench far across the plain.

"What about Reuel and Zelo? Should they not be there?" asked Mordecai.

"No. Zelo has seen enough," said Enoch. "We will spare them this horror." They loaded Jabus and Ada onto a cart and followed it into the sands of the desert. Throughout the afternoon and night the sons of Israel dug trenches and buried their dead: 3,000 men who had died by the sword. Sweat and tears mingled with the acrid blood of the slain. Few families had been spared.

Like a dark cloud overtaken by a darker one, a shadow fell upon the children of Israel. A hot wind from the East whistled through the canyons and grew steadily into a roiling wall of sand. With a roar it chased the mourners from the plain and obliterated the burial site. With each moment, the howling wind grew stronger, the cloud darker. Leaving the wagons behind, the mourners ran.

Mordecai found Rachel under the flapping tent wrapped in a shawl with Kore. "Rachel, help me get the tent down," he yelled. Her look of joy and relief upon seeing him almost made the sandstorm worth it. They rolled up the mats and stashed the poles alongside the cart. Nearby Phinehas and Shelah did the same with the help of Tek and Reuel. "Come over here," Mordecai called, "We will all get under the cart." He tied mats around the donkey's and goats' heads and threw the baby goats under the cart. The women and children lay wrapped with Mordecai and Phinehas spread over them. The sandstorm hit. Seven people, a dog, and a basket of cats squeezed under the cart Mordecai had begged from the master of the wood shop. *How many times has this cart saved our lives,* thought the young wood carver, as the sand and wind drove all thought from his mind.

More than she heard them, Rachel felt Kore's cries against her breast. She remembered the little goddess. *Where did I leave her? What if she is blown away? Should I ask her for help? There is no doubt the god of chaos is at work in this storm.* As soon as the thought formed, she heard a voice shout, "Pray." Kore had stopped crying. Rachel shook the baby. *Still alive. Oh, thank you Yahweh, You gave me back my baby from Sarah. You gave me Mordecai, the best man in all the world. Everything I have that is good came from you. I want to go to the land of milk and honey. Please save us.*

Rachel woke. Mordecai held a bowl of water to her lips. "Oh, thank you Yahweh," she said. "We are alive."

"We are," Mordecai said, "crawl out." He pulled Kore from beneath her. "Poor baby," he said. "I think we almost smothered her." He shook the sand from a mat and sat them on it. He washed their faces with a wad of wet wool.

"Mordecai, did you yell 'pray' when the storm hit?"

"Not that I remember."

"I heard a voice say, 'Pray.'"

"Did you pray?"

"I did. I prayed to Yahweh."

"Who else would you pray to?"

Chapter 13

O NCE AGAIN MOSES WENT UP THE MOUNTAIN. Word spread that he had gone to make atonement for the great sin the people had committed. At the base of the mountain men swept the sand from the twelve pillars Moses had set up. One man, old and crippled in his feet, devoted to the worship of Yahweh, held a shard high and shouted, "Here is a piece of the tablet Moses threw down. It has writing." He crawled to his rug and reverently laid the shard upon it.

Reuel, drawn to the site of his parents' deaths, had persuaded Tek to go to the mountain. Curious, they watched as the man scrabbled on his knees, searched through the sand, and crawling, ferried several more pieces to the rug. Unable to read, he laboriously blew the sand from the engraved words, fitting each piece by its shape. "Let's help him," said Tek.

Soon the boys uncovered more pieces and laid them on the rug, helping the man fit the pieces together. "Here is a word," said Reuel, reading from right to left as Ada had taught him. "I think it says, 'honor you...'" Onlookers joined the search and, after several hours a jumble of broken pieces found order and drifted over the rug in ragged symmetry. Reuel found the left bottom corner then the right top. He laid them in place and heard a chorus of voices: "There, boy, put that one over there. That one goes there." Hour by hour, piece by piece, the people pointed—"No, no. Over there,"— while the nimble youths crabbed across the rug and shifted the pieces. And thus, with ohs and ahs from the crowd, they fitted together a patchwork— some words of the tablets Moses had brought down the mountain.

A middle-aged man of the priestly tribe of Korah, hurrying to his evening meal, stopped to see what had drawn the people into a semi-circle, and bending with his hands on his knees, he read: *Egypt, out of the house of slavery. You shall have no other gods before me...* "These are the same words Yahweh spoke to us the day we heard his voice midst the trumpet, and thunder, and smoke. Do you know what this means?" he addressed the crowd. No one knew. "These are the writ words of Yahweh." He fell to his knees. "Oh, what have we done?" He threw sand on his head and lay prostrate before the broken tablets. The people tore their clothes and wailed. A cry went up: "There is no God like Yahweh!"

"Let's go get Phinehas so he can see it," said Tek. The boys bade the crippled man goodbye and struck out for the camp of Manasseh. Until Shelah finally forced them to bed, they babbled about the crippled man and the tablets they had put together.

"The priest of Korah says they are the same words Yahweh spoke in the thunder that day," said Reuel before he finally managed to sleep.

"This has been good for Reuel," said Phinehas. "Maybe it will help with the terrible memories."

The next morning, Shelah could not get the manna boiled fast enough. With the sun barely up, they headed for the mountain, Phinehas in tow. With high spirits, shoving one another off the path, bragging of their prowess in finding and fitting the shards, they danced around Phinehas. At the mountain, the crippled man, sat alone, rocking in the center of his now-empty rug.

Reuel knelt beside the man. "Where are the parts?" the boy demanded.

"What happened?" asked Phinehas, his voice mitigating his son's. "Let him tell it, Reuel."

Dust and sand, traced with tears, rained from the man's hair and beard. He stopped rocking and studied the boys. "You boys met the priest who came along?" He nodded along with the boys. "Yes. I know you did. I doubt sometimes if what I know happened, really happened."

"What happened?" Phinehas repeated. He sat on his haunches. "From what my sons said, the tablets were marvelous to behold. I believe someone said they inscribed the exact words Yahweh spoke the day we heard his voice..."

"That priest said it! He said he was a priest of the tribe of Korah." The man shook his head in disbelief. "Someone wanted to take a piece. He offered to pay for it. Who to pay? The words were laid out on my rug, but I did not want gold for Yahweh's words."

"Did the priest sell the pieces?"

"Not only that. How a man could calculate so fast, I do not know. He sold them by size and by the importance of the words." He studied Phinehas' puzzled grimace. "I see you do not understand. The word, 'Yahweh,' according to the priest, is worth more than the word, 'serve,' more than the word, 'keep.' I tried to stop them. I lay down on the words." He opened his hand. In his bloody palm lay a small shard engraved with the partial words, *any likeness...*

"Where do you live? We will take you home," said Phinehas.

"My name is Shem of the tribe of Ephraim. I do not live far." Phinehas and the boys helped the man to his feet, rolled up his rug, and adjusted his staffs. They slowly walked to his camp. Neither boy spoke. Reuel held out the man's shard.

"You keep it, boy. Whenever you handle it, remember the joy we found in the words of Yahweh." He limped into his tent and closed the flap.

Tek and Reuel, their thin shoulders slumped, stood looking at the closed flap. Phinehas led them away. "Do you remember what that priest looks like?" They both nodded. "Fix him in your minds. Do you have him firm?" Again they nodded.

Chapter 14

RACHEL WAS POSITIVE MORDECAI HAD TOLD the entire multitude she was with child. "I think he even told the goats," she said to Shelah. Strangers smiled at her knowingly. Women in the latrine lines offered advice. If they were not talking about her baby they were talking about the three thousand dead men and the realignment of families that must take place. And that, too, entailed thoughts of babies.

Hebrew law dictated that upon a man's death, his brother must take the widow into his tent. If the man had no brother, another of his close relatives must marry her. Not only that, but also if the widow had no son, the new husband was obligated to impregnate the woman so the dead man's name would not die with him. Among the women, bittersweet excitement permeated the camps of the Hebrews. And dread. For some it was a chance to start over, possibly with a kinder husband. For others, the opposite might be true. Some might end up with a younger brother, some with an old uncle. A time of uncertainty and anxiety fell upon the Hebrew women.

The war with Amelek had precipitated a realignment. Now, because of sin, three thousand men had died at the hand of Yahweh. Three thousand households would suffer turmoil. Wives must share their tents with a newcomer. Children would be mixed together. Husbands must spread their affection between multiple wives. For good or ill some women had lost a husband in both events.

Four days after the slaughter and sand storm, a tall handsome woman drove her ass-drawn cart into Jemimah's camp. A girl about nine and two small boys road atop their worldly goods. "I am looking for Phinehas," she called to the women who sat weaving under Jemimah's awning. "Someone directed me here..."

Shelah stood. *She must be Phinehas' sister-in-law. The brother must be dead. Why else would she come and ask for my husband by name? And she has brought her children and all her household goods.* In the time it took Shelah to walk to the cart and extend her hand, she thought all those things. She smiled and said, "I am Shelah, Phinehas' wife." *Her handshake is strong,* thought Shelah. *She smiles with her eyes. She is beautiful in spite of her age and the freckles.*

"I am Abigail, Phinehas' sister-in-law. These are my children."

An hour passed while the women visited in the shade of the awning. The boys played with the other children. The daughter, a replica of her mother, red-haired, freckled, with pale lashes, sat close by her mother. Nothing was said that shed light on Abigail's circumstances. For all any one knew, hers was simply a social call. *How can I share my Phinehas with this woman,* thought Shelah, *this Abigail with the amber eyes.* "Here comes Phinehas." Shelah hurried to meet her husband. He dropped his water bag and staff at his tent and, squinting toward the gathering of women, spoke with his wife.

Abigail continued to talk with Jemimah about an intricate pattern she had learned to weave. The girl looked past her mother's shoulder at the man who had come to their house the day they left for the wilderness. Shelah and Phinehas approached the women. "Abigail, will you join Shelah and me?" Leaving the girl with Jemimah, the woman followed the couple the short distance to their tent. They removed their sandals and seated themselves. "Is my brother dead?"

"Killed in the slaughter at the mountain."

So matter of fact, thought Shelah. *She seems almost happy.*

"You are welcome here, sister," said Phinehas. "Shelah and I welcome you and your children. I have thought of you often since I saw you in Goshen." Shelah cut her eyes at Phinehas. "I did not tell you, Shelah, my meeting with my brother was not amiable."

Shelah covered her mouth with her hands when Abigail said mater-of-factly, "Shemida knocked me to the ground in front of Phinehas. Your husband and I were playmates. He was a kind little boy. I am sure his brother's cruelty worried him."

"And you laughed at me," said Phinehas not unkindly.

"I am sorry. You were so endearing with your big, rich coat and your cat in the basket. And the turban..." she smiled. "And you were quite fat!" Her laugh emerged as a hoot. "Sorry." It was her turn to covered her mouth. "Mostly I laughed because I was so very happy to see you alive. Listen, Phinehas...Shelah...I have sons. I do not need a husband. I need a safe place for my children. Phinehas, if you promise not to treat my children unkindly, I would like to set up my tent close by you. For protection."

"We will have to marry. For your safety and the children's. You cannot be left unattached."

"Would that be all right with you, Shelah?" asked Abigail. "I know that is a lot."

Shelah grasped Abigail's large freckled hands in her own delicate ones. With tears in her eyes, she said, "You are my sister from here on. Your children will not be without a father."

They set up Abigail's small tent next to Jemimah's. Shemida had never allowed his wife to have friends. Free at last, she could not contain her happiness. Soon they wondered what they had ever done without her, for she was a midwife.

"Sometimes Yahweh takes a bad thing and turns it to good," said Jemimah. "Was your husband very bad?"

"He was cruel. He was cruel to Phinehas when we were children. I had to watch my children every moment. They had to be quiet."

"We like noisy children," said Jemimah.

The next day Phinehas gathered the family together to introduce them to Abigail. He and Shelah stood with the woman and her three children. Phinehas placed his hands on the girl's shoulders. "This is Jerusha. She is my first daughter, age ten. Is she not beautiful? Have you ever seen such hair? I have four sons now: Tek and Reuel, and these handsome boys are Micah age four and Midian, age five. I am taking Abigail, my dead brother's wife, to be my wife. Shelah has accepted her as a sister." He hung his best remaining ring around Abigail's neck. "Tek and Reuel have killed an antelope. So tonight we will have the marriage feast. I want dancing." Enoch and his family, Mordecai and Rachel, Jemimah and her family, and their neighbors celebrated. Enoch had saved a cask of beer from the Red Sea. Abigail, it turned out, played the lute. Someone brought a flute. By the light of the pillar of Yahweh, they danced.

Mordecai, Enoch, and Phinehas stood apart talking. "What will this mean to my marriage?" said Phinehas. "Another family brought in. An older woman. What will this do to Shelah?"

"Get Shelah with child," said Enoch. "She will be fine."

"Is a baby the answer to everything with women?" said Mordecai.

Enoch nodded. "Just about. Yes. I believe for most women, a child is the beginning and the end."

Chapter 15

O N A HOT SUMMER MORNING, under a cloudless, bright blue sky, Phinehas and Enoch stood with their families in the midst of a throng of Hebrews, waiting for Moses to make his way down the mountain. To Phinehas most people smelled worse than the goats they lived among. He moved away from a particularly fetid man and said, "The first time Moses went up the mountain, I gained a wife. Now, the second time, I gained another wife and three children."

"Let's hope this is the last time," said Enoch. "Do you have any more dead brothers?"

Once again Moses had stayed on the mountain forty days and forty nights. In his absence, although undercurrents of rebellion fomented, no faction had openly risen. Now most of the congregation of Hebrews, along with Enoch and those under his influence, waited with renewed hope. Maybe Moses would take up his staff, the pillar of cloud would rise, and they would get on their way to the Promised Land. *That is what we need to do,* thought Enoch, for although the sand storm had erased the graves of the slain—no pile of rocks, no depression in the sand remained—the blood of 3,000 men called to their brothers. *The sooner the Hebrews say goodbye to this mountain, this unhappy plain, the better,* he thought.

"Look, Moses face is shining," the people marveled. "And he is carrying tablets like the ones he dashed to pieces." Moses did not realize his face shone from the glory of Yahweh's presence. He left the mountain and walked among the people who shied away from him in fear. After that day, he wore a veil when he addressed the people and removed the veil when he spoke with Yahweh in the Tent of Meeting.

Moses assembled all the congregation of the sons of Israel and said to them: "These are the things Yahweh has commanded you to do: For six days work will be done, but the seventh day is a holy day, a Sabbath of complete rest to Yahweh. Whoever does any work on the seventh day shall be put to death. You shall not kindle a fire in any of your dwellings on the Sabbath day.

"Furthermore, take from among you a contribution to Yahweh. Only those with a willing heart may give. They shall bring gold, silver and bronze, and blue, purple and scarlet fabric, fine linen, goats' hair and rams' skins dyed red, and porpoise skins and acacia wood and oil for lighting and spices for the anointing oil, and for the fragrant incense, and onyx stones and setting stones for the accouterments of the priests.

The contribution shall be made in order to build a Tabernacle for Yahweh. And let every skillful man among you come and make all that

Yahweh has commanded: The Tabernacle with its tent, its covering, and all its parts; the lamp stand; the Ark and its carrying poles; curtains; furniture; oil for lamps; the altar of incense; all the utensils for the offering; and the woven garments for Aaron and the priests for ministering in the holy place."

Then all the people departed from Moses' presence and returned to their tents. From the goods they had plundered from the Egyptians, when every slave asked for gifts from their masters, they gathered their offerings.

Enoch emptied his wagon and instructed those he judged: "Come, load your good-will offering into the wagon and we will deliver it to Moses." Since the Golden calf incident and the death of Jabus, a shaky peace had settled over the tribe of Manasseh. No one overtly stirred up trouble, nor, in obedience to Yahweh, did anyone wear gold. Now Enoch passed among his relatives with a pot into which they threw their jewelry. No one dissented.

Abigail happily threw her earrings and bracelets into the pot. They had been acquired during her marriage to Shemida. She held Phinehas' ring in her fist, the thong taut around her neck. "I will give all my other gold, but I will keep this and hide it around my neck. I have waited for it all my life."

Rachel sat in the dim light of her tent, the door flap closed, the sides unrolled to the ground. She had worked so hard to add the sides—spinning the goat hair, weaving the mats, sewing them together, section by section. Some nights her fingers ached. Her handiwork had brought warmth and privacy to her family. She wondered if she would be chosen to weave for Yahweh's house. *Will my skills be acceptable?* she worried.

An afternoon breeze sent pin holes of light zigzagging across Kore at her nap and Rachel's own bent head. She held the pouch Asmath had given her. The mother of pearl disks, small round rainbows, gleamed as she untied the cord. Once bulging with gold, now the pouch lay almost limp in her hand. Where had her riches gone? She poured the last remaining objects onto her lap. So much had happened since that morning in Ramses when Asmath had poured the gold into her lap. *I became Mordecai's wife. We crossed the sea. We found Kore. I am with child.* A torn seam threw a large beam onto Ma'at's small jade body. Since the sandstorm, when she had called upon Yahweh, the goddess held no allure. She set aside the last two toe rings and the nose ring she had never worn. *I will never miss them* she thought. Rachel returned the lapis lazuli combs and Asmath's mirror to the pouch, keeping out the sewing kit. She turned the shell from the sea in the sunbeam and with her finger traced the engraved words of Yahweh on the shard Reuel had given her for safe-keeping. She dropped them into the pouch. Finally, she nestled the goddess behind the combs and tied the end closed. She balanced on her knees, lifted her dress and fixed the pouch around her waist. Her hand lingered over the almost indiscernible rise of her belly. She found her large pelican bone needle and sewed the tear in the roof.

❧

Yahweh chose by name Bezalel, from the tribe of Judah, and Oholiab, from the tribe of Dan, and filled them with his Spirit for wisdom and understanding and knowledge in all craftsmanship. Yahweh equipped them to make designs for work in gold, silver, and bronze; in the cutting of stones for settings; and in the carving of wood, so as to perform in every inventive work. And he gave them the ability to teach. Yahweh enhanced the talents of every gifted person who had skills—skills they had learned as slaves.

Women chosen from the twelve tribes, Rachel among them, began to spin and weave goat hair for the curtains in Yahweh's house. Jemimah and her daughters ground indigo leaves for making blue dye, the color chosen for the Priests robes. They spun linen, dyed it blue, purple and scarlet and embroidered patterns into the finely woven fabrics.

One day Elias, in his red painted box carriage, born by two young priests, came to Mordecai's tent. Morsel frolicked at her feet as Rachel left the women and walked the short distance to her campsite. "May I help you, sir?"

"I am here to see Mordecai. And you are Rachel, the girl with the hair." Rachel's hands flew to her veil.

"The last time I saw you, you wore no veil."

"Elias, the carpenter." She grasped his wrinkled hands.

"These days I am a priest."

"Mordecai is not here. He has gone with Enoch and the goats." Rachel poured bowls of water for the priests and Elias.

"Did I see kittens over there?" Elias pointed toward Phinehas' tent.

"Do you want one?"

"I want two. But I also want your husband. We need him at the building site. I have told Bezalel we cannot begin the carvings for Yahweh's house without our best carver. Mordecai the best; you know that?"

Rachel beamed. "He is something, is he not?" She leaned forward. "Did you ever see this?" She pulled out the bird on its thong."

Elias held the pendant flat on his palm. "Mordacai carved one like it for the portal of Pharaoh's aunt's tomb. Fifteen cubits, the wingspan. It was so massive, he had to travel to the site and carve the tree on the ground. I believe yours was the model. Let's go get my kittens. And you will send Mordecai to us?"

"I will send him today." Her strong promise turned plaintive. "How long will he be gone?"

He dropped his chin, eyed her from beneath his bushy brows, and said not unkindly, "For as long as it takes to complete Yahweh's house." After a short stop at Shelah's tent, the priests hoisted the red box and trotted away,

152

while the old man crooned in a high voice over his kittens. *Now I see why Mordecai loves him so,* Rachel thought.

❧

Mordecai took the time to sharpen his carving tools. "I cannot arrive with dull tools." Rachel packed his sleeping mats and warm coat. She went to the well, filled his water skin, and with lingering hands, hung the strap on his shoulder. "I will come visit soon. I promise," he said. He kissed Kore and his wife and struck out toward the mountain, a little too jauntily for Rachel's taste. She held onto Morsel until his master disappeared in a sea of black tents. *I have never been alone in my life,* she thought, with a sinking heart. That night, to her surprise, Tek and Reuel, announcing, "Mordecai said," rolled into their sleeping mats at her tent door, and there they slept until Mordecai returned.

From his red box, Elias directed the setting up of a shed and work stations for the carvers. He gathered woodworkers from the twelve tribes, but none surpassed Mordecai in talent or dedication. He took Bezalel's patterns, carved prototypes, and set the standard for the other carvers. Using acacia wood, they fashioned the furnishings for the Tabernacle: The Ark, which would house the Ten Commandments; tables and altars for sacrifice and burning incense; boards and tenons for the walls of the Tabernacle; and sockets, clasps and loops to affix the curtains and carrying poles. None of their work would ever be seen. They sent each piece, sanded and perfectly smooth, to the metallurgists where it received an overlay of pure gold, silver or bronze.

Occasionally Mordecai slipped away and visited Rachel. With each visit he marveled at her growing girth. At first, he was shy with her, but she took his hands and placed them on her belly. After that he could not get enough of the baby, listening, feeling its stirrings. Several times Rachel made the half day's journey to see him with a packet of cheese or a bit of meat from a kill Tek had made. On one of his visits she worried that he would miss the birth of the baby. "Send for me the moment it starts. We are almost done with the carving. I can leave." He started down the path, walking backwards, not jaunty at all, which pleased Rachel. Then he turned and walked with a purpose toward the building site.

Reuel and Tek had risen early and gone hunting the morning Rachel's pangs began, so Jemimah sent Zelo to fetch Mordecai. Rachel struggled throughout the day, begging, "Where is he?" But Mordecai never came.

Abigail, frowning, lifted her ear from Rachel's belly. "This baby is butt first. We will have to turn it." With her large strong hands, assisted by Jemimah, she began to push the baby upwards and around. In spite of herself,

153

Rachel screamed. "I am so glad Mordecai is not here," she said. At last the women moved her to the birthing stool. Shelah supported her from behind while Jemimah and Sarah pushed on the sides of her belly to keep the baby straight. "I see curly hair!" said Abigail. "He's almost here," she sang, then she screamed, "Rachel!" The younger women jumped, startled. The mother-to-be had fainted. "If she does not push now, this baby will die," Abigail shouted. They poured water on Rachel's face and washed her down with cold water. They slapped her. Abigail grabbed a shock of her hair and shook her head. "Rachel! Rachel!" At last Rachel roused and summoned the energy for a last ghastly push. The baby girl, fat and perfect slid into Jemimah's hands. She held her up for all to see. "This is what you get when a baby sits upright the whole time. Her head is not misshaped at all." Rachel took one look and fainted again. They left her alone to rest while they salted and swaddled the baby. Mordecai did not know about his daughter or see her until his next visit, two weeks later.

"That Zelo. I feel like beating him," he said. He and Rachel sat in their tent admiring their baby girl. "She is beautiful, is she not? said Mordecai. He shook his head. "There is no excuse for that boy. Look at her little nose. Where is he anyway?" No one had seen Zelo since he had been sent on his errand. "What do you want to name her?"

"I like the name Judith. It was my mother's name," said Rachel. "Forget about Zelo. I was glad you were not here to witness my complaints."

"We are almost done," said Mordecai. "We are working on the last parts, the clasps that will hold the curtains. I see the women are loading the curtains now."

The time came for the women to assemble the textiles for the Tabernacle. Manasseh's women prepared a wagon laden with their share of curtain sections woven according to Bezalel's patterns and plans. At the work site they would lay out the components and sew them into panels connected with gold clasps and hung by gold rings onto gold poles. Rachel held one-month-old Judith and watched her sisters load their handiwork—so much work over the last months. Mordecai left with Shelah and Jemimah, he for his last stint at the work site, they to sew the dyed fabrics into priests' garments. "I will be glad when this is over," said Rachel to Abigail "It has been a long seven months."

On the first day of the first month of the second year after leaving Egypt, the children of Israel finished the work of the Tabernacle. They had arrived at Sinai on the first day of the third month of the first year. Moses went up the mountain twice, for forty days each time. Thus, the people worked on the Tabernacle for seven months and 10 days. Moses examined all the parts and found them to be just as Yahweh had directed. He blessed the people and told them to set up the house of Yahweh.

All the congregation gathered, standing on wagons and carts, and watched the assembling of the Tabernacle: those who had worked and those who had tended the flocks; the old and the young, the infirm and the strong. The families of Levi, the priestly tribe, led by Aaron, erected the Tabernacle with its golden boards, sockets, bars and pillars. They spread the tent over the Tabernacle and laid the covering on top. Then they took the tablets of the Ten Commandments and placed them into the Ark and put the carrying poles in their rings and the mercy seat with the golden cherubim on top. They placed the Ark in the Tabernacle and hung the screens the women had made. They set up the lampstand and lighted it; they placed the altar and burned offerings upon it. The priests washed themselves at the doorway of the tent and donned their robes of blue and gold embroidered linen. Once inside the tent they washed their hands and feet at the golden laver. They erected the court all around the Tabernacle and hung the veil for the gateway of the court. Then the cloud of Yahweh covered the Tent of Meeting, and the glory of Yahweh, his fire, filled the Tabernacle. Even Moses was not able to enter the tent for the glory of Yahweh filled it.

For twelve days, the tribal heads brought to the Tabernacle offerings of silver and gold utensils for performing the rites of worship and grain and animals for sacrifice. Moses sent word among the people and taught them the ordinances by which they were to live and the order of the sacrifices they were to make, and what to eat—whether it be clean or unclean. On the fourteenth day of the first month of the second year they observed the second Passover.

Chapter 16

ON THE FIRST DAY OF THE SECOND MONTH of the second year after leaving Egypt, one month after the Tabernacle had been erected, Moses took a census of the men of Israel, every man from the age of twenty upward, whoever was able to go out to war. The number of fighting men totaled 603,550.

Moses divided the twelve tribes into four armies and arranged them around the Tabernacle. He established marching orders: The first army of three tribes, led by the tribe of Judah, would move out first. Then the priests who had charge over the Tabernacle would dismantle it and load it onto wagons, board by board, with all its curtains, sockets, clasps, and all its furnishings, and those who carried the Ark containing the Testimony of the Ten Commandments would set out. Next, the second army of three tribes would follow. Then those carrying the holy objects of the Tabernacle would go forth. After that, the third army, made up of three tribes, would set out, and last, the fourth army of three tribes would form the rear guard. Thus Moses established the makeup of the armies and the order in which the armies would travel to the Promised Land. Each army camped a distance from the Tabernacle with their families and flocks. Aaron and the tribe of Levi, those charged with carrying, dismantling and setting up the Tabernacle, camped close around it.

Yahweh spoke to Moses and instructed him to make two trumpets of hammered silver for summoning the congregation to the Tent of Meeting, for the commencement of travel, and to mark feast days and the first days of months. A blast of alarm would signal war or attack. Yahweh assured Moses that he would hear the trumpet and save his chosen people from their enemies.

In the second year after leaving Egypt, on the twentieth day of the second month, the cloud lifted from the Tabernacle of the Testimony. The trumpet sounded. The people, after a sojourn of one year, set out on their journey from the wilderness of Sinai and the Mountain of Yahweh. In that year, they had received the Ten Commandments, constructed the Tabernacle, learned the ordinances of Yahweh and formed a four-pronged army. When the Ark set out, Moses said:

"Rise up O Yahweh!
And let your enemies be scattered,
And let those who hate you flee before you."
And when it came to rest, he said:
"Return O Yahweh
To the myriad thousands of Israel.

The trumpet sounded that morning at sunrise, and the cloud lifted from the new Tent of Meeting. Hours passed before the tribe of Manasseh moved a hand breadth. "This reminds me of the morning we left Goshen," commented Enoch to the knot of waiting men.

The tribes of Judah, Issachar, and Zebulun, making up the army of Judah, led out and then stopped and waited for the Tabernacle to catch up. Disassembling the Tabernacle and loading it for transport had taken hours. "I suppose they will get faster with practice," Mordecai said. Now, like an inch worm withering under the scalding sun, the Hebrew nation moved north.

Rachel looked back at the mountain of God still dominating the horizon. Horeb's black top, burned by the fire of Yahweh, stood stark among all the peaks. She had mixed feelings about leaving the mountain. In the months they had sojourned there, she and Mordecai had accumulated goods, increased their goat herd, and had a baby. Kore belonged to them now. The young mother worried that travel would be difficult with the children and how far they would travel before they found water. Would manna continue to fall? She had nestled the new grindstone Mordecai had laboriously made for her in the corner of the cart.

"I think you love that grindstone more than Judith," he teased.

"You made them both. I cannot decide which one I like best." She shook out the sleeping mats and rolled up the tent. She filled all the water bags and jugs. To her dismay, the cart wheels sank into the sand. Mordecai and Phinehas had rigged a yoke and modified the handles so the donkey could pull the cart, and although the donkey had grown into a fine animal, Rachel worried the load would be too heavy. They had not been surprised to learn that Cursing Man died at the golden calf incident. Mordecai's ankle, injured at the wadi and again in the battle with the Amalek, had not healed properly, so they desperately needed the donkey. Mordecai, guilty of theft, according to Enoch's reading of the ordinance, had sought out and offered Cursing Man's widow four goats for the animal. Her new husband had insisted she hold out for six. Mordecai paid five with a profuse prayer of thanksgiving to Yahweh.

Before their departure Rachel stood with her hands on her hips, studying the wheels. "He is all hooked up," said Mordecai, joining her at the side of the cart. "Stop worrying. We won't leave our Goose dying in the sand."

Now they walked on either side of the donkey, engaged in a desultory conversation. "Just think: I am a numbered man," said Mordecai. *And no longer a thief,* he thought. He felt free of a burden he had not known he carried until Enoch accused him.

"Are you sure?" said Rachel. "You might be nineteen. Maybe you should not have been among those numbered men."

"I am twenty. I know that for sure."

"How do you know for sure you are twenty?" Kore rode like a tiny queen atop the sleeping mats, jumping on her knees, squealing and waving her arms. Judith slept in a sling from Rachel's shoulder.

"How old are you, Wife?"

"I was fifteen when we left. Now I am sixteen."

"Wait. I must be twenty-one."

"See. You need a wife to keep up with you."

Mordecai grinned. "I think we're stopping."

"I will not complain," said Rachel, "even though we just started." Mordecai pushed two poles into the sand and draped roofing mats in a makeshift tent from the cart to the poles. They drank sparingly from their water bags, and Rachel poured water for Morsel and Goose. Mordecai spread mats, they settled Kore, and with their legs extended, leaned against the wheel while Rachel nursed Judith. "Look at my shoes," said Mordicai. They look as new as the day you gave them to me."

Rachel studied his shoes, then her own. "Mine, too. Like new. How odd." They sat in companionable silence. After a while she said, "If you are going to be in the army, I hope they give you a better weapon."

"Will you ever forget the tent pole?"

"I don't think so. Going to war with a tent pole seems wrong. Besides, the priests have swords. I saw one."

"What do you think about this? Phinehas and I are going to start making javelins. There was no pay for all the work we did, but Elias figured a way for us to get some bronze left over from the Tabernacle."

"A tent pole called something else is still a tent pole."

They traveled for three days following the pillar of cloud. At last they came to the Wilderness of Paran and camped. The twelve tribes took their appointed positions around the Tabernacle according to Moses' directions. Manasseh's army of 32,000 men, with their families and flocks, spread on the west side between the camps of Ephraim and Benjamin.

Enoch's family and Jemimah's rejoined and camped together, grazing their flocks in an ever-expanding, mingled herd. Their families had blended and bonded, with Jemimah as matriarch and Enoch, the judge, as patriarch. Tek, taking Reuel along, hunted, and they and their neighbors ate well of antelope, oryx and gazelle, and of pheasant and partridge. Jemimah and Shelah became famous for the bowls of stew they took to the sick and old.

Enoch became known as a fair and wise judge, his greatest worry centering on his nephew, Zelophehad. Now thirteen, he had taken up with a rabble gang that gambled and pilfered and complained about the lack of meat. Like his father before him, he spread discontent among the Hebrews. As they had before, people of low character joined with the rabble and murmured about the manna and the lack of foodstuffs they had enjoyed in Egypt. They wanted meat. They cried out, "Why did we leave Egypt?" By now Enoch had gained a glimmer of insight into Yahweh. "This complaining and unrest is trouble for all of us," he told his family. "Be careful that none of it is found among us."

The second night in the wilderness of Paran, Enoch's family ate a stew of partridge, and Abigail payed her lute. Suddenly Jemimah's awning caught fire from edge to edge. The women screamed and ran, grabbing children, throwing them outside the tent. The men ripped the awning from the rest of the tent panels and threw it to the ground, stomping out the fire. While they stood bewildered over the smoking goat hair mats, they saw other tents on fire. They ran to help screaming men and women. "Mordecai! Come back! There goes ours," Rachel shrieked. They ran toward their campsite. Phinehas, his short legs pumping, ran close behind. Halfway there he veered off to his own burning tent.

"The cart!" yelled Mordecai. Before they could throw out the contents of the cart a lanolin-filled bundle of wool ignited, and the fire spread explosively. Enoch, Hazor, and Perez ran to one side of the cart and helped Mordecai tip it over. They took up tent poles and raked burning mats and clothing from the cart. They scooped handfuls of sand onto smoking clothes and poured skins of water over smoldering boards.

Mordecai examined the cart, top, bottom and sides. "A little charred," he said, "no real damage. Your grindstone is all right." He held her destroyed loom over his head. "Don't worry. I can make a better loom than this one. Now that I know how..."

Judith slept in her sling in spite of the jostling and noise. Kore sobbed and pointed to the doll Mordecai had carved, now a charred head. Rachel stood in stunned silence; she wanted to wail for her lost tent, for the lost days and weeks she had sat at her loom, but how could she, when Mordecai insisted it wasn't so bad... *What do you expect,* she told herself, *this is a man who survived the brick yards, who went to war with a tent pole...* She began to chuckle and sat and lay back on the ground, the babies on her chest. *And he came back alive!* Her chuckle grew into a full bellied laugh. Her stomach ached from the position and the laughter.

"Rachel..."

"I will stop." But she could not stop laughing.

Phinehas stood looking down at Rachel. His eyes shifted to Mordecai. "What's that about?"

"Never mind. Let's go see if Jemimah needs any help," Mordecai walked away from his hysterical wife. Later that night they lay beside the cart with the babies on borrowed mats, trying to ignore the smell of charred wood and burned wool. Rachel had tied a fist-size knot in her shawl for Kore to cuddle. Morsel curled up by his master's head and would not be shifted.

"Sekhmet's latest batch of kittens died," said Rachel. "Jerusha and the two little boys cried and cried. I'm sorry I laughed. Sometimes I think if you cut off your hand, you would say, 'it's not so bad.' But sometimes it's more than I can bear. I want to go home, Mordecai."

"Home? What home?"

"Ramses."

"Egypt is not our home."

"I had a good life there."

"You were a slave just like me."

"No, My Love. I had a good home. If we went back, you could open a wood shop and get paid for your work. Asmath's father would help us."

"If we showed up in Egypt we would probably be killed. And Asmath's brother is dead. How do you think his father feels about that?"

"Asaph... He was so handsome..." Rachel said no more. She slept.

Asaph, thought Mordecai. *Handsome, rich, schooled with Pharaoh's sons, everything I am not. I forgot dead.* He smiled, his last thought before sleep: *Asaph is dead, and I am not.*

The next day Enoch learned what he had suspected: Had Moses not prayed to Yahweh, the breakout fire, the result of Yahweh's terrible anger, would have consumed the entire Hebrew nation. He would have destroyed all their possessions, forcing them to trust him.

Moses announced that Yahweh would send meat to the complaining people. "They will eat meat until it comes out their nostrils," Moses had told the elders. From that statement, Enoch knew that Yahweh's anger still burned. "He gathered his family and the one thousand he judged. He addressed them from his wagon bed: "Yahweh will send meat. You are not to partake of it. There is danger in the meat. I do not know how, but the meat will be a punishment, not a blessing."

The crowd mumbled and whispered. "Who are you to tell us not to eat the meat?" a voice spoke from the back of the assembly. "You have fresh kill to eat because of your little monkey with his sling."

"I have told you," said Enoch. "Do not say that I did not tell you." He left the crowd and entered his tent. Tek crawled from under the wagon. He peeked through Enoch's tent door and saw him lying prostrate on his face.

"Uncle Enoch. Can I come in?"

Enoch sat up, wiped his face, and held out his hand. "Come here. Sit next to me." He pulled the boy close.

"Why do they call me a monkey? Is it because my arms are long?" The boy held out his arm and studied it. "Why are my arms so long?" His eyes, with the whitest of whites, gleamed in the shadows.

"Your arms are long because you will grow up to be tall—taller than all those people."

"Maybe it is because my skin is dark."

"The people who call you that are jealous and ignorant. You must ignore them."

"Maybe I should go back to my people."

"That would make all of us very sad. What would Phinehas do without his oldest boy? We are your people now. Do you not know, the people who love you are your people?"

"I will stay. When Kore and I grow up I will marry her."

Enoch's mouth dropped. "But, Tek, she is only three." *And Hebrew,* he thought.

"Well, I am only eight. Maybe I am nine. It is not too long to wait."

"But why have you chosen Kore?"

"Is she not the most beautiful female-child you ever saw? And she is dark, like me."

Enoch, his eyes accustomed to the shadows now, studied the boy's face: the huge brown eyes, no longer bereft, gazed into the future, alight with hope; the nose, finely shaped with the promise of a Bedouin bone. "Kore's parents will decide who she marries. But we will see what the future brings." *Time will have to take care of this,* Enoch thought. *I have told him we are his people, but he will never be allowed to marry a Hebrew girl.*

&

As He had done in the wilderness of Sin, Yahweh sent droves of quail born on a strong wind from the sea. When word spread that quail lay in knee-deep piles a day's journey from the camps, Enoch's dread increased. Why had Yahweh made his gift so inaccessible? A day's journey! The people who trekked to gather the quail Yahweh had sent, filled their baskets to over-flowing for a day and a night and all the next day. Yahweh saw their greed, and before they could swallow their first bite, struck them with a severe plague. Many died where they stood—so many, they named the place, Kibroth-hattaavah—*the graves of greediness.*

While death wails lingered on the lips of the bereaved, the trumpet sounded. The Hebrews abandoned the graves of their loved ones and moved farther into the wilderness of Paran, east of the Red Sea. "It seems we leave graves behind everywhere we go," said Rachel. "Why is Yahweh so hard on his chosen people?" They trekked between low mountains, through wadis and valleys, and across barren expanses of rock-strewn wastelands. A bit of

161

scrub kept the livestock alive. Once, it poured rain. All forward movement stopped while the people danced and played. The wise caught as much as they could in their cook pots. The women laid out their roofing mats, knowing that only with a good soaking would the wool shrink and become waterproof.

Mordecai watched as Rachel turned her face to the rain. He stored her new loom under the cart so it would not warp. "Don't fret. Soon you will replace all our burned mats. Did Jemimah not say she had never seen fingers fly like yours?"

They arrived in Hazeroth and spread their camps. The first morning at the latrine Shelah and Rachel arrived at the end of the line. A woman turned and, arching her eyebrows, asked them, "Did you hear? Moses has taken a Cushite woman to wife."

"A black African?" said Rachel.

"I think Cush is in Ethiopia," said Shelah.

"Sarah was so afraid the Promised Land was in Africa," said Rachel.

"Those people are very black," said another woman up the line.

"I know an Ethiopian man," said Rachel. "He is one of the kindest people I have ever known." She smiled, picturing Hopi, his massive form, his shaven head, his long skirt. Several of the women rolled their eyes and turned their backs.

After a brief silence another said, "And when Aaron and Miriam criticized their brother, she came down with leprosy."

"The Cushite woman has leprosy?" said Shelah.

"No. Miriam has leprosy. She has been sent outside the camp. Shut up in her tent. Not allowed to come out. Someone said she is white as snow from head to foot, so a very bad case."

"Did Aaron get leprosy, too?" asked Rachel. No one knew the answer. By the time the women returned to camp, knowledge of Miriam's plight had spread.

Enoch returned from a meeting of the judges and leaders with the whole story. "They criticized Moses because of his Cushite wife. Yahweh punished Miriam with leprosy. And no, Rachel, I know you are going to ask: Aaron did not get leprosy."

Rachel stood with fists at her waist. "Wait. Yahweh punished Miriam but not Aaron? Now I ask you, Brother, is that fair?"

"Would you question the judgment of Yahweh, Sister?"

"No, but—"

"Leave it, Rachel. Do you not have mats to weave? Sometimes gossip and guessing cannot figure a thing out, but there is probably a good reason for everything. I know Yahweh's reasons are perfect."

"Yes, Brother. Let me get to my weaving like a good female child." Enoch shook his head and walked away, then changed his mind and turned to face his sister.

"Rachel, what if Aaron was all right with the Cushite woman, but Miriam, knowing her brother to be weak, like he was with the golden calf, egged him on and made him go against Moses? Who would be guiltier, Aaron or Miriam? Think about that." He walked away.

Mordecai said, "I think your brother has become a real judge."

"It certainly looks that way."

For a week gossip at the latrine centered around Miriam, banished with leprosy, and Moses' Cushite wife. One morning a woman announced that Miriam had been healed. She had been seen walking around as normal as anyone. "Do you think it's true? No one goes from all white with leprosy to healed," Rachel said to Shelah.

"Maybe Yahweh took pity on her," said Shelah, "how else could it happen?"

"I know how the Cushite wife feels," said Rachel. "I hope she can forgive Miriam as I forgave Sarah."

&

The Hebrews moved farther into the wilderness of Paran and camped in a fertile valley at Kadesh. There Moses chose Joshua and Caleb to lead an expedition of twelve men, one from each tribe, to spy out the Promised Land, the land of Canaan, the land Yahweh had given to Abraham. He told them to go into the Negev, the south country, and then north into the hill country. He charged them to evaluate the land, whether fat or lean, good or bad. Were there trees in it, or not? They were to make an effort to get some fruit of the land, for the season was right for the grape harvest. He instructed them to find out if the cities were open or fortified, if the inhabitants were strong or weak, many or few.

The people camped and waited. Excitement grew and they talked of nothing but the Promised Land. Rachel could hardly concentrate on her weaving. Their new land... "Just think of it, Mordecai. I will have a garden, and we will have goats—not too many. And you can carve and trade your work. And you will not have to carve idols. You can make whatever you like: looms, spindles, tools." Sometimes she would worry, "What if we have to go to war to take our new land? We do not even have a tent pole now." She had said it in jest, but the thought of war brought tears. She thought about her house and how she would arrange it, with a fire pit in the center of the room.

And would her house be of mudbrick or stone? Maybe they would live among their goats in large tents.

Mordecai and the men made their own plans, conjuring their own worries. They speculated: when Moses said they would "take the land," did that mean they must wrest every hill, every valley, every village from the inhabitants? How would the land be parceled out? Who would group together? Would they build houses or would they enlarge their tents? The waiting seemed endless. The spies could be gone many months. They settled in to wait.

After forty days, sooner than expected, the spies returned. The twelve stood together on a hill where a natural amphitheater carried their voices to all the congregation.

Enoch and his family of thirty-eight souls stood together waiting to hear the report from the spies. "They do not look very happy," Enoch whispered to Phinehas.

Phinehas craned his neck. "I would say, grim."

The first spy held up his arms for quiet and spoke. "We went to the land where you sent us, and it does flow with milk and honey. And this is its fruit." He held high a heavy cluster of grapes. The crowd murmured its approval. He stepped back and another spy came forward.

"Nevertheless, the people who live in the land are strong and the cities are fortified and very large, and we saw the descendants of the Anak there."

"Anak! Are those not giants?" the people mumbled.

Another spy spoke: "Amalek is living in the land of the Negev, that is the south country, and the Hittites and Jebusites and Amorites are living in the hill country to the north. The Canaanites are living by the sea and along a river called Jordan, the main river running north and south to the east."

The voices of the people rose as one, a mingling of outrage and despair. Women began to sob and some bent at the waist and wailed as at a death. As each man spoke, Rachel clutched Mordecai's arm, saying, "What? Who are these Jebusites? What did he say?"

Caleb stepped forward and held up his arms for quiet. "We should by all means go up and take possession of the land, for we shall surely overcome it."

The ten spies shook their heads adamantly. One said, "All the men we saw were of great size. We saw the Nephilim, and we were as grasshoppers in our own sight and in theirs."

"*Nephilim!* Are they not also giants?" All the congregation argued among themselves, some weeping. Then people began to grumble against Moses and Aaron saying: "It would have been better if we had died in Egypt! Or that we had died in the wilderness! Is Yahweh bringing us into this land so that we die by the sword? Or that our wives and little ones will become plunder? Would it not be better to return to Egypt?"

Then they said to one another, "Let us appoint a leader and return to Egypt." Moses and Aaron fell on their faces before the congregation and Joshua and Caleb tore their clothes.

Joshua's voice rose above the din. "The land is an exceedingly good land. If Yahweh is pleased with us he will bring us into this land and give it to us—a land which flows with milk and honey."

Caleb shouted, "Only do not rebel against Yahweh. And do not fear the people of the land for they shall be our prey. Their protection has been removed from them, and Yahweh is with us. Do not fear them."

Angry voices overrode Joshua and Caleb. "Let us stone them!" Others took up the cry, "Stone them!" Fearing a riot, Enoch made a circular motion with his finger to Phinehas and Mordecai, his signal to move the family out of the crowd. The men herded the family through the restive assembly and gathered them a distance away. "This crowd is almost ready to break," said Enoch. At that moment, all eyes fixed on the Tent of Meeting where the glory of Yahweh appeared in fire. Enoch's eyes moved over the crowd, taking in the Tent of Meeting. "This is bad. We are in as much danger now as we were after the golden calf. Hurry! Get to our tents."

"But why, Enoch," asked Sarah. "We have done nothing."

"Because they have threatened Moses and Aaron. Yahweh could break out against the whole Hebrew nation. Remember the priests when Moses sent them out and three thousand died."

"And the burning when people complained," said Rachel. "Is it like that?"

"It could be," said Enoch. "I hope not." He addressed Phinehas, Mordecai, Nobah, and all the men: "Hurry. Go now. Get everyone back to our tents. Perez, Hazor, my brothers, I am trusting you; get Sarah and Hannah and the children to our tents. I am going to stay here and see what I can learn." Like a herd of panicked gazelles, the family scurried down deserted paths toward the camp of Manasseh. Enoch watched them go. *Oh, Yahweh, spare us, I pray.* Once the glory of Yahweh fell upon the Tent of Meeting, the mob, panicked and shouting, shoved without direction. Enoch, arms crossed on his chest, feet planted, stood buffeted on all sides. His friend Ishi, with his wife and children, came upon him and stopped.

"Enoch," he yelled, "we are going back to Egypt. Will you help select the new leader?"

Enoch leaned into the man's ear. "Ishi, Ishi. You of all people. You turned away from the rabble and trusted Yahweh."

"But Enoch, the spies say we cannot take the Promised Land. We have to go somewhere."

"Why do you think we called it the Promised Land? We did not make up that name. The land was promised by Yahweh. He was going to go before us and help us conquer it. Do you not see, our lack of faith has thrown Yahweh's promise into his face?"

Ishi pulled away and shouted, "I do not know how to fight a giant. Come, wife." Ishi brushed past Enoch and allowed the flood of humanity to carry him and his family away from the mountain.

Oh, Yahweh, what will become of us? Will everyone be like Ishi? Like the spies who did not trust you? Enoch made his way to the Tent of Meeting and stood off at a distance where a few leaders and judges gathered, for they were afraid to approach. Many, it seemed, had fallen away. As one, the faithful prostrated themselves and waited for a word from Moses. It came: Moses would speak the words of Yahweh to the people. Gather them.

At camp, his family waited for Enoch. They had trusted him from Goshen to Kadesh. He had taught them the ordinances of Yahweh and faithfully imparted every word from the mouth of Moses. Now with troubled faces they crowded around him, pelting him with questions. "What has happened? Are we not going to the Promised Land? Where are we to go?"

Enoch held up his hands. "Stop. I can tell you this: all the spies are dead except Joshua and Caleb." Stunned silence followed, then a chorus of, "Why?"

Enoch looked into the bewildered faces of his family "Do you ask why? I will tell you. The Promised Land was a promise from Yahweh. Would He promise us the land and then not help us take it? Mordecai, you asked once, would Yahweh tell us to take up the bones of Joseph, and then not bring the bones in? Well I ask you, would He not help us take the land? Giants are nothing to Him. Did He not part the sea and destroy Pharaoh and his army? Fortified cities are nothing to Him. Did He not bring water from a rock? Manna from heaven? Yahweh has asked only one thing from us." By now tears coursed down Enoch's face. "One thing: to trust Him. Just that one thing!" Enoch fell to his knees, clutched sand in each hand and threw it onto his head.

"Oh, my brother." Rachel fell on Enoch and rocked with him. The family knelt around them and embraced one another.

"What can we do?" they asked. "What can we do?"

After a time, Enoch sat up, spent. "There is nothing we can do on our own. Moses has called us to hear the words of Yahweh. Maybe He will have pity on us."

By evening hot blood had cooled. Talk of stoning Moses had died down. The great assembly of Hebrews returned to the rocky outcropping to hear Moses speak the words of Yahweh:

"'As I live,'" says Yahweh, "'just as you have spoken in My hearing, so I will do to you; your corpses shall fall in this wilderness, even all your numbered men, according

to your complete number from twenty years old and upward, who have grumbled against Me.

"'Surely you shall not come into the land in which I swore to settle you, except Caleb and Joshua.

"'Your children, however, whom you said would become a prey—I will bring them in, and they shall know the land which you have rejected.

"'But as for you, your corpses shall fall in this wilderness.

"'And your sons shall be shepherds for forty years in the wilderness and they shall suffer for your unfaithfulness, until your corpses lie in the wilderness.

"'According to the number of days which you spied out the land, forty days, for every day you shall bear your guilt a year, even forty years, and you shall know my opposition.

"'I, Yahweh, have spoken, surely all this I will do to this evil congregation who are gathered together against me. In this wilderness they shall be destroyed, and there they shall die.'"

Chapter 17

SENTENCED TO DIE IN THE WILDERNESS; denied the Promised Land. The people fell on their faces and repented before Moses and mourned, tearing their clothes, wailing, throwing sand on their heads, Enoch and his family among them. Yahweh had relented before, surely he would forgive them again and rescind this sentence of death. Dejected, but trusting in Yahweh's forbearance, the people returned to their camps.

"Will he forgive us, Brother?" asked Rachel on the walk back to Manasseh.

"I do not know...he was very detailed in his plans."

Hazor said, "Some men are planning to go up to the hill country and take the land."

"What men?" Enoch stiffened and halted. "Take what land?"

"The land Yahweh gave us," said Perez. "They are planning to muster and go up to the ridge in the morning. We heard them."

"That is not a plan," said Mordecai. "If we are going to go up and fight, we need Moses' blessing, and Joshua must lead us into battle."

"Well, maybe Joshua will be there," said Hazor.

"If an army were forming," said Phinehas, "the trumpets would sound an alarm and Joshua would be calling us to muster. There has been no such call.

"Listen." said Enoch, "We are not going to war tomorrow. Whoever would think such a thing is a fool. We are all exhausted. Go to your tents and rest."

The next morning, the children, oblivious of their parents' death sentence, gathered manna, filling their bowls with Yahweh's life-giving bread. Wives, mothers, grandmothers ground it, baked it, fried it, boiled it. The children could hardly remember the taste of any other bread. Enoch accepted his portion from Sarah and scooped up his boiled manna mush with a fried manna patty, just the way he liked it. Hannah's smallest daughter stood at his elbow as she did every morning, hoping to bring him another patty. Maybe she had done so for her lost father, left behind in Egypt. Enoch had never forgiven himself for leaving Egypt without Jorham. He had married Hannah and adopted her five children. With his own eight, he knew he could never feed thirteen children without Yahweh's bread. *Thank you, Yahweh for not withdrawing this blessing.*

Enoch patted the child's head, declining more food. His thoughts remained on their plight. *What are you going to do Yahweh?* he thought. *Are you going to forgive us, or will we truly never see the Promised Land?* He thought he knew the answer, the rightful and just answer. Sometime during the night he had reconciled himself to the truth: *we do not deserve to go in.*

"Uncle Enoch?" Tek stood before him. "Perez and Hazor have gone to the war."

"What?" Enoch stood, tipping the bowl from his lap.

"They told me not to tell."

"You did right, boy." Enoch threw on his sandals, grabbed his cloak and staff and struck out at a trot for the camp of Judah. He ran along well-worn paths through the camps of Manasseh, along the side of the Tabernacle court, through the tents of Judah and into the edge of the wilderness. In a valley surrounded by low crags and hills, thousands of men milled about, some with weapons, some empty-handed. *Are they waiting for a leader to materialize?* he thought. He ran from one group to another, asking if anyone had seen twins, eighteen years old. "They're tall. They look just alike—like me only younger." A boy no older than the twins pointed toward the war wagon. Enoch found them sitting against the rear wheel in the shade. "What are you doing, going against Yahweh like this?" he demanded. Surprised, they sprang to their feet.

"That Tek," said Perez.

"We are not going against Yahweh," Hazor said, "We are showing Him that we are brave, not like those spies."

Perez said, "Did you know except for Joshua and Caleb, the spies are all dead?"

"And you will be, too, if you join this rabble."

"That is why we are waiting by the wagon. We want to be sure we get a spear and a shield," said Hazor.

"Look how many people we have," said Perez waving his hand over the crowd. "And more coming all the time."

"I came by way of the Tabernacle," said Enoch. "The Ark is not coming. If the Ark does not go with the army, Yahweh is not with you. If he is not with you, you will lose. Are you going to abandon me with no brothers? I need you. And what of the children? You are the Uncle Twins!" The wagon moved away, leaving them exposed.

The twins ran to catch the wagon, leaving Enoch behind. "We have to stay with the weapons, Enoch," shouted Hazor. "Go home. We will see you in a few days. We promise."

Enoch saw other men from Manasseh. He ran to them, pleading, "Please, do not do this. Yahweh is not with you."

"Go home, you coward," growled one of his distant cousins.

Enoch caught up with Perez and Hazor, clutching their arms. They wrestled him gently but forcibly to the ground. Hazor sat on his knees. Perez sat on his chest and looked deeply into his elder brother's eyes. "We mean it, Enoch. We are not children playing in the paddock. Go home." They left

Enoch kneeling in the dust. The army, without rank or reason, flowed around him like water around a stone.

Enoch bellowed, "Yahweh is not with you!" He did not feel the blow to the back of his head.

Mordecai and Phinehas had followed Enoch. They gazed across the churned sand to a dusty smudge on the horizon. Phinehas said, "The army." His attention shifted. "Is that him?" The men ran to Enoch's prostrate body and turned him onto his back. Vomit matted his beard.

Phinehas pushed the beard aside and laid his ear on Enoch's chest. "He is alive. Wake up, Enoch. Enoch." Phinehas shook the unconscious man. "How are we going to get him home?" They rested on their knees.

"I know," said Mordecai. "Elias has a carriage. Can you wait here, and I will go get it?"

With the help of Elias' nephews, they bore Enoch home, slumped in the red box carriage. They laid him in his tent and sat with Rachel and his wives, watching while Jemimah lifted his eyelids, probed his head for wounds, and located the indention in his skull. "This poor man has had his head bashed. Probably with a rock."

"Will he live?" Rachel patted her brother's foot.

Jemimah studied Mordecai for a moment. "That depends on you."

"Me?"

"We need to drill a hole in his skull. To let out the blood. You see, there is no blood. The blood is on the inside. This is very bad."

"But why me?" said Mordecai.

"Because you have a delicate touch. And tools. No other reason," said Jemimah. "Go get a knife and a drilling tool. And a hammer. Go now."

A hammer? When Mordecai did not budge, five people shouted, "Go!"

First Jemimah shaved the indented wound. She took the knife and made a small cut in the scalp. "Here." She pointed. Mordecai placed his awl into the split skin, his hammer poised to strike.

He hesitated. "I am afraid I will kill my cousin." Rachel pulled her veil over her face.

"If we do not do this, he will surely die," said the old woman. "Trust me. I saw this done long ago. Not too deep. Just go through the bone." Taking a deep breath, then holding it, Mordecai struck the awl—thunk!—a sharp blow with his hammer.

Again Jemimah cut, three fingers away from the first hole. "Now here." Again Mordecai struck the awl with his hammer. "Now hold him upside down. Everyone, take hold." No one moved. Jemimah clapped her hands. "Upside down! Can you not hear me?" Grasping Enoch around his knees and waist, they held him upside down. Blood began to drip, then stream from the first hole. As the blood coagulated at the openings, Jemimah wiped it away with a wad of wet wool. With quivering muscles, the holders groaned in agony. At last the blood flow stopped. "Lay him down." Jemimah patted Mordecai on the knee. "You did very well, my son."

&

While Enoch slept, the doomed army went up to the ridge of the hill country. Neither the Ark nor Joshua went with them. The Amorites and the Canaanites who lived in those hills, came down and struck them and beat them down as far as a place called Hormah.

The next day, outside Enoch's tent, Rachel paced and wrung her hands, murmuring, "Oh my beautiful brothers. Where are you?" Word had spread from the few survivors that Hazor and Perez had fought well and died bravely. She refused to believe it. Any minute now they would come sauntering down the path. Feeling through the folds of her dress, she sought and found Ma'at, nestled in the pouch. *What good are you? Chaos reigns in this wilderness and you do nothing.* She wanted to rip the little goddess from her nest and throw her into the desert. Her thoughts turned to Yahweh. *You have taken all my brothers, save one, and he lies dying. Now we are denied the Promised Land.* Last, her thoughts moved to Moses. *I ask you the same question: What good are you? Can you not beg Yahweh to change his mind?*

Mordecai emerged from Enoch's tent. "He is talking."

Like a whirlwind on a straight course her mind could not change direction and take in the good news. "This makes no sense," said Rachel. She stopped pacing, stood with her fists on her hips and contemplated the cloud of Yahweh, bright white against a dark blue sky. "Why is this happening?"

His wife's mouth had settled into a straight line. Nothing he could say would pacify her. Besides, what could he say? She knew the reasons as well as he did. Was she blind? Was she deaf? The people had grumbled about the water and the manna, they had been greedy and ungrateful, they had threatened to stone Moses and Aaron on two different occasions. They had not trusted Yahweh to take the land for them; they had pridefully mustered an army after the blessing of Yahweh had been removed. He had sent punishments: by the sword, by plague, by fire. They had promised to trust and obey and had gone back on their word. Worst of all, they had set up the golden calf. Yahweh had forgiven them time and again at Moses' request. What was left for him to do? *Even an ignorant brick maker, can see it,* thought Mordecai. *Even a dung beetle...*

&

Tek jostled Reuel's shoulder and pointed three hand breadths above the horizon. "Look. Did I not tell you?" Against the distant sky, where it pales, vultures circled. "That has to be it."

Reuel shaded his eyes and nodded. "It's far." He continued the conversation whirling in his head: *don't worry, Aunt Rachel. I will be with Tek. He knows everything about the wilderness.* He would have said just that if he had told her where they were going. They were on a quest for battlefield artifacts: an ax, an arrowhead, a spear point—that's what Phinehas told Uncle Mordecai one day—a *quest for artifacts:* Reuel liked the sound of it.

"We have to go now," Tek had said after the morning meal, "while they're busy with Uncle Enoch. Aunt Rachel will think we're with Phinehas, and he'll think we're with her." Tek dropped a flint and striking stone into his pouch, inserted his sling into his belt, and threw his cloak over his shoulder. A water bag finished his preparations. He watched Reuel copy his every move. "You don't need much."

Accustomed to seeing the boys come and go, no one noticed as they marched down one path and another to the last tents of Manasseh. Leaving the Hebrew camps behind, they emerged into a valley of undulating hills. The settlement of Kadesh lay to the west. They headed north and climbed into foothills, hoping to spy the army's tracks. Climbing, working their way around the mountain, by noon they surveyed a settlement spread below. A thin string of smoke rose into the sky nearby. Crouching behind a boulder, they watched a gray-bearded shepherd who sat on a rock, tending his fire; the aroma of roast meat wafted by. A barking dog jumped onto the ledge above them, sending them to their knees.

Calling off the dog with a whistle, the man watched with narrowed eyes as the boys approached. "You are from that hoard of Hebrews camped across the valley. I saw you coming."

"We mean no harm," said Tek. *But if you do,* he mused, *I have my sling.* He noted the large black mole centered in the man's forehead.

"Sit." The shepherd motioned to the ground by the fire. Watching the shepherd closely, Tek hunkered, then Reuel followed.

"What is that place?" asked Tek, pointing to the village below.

"Hormah."

"Did you see the battle?" asked Tek.

"Battle?" The man snorted. He turned a skewered rabbit toward the fire. "That was no battle. That was a rout. I watched it from the other side of that outcropping." He pointed behind him then traced his finger into the sky. "See those vultures? Straight down."

"What happened?" asked Tek.

Adding a handful of sticks to his fire, the man looked toward the vultures. Pointing his staff as he spoke, he said, "Well, let me see. The Hebrews came over that hill on the other side of Hormah. They went down that hill over there into that wadi. See it? Then the Canaanites and Amorites had them trapped, you see?"

"What did they do?" Reuel spoke for the first time.

"Which ones?" The shepherd chuckled. When neither boy answered, he sobered and asked, "Was your father there?"

"Our uncles," said Tek. "They have not come home yet..."

"They will not be coming." The man studied the two boys, and gathering his thin, white beard into a wrinkled hand, twisted it into a point. His eyes softened. "Why are you here? You should go home." He tore the hindquarter off the rabbit, broke it into two pieces and held them out.

Hesitating, Reuel said, "We are not supposed to eat rabbit." He watched as Tek bit into the thick thigh meat. He took his portion. They ate, wiping juice from their chins and licked their fingers.

When they finished, the man said, "Word has it your god is powerful and defeated Pharaoh and the Amalek. He was not powerful enough to defeat the Canaanites and the Amorites."

Tek stood. "We will go down." He bowed to the shepherd. "Come, Reuel."

Reuel followed Tek toward the outcropping. *Aunt Rachel, I am sorry I ate the rabbit, but I hungered, and it was very good.* At the outcrop they began their descent, taking a well-worn path toward the mouth of the wadi. Encountering no one, by mid afternoon, they entered an opening in the cliff face. Neither spoke. They hugged narrow canyon walls, following the sound of loud chortling, hissing, and barking. Reuel's hand found its way into Tek's as the din echoed and increased. Steeling themselves, they peeked around a bend where hundreds of vultures flapped their wings and hopped from body to body, vying for dominance, ripping and tossing a mass of torn flesh and clothing. Breaking free of Reuel, Tek ran screaming toward them. He repeatedly loaded his sling, swung it, and before they could rise, knocked the pale, rose-colored heads off three buzzards. Then rise they did, in their hundreds, screeching, their dark gray wings beating the stench of death into the air. Both boys vomited the rabbit. An incessant buzzing filled their senses.

"What is that?" Tek looked up at the rough wall. Alive with flies, heads, their mouths drawn into grinning maws, had been wedged into vertical cracks. "The bodies have no heads!" His voice echoed, *heads, heads, heads.*

Reuel slid down the rough wall. *Aunt Rachel...*

Walking sideways along the walls, Tek peered at the faces, periodically launching a stone at a lowering bird. He shook Reuel's shoulder. "I have found your uncles, Perez and Hazor." Reuel reacted with a blank stare. "We have to get them. Get up." He pulled the younger boy to his feet. "Stand up. Look at this." Grasping Reuel's arm, Tek dragged him a short distance down the wadi. "Look at the teeth. The gap. It's one of them. The other one is over there." Reuel's eyes   shifted dully in the direction Tek pointed. "We have to get them," Tek repeated.

"Get them?"

"I will stand on your shoulders." Tek positioned Reuel close to the rock face. The small boy stood, bent knees shaking, while Tek climbed onto his shoulders. "I can reach him." Grasping the beard, Tek pulled. He and the head struck the ground. Their technique proving successful, the boys retrieved the other head. Tek spread his cloak on the ground, laid the heads on it and drew up the ends. "Get that end. I will take this end. Let's go." They staggered from the weight. The sound of many wings ushered them from the wadi into thin sunlight.

By dusk the boys had struggled up the hill, made their way past the overhang, and accompanied by the barking dog, once again came upon the shepherd. He shook his head. "I smelled you coming. I see you found your uncles. Put them downwind. Bury them in the sand. Maybe that will keep the ants off. I do not know about wolves. Or lions," he added.

"I will build a fire and sit with them. I have my sling," said Tek.

"The dogs will guard them. You bury." The boys did as they were told and buried the heads, cloak and all. The man emitted an intricate set of whistles, and soon another dog ran up. The shepherd stationed the two dogs and returned to the fire. "All I have is rabbit. I know you don't eat rabbit." He looked the boys over. "Maybe you could not eat a little just one more time." The shepherd poured water over their hands and motioned them to sit by his fire. They ate and slept under Reuel's cloak, unaware when the shepherd threw a sheepskin over them.

After a breakfast of more rabbit, the boys dug up the heads and bade their host goodbye. As they started around the hill, lugging their burden, he called after them, "Your aunt will not thank you. You should have stuck with artifacts."

By mid day the heads reeked and flies plagued. Tears tracked the dirt on Reuel's cheeks. Tek said, "Maybe the shepherd is right. Maybe we should bury the heads and tell Phinehas. See what he says." They buried the heads at the base of a large stone. Trailing the stench of death and their own swarm of flies through the camps, they made their way home.

Phinehas waited on the path, arms crossed. His lip curled; "What is that smell?" He checked the urge to embrace the boys, taking note of the flies and Reuel's tear-stained face. "We have looked everywhere for you." Reuel hunched his shoulders and clutched his tunic with both hands, blinking back tears. Phinehas relented, but willing to go no closer, patted the boy's shoulder. Then Tek told their tale.

Mordecai and Phinehas, ignoring the disdain of their neighbors, followed the boys to the rock. They dug up the heads and ascertained that they did indeed belong to Perez and Hazor. A groan rose from Mordecai's breast. "How can we go on without them?" Choosing a more secluded site, they reburied the heads and piled a pyramid of stones atop the small grave. "We will bring Rachel here tomorrow," said Mordecai. "She will be grateful to you. The shepherd was right in a way—she did not need to see her brothers, but he was wrong in another way—now she will know where her brothers are buried. That will be a comfort to her."

"I am proud of you both," said Phinehas. They washed with natron at the well, scrubbing the stench from the boy's clothes and their own.

Chapter 18

YAHWEH HAD NOT FORSAKEN HIS chosen people. His glory remained in the cloud and rested in the Tabernacle. The people had broken the covenant, but he would teach them his precepts. He would anchor them with holy days: the festivals of Passover; Unleavened Bread; First Fruits; Pentecost; Trumpets; Atonement; Tabernacles. He would teach them the proper sacrifices. Through Moses he would speak to them, and from the tribe of Levi, Aaron and his descendants would be his priests.

But rebellion festered in the tribe of Levi. From the three branches of that tribe, Yahweh chose one family to be priests in the Tabernacle: Aaron and his sons and their descendants. Upon pain of instant death, no one but they were allowed to lay eyes on the holy objects. The other branches packed the Tabernacle and carried it and all its parts from place to place. Prior to disassembling the Tabernacle, Aaron covered all the holy objects, thereby saving the lives of those who carried them, lest they see and perish.

Korah, a leader of Levi, galled that he could carry the holy objects but not view them, jealous of the priesthood, incited to rebellion, two men, Dathan and Abiram, of the tribe of Reuben. The three drew in 250 leaders of the congregation. As a body they rebelled against Moses and Aaron, proclaiming, "Yahweh has said we are a holy nation. If all the congregation is holy, why do you exalt yourselves?"

Moses prostrated himself before Yahweh. Then he addressed the rebels: "Tomorrow, all of you bring censors of incense and present fire before Yahweh." And they did. But Korah, Dathan and Abiram refused to go before Moses and stayed in the doorway of their tents. "They have taken the land of milk and honey from us," they accused, "why should we go to have Moses lord it over us?"

The congregation, fearful of Yahweh's wrath, watched the goings-on from afar, among them, Phinehas and Mordecai with the males of their families. As he craned his neck to see over the crowd, Phinehas felt a tug at his sleeve. "There is the priest who stole the shards," said Tek.

"It's him," Reuel agreed. They watched as the man strode across open ground and joined the people at Korah's tent.

Then Moses said to the congregation, "If these men die a natural death, then you will know Yahweh is not with me. But if Yahweh does a new thing and the ground opens its mouth and swallows them up, then you will know that these men have spurned Yahweh." Immediately the ground split and swallowed up Korah, Dathan and Abiram, their households, and all their possessions. The congregation stood with mouths agape then fled as one, lest they, too, be swallowed up. "We will be back," shouted Tek, running toward the camps with Reuel at his heels.

Phinheas called after them, "Where are you going?"

Over his shoulder, Reuel shouted with a grin, "To tell Shem what happened to the man who stole his shards." Phinehas watched them go, a grin spreading over his own face. *It is good,* he thought, *for them to see that the justice of Yahweh pours out on the great and satisfies the small.*

Then fire came forth and consumed the 250 men with their censors—those who had rebelled against Yahweh. Again, the people fled, but the next day they continued to congregate and grumble, accusing Moses and Aaron: "You are the ones who have caused the deaths of Yahweh's people." Then Yahweh sent a plague among the people. Aaron ran between the living and the dead with his censor and took a stand; Yahweh relented. In that plague, 14,700 people died, among them Jemimah's elder son, Nobah.

Jemimah never knew why Nobah died. "He was not rebellious. You all know that." She asked everyone she knew, "Why was he there?" As rushing water hones river rock, so sorrow and time wore Jemimah to her essence. At her end she had one thing left: her trust in Yahweh. One day she lay down and did not rise. "It is my time," she said, so they laid her on her sleeping mat and the family gathered. "Obey Yahweh," she said, "and do not be bitter. Teach the children his wonderful deeds, so when the time comes, they can receive the Promised Land." One by one they sat with her for a blessing.

To her daughters, she said, "You have made my heart glad all the days of my life. Even at the dying vats you were a support to me."

To Rachel she said, "Cling to Mordecai. He is like a tree planted by the water."

"Oh Mother, how can you leave me?"

"Rachel, would you keep me here to suffer? You must let go. Let go of me. Let go of Egypt and your old life. In the vizier's house you were a beloved slave, now your heart is divided."

"Mother, have I been so wrong?"

"Yahweh is your strength. Trust Him and Him only."

To Phinehas she said, "The places we have gone, the things we have seen and done, write it down. Yahweh is in it all."

The men hollowed a cave into the cliffs at Kadesh and buried Jemimah. The trill of mourning echoed among the hills.

&

A pall settled over the nation of Israel. Yahweh did not relent. He would cleanse his chosen people of the slave mentality born in their 430-year sojourn in Egypt. He would inculcate them with his laws, his ordinances, his holy days, designed to teach them his great interventions and blessings: Passover to remind them of his rescue, the Sabbath to give them rest.

Because of their unbelief, the great assembly of Hebrews remained at Kadesh in the Wilderness of Paran. There they dwelt, circling the mountain, spreading their flocks over the hills and valleys, centered by the Tabernacle, tethered to the pillar of Yahweh. Sometimes they camped a year, sometimes a month or two, following the cloud to fresh grazing, to the next well. The manna never ceased; their feet did not swell; nor did their clothes wear out.

For forty years Israel wandered, buried their dead, and mourned the loss of the Promised Land.

Book Two

Chapter 1

ZELOPHEHAD, A MAN OF MEANS, A MAN of the tribe, Manasseh, stood watching the women's tent from the shadowed recesses of his awning. Bitterness twisted his mouth as one by one his four daughters stepped through the door flap into the breaking dawn. *Not a male child among them,* he thought.

The pillar of fire had transformed to cloud. The sky behind it displayed a panoply of colors. Playing downward, a dome of purple faded to pale blue, then pale green, and low on the horizon, a strip of orange stretched above the dark mountain. The blue haze of dung smoke dulled the rising sun to the color of pomegranate. Few could name that color; no one had seen a fresh-plucked pomegranate in almost forty years. Dressed in black wool cloaks, the girls huddled a moment while Tirzah, the oldest at sixteen, established her authority and handed rose-colored, earthenware jars to her sisters. She straightened the smallest girl's hood. The cool night air would not linger. By the time they finished gathering the day's measure of manna, the cloaks would be a burden, the hoods thrown back.

The girls started down the path. Mordecai brushed past Zelo and fell in behind his granddaughters. They had strict orders not to leave the old man's sight. Long-legged Tirzah forced herself to accommodate her grandfather's slow pace. His limp grew worse by the day, but Nana said the walk did him good. They walked single file along the right side of a wide path, threading between the black tents of Manasseh, Tirzah first, then Milcha, nine, Mahlah, six, and last Hoglah, fourteen. Hoglah dropped back and grasped her grandfather's calloused hand as she did every morning. Was she not his favorite? Did his eyes not smile every time he looked at her? Everyone knew she was the most beautiful of the daughters, and except for her straight hair, the one who looked most like Nana.

In the women's tent, stooped under the low roof, Rachel moved about and banked the coals in the small fire pit. Judith, pregnant with her fifth child, rolled sleeping mats and piled them to the side of the spacious tent. "Go outside," said Rachel, "I will finish." She noticed her bags and baskets had been disturbed. *Mahlah has been meddling again,* she thought. She examined the pouch Asmath had given her so long ago. The mother of pearl disks rattled and reflected the light in rainbow colors, an irresistible fascination for her youngest granddaughter. Rachel could tell the child had not opened the pouch. She untied the cord at one end and took out the four remaining items: Asmath's mirror, the shell from the Red Sea, the shard from the Mountain of Yahweh and the goddess, Ma'at. She wondered if Ma'at had been kind to Asmath. Was her beloved mistress alive or dead? A grandmother herself?

Rachel remembered the morning she left Ramses. Asmath had emptied the pouch into her lap. How many times had they dipped into the pouch over the years? The amulet had bought the cook pot, the silver compact, another stud donkey after Goose died. The pearls had added quality to their lives in so many ways. As if it were yesterday she could see her mistress displaying the most precious items the pouch had contained—the gold combs inlaid with lapis lazuli. Rachel had given them to Kore the first time she left with Tek.

&

When Enoch was injured, Sarah renewed her determination to deny Kore a betrothal within the family. She added to her argument that with each passing year, the girl looked less Hebrew. Rachel secretly agreed. Kore's skin darkened; her hair had an unusual texture. Yet Rachel never admitted what she knew in her heart—her baby bird was not a partridge, but an indigo bird—one that lays its egg in another's nest. No betrothal had been arranged.

They had known Tek would take her away someday. Had he not declared his intentions to Enoch when he was just a boy? He would wait for Kore to grow up, and he would marry her. He never wavered. Rachel remembered the day they stood hand in hand before Mordecai and asked if they could marry. Kore, fifteen, tall and straight, had looked boldly into her father's eyes and had said, "I love him, Papa." And Tek, twenty, his Bedouin nose now a full-formed beak, his gaze piercing, had said, "I will take care of her all my life."

But what do they know of life? Rachel had thought. Kore, raised as a Hebrew, a child of tents and flocks; Tek, a Bedouin, with a faraway look in his eyes. "It is against Hebrew law to marry a foreigner," she had said. "Tek, we love you, but you are not Hebrew. Would you have Kore give up her inheritance?"

Kore and Tek exchanged a look. "What inheritance, Mama? I am not betrothed. I know the truth. You know the truth. Tek and I have always been a match. Yahweh is still my God. Tek is my husband. Would you have me be a widow before I am married?"

"Who would you trust more to take care of her?" Mordecai had said to Rachel. "Certainly not me with my tent pole." They had laughed and Rachel had given her blessing. Now she rattled the disks just to hear the

182

tender, sentimental sound. *Did I have a choice? No. With no betrothal, Tek was her one chance for happiness.*

So they had married. Never had two people been more suited. Then Tek bought an unbroken camel and began to train it. He inspected every caravan that came along, until one day he found a head driver, a man named Suli, whom he trusted. With no time to tarry, family and friends donated food and goods for trade and piled the parcels near the camel. Kore's cousins loaded water bags.

Rachel led her daughter into their own dark tent where Judith, twelve, sat alone, sobbing. "Things will never be the same without my sister," she said.

"Judith, Sister," Kore said, embracing the girl, "I will come back and I will bring you a present."

Rachel opened the pouch and took out the combs. Pressing them into Kore's hands, she said, "Do not keep these for my sake. Save them until a dire need arises—and someday it will. This is your inheritance."

Family and friends followed Tek and Kore to the meeting place and watched the single-file procession of sixty grunting camels, heading west, their dark drivers dressed in white robes and head cloths. Tek mounted, helped Kore onto the saddle, and pulled his camel into line. Kore turned and waved many times, an east wind carrying her veil high into the air. By the time a mirage swallowed her baby bird, Rachel, Mordeai and Phinehas stood alone, shielding their eyes against the sun.

"I knew that boy could not be tamed." The words echoed in her memory, but she could not remember which one said it.

They would not see the two again for three years. One day Rachel looked up and Kore stood framed in the tent door, a dark Bedouin woman, an apparition in white robe and veil. Rachel fainted. "I thought you were dead," she said. Since then there had been other visits, brief and bittersweet. For twenty years they had traveled with the caravan. There had been no children. Rachel said the rolling gait of the camel killed them before they started.

&

Tirzah led her sisters down a side path toward her favorite spot for gathering manna. She noticed Great Uncle Enoch had penned several baby goats. He had tied a string around the neck of one with a twisted ear, the flaw making it unacceptable for sacrifice. She had raised a baby goat once, but it was perfect and Papa had taken it to the Tabernacle for sacrifice. She had cried.

Enoch rounded his tent and called, "Tirzah, I've been waiting for you." He picked up the kid with his good arm, shuffled to the fence and held it out. You can have this one if you want it."

She stroked the tight whorls on the kid's face. "I'll ask Mama. I'll be back. Thank you, Uncle Enoch." Great Uncle Enoch was the kindest person she knew. Nana said he had been a judge but was injured long ago and had never been the same. Although in his sixties, his hair and beard had never gone gray, but one side of his face sagged and his left leg dragged. Now he tended the goats confined to the paddock.

They passed the pens where a cousin raised turtle doves for sacrifice. Mahlah whined to stop. "For a little bit." Tirzah said. Maybe Gershon and Gideon, twins, eighteen, would catch up to them. Gershon, the best looking of all Uncle Enoch's twenty-four grandsons, had long been betrothed to Tirzah, Gideon to Hoglah. They had been in the hills with the goats; but Tirzah heard the brothers had finished their turn. With so many grandsons, work had to be rationed among them. Some shepherded the flocks of other families; several worked for her father since he had no sons.

Tirzah tugged her sister into motion. "Come on Mahlah. Mama said no lagging. We have to get back or Papa will be upset." She would never forget the time Hoglah sprained her ankle, and the manna had melted on the way home. They walked steadily until they reached a stretch of clean ground where manna spread white and thick and hundreds of children bent to the task of filling their containers. Working steadily, the girls filled their jars. Mahlah whined in earnest now, adding tears.

"Give me your jar." Tirzah handed her sister's jar to Mordecai. "I told Mama you were too young to come, but she said you are not too young, and if Mama says so, that's that." Tirzah knew her mother, great with child, needed a rest from Mahlah. Who could blame her? Mahlah had been the spoiled baby of the family for too long. That would end soon.

Milcha stopped. "Quail eggs."

"We'll get them. Nana will be pleased." Tirzah nestled thirteen eggs in Milcha's hood with orders, "Do not bend over.". Mordecai grinned. If thirteen eggs made it to Rachel's cook pot, he would be surprised. One of his greatest joys lay in this morning ritual with his granddaughters. He knew Hoglah thought of herself as his favorite, but what the harm? His heart lay at Tirzah's feet. Of all the girls she alone had her grandmother's hair and ways.

Judith left her mother to her chores and sat with a groan by the large family fire pit. Zelo crossed from the men's tent and threw a double handful of dried dung on the coals. He sat and tapped his feet on the ground, a vain attempt to wake up his increasingly numb feet. An old yellow dog gave the man wide berth and laid its head in Judith's lap. "It is time for that dog to go," he said.

"Papa will decide when the dog goes. It's his dog. Maybe the baby will come before we move again."

Through one slitted eye, Zelophehad examined his wife. Her heavy breasts rested on her belly and her belly on her knees. The baby stretched against the taut tunic—*another girl, no doubt.* She pushed her hands into the small of her back, dislodging the dog. *Still comely, at thirty-nine,* he thought. *If this is another girl, she will have to try again.*

"The grass is good here," he said, "I do not expect us to move anytime soon."

"Whether the baby has come or not, moving is always hard." The baby shifted. She brightened. "This baby moves like a boy." The twin boys would be two years old if they had lived. She did not blame Zelo for his bitterness. "Maybe it will be a boy this time."

Maybe, maybe, he thought. He had long since despaired of getting a boy. *There is something wrong with my wife. The boys born dead; the girls thrive. Something very wrong.* The first boy had been his dead brother's child. That had not been so bad; who wanted a weakling like Reuel for a son? But the others—*my sons...*

Judith stroked the dog's muzzle. "He does not follow the girls anymore."

"They have Mordecai. Why do they need a dog?"

Rachel heard the remark but decided not to confront her son-in-law. He would take his ire out on Judith or the girls. Since Reuel's death and Judith's marriage to Zelo, sorrow had settled upon Rachel's heart. Day by day she had watched the man kill her daughter's spirit. With the birth of each daughter, he had grown more petulant, blaming Judith and Yahweh equally for his bad luck. Four sons had died. Sometimes Rachel wondered what Yahweh was thinking, but Mordecai said that wondering was not trusting. "Here comes the manna," she said. Milcha turned and walked backwards toward her grandmother. "Eggs. Oh, are you not a clever girl?"

The dull red sun rose a hand span into the sky and turned orange, then yellow. It would be a hot day. A breeze blew away the morning smoke.

In many ways, almost forty years of wandering, moving, and setting up camp had taken a toll on Rachel. Still handsome at fifty-five, desert wind and unforgiving sun had coarsened her skin. The veil had spared her hair, now streaked with white. Her luminous dark brown eyes had faded to hazel. *What would I do for a little garden,* she often thought. *Rooted plants. Rooted feet.* Sometimes she wanted to give up, but she could not leave Judith alone with Zelo.

Chapter 2

RACHEL BUSIED HERSELF ROLLING UP the sides of the tent. *Not a breeze to be had,* she thought. *How can Judith rest in this heat?* Tirzah's head appeared under an open side. "Nana, Kore and Tek are here." The mat unrolled from Rachel's hand. Agile as a girl, she crossed the tent and ducked under. She hugged Tirzah as if the girl herself had brought Kore home, then struck out for Phinehas' compound.

Kore, deeply bronzed, tall and stately in her white Bedouin robe and veil, held out her arms to receive her mother. "I thought it better to stay here," she laughed, "I did not want you to faint."

Rachel buried her face in her daughter's neck and relaxed into the strong embrace. Following their tradition, she said, "You smell of camel." Holding her hands, pushing Kore to arms length, Rachel assessed the effects of two years. Only thirteen years younger than herself, age did not seem to touch her lovely daughter. Her brow unlined, her eyes, with only a few wrinkles, seemed to focus in the distance; *from years of gazing across the wide desert,* Rachel thought.

"Aunt Rachel!" Rachel whooped as Tek's strong arms swung her around.

"Stop, you kidnapper," she squealed, raising a belly laugh from her beautiful Bedouin son-in-law. Tek's hawk nose dominated his dark face. With each visit, Rachel noticed his kind eyes grew more wary. "Here comes Papa." It seemed all Manasseh must greet Kore and Tek before they settled under Phinehas' awning. The children had come to expect camel rides. Tek, good natured, obliged them, then removed the finery, bells and fringes from the camels and turned them into Enoch's sturdy paddock. Phinehas' sons killed a lamb and enlarged the fire pit to accommodate a sizable gathering. Kore and Tek brought flour, spices, and gifts.

On every visit, the travelers had to tell where they had been and what adventures they had experienced. Rachel always suspected they removed from their tales any dangers they had faced. "You tell it," Kore said to Tek.

"No, you. You are a better story teller," he said. So Kore began:

"You will not believe where we have been..." she paused.

"This is what makes her better," said Tek.

"...to the Promised Land!" Murmurs of wonderment sufficed for everyone but Rachel.

"By *yourselves?* That is too dangerous."

Mordecai gave Rachel a look. "Let her tell it."

"Mama, we are in a caravan of eighty-five camels. We are safe. We have never been that far north, but we went all the way to Damascus, on the far side of Canaan." Rachel covered her mouth with both hands.

"You saw the Promised Land?" asked Mordecai, avoiding Rachel's look.

"We did," said Tek. "From Damascus we came south by way of Canaan. And all the stories Joshua and Caleb told are true. There are beautiful hills and valleys and vineyards and flocks."

Phinehas spoke up. "What about the fierce tribes and giants?"

"We did not see a single giant," said Kore.

"Did you see the milking honey?" asked Mahlah, saddened by the laughter that followed her question.

Kore grabbed the girl and tickled her soundly. "We did see the milking honey, and I brought you a jarful."

"Most of the cities are large and fortified," said Tek. "just as the spies reported. But the ones we saw—I know we could have taken them with Yahweh's help." Silence fell over the listeners. Those who had been there remembered how the crowd rejected Yahweh and his help.

"We have a surprise for you," said Shelah. Old now, but spry, she dashed into Phinehas' tent and brought out a scroll the length of a man's arm, made of sheepskin, attached to intricately carved dowels. She handed it to Tek.

"Who did this?" he asked, stroking the butter-soft sheepskin, running his hands over the handles.

"Your father, Phinehas himself, tans the hides and writes the words. Mordecai carved the wood and does the painting." she said.

Phinehas, gray and bent, shrunken to a tiny husk, had always thought of Shelah as his young bride. Now he spoke up proudly. "Shelah makes the paint." Tek stroked the length of the scroll.

"Unroll it," said Phinehas. It is not delicate. Unroll it all the way to the right." With Kore and children looking over his shoulder, Tek unrolled the scroll, rolling up the left dowel as he went. At the beginning he revealed pyramids, and palm trees, and water birds, and a blue river, interspersed with writing. "It is our story," said Phinehas.

"It's Egypt," Kore marveled. We have been there. This paint. How did you do it?"

"Making paint is not difficult. A little oil, a little ground up rock, a little dye." said Shelah.

Tek continued to unroll: deserts and mountains, the sea divided, smoke rising from the Mountain of Yahweh, the Tabernacle, desert vistas, caravans, until he came to blank sheepskin. "Our story is not yet finished," said Phinehas.

They celebrated into the night with tambourines and dancing. At the end of the evening Abigail played her lute. Kore retired to Rachel's tent and sat talking with her mother while Judith, exhausted by the long day, and the girls slept.

"How is Judith, really?" asked Kore. After Rachel told of Zelo's worsening behavior, she said, "I know someone who would do away with him for a price."

"I am trusting Yahweh to take care of Zelophehad. Now, daughter, I want the truth for once. Are you safe?"

"Oh, Mama. We are safe for now, but Suli is old, and his son hates Tek. Before long we will have to find a new caravan or come home for good. I would like that, but I do not know if Tek could live this life."

"I have never asked. Do you still have the combs?"

"I do. The dire event has never happened. Yet."

"I hope it never does."

The next morning the camels chewed their cuds as Tek dressed them in their finery and loaded them. "They seem to know how beautiful they are," said Rachel.

"I don't like camels. They spit," said Tirzah.

Kore linked her arm in Tirzah's and walked her to the smaller cream-colored camel. "This is Kizia. I raised her from birth. Whenever she spit she got a tap on the nose. It is safe to pet her." Tirzah sank her fingers into the wiry hair. "She is my baby. Is she not lovely?" said Kore.

When the long caravan passed, heading south to Midian, a gap opened for Tek and Kore near the front. Milcha informed everyone that they went in at eighteen and nineteen.

How many times can a heart break? thought Rachel. Once again she, Mordecai and Phinehas stood alone until the caravan disappeared over a hill. *Watch over them, Yahweh, watch over my baby bird.*

Chapter 3

Z ELO LED THE DONKEY, PULLING MORDECAI'S ancient cart, to the men's tent and flopped down in the shade. *If only I had sons to help me,* he thought. Mordecai kept the cart repaired, but he could no longer haul stones, and his wife wanted to enlarge the fire pit. He removed his wide, tooled leather girdle, his most treasured possession, given to him as a wedding gift by Phinehas. The thing made him sweat, but it was a girdle fit for a Pharaoh. He stretched out under the awning for his afternoon nap. He woke to Mahlah's singing, and watched as she made a toy hop along to the rhythm of the tune. "What have you got there, Mahlah?" The girl held out an object he had never seen. He turned it over in his hand. Jade. A little naked woman carved out of jade, with breasts, and a feather on her head. His hair prickled.

"Where did you get this, Daughter?" he asked in a level tone. The little girl raised her shoulders, clutching her hands under her chin. "It's all right. I'm not angry. Where did you get it?"

"In Nana's pouch."

"I do not think you are supposed to have it. Go put it back." Mahlah plucked the tiny woman from his hand and ran into the women's tent. *An idol! Rachel has an idol in my tent. Where would she have gotten such a thing? How long has she had it? Such a secret to keep…*

Wide awake now, Zelo wondered if Judith knew her mother had an idol. *In my tent.* He had to admit he knew very little about idols, having never seen one. He supposed people worshiped them or asked favors from them, or maybe thanked them for good fortune, much like they did with Yahweh. Had he not asked Yahweh for a son again and again? He had not had much luck, had he? His mind churned. *Abomination! This is a bad thing. A very bad thing. Yahweh could get angry and punish the whole family.* Had he not forbidden graven images? His heart surged, reddening his face. *Maybe he already has punished us.* Did the son by Reuel not die? And the next son? And the twins? Why did he have nothing but girls, shaped like that idol? Was he the only one upset about having no sons? Women. They had their hair to braid, their secrets, their satisfied, rolling eyes. *Maybe the idol killed the male babies…Yahweh or the idol—someone is killing my sons!*

In the women's tent, Mahlah hovered over Rachel's bags. "What are you doing Mahlah?"

Rachel stood over the girl. Mahlah dropped the pouch. "Go help Tirzah." The girl cringed past her grandmother. *You are not as sorry as you should be,* thought Rachel, and she gave the girl a sound thump on the head.

&

Judith leaned across her belly and pulled the comb through Tirzah's hair. It seemed to Judith her belly grew bigger by the minute. Maybe this would be a boy after all. How happy Zelo would be. With no son, his line would die with him, and his portion would fall to other members of Manasseh, to Enoch's sons. The girls would marry within the family, according to Hebrew law, so they would be taken care of no matter what. *But oh, Yahweh, what a blessing a boy would be.* "Ouch, Mama!" Jolted from her reverie, Judith contemplated the top of Tirzah's head. Her comb had hit a snag of gigantic proportions. Like her grandmother Rachel, the girl had wool instead of hair. Defeated, Judith said, "Mama, can you finish Tirzah? I am about worn out."

"Let me finish Hoglah. I'm almost done." The Sabbath meant the oiling and combing of hair. Rachel insisted all the girls have perfect hair for Yahweh's meal.

Taking her leave, Judith said, "Tirzah, do not move. The sun is getting low." She stepped through the tent door and spied an open-weave basket with a tiny black body inside. "Tirzah!" she called.

"I'm not moving, Mama. Much."

"Well, move yourself out here." Tirzah appeared at the door, hair a-frizz. Judith stabbed her finger at the basket. "What is this?"

"Oh, Uncle Enoch...I was going to ask you first."

"Well, get it out. Let's look at it."

Tirzah bent to the basket, opened it and took out the tiny kid. "It's an orphan, Mama. And look, it has a twisted ear. Papa will not sacrifice it. Uncle Enoch said I could have it and raise it. Can I Mama?"

"If it's a female you can keep it." She knew Enoch would not give the girl a male kid.

"It is, Mama. Thank you, Mama."

"Go get your hair done. It's almost sunset." Judith took the kid and rocked it from side to side. "You are just a little baby, aren't you?" Judith knew the mothering instinct had awakened in Tirzah. *It is beginning,* she thought. *Time for her to marry. What are we going to do?* Tirzah had said she would not marry until she set foot in the Promised Land. *Where did she get such a notion?* So far, Gershon had agreed. But would he continue to cooperate with this willful girl? Would her father?

The Sabbath. From sundown on the sixth day until sundown on the seventh, the people rested. As Yahweh had rested from six days of creation, so they rested. No gathering of fire wood. No work. No cooking. Yahweh had blessed the seventh day and declared it holy. At sundown, they would eat the Sabbath meal. The double portion of manna, gathered that morning, would carry them through the night until sundown the next day.

Like the lowing of cattle at evening, the great congregation of Israel settled and quieted at sundown on the Sabbath. No loud noise could be heard in all the camps. Rachel and Judith smoothed the floor mats and spread linen cloths, precious keepsakes woven by Jemimah. Zelophehad and Mordecai sat cross-legged across from one another, joined by the girls. The women placed platters of food on the cloths, manna prepared several ways and the quail eggs, and then they sat, completing the circle.

According to rituals developed since Yahweh had given the Ten Commandments, Mordecai said the Sabbath blessing: "Blessed are you, Yahweh, our God, ruler of the universe, who brings bread out of the earth."

Rachel said a blessing for female children: "May Yahweh make you as Sarah, Rebekah, Rachel, and Leah." She raised her head, unsettled to find Zelo, who had neither closed his eyes nor bowed his head, staring coldly in her direction. Breaking his gaze, he wrapped a manna cake around some mush, and resuming his stare, ate it. Mordecai dipped in, then the women and girls.

In keeping with the solemn occasion, Mordecai allowed the girls to speak at the Sabbath meal, but he did not allow them to jabber. He welcomed anyone to express thanksgiving for Yahweh's blessings over the week. Mahlah proudly announced, "Uncle Enoch gave Tirzah a baby goat."

"Mahlah," Tirzah objected, "that's my praise."

"I found the quail eggs," said Milcah.

"Yahweh showed you to the quail eggs," said Mordecai. And so it went around the circle.

"I have a praise," Zelo announced. Rachel and Judith, eyebrows raised, exchanged looks. The girls stopped chewing. Mordecai suspended his reach for another helping.

"Yahweh showed me something, too. A secret." He pinned Rachel with a level gaze.

Rachel grew hot. She stifled the urge to fan her veil. Still the man stared. "What would that be, Zelophehad?"

"Someone," he paused, "has brought an idol into my tent."

Mordecai followed Zelo's stare straight to Rachel. His wife had turned white. She was going to faint. He knew all the signs. "Rachel!" He was on his feet before she crumpled into Milcha's lap. Zelo remained seated, watching the hubbub, his hands resting on his knees.

The girls had been put to bed. Rachel, arm thrown over her eyes, lay on her sleeping mat fully clothed. She knew her ordeal had just begun. Judith knelt by her mother's side. "What is he talking about, Mama?"

"Did you never look in my pouch, Judith?" Of course she had not. Judith had been, of all children, the most obedient. *But that Mahlah...* "When I left Asmath, she gave me a little idol. I've had it ever since. Go get my pouch. I'll show it to you."

"I do not want to look upon it."

"How like your father you are." At the door Mordecai cleared his throat. "Speak of him and there he is. Go get the pouch. You do not have to look." Rachel gathered her strength. She and Judith joined a silent Mordecai and followed him to the men's tent where Zelo waited cross-legged under the awning. The three sat opposite. *We look like scolded children*, thought Rachel. She squared her shoulders, narrowing her eyes at her son-in-law.

A familiar voice said, "I heard a commotion during the Sabbath meal. What is the matter here?" Phinehas stood peering from beneath quizzical eyebrows, bushy with age. After Enoch's injury, Phinehas' ability to write propelled him into the judgeship and established him as a leader in Manasseh. He leaned on his staff, taking in the scene.

"This is none of your business," said Zelo.

Mordecai pointed to the mat. Phinehas eased down behind Judith, who slumped in submission, for once allowing him a clear view. To Zelo, he said, "Pay me no mind."

Ma'at had warmed in Rachel's closed hand. She laid the idol on the mat, equidistant from herself and Zelo. The little woman seemed to glow in the dim light. All eyes focused on her; Phinehas leaned over Judith, peering through rheumy eyes.

"What is it?" asked Mordecai.

"I suppose it is an idol," said Rachel.

"You suppose?" said Zelo. Rachel had come to hate the scoff inherent in almost everything he said.

"It is an idol. Asmath gave it to me the day I left Ramses."

"And you kept it," said Zelo, triumph reverberate in his voice.

"I never worshiped it." *Even though I did consult it*, she thought. *From time to time...*

"Why did you keep it?" Mordecai asked, as if to say, *are you a fool?*

Judith stood suddenly, barely making it to the sand before vomiting her Sabbath meal. Rachel embraced her daughter. "Go to bed. I will be there soon." Seating herself, she addressed Zelo. "Your wife is about to have a child." *Another girl*, she thought, *you wretched man.* "She does not need this upset."

"The upset lies at your feet."

"I kept it, Husband, because it was a gift from my dear friend whom I loved."

"You love the idol," said Zelo. "If it was so innocent why did you keep it a secret?"

"I do not love the idol. It was just a gift. A keepsake." How could she explain? *Can I not have just one thing that is all my own, not fingered by anyone else, not considered a trade item?*

Zelo stabbed his finger at the idol. "This," he said, "is the reason I have no sons. This is the reason I only get dead sons." He spit on the idol.

"No!" bellowed Mordecai.

"Do you not see, Zelo," said Rachel, "You are the one giving power to the idol, not me."

"Maybe she does it herself, or maybe she has brought a curse from Yahweh. I do not know." His opponents gasped.

Phinehas spoke. "Give the idol to me. I will dispose of it."

Zelo snatched up the idol and closed his fist. "I will see to this abomination. I may take it to Moses."

"Now, Zelo," said Phinehas, "I am a judge. Do you not trust me to get rid of it?"

"When I was a boy, you threatened to break my arm just for throwing a rock at your beloved cat. My father called you a worm. I trust his judgment."

"But, Zelo, that was long, long ago." said Mordecai.

"And you are a talking bird. See, I forget nothing."

"You are Jabus' son," said Mordecai. "Maybe that is the reason Yahweh does not give you sons. He wants no more like you on this earth."

"We will see what Moses says." With that, Zelo rose and left them.

Mordecai pondered. "I should not have said that."

"But there may be truth in it," said Phinehas. He peered around the side of the tent. "He turned onto the path to the latrine."

"Maybe he's going to throw it in," said Rachel.

"I doubt that," said Phinehas.

"What are we going to do?" She wanted to wail. Unconsciously mimicking Ethan's mannerism, she laced her fingers and squeezed her palms together.

"Watch him." said Phinheas. "See what he does. Let's go to bed."

Judith had not slept. Rachel sat beside her. "Mama, I am so sorry I brought this curse on our family." Rachel knew she meant Zelo.

"None of this is your fault," said Rachel. *Is it your fault our wonderful Reuel died? Is it your fault a widow must marry her dead husband's brother? Is it your fault Zelo is such a horrible man?* Without warning, her voice broke through her thoughts: "He was a horrible boy."

"Was he, Mama?"

"Horrible. Yes. I wish that scorpion had bitten him instead of his sweet brother. I have thought of putting one in his bed."

"You have not."

"No." They grew thoughtful. Reuel had waited so long for Judith to grow up. His patience astounded everyone. Married less than a year... Many people had been bitten by scorpions. It seemed the vile creatures lived under every rock. But Reuel—his foot swelled, then his leg, to twice its size, and his fever could not be tamed. He had suffered until everyone, even Judith, wished for his death. Then Zelo had appealed to a judge of high rank, demanding his right to marry his brother's widow.

Judith had miscarried after one night with Zelo. Rachel would never forgive him. The baby had been a boy—Reuel's son. Mordecai had beaten Zelo senseless and they refused to allow him to keep Judith in his tent. Instead, Zelo moved into their compound where he festered, no less poisoned than his dead brother. Mordecai gained control over the man, although he continued to demand his rights with Judith. Now the fifth baby was due any day.

Rachel drew her daughter to her bosom. "Don't worry. I am not going to leave you. Papa is not leaving you. We will work it all out somehow. Phinehas will help us."

Chapter 4

BEHIND THE SCREEN AT THE MEN'S latrine, Zelo relieved himself with a powerful stream. Grinning with satisfaction, he kicked sand over the wet spot. He marveled. Gone, the low urgent aching, the dribbling, the burning pain. Completely gone. No wonder Rachel had kept Little Green Woman. He chuckled. Did he not ask her to heal him and did she not do it? The idol nestled in a secret pocket on the underside of his leather girdle. His constant fingering made a greasy smear where the small body made an imperceptible rise on the tooled side.

An uneasy truce had settled over Mordecai's family. Zelo's zeal to accuse Rachel before Moses seemed to have cooled. "Maybe he took pity on me and smashed the idol," Rachel had said to Mordecai.

"Do not question or anger him. Just stay in your tent."

"I will not cower in fear of my daughter's husband."

"Well then, fear Moses and his ordinances, as I do."

"I think he has changed his mind."

"Only for as long as it suits him. He is a snake, loose in the tent."

Moses and the ordinances, thought Rachel. *"You shall not allow a sorceress to live."' Did Moses not proclaim those words? Is idol worship the same as sorcery?"* Rachel did not know. *But I did not worship the idol,* she thought. In her innermost self, she knew she had talked to Ma'at and consulted her. *Yahweh must know it, too. Of that I am guilty. Shall I be stoned for that? But I did not make sacrifices. I did not bow down!* Maybe her hatred for Zelo had awakened the idol. Zelo created chaos and Ma'at fought against chaos. Did she kill his sons? *I hate the man, but I would never wish the death of his sons. Oh, Yahweh, I did not bow down.*

"What's the matter, Mama? Do you have a headache?"

"Yes. I am going to lie down. See if you can keep Mahlah off me."

Finding no company inside the tent, Judith joined Tirzah under the awning. The baby goat sprawled limply across the girl's lap. Judith sat and said, "Here, let me hold her. Is she sick?"

"She will not stand up. I took her to a nanny goat, but she would not nurse."

"She's hot. Let's take her to Enoch and see what he says. Help me up."

Zelo watched his wife and daughter head off to Enoch's paddock. Enoch and his sons had prospered with flocks and more sons. Gershon and Gideon had been betrothed to Tirzah and Hoglah, good matches for his daughters. But Tirzah refused to marry until she reached the promised land. *What nonsense. I know a young man richer than Gershon who would marry her today.*

*All I have to do is go to a judge and say, Gershon has shown no willingness to marry. Maybe there is something wrong with him...*He stroked the rise in his girdle. *What do you think I should do, Little Green Woman?* Lost in his ruminations, Zelo did not notice smoke rising from Enoch's compound.

"Fire!" shouted Mordecai. "Zelo, get the women's water jug. I'll take ours." The men gathered water jugs and mats and headed for Enoch's tents. Neighbors ran carrying water and mats for beating out the fire, but water and mats and willing neighbors could not help Enoch and his sons.

A hundred onlookers stood in silence with Enoch at his paddock, watching acrid smoke rise from a mound of burning goats. As if alive, the pyre moved and shifted, legs thrusting, bellies bursting, tails curling upward. Enoch leaned heavily on his staff, supported by his second wife, Hannah. The stench of burning hair gave way eventually to the aroma of roast goat, then to the smell of charred meat. Enoch, his sons, and his grandsons had cut the throat of every goat, piled them in the center of the paddock, and set them ablaze. On a hillside far away, other sons had done the same with the herd in the field.

Tirzah stood stone-faced with her mother. Gershon had taken the baby goat from the girl's arms and turning his back, killed it. He laid it on the far side of the pile away from Tirzah's view. Zelo joined his wife and daughter. "What of our herd?" asked Judith.

"The ones on the hill are mingled. They are lost. The ones in the paddock may be safe."

A breeze came up, twisting the smoke high into the air. *Maybe the wind will carry the plague away from us,* thought Julia. Yahweh had promised He would not put the plagues of Egypt on them if they would trust Him. If only they had…

A priest, an emissary from Moses, set up a small tent and camped near Enoch. Every day he examined the surrounding flocks. His presence added to the dread and fear, but so far no other flock showed signs of infection. Word had gone out: no flock should be moved from its present location. Further, the tribes of Israel would remain in place.

Four days passed. Under a bright blue sky, Zelo leaned on his woven brush fence and watched Enoch's grandsons fill the water troughs. Enoch's five sons had so many sons he put them to work among his relatives and neighbors. Two had been assigned to Mordecai's and Zelo's paddock and four to their herd in the hills. Needing the help, but shamed by having no sons of his own, Zelo chafed under this favor. Even that little worm, Phinehas had sons. His brother's wife, Abigail, had brought two and made three more for Phinehas. Once Shelah got started, she produced five. *Now that the Little Green Woman belongs to me,* he thought, *this new baby is bound to be a son.* He exulted in the thought: *Redemption is coming.* Suddenly, as he stood there musing, a fat ewe—his best ewe, hugely pregnant—collapsed to her knees.

"Jotham! Achim! Check that ewe." Before the boys, shocked and pale, turned to face him, he knew what they would say. His knees buckled. He sat by the fence. *What have I done to deserve this*, he thought. *Enoch has sons to help him rebuild his wealth. That's where a man's strength, his wealth, really lies—in sons. Now I will not even have goats.*

Enoch found his nephew sitting by the paddock fence. He wanted to kick the man, but pity gentled his voice. "Zelo, we have work to do."

"Let Yahweh burn his own goats." Zelo brushed off his knees and walked away.

Enoch had watched his own sons and grandsons cut the throats of goats they had raised from kids. They had burned their inheritance. They had shed tears, but none had questioned or railed against Yahweh. They knew their father would not tolerate disrespect. Had they not been taught from childhood?

Mordecai limped to the paddock carrying his knife and strop. Phinehas and his sons joined Enoch's sons and they set about slaughtering the confined herd, mostly ewes and newborns.

Days passed. No new infection showed among the surrounding herds. At last the priest declared the plague over, rolled up his tent and returned to Moses. The question remained: why had the plague struck only the flocks of Ethan and Mordecai?

Chapter 5

KORE ALWAYS CRIED WHEN SHE left her mother and father. And so her tears did not surprise or dismay Tek. He allowed her sorrow to have its way. After several days, she would focus her eyes on the horizon, and her heart would come back to him. For twenty years this had been the way of it.

They had left Kadesh in the Wilderness of Paran and headed south, taking the route through the Arabah, a wide, barren valley that lay south of the Dead Sea between tall mountains. With stops along the way they headed for Elat where the Sea of Reeds meets the shore. Wrapped against the unforgiving sun and desert wind, Tek and Kore sometimes traveled half a day without speaking. At night they built a fire, unloaded the camels, and hobbled them nearby. They joined friends for story telling or singing then slept under the stars or under a simple tent. They had few possessions: water bags, sleeping mats and warm covers making the bulk of it, with a few cook pots. They carried trade goods and bundles of hay for the camels. At forty, Kore struggled with the morning's loading of Kizia, tying ropes with cold fingers, balancing the load. It had to be done correctly, or throughout the day, the camels would grumble and complain with loud groans. Kore had begun to wonder how much longer she could hold up. Her joints ached. During the cold hours of morning, they walked beside their camels, mounting after the sun heated up. Only then did she find relief. She found herself dreaming of her mother's tent, of the laughter of her nieces, of manna.

On the eighth day out, Kizia lowered her head and began to drool and grunt. Kore and Tek dropped back in line repeatedly, motioning other riders around, until finally, they brought up the rear. When they stopped for the day the beast collapsed heavily. Panicked, Kore forced the animal's mouth open, raised her eyelids, checked for ticks in her ears, lifted her tail. Diarrhea. Too sick to flick her tail, flies buzzed. Kore threw a mat over Kizia's rear end and paced. "She's sick. She refuses to drink. She will not take a date from my hand." Tek stood watching with his arms crossed, not commenting. Kore waited. "Well, what do you think? Say something."

Tek laid his hand on the soft, velvety muzzle. "She has fever." He scratched between Kizia's ears. The camel huffed wetly and rolled onto her side. Kore began to cry. She sat and took the lovely head onto her lap, crooning, begging her pet to be well. Tek said, "We will wait until morning and see." He built a fire close by and lay down, but sleep would not come. Finally, he sat with his back to Kore's and listened to the camel's heavy breathing. He watched the stars traverse the black sky and prayed, as Mordecai had taught him so long ago. He remembered the carver's words and his own: *The one who made the earth and the stars made you, Tek.... But Mordecai, why did Perez and Hazor die?... Everything dies. While we live, we must trust Yahweh to know best. Will you do that?...I will try.*

Sometime during the night his own camel's raspy breathing woke Tek. He left his wife asleep on Kizia's neck. He prodded and coaxed, but his beast would not rise. At daybreak Suli walked into Tek's camp with his father, the ancient patriarch of the caravan. It always surprised Tek that the man could still mount a camel. Tek shook his wife. "Kore, wake up."

The men examined the camels. After much gesturing and head shaking, they made their decision: the beasts must be destroyed. Tek had already come to the same conclusion.

"My father says this sickness will spread, probably already has," said Suli. "I have a spare. You can ride it to the next town. There you can buy another." He whistled. Soon a boy stood at a distance with the spare.

"No," said Kore. "We can nurse them. Give them a chance. We will catch up."

Ignoring Kore, Suli said, "Get it done. We need to go." The men walked away, stopping to examine other camels on the way to the front.

Bells and brass disks played a small discordant tune as Tek removed the camels' halters. Had he not told Kore that a camel is a tool, not a pet? He made a pile of the fringed saddle pads which had their own bells and tassels. Had he not told her she was getting too attached? Carrying both sets of tack, he saddled and loaded the extra camel. Kore watched, still holding Kizia's head in her lap. "Come on Kore. You have to get up now." She had begun to rock, a hum forming in the back of her throat. "No. We are not doing that. Get up." He pulled her gently by the arm and disengaged her grip on the dying camel. The boy made the extra camel kneel and helped Tek push Kore onto the saddle.

Tek's friend walked his camel forward to block her view. "Do you want me to do it?" he asked.

"No. A man is duty bound to slay his own animals." Tek spent long days in the saddle honing his knife to razor sharpness. He spoke softly and drew the knife across the necks of the gentle creatures. Neither made a sound, evidence they had felt very little. He kept his back to the caravan, talking to them as they bled out and died.

Mounting the spare camel, Tek kicked it forward and entered their customary place in line. "Do not look back," he told Kore, but she did, until her beloved Kizia became another tan rock in a wide expanse of tan sand.

One by one, over a span of three days all the camels sickened. When old Suli's camel collapsed under him, the man pitched forward and fell. They carried him a distance from the slaughtered camels, made camp, and waited for the man to die. At last the people loaded their goods on their saddle boards and dragged their possessions across the sands away from the circling vultures. Once proud, high on the backs of their camels, now they trekked on foot like Hebrew beetles, their name for the tribes of Israel. Once proud, the Bedouin caravan became a desert terrapin on its back.

Chapter 6

For three days Mordecai had not spoken to Zelo. "I have no respect for a man who forces someone else to kill his animals," he told Rachel.

"Well, you never respected him in the first place. Listen, I am worried about Judith."

"Is it time for the baby?"

"Yes, but this is something else."

Judith lay feverish on her sleeping mat, refusing to eat. Tirzah bathed one arm with cool water, Hoglah the other. The two younger girls sat at her feet. Tirzah understood the gravity of her mother's condition, but the other girls chattered, oblivious. Rachel entered the dark tent and said, "Judith let me check the baby. Back up girls." She raised Judith's tunic, and noticing the rash across her daughter's smooth navel, put her ear to the great belly, listening intently. After a few moments, she re-positioned and listened. Sitting cross-legged she looked into Judith's worried eyes.

"What, Mama? Is the baby all right?"

"She's fine."

"She. So it is a girl-baby?"

"I think so."

"What is Papa going to say." said Tirzah.

"He'll be angry," said Hoglah.

"Let's don't tell him," said Judith. She wiped away tears.

Rachel cupped Mahlah's chin into her hand. "Now that you will be a big sister, can you keep it a secret?" The girl nodded solemnly. "All right. Take your naps." Rachel left the girls sleeping and moved quietly to the men's awning where Mordecai and Zelo snored. She kicked Mordecai's foot until he woke and motioned him to follow. Hidden behind her tent, she whispered, "Where does Zelo keep the idol?" Mordecai blinked.

"Wake up. Where is it hidden?"

"I think in his girdle pocket. He rubs it all the time and mumbles to himself."

"You have to get it. Does he sleep in his girdle?"

"No. It's too hot."

Rachel remembered the day Phinehas presented the girdle to Zelo as a marriage gift. Wide and finely tooled, a belt of the finest leather, fit for a Pharaoh, Rachel had asked him why he gave it to Zelo. "You cannot stand the man," she had said. Phinehas had grinned and said, "I have not worn it in years. That girdle is a miserable thing. It is so wide and hot I could not stand it. Now Zelo will be chafed and hot all the days of his life, may they be few."

After all these years, she felt joy, thinking about the satisfied look on Phinehas' face. "Husband, we have to get that idol. I'll think of something."

Judith grew worse in the midst of labor. The rash had spread across her belly and up her chest. Rachel banned the girls. She sent for Abigail, Phinehas second wife. Judith did not have the strength to push the baby out. After hours of struggle, the tiny creature pushed herself into the world. Abigail held the baby up for Judith to see. With her last breath, she said, "Her name is Noah—*rest*."

"Oh, my sweet girl," said Rachel stroking Judith's hair. "You were so good. You are free now."

Abigail said, "I think the baby is blind."

A wet nurse came. Word spread about the circumstances surrounding Judith's death. Abigail and Shelah helped Rachel wash and dress the body. Now they sewed the shroud. Mordecai called, "Rachel, two priests are here."

"Priests! Why?" She opened the flap. "What is it?" Two men in priestly garb, one old, one young, waited.

"We need to see the body," said the elder. Rachel wanted to pull the long white beard and scream, *her name is Judith.*

"In case of plague..." said the younger. They brushed past Rachel and stood over Judith, laid out on her shroud.

"Please pull back the bodice," said the elder. Abigail, Shelah and the wet nurse fled. *What difference does it make now,* Rachel thought. *My daughter is past shame.* She folded back the shroud and the bodice, revealing a dark red rash across the pale flesh. Without speaking the priests left the tent and joined Mordecai and Zelo under their awning. Rachel set her teeth and continued with her sewing, wondering at their mumblings. She heard Zelo yell, "No!" She gazed at her daughter, fixing Judith's face in her mind, and set about sewing closed the top of the shroud.

The priests allowed them to bury Judith. Enoch's and Phinehas' sons dug a cave, and with all the family gathered, they placed her body inside and rolled a large rock over the opening. For the first time Rachel's granddaughters joined the women in their wailing. Judith's sleeping mat and all her possessions had to be burned. They dismantled the tent, washed it and everything in it, and spread it all in the sun to bake dry. They waited.

After two Sabbaths, the priests declared Mordecai's camp clean and the family reassembled the tent. The frightened wet nurse returned and taught the baby to nurse. The baby's eyes clouded to a hazy blue. She was indeed blind.

&

Zelophehad pondered. First the plague. Then his wife dead and the baby born blind. Yahweh had had enough of the Little Green Woman. *Will I be next?*

He visited the latrine one last time before making his final decision. *No burning pain. Strong stream. I am truly healed,* he thought. Before the Little Green Woman changed her mind, he would do it. He would take Rachel before Moses. A sorceress would not be allowed to live. The priests would be on his side. Had they not seen the trouble Rachel and her idol had caused?

Rachel felt Zelo's hot eyes upon her. Whatever she did, wherever she settled, whether at her loom, at her cook pot, or while she told stories to her granddaughters, he watched. And then he stopped watching. *He has made his decision,* she thought. *He is going to accuse me before Moses. Look how peacefully he sleeps beside my husband. I must do something or lose my life.* She remembered Miriam. Had Yahweh not struck Moses' own sister with leprosy? And this for criticizing Moses for his Cushite wife. Accused of sorcery, of worshiping an idol, what would her fate be? She would be taken out and stoned.

At midday man, woman, child, and beast succumbed to the oppressive desert heat. Yahweh understood. When they traveled, even the cloud rested. Rachel waited. Not a soul moved about the camps. She heard only the rise and fall of locust music and a screeching hawk. The sides of Mordecai's tent had been rolled up. She ducked under at the back and made her way to the front where the men snored under the awning. She watched their even breathing for a moment, then without hesitation, pulled Zelo's girdle and Mordecai's staff toward her. Clutching both, she hurried to the back of her own tent. The secret pocket—she located it and peeked inside. *Yes, I see you, Ma'at.* The idol lay snug against the sweat-stained leather, unaware that she was about to enter the underworld born on a sea of human dung. Rachel stuffed the girdle into a woven bag, added several fist-sized rocks and headed for the women's latrine. Once behind the screen, she knelt out of sight beside the waste hole. The stench nearly took her breath. Filth, alive with flies, came almost to ground level. Rachel laid the bag on the surface and pushed it down with Mordecai's staff—*slump*—until her hand sank into the muck. Afraid the staff would bob to the surface she pulled it out. She threw it on the ground and rubbed it with sand. At her tent she cleaned her knees, her hands, and the staff with ashes, natron, water and wet sand. She leaned Mordecai's staff against his tent, went into her own, and lay down. She slept more peacefully than she had in days.

Rachel woke to the stirrings of her granddaughters. Her sense of well-being lingered as she peeked through the door flap. Mordecai woke and rose, taking his staff in hand. He walked a few steps, and sniffing the staff, threw it down. He continued down the path. Rachel clamped her hand over her mouth holding back laughter. She watched with fascination as Zelo stretched and sat up. He patted the rug where he had laid the girdle. He shook his head. Surely his eyes deceived him. On hands and knees he crawled into the tent, patting and lifting sleeping mats and water bags. Soon mats, coats, bags and jugs came flying out, and everything he and Mordecai owned lay around the open-sided tent. *I must not laugh*, she thought, but laughter continued to bubble up, until Zelo emerged and headed for her tent. Mirth dissipated instantly. She threw herself onto her sleeping mat, feigning sleep. The tent flap flew back. "*Rachel*," he bellowed. The wet nurse and girls sat up; the baby cried. They all ended up on Rachel's mat with Zelo standing over them. "You did this," he said through clinched teeth.

Rachel stayed on her knees, cowering in submission, arms around her granddaughters. "What, Zelophehad? What have I done?"

"You know."

"I do not know. What is it?"

"My girdle is missing."

She shook her head. Bewildered. Puzzled. "Unless..." she ventured.

"What? Do you know where she—it—could be?"

Rachel almost burst out laughing. "Well, we have had a rat..." The corners of her mouth quivered. "One of those that carries things off..."

"A pack rat," Mahlah piped up, beaming, the bearer of information. Did her grandmother not tell her all about them?

"Yes, one of those, you clever girl," said Rachel. "I myself am missing a bag. But there should be tracks in the sand. You haven't disturbed the sand have you?" She watched as Zelo's shoulders slumped. His fists fell open. He turned and left the tent. Rachel could hold it no longer. She buried her face in her pillow and laughed.

"Don't cry, Nana," said Hoglah, patting her grandmother's shoulder.

❧

Hundreds of relatives had replenished the herds of Enoch and Mordecai, esteemed men of Manasseh. Rachel stood at the paddock fence and watched as Enoch's sons and Mordecai tended the new goats, sorting those going to the hills from those staying in the home paddocks.

Peace had settled over her since she had launched Ma'at on her journey. *I should have done it long ago*, she thought. *Yahweh is my God. Why would I displease him?* She contemplated her shoes, bought in Ramses so long ago, and Mordecai's, taken from the feet of a soldier at the Red Sea. She wore the faded, blue linen dress Asmath had drawn over her head the morning she left Ramses. Only Yahweh had the power to suspend the ravages of time. *Even in our disobedience and punishment, he has watched over us,* she thought.

Her thoughts drifted to Kore and Tek. They had left the fold. Would Yahweh's protection extend into the desert to them? Kore did not know her sister had died. What a wonderful time they had on their last visit. The feasting, the children riding the camels...*the camels*. Rachel's heart pitched against her chest. The camels had brought the plague. Why did they not think of it sooner? Judith had been pregnant. None of the goats was sick. They had sickened after Kore and Tek had been gone two Sabbaths. "Mordecai," she called, "come here husband."

Chapter 7

"Kore." Tek covered his wife's mouth and whispered in her ear. "We are leaving." She nodded. "Now." Again she nodded. Tek had already rolled his sleeping mat and packed a bag. He cut the bells and medallions from all the tack and draped one set over his neck. Kore stashed the metal with her valuables in a pouch worn under her clothing. She rolled her bedding. She tied her small cook pot to her belt and hung Kizia's tack around her neck. They shouldered water bags. He whispered one more thing: "You are the best Bedouin wife I ever had."

Staying low, by the light of the stars, they struck out across the wide sands of the Arabah. They headed northwest toward distant mountains, lying black against a blacker sky. They did not speak until daybreak when they came upon a cluster of boulders. "Are we safe?" asked Kore.

"Yes. They are no better off than we are." They found an opening and entered a small sheltered room with a sandy bottom. Tek searched for snakes and killed a scorpion. A fire circle centered the space. "Look." Kore pointed to shapes carved in the rock: a gazelle, a stick figure with a spear, ten men clustered around a fire pit with rising smoke. Wrapping their bodies against the cold, they settled shoulder to shoulder with their backs to a rock.

"What do we have to eat?" asked Tek. Kore fished out a hand-sized piece of flat bread and broke it, handing him the larger piece. "They blamed us for the plague," he said. "When the old man died, I knew we were in trouble."

"Why us?"

"Our camels were the first to die. They said the Hebrew goats had the plague." They slept, waking late in the afternoon, waiting for night to fall.

Kore reached into her pouch and retrieved a brass medallion and one of the gold combs. She held out the comb to her husband. "Will this buy a camel?"

"Where did you get this? This will buy two camels. Maybe three."

"My mother gave me two of them twenty years ago. She said to save them for a dire need. Now we do not have to follow these foothills and cut across on foot to Kadesh. There are oases on the other side of this mountain, are there not? We can buy camels."

With the brass medallion Kore began to scratch into the rock wall: two camels, each with a rider; two camels with legs folded, the riders with bent backs, walking away. She wiped her tears and added details: the distant mountain, and stars, gouged with a twist of her wrist. Last, above the stars, she carved the letters, YHWH. She buried the worn medallion in the sand below the carving. "Someone will find this someday," she said.

Tek displayed the comb in his open hand. "You are the best Bedouin wife I ever had." Under a deep purple sky, they gathered their belongings, left the ancient shelter, and walked into the starry night.

By first light, they entered foothills and started climbing through mountain passes ever upward toward the crags of the mountain. One range led to another. They scrambled over boulders and navigated around outcroppings. Kore learned she feared heights. Tek learned he had little patience with people who feared heights. Like a pair of hyrax they became mountain dwellers, living off the land, spare as it was. Kore had learned to use a sling, so between the two of them they killed enough. They drank from dribbling mountain springs. At night they camped, keeping their fires and voices low. They encountered no one. At last they topped the last ridge and looked far below where a small oasis and settlement nestled at the foot of the mountain.

Reaching the foothills, they camped under a deep overhang. "We cannot just go walking in," said Tek. "That would not be safe for you. You'll have to stay here and I will go."

"Stay here by myself?" *What was the man thinking?* "I will not." Ignoring her protests, Tek ticked off his plan on long elegant fingers: "One— we will wait for a caravan to come by. Two—I will go down and purchase a camel. If the caravan is trustworthy, I will come get you and we will join it. If not—see that outcropping down there?" he pointed north—I will meet you below that with the camel."

Two nights passed. Kore grew silent with dread. Finally, at mid morning on the third day, they saw a line of camels coming from the south. "They are headed in the right direction," said Tek. "Stay here. Do not leave this overhang." If I am not back in three days, head for that outcrop." He kissed his wife soundly and started down. Kore craned her neck around the wall of the overhang and watched until he disappeared. She leaned against the back wall. *I am alone,* she thought. *For the first time in my life, I am alone. How could he do this? Leave me here. How can this be safe?"*

She woke to the sound of voices. *Voices. Men talking. Laughing. Above me!* She pressed against the wall and drew back her feet. Pebbles from the rocks above peppered the ground. She eased her sling from her belt and nestled a stone in the supple leather. Her knife slid easily from her ankle scabbard. Suddenly a body fell at her feet. Within seconds, another hit the ground. She bolted, and stumbling over the bodies, ran from the overhang, dashing between boulders. She saw a crack and wedged herself far into it. She slowed her breath and listened. Nothing. *I am safe here. Like Moses,* she thought. *Had Moses not told the story of Yahweh placing him in the cleft of the rock? Yahweh showed me this cleft.*

"Kore! Kore! Come out!"

Tek! She shimmied out of the crack holding her knife in one hand, her sling in the other. Standing on a rock above her, grinning, legs spread, hands on his hips, stood her husband, his white kaftan blowing in the wind. "I told you not to leave the overhang. Where are you going?"

"To get my cook pot." At the overhang, Kore stepped over the two dead men and crouched against the wall, while Tek dragged the bodies away and threw them into a crevasse. Refusing to speak, she wiped angry tears.

"Kore. Listen. I saw them following two days ago. I could not leave until I had killed them. You were never in any danger."

"You used me as bait. Like a piece of meat in a snare." The thought of it brought more tears.

He shook his head, took her face in his hands. "No. If that were true, then I would take you with me now. But the plan is the same. I will go, and you will wait here." He held her tight.

"Why did you not tell me they were there?"

"You would have let on in ways you could not help. Maybe with just a backward glance. They had to think I had gone. Now I have to go to meet the caravan. Can you trust me again? If I have lost your trust, I cannot live."

She looked deeply into his tear-filled eyes. "I trust you, my husband. I am sorry. I will do as you say. I will wait."

"You are the best Bedouin wife I ever had." He kissed her and left. Once again, she peeked around the rock and watched him go. She waited three days, marking the rock face lest she lose count. On the fourth morning at first light, she left the overhang, staying low, working her way around boulders, heading down toward the outcropping to the north. *What could have happened? He will surely be there with a camel, waiting for me. He will say, where have you been, my Bedouin beauty?* She inched along a ledge, startled to see a flash of white below. Hugging the rock face, she waited. She peered over the ledge. The white had not moved. *Tek.* He lay splayed near the bottom of a ravine. She followed the ledge until the incline lessened, slid down on loose rock, and ran back to her husband.

"Tek! Wake up. What has happened?" She poured water in her hand; smeared it on his face; slapped his cheeks. His eyes opened, widened in recognition, then drifted to the side and fixed. "You waited for me," she whispered. She clamped her hands over her mouth and stifled the urge to wail, to set her tongue in motion, to sound that magnificent trill of agony. "What should I do, my husband?" She dragged his body, made easier by loose rocks and momentum, to the bottom of the steep slope. She made a pile of the water bags, his sling, and his pouch, which held his knife, whet stone, flint and the gold comb. She kissed his hands and crossed them on his chest. His lips were still warm. She covered his body with his sleeping mat. She scraped handfuls of loose rock, followed by larger rocks, then the largest rocks she could lift, and mounded his body. At last she combined his meager pile of belongings with her own, draped the second set of tack around her neck, shouldered the water bags, and turning away, followed the ravine until it abutted a rock face. The cliff sloped downhill to an ell. At last she rested. Speaking low, as they had for many days, she spoke to her husband. "There will never be another like you, Tek. Only a mountain could take your life. But it will not take mine. You would not desire that." She made a plan and sheltered in the ell until dusk.

Kore left the ell and followed the cliff face downward. She hid behind a boulder and watched the comings and goings of people below. South of the town she spotted the caravan, the camels hobbled now, the Bedouin gathering around their cook fires. A man led six camels to a paddock, hobbled them, and returned to the caravan. She knew these were camels that would be sold or traded. The sky darkened to purple. Dim lights glowed in narrow windows of hovels throughout the settlement. The mad chirrup of night creatures drowned all sound from the town, and small animals scurried among the rocks. The north star brightened. She waited until no light showed in any window, and the fires of the Bedouin, lowered to coals, dotted the night. She girded her skirts, stuffed her white veil into her bag and threw on her black shawl. Last she rubbed dust on her face, hands, and legs. *Help me, Yahweh.*

Kore left the safety of the rocks. Staying low, moving slow, hugging walls, she worked her way to the lean-to at the back of the paddock. She clutched a rock in her hand, relieved to find she would not need it. The watchman snored loudly, a skin of beer on his lap. She moved into the stench of his breath, its heat damp on her hand, and laid the gold comb on the skin. She hoisted a saddle and blankets from a pile, entered the paddock, and staying low, moved among the camels. Choosing two, she saddled one, and pushing the bits into place, harnessed them both. She untied their hobbles, looped the ropes around her neck, and mounting one, kicked it up. Moving forward she snapped and pulled the reigns of the second camel. It rose with a protesting bellow, sending her cowering flat in her saddle. No one stirred. Staying low, she rode through the opening in the paddock and walked the beasts into the desert. Their wide padded feet made no sound. She counted to one hundred, then set them into a steady trot, heading east of the north star. *Thank you, Yahweh.* Every footfall seemed to repeat a soft shuffling rhythm: thank you... thank you... thank you...

Chapter 8

RACHEL PUSHED THE SHUTTLECOCK THROUGH the taut strands of wool. In and out to the end of the row, pack the threads, back across. Over the years Mordecai had crafted many looms, each one better than the last. Her hands needed no direction. Her mind wandered to Kore and Tek. If they had indeed brought the plague, what had happened to their camels? Had they died somewhere in the wilderness, leaving them on foot? She took little comfort in the gold combs. Bandits roamed the desert. Were Mordecai and Phinehas not proof of that? How many times had they entertained the children with the wadi story? Had it not been for Tek and his brothers they would have lost everything. Mordecai's words echoed. *Who would you trust more to take care of your daughter? And Tek had promised: I will take care of her all my life.* She knew Kore could not be in better hands than Tek's.

"Rachel." Zelo stood behind her. His voice squeezed between clinched teeth. She fully expected him to club her to death someday. Lately she made the dog lie behind her, but the old fellow had gone off and not come back. "Rachel." Rasping, pleading. Her scalp itched. She looked over her shoulder. His skin had turned as green as a half-ripe olive. "

Rachel dropped the shuttlecock and swiveled, tilting her face up to meet the yellow eyes. She said, not unkindly, "I do not have it. I have told you."

"You have her. I know you do. Give her to me, and I will not tell Moses."

"Zelo, go lie down. You do not look well." The man's face sagged on one side.

"You know, the Little Green Woman healed me once."

The little green woman... Laughter bubbled, but curiosity dispelled mirth. "No, I did not know that. When?"

"It does not matter. Listen. I cannot make water. The sickness has come back."

Surprised by the pity she felt, Rachel's face softened. "Zelo, I am sorry for you. The idol is gone. She will never return. Never. Now go lie down." She watched as her son-in-law turned and crossed to his tent. She picked up her shuttlecock and finished the row.

&

No one mourned the man, Zelophehad, of the tribe Manasseh—neither his name nor his deeds were mentioned around the camp fire—but his absence was surely felt. Like a bird miraculously escaped from the jaws of a fox, Rachel struggled to regain her wings and adjust to his absence. For days after his death she expected him to appear and reclaim his hold. Then one morning she awoke and his oppressive spirit had drifted away. She was free.

Zelo's death had the opposite effect on Mordecai. In a way, Zelophehad had kept his father-in-law alive. Mordecai seemed ready to relinquish his hold on life now that Judith, Rachel, and his granddaughters no longer needed his protection. As for Tirzah, Hoglah, Milcha and Mahlah, they no longer sought approval that would never come, warmth that would never be given. His threat to nullify Tirzah's betrothal to Gershon had died with him.

&

Tirzah stood on one foot, both hands flat atop the low rock wall at Great Uncle Enoch's goat paddock. Unlike her sisters, she loved the earthy smell of goat and never complained when her turn came to gather dung for the fire. When she returned to the women's tent, they would all hold their noses. Her twin cousins, Enoch's grandsons, Gershon and Gideon, had brought pregnant goats into the fold for birthing. It amazed Tirzah that one of Yahweh's creatures could be so stupid about something as natural as producing offspring. But with a little help they could deliver twins or triplets.

Gershon, clearly in charge, directed his brothers; Gideon was happy to let his twin take the lead. She always referred to her betrothed as "my Gershon." She took in the bend of his back, every angle of his muscular, sunbaked arms, and his black, kinky hair. His beard had decided to thicken. *Our girls will have impossible hair like mine,* she thought. She caught his eye and smiled. Startled at her grandmother's voice, she straightened her hips. "Nana, you scared me."

"You do not look scared to me. Maybe you should be. He is pretty."

"What do you mean, I should be scared?"

"When are you going to marry that boy?"

"You know. When we get to the Promised Land. Uncle Enoch says it will not be much longer—maybe only a year. We are supposed to wait for as many years as the spies took in days. And Uncle Enoch says we get to add the year it took to build the Tabernacle."

"Well, I'm glad you and Uncle Enoch have it all figured out."

"Gershon and I will be married in the Promised Land."

211

"Does he agree with all that?"

"Not as much as he did when I first told him."

"That is what I feared. Hear me girl." Rachel leveled eyes without pity upon her granddaughter. "Hoglah is beautiful. She is fourteen, and I have been watching her. She likes Gershon."

"Nana, everyone likes Gershon." Tirzah crossed her eyes and pulled a face at her grandmother. "Besides, I am betrothed to Gershon. Hoglah is betrothed to Gideon." She turned and watched a drama she never tired of: A dead kid lay on the ground. Gershon cut the skin from around its legs and neck, pulled off the skin and fitted it like a coat onto a newborn triplet. He allowed the mother of the dead kid to smell the dressed kid. Thinking it her own, she licked its head and allowed it to nurse. Now both nannies would have kids. "That is my Gershon," she said to no one. Rachel had walked away.

Rachel stopped at Enoch's tent and found him lying on his sleeping mat. Sweet Hannah, wife of Enoch's lost brother, in her late fifties now, held his hand. She had proved to be the wife Enoch deserved. When Sarah died, Rachel did not mourn her sister-in-law, the woman who had the power, and used it, to crush her baby bird. Even now bitterness crept into Rachel's heart. Enoch said, "I can see the bend in the road." She leaned close to hear.

"Maybe not today, Brother."

"Tomorrow for sure. Hannah has told the children to come for their blessing. I wish Sarah were here to see them all grown up with tents of their own." His voice grew weaker. "Sister, did you ever forgive me for taking you away from Asmath?"

Rachel laid her head on her brother's chest. "Long ago. I should have told you. You saved my life. I so wanted us to go to the Promised Land together. To die there together."

"…Yahweh's will." Enoch patted his sister's head.

"I know." She kissed him, hugged Hannah, and left.

&

Mordecai stood talking with Phinehas, Shelah, and Abigail at their tent, where Phinehas and Shelah poured over their scroll, their account of the Hebrews and their travels. The wives had lived in harmony since Phinehas' brother had been killed at the golden calf incident. When Abigail arrived with her three children, she vowed she wanted only protection, but Phinehas could not resist the tall red-haired woman he had adored as a child, and Shelah had complied. Abigail had produced three ruddy and handsome sons.

Chapter 9

THE TRUMPET SOUNDED MUSTER BEFORE dawn, jolting awake the camps of Israel. "Sometimes I think Moses takes joy in yanking us from our warm covers," Rachel groused to Mordecai. Knowing hours would pass before Manasseh moved out, they built up the fire and sent the girls for manna. The wet nurse finished feeding Noah so the women's tent could be dismantled. Over the morning meal, Rachel said, "Hurry girls. We are going to visit your mama before we leave."

They had been camped a year at that location—by all reckoning, the thirty-ninth year at Kadesh-Barnea, the fortieth since leaving Egypt—a year marked neither by spring planting, nor fall harvest, but by burials and wailing. It had been a year of death. Most of the remaining numbered men had died, Enoch among them, leaving but a handful. *Oh, the graves that litter this mountain,* thought Rachel. *The wailing will echo through these hills for all time.*

So much had happened during that year: they had lost their herd to plague. Judith had died. Noah had been born. Zelo had died. Rachel's thoughts churned: *How can I bear to leave Judith behind...and Kore has been gone four Sabbaths now...* Rachel had convinced herself the camels had brought the plague. Worry like never before had taken root in her heart: for her dead daughter, left in a cold cave for all eternity, for her baby bird, lost in the cold desert, for Tirzah, blind to her sister's cold designs on her beloved Gershon.

"Wife," said Mordecai, not unkindly, "we need to busy ourselves if we want to visit Judith.

Rachel threw off her reverie and began to load her cook pots and grind stone. "Shake the mats before you roll them, girls. We do not need to lug extra sand."

The packing almost finished, the girls assembled, dressed in their warm black cloaks. The sun, rising orange, painted the sky gold behind gray, streaked clouds. "Nana, can I take the puppy?" asked Mahlah. *Even the dog died,* thought Rachel.

"Mordeci, who does that black puppy remind you of?" she asked.

"Morsel." He grinned.

"He does." That first night they had sat on a log, and Mordecai had handed her the puppy... Mahlah, would you mind if we name the new puppy Morsel?"

"All right. But that is not a pretty name." They walked through Manasseh down familiar paths, hailing neighbors and family, everyone busy piling belongings and loading carts. They pushed through goat herds where shepherds whistled and barking dogs worked. Finally they climbed a short distance into the foothills and reached a shady cliff face where hundreds of graves had been dug into the wall.

Mordecai, carrying Noah, led them to Julia's grave site where a large boulder stood guard. The men had worked half a day to wedge it there. At its base, a circle of rocks marked the old yellow dog's grave. Rachel stepped to the boulder and laid her hand flat against it. She had planned to have all the girls do the same, while Mordecai said something hopeful, but the cold rock seemed to pull all the warmth from her arm, from her soul. Tirzah reached out—"Don't touch it," said Rachel. "Better to remember your mama's warm hugs than this cold rock." The sun topped the hill casting a fan of golden rays. "Look at the sky. Your mother loved sunset and sunrise."

"Your mother *was* my sunrise..." Mordecai began. While he spoke Rachel contemplated her granddaughters: Tirzah, tall, somewhat plain, strong-willed, and brave; Hoglah, beautiful, cunning and intelligent; Milcha, snapping almond-shaped eyes in a moon face, clever and always smiling; Mahlah, spoiled and demanding; who could resist her energy and those piercing, hazel eyes? Who could tell what little blind Noah would be like. She certainly let the wet nurse know when she wanted to feed.

Rachel asked all the girls to share a good memory about their mother, then she said, "When your mother was a girl, Grandpapa used to carve baby dolls for her. And I would weave tiny blankets. She was the best little mother. Those babies were put to bed every night and kissed. She fed them their manna and sang songs to them. So I was not surprised at how wonderful and gentle she was to you. You were the light of her life."

On the way down the hill, Rachel fell to her knees and allowed her forehead to go over to the ground. She began to wail. Mordecai watched as the four girls fell on their grandmother, a sobbing black mound of females. After a time, he heard a husky chuckle from deep in the pile. It grew to a lusty laugh. Morsel had burrowed in to find Rachel. Then Tirzah began to giggle, then the others. Soon they all lay on the ground, laughing, tears running down their faces. Mordecai walked away, murmuring to Noah, "Women. You are going to grow up to be one. I would like to be there."

Feeling his age, Mordecai loaded his tool box onto the cart and waited for Rachel and his granddaughters. He had grown accustomed to waiting for females and was long past trying to hurry them. He sat on the back of the cart, dreading the move. His ankle had never fully healed. His thoughts drifted. *What would I have done without Goose?* He believed Yahweh had led them to that poor dead donkey. A new thought came to him: *before my ankle had been injured.* Goose had lived twenty-three years and sired a line of fine offspring for trade. He tethered the jenny, the female, to the cart and yoked the strong young male.

Flexing their muscles and swaggering, two other strong young males came to help: Gershon and Gideon. The identical twins reminded him of

Perez and Hazor. They had the beauty of Enoch's line, complete with the kinky hair and the gap in their teeth. Gershon, always smiling, and Gideon, a bit dour, made themselves identifiable by their demeanor. "You can settle down," Mordecai told them. "Do you see any girls here?" They elbowed one another, embarrassed. *No wonder my granddaughters love them,* he thought. "But here they come now," he announced, catching sight of Rachel and the girls coming down the path. An apparition in black, his herd of women came into camp. The young men resumed their poses. Mordecai caught Rachel's eye with a wry twist of his lips. When he was their age, he had spent his days slaving in Pharaoh's brickyard. He wondered if they realized what a magnificent thing Yahweh and Moses had done, how far their people had come.

The army of Judah led out with the Tabernacle following. By late morning, Manasseh, in their thousands, moved into position with flocks of sheep and goat herds. They followed the pillar of cloud eastward into the Wilderness of Zin, heading, word went out, to Kadesh on the border of Edom. Would they at last be allowed to enter the Promised Land? And what of those few who had survived the curse of unbelief? Would Yahweh relent and allow the remaining counted men to go in? *He has no reason to,* thought Mordecai.

They moved forward: Mordecai and Rachel, holding the halter on each side of the donkey; following behind the cart, the wet nurse with Noah; then, Milcha and Mahla, leading three nanny goats; and last, Tirzah and Hoglah, walking with their betrothed. Three baby goats, bawling for the teat, rode in the cart with Morsel.

Mordecai suffered. His ankle flared and swelled as he had known it would. He leaned heavily on his staff, and though it galled him, he gave up and rode on the cart. "Do not be so proud," Rachel chided. "Be glad the cart has lasted this long." By mid afternoon she surrendered to aching hips and joined her husband. "And we thought the days to the Red Sea were hard," she said, dangling her legs, enjoying the ride. Getting no response, she studied her husband, dozing with his mouth agape. *That is what he will look like in death,* she thought. She felt the burden of Yahweh's edict pressing, pressing.

The couples took turns leading the donkey. To Rachel's surprise, at some point they traded partners.

And so the great Hebrew animal crawled toward Kadesh and the border of Edom. The Promised Land lay somewhere beyond.

&

"Mama." Kore woke. Where was she? The camels stood sleeping. Long shadows stretched across the sand behind her. *I am heading west. West! How long?* She pulled the reigns, kicked the camel and turned her north. The sun stood two hands into the sky. She had lost count of the days.

Kore had tied herself with the hobble ropes to the front and back saddle horns, also tethering the second camel to the back horn. The one time she had dismounted, the camel had tried to bolt, swinging her around, biting, pulling out a clump of her hair. She had wrapped one arm around the reigns and struck the beast between the eyes with her fist. Forcing it to kneel, she had remounted. From then on she had urinated by positioning herself to the side of the saddle. She dared not dismount; the camels were too thirsty.

Three empty water skins hung off the saddle. The last skin had very little in it. She had had nothing to eat for days. Oddly, she was not hungry. She licked her lips; dry skin scraped her tongue which felt thick in her mouth. Her eyes felt dry and small. She took a sip of water, dropped the water bag, grabbed for it, and missed. *Should I try to get it? No.*

The sun set gloriously behind a mountain range, sucking the heat up to a fiery sky, leaving behind nothing but cold, and it more brutal than the heat. Black dark fell fast with stars, then the moon rose, yellow, a friend. She spotted the north star. She studied the silhouetted mountain range to her left. It looked familiar. She rode at a steady pace into the night. Then she saw them, in the moonlight—*tracks*—leading from the mountain, heading east. She turned the camels onto the tracks. "We are going to live," she told the camels. *Thank you, Yahweh.*

The night seemed endless. Cold penetrated her wool shawl. Elation turned to worry. How far behind was she? *I could trail behind these tracks until I die, tied to this camel,* she thought. She kicked the camel's shoulder brutally. Again. Again. When the beast bared her long yellow teeth and reached around to bite, Kore, in anticipation of the move, whacked the side of her face with a leather water bag. Finally, the camel moved into a trot, dragging the spare along.

Brooking no misbehavior, Kore kept the camels at a trot until she saw a glow on the horizon. Not sunrise—too white. The pillar of fire. Then she came to flocks of sheep and walked through them to the other side. Then goats. Tents. Banked fires. A shepherd called to her. She stopped. "What tribe are you?"

"Ephraim," the young man answered.

"What direction is Manasseh?"

"Straight ahead mostly."

"I will trade you two camels with all the tack for a donkey. And this." She untied Tek's bag and pulled out brass medallions and bells, holding back one bell, displaying them in her cupped hands.

And thus, Kore, daughter of Mordecai, entered her father's camp, on the way to Kadesh, riding on a donkey. She found a water bag and drank long. She tethered the donkey to the cart, slipped into the women's tent, and lay down beside her mother. "You smell of camel," said Rachel. They slept.

Chapter 10

AT LAST THE PEOPLE OF ISRAEL CAME to Kadesh near the border of Edom and camped. And Miriam died there, and they buried her and stayed there and mourned.

At the women's latrine those in line speculated about Miriam's age. Some said she was one hundred years old. Some said, since Moses was one hundred twenty, she must be at least that. At the evening meal, Rachel reported what she had heard. "There is a story that Miriam tended to Moses when she was a girl," said Rachel. "It is said she was there when Pharaoh's daughter discovered him in the water. Speaking of water, Mordecai, we are just about out."

"I know. No wells have been found. There do not seem to be any streams nearby. And that is one thing, but Phinehas heard the people have gone to Aaron and Moses with the same old complaints of no grain, no pomegranates and no figs. Then they started saying, 'Why did you bring us out of Egypt?' The same old complaints we have heard for thirty-nine years."

Because the people contended with Moses and Aaron, Moses took his staff and struck a rock twice. Water gushed forth, and the people and their beasts drank. "They will never learn," said Mordecai to Phinehas. "These younger people are no better than all the rejected dead."

At the latrine, Rachel learned, Moses named the site, Meribah—*contention*, for there the people contended with Yahweh.

Rachel and Mordecai stayed close to camp while Rachel tended to Kore. She still could not believe her baby bird had come home. They expected her first words, "Tek died..." to be followed by an explanation of why she had come home alone, riding a donkey, but none came. She lay on her bed dry-eyed, not speaking. Rachel bathed her, rubbed her lips with olive oil, and fed her goat's milk and mush made with manna. At last she sat up and said, "I chose female camels because they are easier to manage. But that one...will my hair grow back, Mama?"

Exchanging a look with Mordecai, Rachel studied her daughter. *She may never be well,* she thought. "In time, I think it will grow back. Time heals everything."

"Kizia would never pull out my hair like that...my Kizia..." Kore sighed deeply and lay back.

From Kadesh, Moses sent messengers to the king of Edom, reminding him that they shared a common ancestry. Moses requested safe passage through his land. Moses made promises, not to drink from Edom's wells, not to wander into the fields, to purchase and not to steal anything, but the king sent out an army to threaten Israel. His refusal was final.

At the evening campfire, Gideon adamantly denounced Edom. "Why do we not go in and take what we want? We are powerful. With Yahweh's help we could trample them into the ground."

"I am happy you admit we need Yahweh's help," said Mordecai. "Your grandfather taught you well, but Yahweh does not want to help us destroy Edom."

"Why not Grandpapa?" asked Tirzah.

"There were twin brothers, Jacob and Esau, sons of Isaac. They fought over their birthright, and Jacob ended up in Egypt. Esau settled in Edom. So they are our kin from long ago." Rachel noticed Gershon and Hoglah played a game with yarn, twisting it around their fingers. Neither showed interest in the discussion.

"But that was so long ago..." said Gideon. "More than four hundred years..."

"Yahweh promised that land to Esau. Yahweh does not go back on his promises, no matter how long ago they were made. We will not fight them. We will go around them," said Mordecai.

The next day the congregation of Israel set out for Mount Hor, near the border of Edom. The people watched as Moses, Aaron, and his son, Eleazar, went up the twin-peaked mountain. Only two came down. Eleazar wore the priestly raiment, for Aaron, one hundred, twenty-three, had died on the mountain. He died on the first day, in the fifth month, of the fortieth year, after leaving Egypt. Moses declared a thirty-day mourning period. The Hebrews set up their tents and wept for Aaron thirty days.

&

The twins had been sent back to their parents' compound. Rachel charged Milcha and Mahlah with tending Kore and left to find Tirza. At her granddaughter's request, she carried a rolled papyrus in the folds of her veil. She found Tirzah, sitting with the nanny goats on the far side of the cart, holding a black kid. "Tirzah-girl, what are you doing? May I sit?"

"I am thanking Yahweh, Nana," she said, her voice spongy with tears. The girl patted the mat.

Rachel sat. "For what are you thanking him?" She laid the scroll between them and held out her arms.

"No, Nana. I am not sad. Well, I am sad for what was supposed to be, but I am happy for being rescued."

219

"Rescued?"

"Yahweh has rescued me from a life of trouble. There will be much to do in the Promised Land. I cannot be tied to a turd." At Rachel's sharp intake of breath, she said, "Forgive me, Nana, I meant to say, fool."

"You said it right the first time." Rachel chuckled. "This is your marriage contract to Gershon." Tirzah dismantled the papyrus by its glued strips and fed it piece by piece to the goats.

&

One day Mordecai summoned Rachel. Gershon waited at the fire pit, his cocky look suppressed. "Aunt Rachel, Uncle Mo, can I talk to you?"

"Of course," they answered in unison.

"Well, Hoglah and I want..." Rachel saw Hoglah peeking from behind the women's tent. She motioned for her to join them. Hoglah, never one to be shy, minced forward. *How does a girl make her cheeks flush,* Rachel wondered.

"Hoglah, Gershon joins your name with his own. How do you feel about this?" *Maybe she pinches her cheeks. Has she been looking in my mirror?"*

"I want to marry Gershon," the girl murmured.

You poor boy. You poor, poor boy, thought Rachel.

His father paid a bride price of ten goats, and Gershon erected a tent near his parents. The families stocked it with gifts: oil lamps, rugs, pillows, a grindstone for Hoglah. The families gave their blessing at the wedding feast, a quiet celebration, for Aaron's mourning period had not ended. Gershon's parents and Rachel and Mordecai watched the couple enter their tent for the first time.

Later, Rachel said to Mordecai, "Never have I felt so sorry for anyone in my life."

"She will be all right. We can keep an eye on her."

"I am not thinking of her."

"He will feel like a dung beetle sometimes, but he will learn to get by."

"A dung beetle! Where did you get that?"

&

The days of mourning came to an end and the Hebrew nation moved south along the border of Edom. Now that Gershon had married Hoglah, Gideon and a younger brother helped Mordecai with the cart. Kore walked with her parents and nieces, content to be left to her own thoughts. Rachel remembered the days when Sarah had forced her to give up Kore. *She must be feeling as I felt,* thought Rachel. *Her spirit is broken. Only Yahweh can help Kore now.*

Mordecai and Rachel talked as they walked. "Mordecai, I have to tell you something before you die."

"You can tell me after. I will hear you." She shouldered him sideways then helped him regain his balance.

"It's about Ma'at."

"You said you got rid of it."

"I did. But you never asked me how. Were you not curious?"

"No. I just wanted it to be over."

"She was in Zelo's girdle, just like you thought. I pushed the girdle down to the bottom of the latrine." She cut her eyes toward her husband, laughter bubbling up to play around her mouth. "Using your staff." Her chuckle grew to laughter, then to uncontrollable guffaws. She bent over, eyes streaming, unable to walk—until she saw the expression on his face—then she ran.

"Ghaaah!" Carts and wagons halted, dogs barked, and people stopped to watch the commotion. Elbows pumping, Mordecai chased his wife across the sand, unable to get traction with the infamous staff. She stood at a distance laughing, hands on her hips. "Don't come back," he yelled.

Noah began to cry. "Oh, no," said Rachel, reaching the cart first. Mordecai enveloped them both in his arms, swaying.

Tirzah, leading Kore's donkey, said to Gideon, "That is the kind of marriage I want."

Gideon waited for Tirzah to meet his gaze. "So do I."

Chapter 11

A CRY WENT UP FROM THE PEOPLE, the likes of which had not been heard since Pharaoh amassed at Pi-Hihiroth at the Red Sea. From the north in the Negev, the desert west of the Dead Sea, Arad, the king of the Canaanites came out against Israel and took some of them captive. Rumors had spread that as a warning they staked the heads of the captives at their border.

Those families missing members formed a search party, among them Gershon's family, for indeed, they could not find him anywhere. His mother had taken to screaming at Hoglah, "What have you done to my son?" A rumor started that Hoglah had murdered her new husband. Searches had been made. Sand had been dug up in their tent. Women at the latrine spoke ill to Rachel, Kore and the girls. Finally, Mordecai and Rachel took Hoglah home with them. One day Gershon's mother came to Mordecai's camp screaming, "Hoglah, Hoglah, where is my son?"

Rachel motioned for Hoglah to stay in the tent. She went out to meet the distraught woman. "Magdah, why do you think my granddaughter is at fault? She is just a girl."

"She is an evil girl. She thinks her beauty is the answer to everything. At night my son leaves their marriage bed and goes out into the desert. I want to know why. Why?"

"Magdah. Young love is difficult sometimes. Give them time to adjust."

"How can they adjust, Rachel? My son is missing."

When the search party returned, they bore the head of Gershon. They buried the dead in a communal grave, mourned, and made a vow: if Yahweh would deliver the Canaanite, Israel promised to utterly destroy their cities. Deep hatred for the brutal Canaanite burned in Israel, for the rout at Hormah thirty-nine years before. Israel prepared for war.

Rachel remembered the day so long ago when Phinehas and Mordecai came to her and told her Tek and Reuel had dragged home, out of a wadi near Hormah, the heads of her brothers, Perez and Hazor. Slain by the Canaanite, their heads wedged in the walls of the wadi, they had never been avenged. Now they would be. The Canaanite had beheaded three men of Enoch's clan. She wished her brother were alive to see the destruction the men of Israel had promised—utter destruction of them and their cities.

The wails and screams of Gershon's mother and sisters followed Tirzah as she sought his twin in the foothills of Mount Hor. She found him sitting alone, his tunic rent from neck to waist; tears had channeled the dust on his face. She knelt by his outstretched legs and patted his foot. "Gideon." Her voice implored him to look at her.

"It was like looking at my own face, my own head cut off." He drew up his knees and buried his face in his arms. "His eyes were open. His mouth..." Tirzah encircled her cousin with her arms and rocked him.

"You must not touch me. I am unclean. I have touched a dead body." He shook with sobs.

Tirzah laid her head on his. "You could never be unclean to me. What is an ordinance to us? You must wash and clean yourself. They are begging Yahweh to help them defeat the Canaanites. You must be among them. For Gershon. For your great uncles Perez and Hazor. And when we get to the Promised Land, we will be wed."

Gideon wrote *Gershon, Perez, Hazor* on his shield. With his uncles, cousins and brothers, under the banner of Manasseh, he marched to war, one young man in an army of thousands. Tirzah stood with the women, children, and those unfit for battle and watched Gideon's back, until his shoulders, his head, became indistinguishable, and the army stitched him into its fabric.

The people waited. Yahweh heard their prayers and laid the Canaanite out like a feast to satisfy the hungry souls of the Hebrew people. Blood lust and revenge raised the people's spirits as no amount of mourning could.

Phinehas wrote a marriage contract for Gideon and Tirzah. In spite of their hatred of Hoglah—Magdah spit on the ground whenever she sighted her son's widow—his parents signed it. Inseparable now, the betrothed planned every aspect of their future in the Promised Land: what their house would look like, what their garden would grow, their children's names.

"You know, Nana," Hoglah told her grandmother, "by law, Gideon should take me to wife. I am his brother's widow."

Rachel studied her granddaughter. *Did her gall know any bounds?* "Your husband has other brothers, but I think we will have to look elsewhere."

After the defeat of the Canaanites, Moses announced they would proceed on their journey southward, skirting the border of Edom. On the way the people rebelled, because of the difficult terrain, the scarcity of water, and their disgust with the monotonous manna. Yahweh sent fiery serpents among the people as a punishment; they bit the people and many died. "Well," Phinehas mused, "they will not have to eat any more manna, will they?"

During the plague of serpents, Phinehas added lengths of sheepskin to the illustrated scroll, Shelah mixed paint, and Mordecai illustrated the war and the fiery serpents. He had stared long at the pale cream sheepskin. "How do I illustrate a war?" He finally settled upon Gideon's shield with the three names, and a spear.

As for the curse of the serpents, he painted a rectangle of snakes bordering a tall pole with a bronze-colored snake coiled at the top. "What do you think?" Mordecai asked his wife and friends. They deemed it perfect. Except," Phinehas said, "At the bottom you should write the number of fools who died." When the serpents had been let loose, the people repented and went to Moses, begging relief from Yahweh. He did not remove the serpents, but Moses cast a bronze serpent and attached it to the top of a tall standard. He stationed it outside the Tent of Meeting. If bitten, a person who gazed upon the bronze serpent would live. It became common to see people racing to the bronze serpent with a bitten family member.

Mordecai wrote the number, 24,000, under his illustration. "That is a lot of people. Will we ever learn?"

"I have come to doubt it," said Phinehas. "In any case you and I do not have much longer to worry about it. The closer we get to the Promised Land the heavier I feel the hand of Yahweh on my neck." As if to illustrate his point, he stood. His back had bent to an alarming degree.

&

The Hebrews skirted the southern border of Edom. From there they turned north and traveled along the eastern border of Edom until they came to Brook Zered east of the Dead Sea.

Heavy rains made the brook impassable, so spreading for miles along the banks and southward, they camped. Had they followed the brook toward the west, they would have ended at the southern end of the Dead Sea near Sodom and Gomorrah, for generations a favorite subject of moral lessons.

After two days at the river, Mordecai, age sixty, of the tribe Manasseh, lay on his deathbed. For forty years, Rachel had wondered when and where it would happen. *It seems Yahweh has chosen the banks of the Brook Zered,* she thought. At the beginning she had watched her husband keenly: would a boulder fall on him? would he keel over dead? would he die on his bed? One day he said, "Stop watching me. I feel like a fly, and you're that lizard whose eyes go different directions."

Rachel calmed herself. Family and friends clustered outside the tent. The sun peeked through low clouds, haloing each shape, as a fine morning mist settled upon wool shawls and cloaks. She sent them away. Neither she nor Mordecai had the strength to bear their sorrow.

"Kiss your grandfather, and let him rest." One by one the girls said goodbye. Hoglah smiled prettily, giving her grandfather a final blessing. Mahlah laid her head on his chest and cried until Rachel lifted her away. Milcha, repulsed by beards, kissed his hands over and over. Noah patted his face, fascinated by the feel of him; her fingers explored the crevasses and creases, the excitement of his long eyebrows.

Tirzah handed the baby to Hoglah and sat. Tears watered her voice. "Grandpapa, I want you to know, Gideon and I will take care of Nana and my sisters. You do not have to worry." Mordecai mustered the strength to pat her back. She laid her head on his chest, heard the wheezing, and continued, "And I will remind them of everything you taught us. And I will name my first boy Mordecai." Rachel pulled Tirzah away. "Go now. Grandpapa loves you all very much."

Phinehas groaned his way to a sitting position by stages. "I do not know if you are worth it," he chuckled. Mordecai smiled. Phinehas shook his head in wonder. "Remember that day those camels spit on us and we thought we were dead men?"

"Naked."

"We were not entirely naked. You at least had on shoes. You were so happy about that."

Rachel said, "Have you two been keeping secrets?" Mordecai raised a finger.

Phinehas said, "All right, we will tell her all about it later. You rest." A dry husk now, weighing no more than a child, Phinehas allowed Kore to help him up.

At last only the three remained in the yellow lamplight. Kore sat beside her father and spoke: "We left, heading for Elat, by way of the Arabah. After two Sabbaths the camels went down, and Tek had to kill them. He killed my beautiful Kizia. She did not make a sound..." Mordecai closed his eyes. Whenever she paused, thinking him asleep, he squeezed her hand and she continued. "When I saw the tracks, I was so happy. I had to get home to Mama and to you, Papa." He opened his eyes and nodded. She kissed her father and left the tent.

"She will get well now," said Rachel. "As for you, I am going to make Phinehas tell me all the bad things you ever did." She thought she saw a twinkle, or was it a tear? He took a last shallow breath and died. Rachel closed his eyes.

She pushed out through the door flap. Fresh rain born on a west wind scented the air, and cooled her face. *Good,* she thought, *the river will stay high, and I will have plenty of time to bury him.* She heard the girls teasing in their tent. Kore laughed. *Thank you, Yahweh.* She went inside, and tied the door flap shut. She wanted to be alone with her husband, to wash his body, to tell him some things.

&

While the great assembly of Hebrews waited for the River Zered to return to its banks, for the wadis to drain, the last of the counted men died. Shelah had awakened to find Phinehas dead on his bed, his current cat curled in the bend of his arm. "What do you think, Rachel, about burying our husbands together? Abigail likes the idea."

Enoch's sons and grandsons dug a tomb in the cliffs at Zered and the families laid the two old friends side by side. At last Yahweh had cleansed the nation of Israel of the men counted in the first census. Rachel could find no comfort in that notion. Enoch, Phinehas, and Mordecai, her rocks, her loves, were gone. They had never rebelled. They had tried to do Yahweh's will. Yet they had been caught up in a whirlwind…

There would be no more stories of the patriarchs around the campfire. No more wood shavings to complain about. How many times had she teased her husband about his tent pole? Long after the Amalek blood had worn off, she would say, "Here is your weapon, let's set up the tent." And they would laugh. Well, she admitted, to herself, she would laugh. What would happen to the illustrated scroll? Who would finish it? She held the carved bird she had worn around her neck since he had built the balustrade on the vizier's porch. The back had turned black, the front worn smooth by her clothes. It hardly looked like a bird in flight anymore.

The families mourned until the river receded, then Judah found a crossing and the tribes moved north.

Chapter 12

NOW THE PILLAR OF CLOUD, WITH the Tabernacle in the midst of the tribes, led the people into the land of Moab. As he had forbidden violence against Edom, so Yahweh forbade the people to disturb Moab, for he had promised that land to Lot, Abraham's nephew. Staying east of Moab, they crossed the Arnon River, the border between Moab and the Amorites, and they entered the wilderness of the Amorites. They camped in Beer where Moses led the people to a well of water, and he composed this song:

Spring up O well! Sing to it!
The well which the leaders sank,
The well which the nobles of the people dug,
With the scepter and with their staffs.

Then Israel sent messages to Sihon, king of the Amorites, asking for peaceful passage, just as they had with Edom. But Sihon forbade them passage and sent an army out to prevent them. Now Yahweh had not promised anyone that land, so Israel went up against the Amorites and defeated them and dispossessed them of their land and their cities. And Israel moved into the cities and villages of the Amorites, into Ar and Heshbon and Jazar.

The camps of Israel with all their flocks followed the army and when the warriors cleared the land of the enemy, the people walked amazed through the streets and into buildings, for most had never seen a street or entered a house. Shy at first, they moved tentatively, half expecting someone to shout, *thief!* When it became evident that the land had indeed been conquered and that everything belonged to them, the people began to fight and vie for the best houses, the best cook pots, the best clothing. They plundered the Amorites with abandon.

"No," Rachel stood with fists at her waist and spoke to her granddaughters. "I will not sleep in one of those filthy houses. Nor will you. They probably have lice. We will stay here in our tents. This is a beautiful land but it is not the Promised Land. We will build our own house there."

Disgusted with their grandmother, the girls argued and pleaded.

Tirzah: "Everything will be gone by the time we get there."

Hoglah: "We can clean it. Sweep it. Wash it. We have lice sometimes."

"Hebrew lice are different," said Rachel.

Milcha: "I want to go to the market. What is a market?"

Mahlah: "I want to go to the market."

"You have all you need. You do not need to go to the market."

Kore: "Mama, let's at least take the girls into town, let them see."

"Who is going to watch our tents? I will stay here with Noah. Kore, you take the girls. And do not lose them! Take some empty bags. There may be something to get. See if you can get some flour. And some leaven. I'll make bread. And do not talk to anybody not from Manasseh."

She watched her granddaughters, holding hands as instructed, walk away toward the town. *This is going to change everything*, she thought. *I'll have to make sure they do not become grasping and worldly. Maybe I can get some olive shoots.* She had thought for a long time how wonderful it would be to have an olive grove. *I wonder how long it takes an olive tree to produce?*

On the way, the young women met Hebrews who thought like their grandmother. They had grabbed what they could carry and headed back to the safety of their tents. Still holding hands, Kore on one end and Tirzah on the other, the girls joined a growing, noisy throng and followed a road through what had once been the entrance to the walled town—broken stone columns and shattered, heavy gates thrown to the side. Caught up in the tide of people, they walked into the markets place where shouting people fought over rugs and lengths of cloth, and broken pottery littered the ground. Milcha stooped to pick up a broken loom. "Nana would like this if it wasn't broken," she said. She laid the loom carefully on the ground. Dumb-struck by the goings on, the girls had stopped, open-mouthed. Kore pulled them into motion; they walked through the markets to the other side, stepping over broken wares.

Shouting above the racket, Kore said, "Let's go see what a house looks like." She led them from the markets with its clamor and din into an equally noisy, narrow alley. Mortared stones proved to be the walls of houses, for skins hung at intervals over doorways, and narrow spaces in the stones turned out to be windows. A trench, centering the alley, stank of excrement. Buffeted by people coming and going, avoiding the trench, the girls walked single file close to the wall. Kore stopped and pulled aside a skin. In the dim interior a woman stood at a corner fire pit stirring a steaming pot. Smoke rose through a hole above. She grinned and motioned for Kore to enter. "My nieces have never seen a house." Holding Mahlah's hand Kore stood in the doorway. The woman laid her wooden paddle across the pot and peered past Kore around the animal skin. Seeing the group of girls, she produced a broad toothless grin and motioned them inside.

"I am Dinah, of the tribe, Judah," she said. "We came in behind the army and got a good house." She motioned to steps on the back wall, leading to a square room above. "We sleep up there." On the other side a ladder led to the roof, revealing a patch of bright blue sky. Baskets and jugs had been neatly piled in one corner. A small fenced area held two goats. From a built-in ledge of rock, Dinah took a bowl and poured water from a goat skin that hung from a peg fitted into the wall. She handed the bowl to Kore who drank and passed it around.

Mahlah asked the woman, "Do you have lice?"

"Mahlah!" Tirzah clapped her hand over her sister's mouth.

Dinah threw back her head and laughed. "Most of them ran away with the people." She lifted her thatched broom. "This is for the ones that did not go."

"Do you like living in a house?" asked Milcha.

The woman thought a moment. "Not very much. I like to walk outside my tent and see the mountains, feel the breeze. The noise and smells are not pleasant. My son is keeping the goats in the hills. He says we will receive a large inheritance when Moses and the army moves us into the Promised Land. We will build our own house there, not in a row, like this one."

"When we get to the Promised Land I will marry," said Tirzah.

"It has been a long time coming," said Dinah. "I have had three husbands. One died in the first war. One died at the golden calf. One just up and died. Now my son takes care of me."

Chapter 13

AT THE CAMP OF MANASSEH, THE YOUNGER girls jabbered to their grandmother for hours about the town and Dinah's house. Kore, who had been in markets from Damascus to Cairo, remained silent, happy to enjoy her nieces' excitement. Of particular interest to Milcha had been the shelf built into the wall. "They set things on it," she said. "It is called a shelf. I want a shelf someday." They had come home empty-handed.

Tirzah seemed quiet to Rachel, then, "Nana," she said, "the woman who was in the house has got me thinking. She said they would build a house on their inherited land. When we get to the Promised Land, where will *we* live? Gideon says the land will be divided and *everyone* will receive an inheritance."

"Well, I suppose we will live near Gideon's family, Uncle Enoch's kin. After all, his mother, Magdah, is Enoch's daughter-in-law."

"But, Nana," protested Hoglah, "Uncle Enoch and his son are dead. Aunt Magdah is married to another cousin now, and besides, she hates us because of me and Gershon. Do we have to live with them?"

Tirzah spoke. "I want to know what happened to *our* inheritance. What happened to our father's inheritance? What happened to Grandpapa's inheritance?"

"Well," Rachel ticked on her fingers: "Grandpapa had no brothers, no sons, so his inheritance died with him. Your father, Zelophehad, had no sons, so his inheritance died with him, also."

"Our inheritance *died?*" Tirzah covered her mouth.

"Females do not inherit." Rachel said, shaking her head. "Did you not know this, girl?"

"We will not have any *land?* Of our *own?* Are we not a Hebrew family?" Tirzah paced with a stricken look.

"Yahweh will take care of us," said Rachel. "You will have Gideon's land. We will all live under his wing.

"With his mother, that Magdah, spitting on the ground every time I pass." said Hoglah.

❧

Rachel stood in line at the latrine which had always proved the best place to get news. She was seldom disappointed.

The woman ahead of her said, "Have you heard about that diviner the king of Moab hired to curse the Hebrews?" Several women laughed.

Another spoke up. "No. This story is true. I heard every time he tried, he ended up blessing us instead. Then Balak, the king would send him to a different place."

"As if a different place would be a better place to make a curse?" someone asked.

"How could that happen?" said another. "How do you know this?"

"My son in the army. They captured someone from Moab. He told it. Three times the man, Balaam, went to a different place to say the curse, but every time, Yahweh made him change the curse into a blessing. Finally, the diviner said, no one can curse someone Yahweh has blessed. Anyway, he gave up and went back to his own land. They say he has a donkey that talks." Again, everyone laughed.

Another day Rachel and Kore stood in line listening to the latest gossip. The story was so terrible, a crowd formed. "There was this man named Cozbi, and he had a Midianite woman named Simri, and Cozbi took this Simri to meet his relatives—right there in front of the Tent of Meeting— in front of Moses and everyone." The women gasped and covered their mouths.

"Then Cozbi took this Simri into his tent..." Some of the women covered their faces. "Then Phinehas, the priest, followed them and stabbed the two of them through with his spear."

"Moses was already furious," said another woman who knew the story. "Some Moabites invited some Hebrews to a feast, and they ate and bowed down to the Moab god, Baal-Peor. The priests executed 24,000 people who were guilty." The remainder of the women, including Rachel and Kore lowered their veils.

On the way back to their tent, Rachel said, "If we do not get to the Promised Land soon, no one will be left to go in."

Kore had her own news: "Mama, I think Tirzah is planning to go to Moses about our lost inheritance. What do you think about that?"

"I think she is in for heartache. She should marry Gideon and let him be our head. I think he can control his mother."

"I do not think anyone can control Magdah" countered Kore. "She hates Hoglah. I would not gainsay an intention to poison your granddaughter."

&

The nation of Israel, the women and those not fit to fight had moved camp to the Plains of Moab, a wide grassy plain east of the Jordan River, the very river they must cross. Rolling hills covered in trees surrounded the plain, and Phinehas' sons moved their flocks and Rachel's into valleys with streams. With every move since leaving Kadesh, they came closer to the Promised Land. A knot of worry had taken hold in Rachel: could the sin of people like Cozbi cause Yahweh to send them back into the wilderness, back to that land of sun and sand and rock? They had been so near before; now they had come near again...*Mordecai would be disappointed if he heard these worries,* she thought. *He would say, worry is not trust.*

On a windy day heavy with the smell of rain, Rachel, Kore, and the girls stood on a hill overlooking the vast Jordan valley to the west. To the east, black clouds rolled over a mountain range running from north to south fading into the hazy horizon at each end. Somewhere to the north, the army fought the inhabitants for the land. "I do not understand," Tirzah told her grandmother, "why we are fighting there? This is not the Promised Land, is it? Will there not be enough fighting when we cross the river? Will Gideon always be off fighting somewhere?"

Rachel said, "At least he has a weapon and a shield. Your grandfather, Uncle Enoch, and Phinehas went to war with sharpened tent poles." She settled her gaze over the Jordan valley. "I hope this is the last camp before we go across the Jordan. Forty years of moving is enough. I want a garden before I die, then you can bury me in it. I want to be in the sun." *Not in a cold, dark cave like Judith,* she thought.

"We will plant a tree on top," said Mahlah without sentiment. "What kind do you want, Nana?"

"Well, it should be beautiful and useful. A fig tree."

&

The steady attrition of the older men had not diminished the size of the vast Hebrew army. Did the midwives not tell the Egyptians the Hebrew women were hardy in childbirth? After taking Ammon, the army fought against Og, the king of Bashan and defeated his cities, leaving no remnant. They completely cleared the land east of the Jordan River. Then they returned to their tribes and camped with their families east of the Jordan.

Gideon, always slow to speak, came home from the wars silent and withdrawn. To Tirzah, he seemed as sad as he had been after Gershon's death. "So you defeated Sihon, king of the Amorites first. Then what happened?

Tell me about that king of Bashan, that Og," she coaxed. "Was he really a giant?"

"His bed was nine cubits long and four cubits wide, made of iron. I saw it myself. They pulled it out into the street and laid his dead body on it. He was a huge man. They say he was a descendant of the Nephalim."

"And everyone celebrated..."

"Yes. Then we slew them all," he said, "every last one."

"And the women and children...?" Tirzah knew the answer before she asked. "Did you kill the children?"

"Tirza..." Tears sprang from Gideon's eyes; he covered his face and sobbed. After a while he raised his head, embarrassed. "We had orders. I should be ashamed, but I cannot help it. I am glad. When I saw what they were doing—dashing the children—I went into a shed to hide myself. There was a pile of hay at the back. Some men were already there. They thought I was a commander; they almost killed me. But they took me in and we stayed there all night...The screams...One man had a little boy with him. He kept his hand over the child's mouth all night. The next morning, while everyone slept, I found a basket, and we put the boy in it. That is the last I saw of them. I smeared some blood on my shoes and tunic and joined my troop."

"Why? Why must they kill the children?"

"Because they grow up to avenge their fathers; their blood lust makes them more fierce than their fathers ever were."

☙

When the army returned from the wars, Moses declared a census of all the men over the age of twenty. Each tribe would be counted and the number would be the basis for establishing the inheritance, the allotted portion: the greater the number, the larger the inheritance. But the location of the tribal land would be decided by lot, and within that location, individual family plots would also be distributed by size and by lot.

Once word went out about the census, and that it would be the basis for determining the inheritance, Tirzah knew she had to act. If she were going to appeal to Moses for an inheritance, now was the time. *I may be young and only a female*, she thought, *but if I were Zelophehad's son, I would speak for this family.*

"Go to *Moses*?" Fear and shock distorted Hoglah's mouth.

"Go to Moses. You would do that?" said Rachel.

"If our father were alive, he would have an inheritance. If we were sons, we would have an inheritance." Tirzah had called a meeting of the family. She held Noah on her lap while she told them her plan: As she spoke, horror settled on the faces of her sisters. "We will all go together, the five of us."

"Oh, Tee. I'm afraid," said Hoglah. "Moses..."

"I'm not afraid," said Mahlah—anything to be different from Hoglah.

"I am," said Milcha.

"I am," parroted Noah.

"No you're not." Tirzah jiggled her baby sister. "We are going. Tomorrow morning. None of you has to open your mouth. Just stand with me. Can you do that?" Only Mahlah nodded.

"Tomorrow morning after manna, we will leave. It will take a while to get to the Tent of Meeting."

Sleep would not come. Tirzah had practiced what she would say. She must not whine. She must sound strong. She must look Moses straight in the eye... *Should I? What if he thinks me brazen?* Who did she think she was? Would she be scolded? What if he laughed? He would not do that. Could she be punished for such impudence? *Oh, Yahweh, help me to be brave. Make Moses take pity on us.*

Tirzah woke, surprised that she had slept. Noah had wedged herself under her armpit. She eased herself from the covers she shared with her sisters and draped her cloak over her shoulders. She left the warmth of the tent and added a double handful of dung to the banked embers. A spark rose with promise into the air then died. *That is me,* she thought. *I will not last any longer than that.* She began to feel sick. They did not have to go today, did they?

She thought about Moses. He must be very old. She had only seen him from a distance. When Aaron died at Mount Hor, she watched them go up. His long white hair and beard...he must be fierce and strict. Did he not send plagues and snakes to punish the people? No. He only did what Yahweh told him to do. Grandpapa had said so. Grandpapa said Moses was humble and good. It was the people who were bad. She paced, gesturing, convincing the flickering fire with a mute soliloquy.

"It all sounds very good," said Rachel. "Say it just like that."

Tirzah laid her head on Rachel's shoulder. "Oh, Nana, what will happen?"

Rachel patted Tirzah's back. "You will be brave. Moses will be kind. Those two things I know."

"Why should we not have an inheritance? We had a father. And a grandfather."

"That is what you will say to Moses."

Tirzah did not ask her grandmother to go with them. After the last move her hips had stiffened. Kore offered to go, but Tirzah refused her aunt.

Somehow, she knew the thing must be kept simple: five orphaned females seeking an inheritance. No Nana, no aunt. When Gideon offered to accompany them, she refused him, also.

They walked steadily, taking turns carrying Noah. Soon they moved beyond familiar faces and greetings and passed tent groups where curious stares followed four black-caped girls, carrying a baby. Coming up on the back side of the Tent of Meeting, they turned right and followed the curtained wall to the corner. "Nana wove some of these panels," she informed her sisters. They turned left and followed the side wall to the front where a crowd of petitioners stood in a ragged line, seeking an audience with Moses.

Black-robed priests moved along the line speaking to the people, sending many away. As the line thinned people shuffled forward, pushing Tirzah and her sisters toward an inevitable encounter with a young priest who worked his way toward them. Watching him, dreading him, Tirzah noticed he seemed to wear his priestly black robe and hat proudly, his hands clasped at his waist, long fingers white against the black. He stopped, surveying the huddle of females standing in his line. Tirzah wanted to adjust her veil but did not. She shifted Noah away from the priest to her other hip. Milcah and Mahlah cowered behind; she felt their faces pressing into her back. His eyes settled on Hoglah and lingered, until she dipped her head and abandoned Tirzah to face the man alone. She squared her shoulders and met his piercing eyes.

"Where is your father, girl?"

"Our father is dead."

"What do you want with Moses?"

"We are seeking our inheritance." Several people laughed.

The priest pulled his top lip into a smirk, and with a look, invited the surrounding people to join in his disdain. "You will not find that here. Go home." He moved down the line. They inched forward. Through the crowd, Tirzah caught a glimpse of Moses sitting at a table just outside the entrance. Eleazar, the head priest and the tribal leaders sat with him.

"I told you to leave," said a now familiar voice. The priest gripped her elbow.

"We are not leaving," she said over her shoulder. "We came to see Moses." The priest tightened his grip and pulled her arm downward, forcing her to the ground. The crowd drew back, arguing, speculating. Tirzah handed Noah, frightened and bawling, to Hoglah. Having lost their shield, Mahlah and Milcha cringed behind Hoglah. *Well, here we are. I have created a spectacle,* thought Tirza. She wanted to gird up her skirts and run.

"What is this commotion?" Two young priests set a red box carriage on the ground beside Tirzah. An ancient man, his pink head visible through long wisps of white hair, peered over the side. Men in the crowd shouted, *that girl...*The old man waved off the bystanders, and motioning to the bearers, ordered, "Help her up." Strong hands lifted Tirzah to her feet. "I know you, young woman."

"And I know you. You are Elias. You honored us when you came to my grandfather's burial." Tirzah dusted herself off, resettled her veil, and cast a wary eye at the priest.

"I hope you will forgive my great nephew. He is over-zealous at times."

"Uncle Elias..."

The old priest dismissed the man with an impatient wave. "Go tell your mother to prepare for guests." Elias directed his attention to the stricken girls and motioned them to come near. "Do not be frightened. You are here to see Moses. Follow me." The carriage cut through the parting crowd, the girls trailing behind like four black ducklings. He led them straight to Moses where he sat at his table. They waited for an old couple to leave, then the men set the carriage down before the table. Peering up from the ground, Elias said to Moses, "These are the granddaughters of Mordecai, of the tribe Manasseh, the man who made this table, who carved the holy articles for the Tabernacle." Motioning them forward, Elias said, "Speak, girl."

Tirzah pulled her sisters forward and stationed each one to face Moses: Milcha and Mahlah to her right and Hoglah to her left. She took Noah in her arms. Only then did she gaze into the kindest eyes she had ever beheld. Tears immediately ran down her face but her chin did not tremble, nor did her voice waver.

"Our father died in the wilderness, yet he was not among the company of those who gathered themselves together against Yahweh in the company of Korah; but he died in his own sin, and he had no sons. Why should the name of our father be withdrawn from among his family because he had no son? Give us a possession among our father's brothers."

Dazed and unsure of what she had said, Tirzah gathered her sisters. They followed Elias' carriage to a nearby canopy, where his nephews lifted the old man from the carriage and sat him on a rug with the girls. His granddaughter served them meat pies, dates and goat's milk, while he told them stories of their grandfather and their time together in Pharaoh's wood shop. He told them about the awful food the master's daughter served them every night and made them laugh. He told them about the sarcophagi their grandfather carved and the day he first saw their grandmother at the vizier's house. "Once he realized it was really Rachel, he could talk of nothing else. Your grandmother was comely," he said. "and you all look just like her."

"Everyone says I look the most like her," said Hoglah.

He told them how their grandfather had become a master carver and how the objects in the Tabernacle had been carved by him. "Mordecai was like a son to me," he said. "He even saved my life one time."

"You are Elias who taught Grandpapa about Abraham and Joseph," stated Milcha. "Did you know them? You are very old."

"Milcha!" Sometimes Tirzah wished for a rag to stuff in her sister's mouth.

A wide toothless grin spread over Elias' face. "Listen," he said, "I do not know what the answer will be about your inheritance, but I know Moses will do what Yahweh tells him to do. So it will be the right thing, no matter what." He spoke to Tirzah, "As for my nephew, he will be disciplined."

"Don't beat him," said Mahlah, stuffing another date into her mouth.

Chapter 14

THE HEBREWS CAMPED IN THE PLAINS of Moab across the Jordan River from Jericho. Mount Nebo rose to the south, half a day's journey away. Word came that Moses would speak to the people from the mountain. Surely he would give instructions for the last leg of the journey. Maybe he would praise the army, for they had routed the enemy from the land.

"We will travel light," said Rachel. "Each one take your warm cloak and your bedroll. Take a water bag. Mahlah, you may take Morsel. Don't forget his tether. I will take cheese and manna cakes. Where is Gideon? I thought he was going with us."

"His mother wanted him to travel with them," said Tirza.

"I hope we get our inheritance," said Hoglah, "or that woman will be running our lives forever."

The great assembly of Israel left their tents and gathered at the foothills of the mountain, spreading across surrounding hills, carving out space for their families. When Moses walked from the Tent of Meeting and made his way to a flat rock, excitement filled the hearts of the Hebrews. Even blind Noah felt it and began to bounce in Tirza's arms. She gazed toward the mountain as if she could see it and he who stood upon it.

Tirzah said, "Oh, Nana, if you could only see him up close...I was so afraid until I looked into his eyes—so kind and gentle. Just remembering it makes me cry.

Moses spoke. His voice carried perfectly to the surrounding hillsides where the great assembly of Hebrews gathered. Rachel remembered how perfectly his voice could be heard at Mountain of Yahweh. How did Yahweh accomplish such a thing? Did he carry the words on the air? Did the rocks echo them across the hills?

"You have seen all that Yahweh did before your eyes in the land of Egypt to Pharaoh and all his servants and all his land..." Milcha stretched her eyes and shrugged, palms raised. Rachel's reprimand died on her tongue. It was true, most of the people had not seen what happened in Egypt or did not remember.

"...and Yahweh has led you forty years in the wilderness; your clothes have not worn out on you and your sandal has not worn out on your foot. You have not eaten bread nor have you drunk wine or strong drink in order that you might know Yahweh, your God.

"You stand today, all of you, before Yahweh that you may enter into the covenant and into his oath which Yahweh is making with you today, in order that he may establish you as his people and that he may be your God, just as he swore to Abraham, Isaac and Jacob.

"...you have seen abominations of idols of wood, stone, silver and gold...if anyone, whether man, woman, family or tribe, will go and serve these gods, and boast saying, 'I have peace, though I walk in the stubbornness my heart, Yahweh will never be willing to forgive him... Yahweh will single him out for adversity...

"If you return to Yahweh and obey him, with all your heart and soul, then Yahweh will restore you...and have compassion on you...If you obey Yahweh and keep his commandments and his statutes which are written in the book of the law, if you turn to Yahweh with all your heart and soul, he will prosper you.

"This commandment is not too difficult for you or out of reach.

"It is not in heaven, that you should say, who will go get it for us?

"Nor is it beyond the sea, that you should say, who will cross the sea for us that we may observe it?

"The word is very near, in your mouth and in your heart that you may observe it."

Then Moses said, "I am a hundred and twenty years old today; I am no longer able to come and go, and Yahweh has said to me, 'You shall not cross this Jordan.'

"It is Yahweh who will cross ahead of you; he will destroy these nations before you and you shall dispossess them. Joshua is the one who will cross ahead of you, just as Yahweh has spoken.

"And Yahweh will do to them just as he has done to Sihon and Og, the kings of the Amorites, and to their land when he destroyed it...

"Be strong and courageous, do not be afraid or tremble at them, for Yahweh is the one who goes with you. He will not fail you or forsake you.

"At the end of every seven years, all debts will be forgiven. At that time, read the law which I, Moses, have written and given to the priests. Read it to all the people, so your children, who have not known it, will hear and learn to fear Yahweh, as long as you live on the land which you are about to cross the Jordan to possess."

Then Moses spoke the words of a song-poem he had written—one for the people to recite and teach to their children—a history of Yahweh's provenance, a prophesy of times to come and a warning to the people to keep faith with Yahweh.

Moses left the mountain, and Joshua, the son of Nun, went down from his place on the hillside. They met at the Tent of Meeting, and the pillar of cloud covered the doorway. Thus in sight of the nation of Israel, Yahweh commissioned Joshua: "Be strong and courageous, for you shall bring the sons of Israel into the land which I swore to them, and I will be with you." Moses wrote the words in the book of the law and gave them to the priests to keep for all time.

Moses walked again to the rock and gave a blessing to the twelve tribes, each one unique:

May Reuben live and not die, nor his men be few.
May Judah be a help against his adversaries.
Of Levi, Yahweh proved the godly man at the waters of Massah and
  Meribah.
May Yahweh bless Benjamin and shield him all the day.
Of Joseph' sons, may He who dwelt in the burning bush favor Ephraim and
  Manasseh.
Zebulun, rejoice in your travels; you shall draw out the abundance of the seas.
Issachar, rejoice in your tents; your sacrifices shall be righteous.
As for Gad, he executed the justice of Yahweh.
Dan is a lion's whelp that leaps forth from Bashan.
Naphtali is full of the blessing of Yahweh.
Asher, may you be favored by your brothers and may your life be a leisurely
  walk.

The people returned to their camps and Moses climbed to the top of Mount Nebo, in the plains of Moab, and he died. It is said Yahweh showed him the Promised Land as far as the western sea. It is said, Yahweh buried him in the valley of Moab, but no man knows his burial place to this day. It is said, since then, no prophet has risen like Moses, whom Yahweh knew face to face. And the people wept and mourned for Moses thirty days.

It seemed the days of mourning would never end. The Jordan River, like a tantalizing fruit hanging just out of reach, flowed deep and verdant to the west. Mahlah asked the question every child wanted to ask: why can we not mourn from the other side? And Rachel answered, "Yahweh's timing is perfect When it is time to cross, we will cross." But in her heart she echoed Mahlah's sentiments.

Since the trip to Nebo, Rachel's hips ached as never before. She spent most of her days sitting under her awning telling her granddaughters stories of Egypt and her childhood and the time of the plagues. They could not get enough of Asmath and Hopi and the market and the Nile River. Crocodiles loomed large in their imaginations. She told them of the murals painted on their sleeping room walls. "They looked like Phinehas' scroll," she explained, "only much larger—Hepsut and Marwat were as tall as you."

"Did you know them?"

"No. They were not real. A man came and painted them on the wall. We made up their names and the things they did."

"But how did they do things if they were painted on the wall?"

"Close your eyes," Rachel directed the girls. Now make a dog come into your mind. What color is he?" Milcha: Black; Mahlah: yellow. "Make him wag his tail." The girls smiled with closed eyes. "Now throw a stick and make the dog go get it." The girls watched their dogs, laughed, and opened their eyes.

"That is how you make stories in your mind." Their game ended abruptly when a young priest stopped at the edge of their rug. Following Tirzah's lead, all the girls rose. Mahlah and Milcha moved behind their grandmother.

The priest glanced repeatedly at Hoglah, who returned his gaze, while he addressed Tirzah: "Please do not fear me. I bring news from my uncle, Elias, and my cousin, Moses."

How humbly he stands, thought Rachel, *holding his own hands. My cousin Moses, he says...* "Mahlah, Milcha, go in the tent. You too, Hoglah," said Rachel.

"But Nana..." Hoglah protested.

"Go on." Hoglah entered the tent behind her sisters, flipping shut the flap. Rachel saw the three, peeking from a slit in the door. "Tirzah get the priest a bowl of water." To the priest she motioned and said, "Please sit. Why should my granddaughter fear you?" She knew this must be the priest who had treated her granddaughters badly. *My cousin, Moses...*

The priest set free his hands and accepted the cup from Tirzah who remained standing.

"It is my duty to go along the line and cull those who should seek a lower judge. My cousin cannot see everyone. I should say, *could* not see everyone."

"And?"

"When your granddaughter said she came to ask for her inheritance, the idea seemed so outlandish, I told her to leave."

"And?"

"She did not leave."

"You mean she did not obey."

"Yes."

"And you are accustomed to being obeyed..."

"Well, yes. I am a priest."

"What is your news?" Rachel tired of toying with the man.

"I have good news and sad news. My Great Uncle Elias has died."

"Oh, no."

"He was as old as my cousins, Moses and Aaron. Very old."

"I know. He was such a good man. My husband loved him."

"We will take his body to the Promised Land. It was his desire. Now for the good news: your granddaughters will receive their inheritance among their male relatives." He said it so matter-of-factly, Rachel almost missed it.

"What?" Her hand pressed against her heart.

"My cousin Moses asked Yahweh and consulted with all the leaders. I would have come sooner, but we have been at the mountain. "Zelophehad's daughters, your granddaughters' names have been written down. Whenever this statute is cited, their names will be spoken. Moses has decreed this and it shall never be revoked."

*Their names...*thought Rachel. Again her hand pressed against her heart.

"There is just one more thing...When the leaders of Manasseh heard of this thing, they worried that their inheritance might be passed on to another family through marriage. They appealed to Moses, and he agreed: when women inherit, they must marry within their father's family.

"That seems reasonable and wise." Rachel rose. "Thank you for coming." She noticed with satisfaction the priest's look of chagrin at being dismissed so abruptly. *You are in my house now,* she thought. He glanced at the tent door, donned his sandals, bowed, and walked away.

"What a horrible man," said Tirzah.

"More horrible to some than others," said Rachel. "I do not think we have seen the last of Moses' cousin."

Milcha's round face appeared in the doorway. "Can we come out?"

Tirza, wonder and delight written on her face said, "I can hardly take it in. Sisters, we have our inheritance. We will have our own land in the midst of our cousins." She broke into laughter, grabbed her sisters and swung them around.

Chapter 15

J OSHUA COMMANDED THE LEADERS of Israel to pass among the people and inform them that in three days they would cross the Jordan River and enter the Promised Land.

"Why do I need three days," Rachel said to Kore, "have I not been packing and unpacking for forty years? Can I not do it in my sleep?" Her hips ached. She was ready to cross the Jordan River, set up her tent and rest.

"I love the smell of grass," said Kore.

Their tents stood on a knoll, giving them a commanding view of the surrounding camps. Rachel shielded her eyes from the sun—a gentler sun, it seemed, from the merciless ball that tortured them in the wilderness. Shepherds had started bringing the flocks closer for muster, their sharp whistles echoing through the valleys, rising to the hilltops. Dogs dashed back and forth, tails low, ears back, a flash here, turning, a nip there, working to control the mass of animals. Goats and sheep know the sound of their master's voice, his whistle; they know their dogs; now thousands of confused sheep, goats, donkeys and cattle, spoils from the wars, had been added to Manasseh's herds, causing chaos.

Another kind of spoil had been shared among the tribes. Sixteen thousand virgins, spared from the great slaughter the Hebrews exacted upon their enemies, had been taken in by the twelve tribes. When offered a young female-child, Rachel had said, "What do I need with another girl? Give me a boy." But all the male children had been slain.

"Nana," said Milcha, "Did Pharaoh slay all the boy babies when Moses was born?"

Rachel knew Milcha never asked a simple question. She came at it sideways. "Yes, he did that." *I know where you are going with this,* she thought.

"My friend said our army killed all the boys. Why did they do that?"

"It is the way of war. Do not ask me. I think it is terrible."

Hoglah gave the skin for churning butter a vigorous shake and whined, "Where is Tirza? Must I do this by myself? I hate churning and Tirzah likes it."

"She and Gideon are making plans," said Rachel. "Tirzah wants to be wed the moment the Promised Land is under her feet. How she plans to do that I do not know."

"That is what she told Gershon. He grew weary of hearing it."

"Well, now she is saying it to his brother. And he is not weary."

"Gideon will have to marry me now. The inheritance has to stay in the family. Besides the patriarch, Jacob, was married to sisters."

"And you have heard the stories of jealousy and strife between Rachel and Leah. No, Hoglah. We have a large family. Your Great Uncle Enoch has more grandsons than I can count. Most of them are of an age to marry. There is a husband somewhere in there for you." *If any will have you,* she thought. *Maybe between the inheritance and your beauty, you will be able to entice some poor boy.*

Rachel spied Tirzah and Gideon standing with two small girls four or five years old. She left Hoglah to her complaints and Milcha to her questions and joined them. "Who are these? Look how thin they are. And dirty. Where are their shoes?"

"Captive children," said Gideon. "I do not think they are native Amorites. I think they are captives from somewhere else. But they refuse to talk. I checked; they still have their tongues. We may never know where they came from."

"What are you going to do with them?" Before he could answer, Rachel cupped their chins in her hands and smiled into their filthy, tear-stained faces. Choosing one, then the other, she parted their matted hair and peered at their scalps, fulfilling an unspoken prophecy: "Lice."

"We are taking them, Nana," said Tirza. "Gideon took them from his cousin Eli. He had to fight him to get them."

Gideon rubbed his knuckles as if to affirm the account. "He had tied them to the back of his wagon with the goats."

"Well, we cannot have that...come on Tirza, let's get them cleaned up." Speaking softly, Rachel took the barefooted, frightened girls by their hands and headed for her tents. "I know some of Mahlah's clothes will fit you. And from the looks of you, Hoglah will lose her claim to be the most comely female in the family."

"They'll be spoiled, fat ticks before the week is out," said Tirza.

"Before the week is out, we will be married across the river," said Gideon.

"Have I not said? And you will be marrying a woman with an inheritance. Do not forget that, husband." Tirzah left her betrothed and joined her grandmother under the awning.

Rachel, it seemed, had forgotten her sore hips. "Milcah, you and Mahlah heat some water. These girls need washing. Hoglah, heat up the oil. We'll have these lice out in no time."

"Lice!" said Hoglah. "They are not sleeping near me."

"Hoglah-girl," said Rachel, "Moses wrote an ordinance concerning the alien who lives among us. They are to be treated with kindness. If you prefer to sleep under the awning, we will move your bed."

&

Early on the morning of the third day, Rachel stood beside the cart, whereupon her granddaughters and the slave girls, now indistinguishable from the rest, crowded for a better view. The early yellow sun warmed their backs and lifted the fog from surrounding valleys and the river. Haze cleared from the azure blue mountains, revealing their rugged form. Circling low, waiting for warm air currents to carry him aloft, a hawk, like a herald of momentous events, screeched, *kee-arr, kee-arr.*

From their vantage point on the rise where they camped, Rachel, her family and all Manasseh watched the priests carry the Ark of the Covenant and the Tabernacle in their march toward the river. Rachel spotted a red box carriage in the throng of priests following the Tabernacle. Like Joseph's bones, it seemed their old friend, Elias, would make it to the Promised Land. The priests carrying the Ark moved to the edge of the flooded Jordan. When their feet touched the water, the people gasped open-mouthed, for the river stopped flowing from the north and drained away to the south.

"Look," Rachel pointed north where the waters heaped up at a town they could barely see, a town called Adam. "This is exactly what happened at the shores of the Red Sea. I was your age, Hoglah. Now you will see for yourselves." The priests carried the Ark to the center of the river and stood on dry ground. Below them, many cubits to the south, the tribe of Judah moved out and began to cross the dry river bed. Thousands upon thousands of people and flocks of sheep and goats from seven tribes must cross before Manasseh. Rachel knew it would be hours before they moved out, so she allowed the girls to watch from the empty cart. *They will tell their children stories of this day,* she thought, *just as I have told them my stories. Surely no one will ever doubt that these things happened...*

Finally, Rachel motioned for the mesmerized girls to get down. "Time to load." Everything had been piled nearby and the girls quickly packed the cart to their grandmother's standards. *Oh, Mordecai,* thought Rachel, *how many times have we loaded this cart, your most prized possession? Sometimes I thought you loved it more than me.* Her mind a-whirl, she remembered how her husband, with blistered feet, had toiled to push the cart across the sand. Most of the char from the fire, when they lost everything, had worn off. Goats had gnawed the boards; the wheels had not matched in years. *Oh, my husband, I said goodbye and left Asmath at the Red Sea. I will take you with me. It will make you so happy to see your cart carrying us safely into the Promised Land.*

The hawk sailed high on a warm updraft by the time the tribe of Manasseh, in their thousands, with their carts and wagons, their dogs and herds, stepped onto the dry riverbed. With hushed voices they crossed the Jordan. Among them walked a woman named Rachel and her five granddaughters, the daughters of Zelophehad. Because of them, Hebrew women would be blessed for all time, and their names were Milcha, Tirzah, Mahlah, Hoglah and Noah. They climbed the far bank and entered the Promised Land.

The End

The eternal Yahweh is a dwelling place,
And underneath are the everlasting arms,
Blessed are you, O Israel;
Who is like you, a people saved by Yahweh.

Rachel's Stories of the Ten Plagues
(as told to her granddaughters)

Plague of Blood

"Well now...

"The year I was fourteen, Asmath and I were learning to weave one afternoon. Hopi, our bodyguard, had taken us to the yarn dyers, and we had chosen our colors. Mine was a beautiful blue. The woman at the vats said it was made from a crushed beetle bug. Asmath chose yellow made from the center parts of a flower. The yarn was soft and very expensive, especially the blue.

"We thought Hopi was teasing when he came running onto the porch blabbering like a mad man. He did tease us sometimes. One time he put a lizard in Asmath's pocket. I can see him now: he had large, very white teeth and he was very black. When he smiled his eyes disappeared."

"What did she do Nana?" Mahlah hugged herself.

"She ran around the room throwing off her clothes."

"Did she scream?"

"Mahlah please," said Tirzah, "let Nana tell it."

"Oh yes, she screamed. And if I remember, she knocked over a vase and broke it and then we were all in trouble."

"But you didn't do anything wrong," said Milcah.

"Well, sometimes life is not fair."

"Milcah, please," begged Tirzah.

"Asmath's father forgot all about the vase when he heard Hopi's news: the water in the Nile River had turned to blood. And not only that, the water in the pools and canals and reservoirs were also blood. So Asmath's father went to see if this was all true. And it was. All the water everywhere had turned to blood. Well, Asmath's mother said we would just have to drink the water we had in the house, but when she looked in the urns, that water was blood, too. So we had no water to drink. No water to bathe in.

"Then the fish in the Nile died and began to stink and the blood began to stink. Crocodiles crawled out of the water onto the banks. Now Asmath's uncle had a villa on the water, so one day we stood on his balcony and looked down at the river and the floating dead fish and the crocodiles. We knew crocodiles lived in the river, but it was frightening to see so many. I will never forget that blood-red water and all those crocodiles...

"Asmath's father sent Hopi to buy goat's milk, and cow's milk, and we drank that, until the animals quit giving, because they had no water either. Some people discovered that fresh-dug wells produced clear water, so every day Hopi went to buy water, and the people would be fighting over it. This went on for seven days.

"Now rumor had it that two Hebrew priests named Moses and Aaron were behind all this, but who could prove such a thing? At that time we did not know anything about Moses and Aaron.

"Finally, after seven days, we heard shouts and whistling beyond our garden. Asmath's mother checked the urns, and the water had turned clear. To celebrate, the cook made a basket of food for the family, and we went to a tributary of the Nile toward Goshen, to bathe and eat. As you know, Goshen is where our people, the Hebrew slaves lived. When we approached in our carriages, they bowed and moved to the side so we could pass. In my heart I knew I was a slave, but no one treated me as such. I was treated like a daughter. When my mistress bought new shoes for Asmath, I also received new shoes.

"After we ate, even though Hopi assured me he had scared off all the crocodiles, I refused to get in the water."

"I would not get in it either," said Mahlah.

"You are a wise woman, Mahlah."

Plague of Frogs

"Well now…·

"Asmath and I woke to the sound of a commotion in the hall outside our sleeping room. Hopi slept on the floor there, because he was our bodyguard. The sun had not risen, but it was dawn, so we had a little light, and of course the corner shrine where the gods lived always had a lamp burning. Hopi was jumping around shouting and cursing. We had never heard such words I must say."

"Gods lived in the corner?" This from Hoglah.

"They were idols. Some were made of stone and some of wood. The Egyptian people worshiped them."

"We slept on a raised platform about knee high. Before we knew it, we had our backs to the wall, and we were screaming and crying, beating back huge jumping frogs. Asmath's older brother and parents ran in, and Hopi, too, of course. Thousands of frogs hit our legs and piled up around our feet and heaped up on our bed and against the walls. The men carried us out, but by then the frogs had taken over the house. "There was nowhere to step without stepping on a frog. We could not hear ourselves for the croaking."

"What color were they, Nana?" Milcha asked.

"In the dark the frogs looked black, but by the light of day they were green. The ugliest color green in all creation. And they were big. If you made a circle with your hands—that's how big they were.

"Hopi and my master carried us down to the kitchen, slipping and sliding, kicking at the frogs. But there was nowhere to go. The cook had backed into a corner and stabbed at the frogs with her knife. Her helpers had fled, where I do not know. And still the frogs came, and they could jump high. Asmath's father and brother and Hopi stood us on the table and did their best to beat the frogs off Asmath and me."

"You had a table in that house?" Milcha asked.

"The vizier was very rich. They had chairs, too."

"I want a table someday," said Milcha.

"Milcha, please." Tirzah said.

"So finally, Asmath's father and brother took the table and made a barricade the frogs could not jump over. They blocked the windows and killed all the frogs in the room. You can imagine the mess that made. Then we waited. We stayed in there all day and all night and most of the next day. Then the thumping stopped, and Asaph—that is Asmath's brother—peeked out. It was over.

"Every single frog had died. We worked all that day sweeping them out and throwing them out the windows. Hopi and the other slaves shoveled the odious creatures into to a huge pile and set them afire. Now this was going on all over Egypt, and the smell of dead and burning frogs in the streets and fields was worse than the smell of the blood. My masters burned incense day and night, but it did not help. The stinking smoke hung in the air, and we smelled of it. We could not get to the bath house soon enough.

"Then Pharaoh's palace slaves spread rumors and gossip that whenever Moses and his brother, Aaron came to the palace, bad things happened. Yahweh must have protected them, or they would have been mobbed and killed."

Plague of Lice

"Well now…

"Tirzah, do you remember that time you picked up that baby bird and it was covered with lice, and the lice got all over you?"

"It was awful."

"Well, no sooner than the frogs were dead, we were all covered in lice. Every last one of us, even Asmath's mother. She was a very clean lady and bathed every day at the bath house, and she oiled our hair and hers. Lice did not exist in our house."

"But now it did!" Hoglah clapped.

"They had a house to bathe in, I suppose," said Tirzah.

"Everyone bathed in it. One for the women and one for the men. And slaves poured water and served us."

"But you were a slave," said Tirzah

"I know. As I have said, they were kind to me."

"We could hardly breathe for lice up our noses. We had to keep a cloth over our mouth and noses. They crawled into our ears. And the itching! They were under our clothes and in our beds, jumping in our food.

"The animals suffered, too. The cats froze and would not move. Their bodies were alive with lice. And rats ran from their holes, unafraid of us, crawling with lice. Cattle went mad and broke loose from their paddocks.

"One of Pharaoh's servants told it about that Moses and Aaron wanted Pharaoh to let the Hebrew people go free. The story went that if Pharaoh would let the Hebrews go, the troubles would stop. And who do you think was doing all these things?"

"Yahweh!" shouted Mahlah.

"And why was Yahweh doing it?"

"So we could go free," said Mahlah.

Plague of Insects

"Well now…

"As if the blood and the frogs and the lice were not enough, Yahweh told Moses and Aaron to send a plague of insects."

"Lice are insects." Hoglah opined.

"Yes, but these were big insects."

"I was there, and I can tell you the insects were truly terrible. I suppose Yahweh brought all the insects that lived in Egypt into a swarm, those that flew through the air and those that lived on the ground. Great swarms of biting flies blackened the sky—the big flies that get on cattle and donkeys. And wasps and hornets stung the Egyptians. And of the ground dwellers: centipedes and ants and fleas and ticks bit them.

"The swarms covered the ground, the houses, the streets, and the animals. There was no safe place. My master came up with a plan. He decided to take us to the Nile where we could get under the water. Only our heads would be above the surface, and we would cover our heads with baskets. I refused to go. I was terrified of the crocodiles, especially after seeing how many there were. So off they went, servants and slaves, too, and left me alone at the house.

"As soon as the last person left the house, the insects left the house. They flew away and crawled away, and none of them bothered me. I did not know at the time that Yahweh had set a hedge of protection around the Hebrew people. Milcha, you will like this: I went down to the kitchen and ate a fig cake.

"One of Pharaoh's servants was like a talking bird. Whatever happened at the palace was told about within a short time. It seems Pharaoh promised to let the Hebrews go, so Moses stopped the insects.

"Well, when my masters and their servants returned from the Nile, they were wet and miserable. The plan had worked only partly. Hundreds of people had the same idea; they could barely get into the water, much less under it. Asmath's eyes were swollen shut, and she was put to bed, so I sat with her and put wet cloths on her bites and held her hand. No one seemed to notice, so I did not mention my secret."

"That you ate a fig cake without permission, Nana?" asked Milcha.

"No, that I had not been stung nor bitten."

"Did Pharaoh let the people go that time?" asked Hoglah.

"No. Even though the swarms came into the palace, he was stubborn and he did not want to obey Yahweh."

Plague on the Cattle

"Well now…

"Pharaoh was a bad man, and he did not keep his word. He kept saying he would let the people go, but no matter what Yahweh did, he refused."

"If he had done the right thing, would Yahweh have stopped punishing Egypt?" asked Tirza.

"I do not think so. We learned from Moses that Yahweh hardened Pharaoh's heart. I think Yahweh wanted to punish him because he had made slaves of the Hebrews. And also because he killed the boy babies that time."

"So Yahweh was angry at Pharaoh before any of this happened?" Hoglah asked.

"I think so."

"In today's story Moses tells Pharaoh ahead of time what will happen if he does not let the people go: Yahweh will send a plague the very next day on Pharaoh's livestock, horses, donkeys, camels, herds and flocks. But the livestock belonging to the Hebrews would not die. But Pharaoh would not let the people go, so the very next day pestilence struck all Pharaoh's animals, so that many of them died."

"But Nana, the donkeys are not to blame." Mahlah started to cry. Milcha followed.

"I know, but if you take a man's cow or his donkey, it really hurts the man."

"Well, how did that hurt Pharaoh?" Tirzah demanded.

"Pharaoh owns the man and the cow and the donkey, so his property is destroyed. Do you not see? Yahweh punished Pharaoh and killed all his animals, but he spared the animals of the laborer and Israel's animals and none of them died at all. Is that not a good ending?"

Plague of Boils

"Well now...

"Everyone knew that Yahweh was telling Moses and Aaron to do these things to the Egyptian people and their animals so Pharaoh would let the Hebrews go free. But Pharaoh would not let them go. After all, who would make the bricks and who would do the work? Someone had to work in the mines and grow the crops.

"So one day Moses went to see Pharaoh, and Yahweh told Moses to take a handful of soot from a kiln and throw it into the air, and it would spread all over the land and become boils on the people and the animals. So Moses threw the soot into the air.

"There were no secrets now; the palace slaves spread the news of what was to come. Fear and dread filled the hearts of the people. That night at the vizier's house, we hung mats and cloths over the windows to keep out the soot. I watched Asmath as she knelt before the gods in her corner shrine. Many times she asked me to kneel and pray with her, but I would not. I was as afraid of those gods as I was of the crocodiles. In fact one of those gods had the body of a man and the head of a crocodile. One had the body of a woman and the head of a bird. I know now that Yahweh made me fear and hate those gods. I will tell you now, that when I left Ramses, Asmath gave me a little female god to keep. I kept it for many years but I never prayed to it."

"Can we see it, Nana?" asked Hoglah.

"No. I finally pushed her to the bottom of the latrine. Just having her in my possession caused trouble. When you get older I will tell you the whole story."

"Some of that soot found its way into the house, for two nights later, we had not been asleep very long when I woke to the sound of Asmath crying. I lighted several lamps. What a horrible sight. Asmath was covered from head to toe in huge purple boils. She was in such pain she could not lie still. At the doorway, I stepped over Hopi, who whimpered pitifully, and I ran to the kitchen to get a wet cloth. From every room I passed, I heard sorrowful moaning. The cook, on her mat, begged the gods for mercy, and her helpers writhed and groaned.

"Asaph cried in his room. Asmath's father saw my lamp and cried out, 'Rachel, come here.' I went in and saw him and my mistress covered in boils. He begged me, 'Ask your god to help us.'"

"All the next week I went from room to room trying to keep wet cloths on everyone's forehead. I cried for Asmath's family until I had no more tears. And I did ask Yahweh to heal them. I surely did.

"After a while the boils began to drain, and the people in the house began to hunger. I took some bread and soaked it in soft cheese and fed the family, Hopi, the cook, and the slaves. They were still in the bed when the next plague arrived, so they did not know much about it. But I will say, the boils left horrible scars, and Asmath lost her beauty forever. I did not know it then, but Asmath's father began to make plans to sell me at the slave auction. I believe he hated me for what Yahweh had done. My God had condemned the vizier's daughter to a lonely existence, for she would probably never marry, and he had spared me, a Hebrew slave."

Plague of Hail

"Well now…

"While Asmath and her family and their slaves lay on their beds recovering from the boils, word spread across all Egypt that a terrible thing was about to happen. But this time things were a little different. Moses and Aaron warned Pharaoh, and word spread from town to town: hail and fire from heaven would be coming. Any person or animal left outside would surely die.

"Now pharaoh's servants and officials had begun to believe in the power of Yahweh, and they heard what Moses and Aaron said. They begged Pharaoh to let the Hebrew people go. But he hardened his heart and would not listen to anyone: neither his magicians, nor his priests, nor his trusted physicians.

"The Egyptians who believed in Moses' warning brought all the livestock they could into caves and under shelters and into their homes. Some only had room for their best ewes, their best oxen and their best donkeys.

"Those who did not believe stayed outside with their animals and continued to plow their fields. They laughed at the people who scurried inside, those who crowded all their animals into their houses.

"Before long it began to thunder—the loudest thunder I had ever heard—cracking and rumbling endlessly. I put my hands over my ears and ran to the window. dark clouds, black, black, came up from the west, and bolts of fire as wide as my finger began to rain down on the earth. I could smell the fire in the air, like burning hair. Then it began to hail—the worst hail anyone had ever seen—chunks of ice the size of a man's head. And it happened so quickly, no one could get inside before the fire and hail began to fall. The fields with ripe crops were destroyed, and the trees were shattered. Every living thing that was not under shelter died—the farmers, the shepherds and all the livestock. I watched as the hail crashed down on my master's garden and the lattice and vines that used to shelter Asmath, Hopi, and me. All torn and broken and destroyed. But it did not hail on Goshen where the Hebrews lived. No Hebrew nor his animals was killed."

"Why were they not killed?" asked Mahlah.

"Because Yahweh protected them." said Hoglah. "Even I know that."

"But why?" Mahlah insisted.

"Because Yahweh promised Abraham many years ago that the Hebrews would be his chosen people forever. We are those people. You are those people. Did Grandpapa and I not teach you this?"

"So Yahweh *chose* not to hurt them," said Hoglah.

"That is right."

"Then why are we in this desert?" asked Hoglah. "I do not feel *chosen*."

"After Yahweh rescued us, we did not trust him. So we are being punished. But soon the time of punishment will be over."

"And we will go to the land of milking honey," said Mahlah.

Plague of Locusts

"Well now…

"The hail had beaten down the trees, and all the crops but a few sprigs and twigs remained and began to straighten up and sprout a little. The people who were alive turned out their animals. They buried all the people who had been killed by the hail. They piled up the dead animals and burned them. Oh the smoke was terrible. The whole land was covered in smoke from the burning piles of animals.

"Now the people who had gone inside believed in the power of Yahweh which is different from trusting in him. They feared Yahweh just as they feared their own gods, who we know were idols, because they made them out of wood or clay and stood them up in the corner. Can you imagine believing in a god you could stand in the corner?

"Well, once again Pharaoh refused to let us go, and he drove Moses and Aaron out of the palace. Pharaoh's servants knew Yahweh would not be happy about this, so they said to Pharaoh, 'Can you not see that Egypt is destroyed?' Word spread of their bravery before Pharaoh.

"Now Asmath lay on our bed. I had to sleep on the floor because she could not bear to be touched. It is true, I was a slave and she was my mistress, but she was my beautiful friend and my sister, and I could hardly make myself look at her. First the boils turned to black scabs, then deep red scars. She was as ruined as the hail-torn vines that grew over our balcony. It took Hopi three days to clean up the broken lattice. Just as the land bore the scars of the hail, so all the Egyptians bore the scars of the boils.

"Then one day my mistress, Asmath's mother said to me, 'Rachel, the wasps did not sting you nor did the boils touch you. Your God is very strong. We will make a statue of him and place it in Asmath's shrine so she can pray to him.' How could I tell them that Yahweh has no image, that Yahweh had forbidden the people to make an image of him?

"As we were speaking, a hard wind from the east began to blow through the house. The room became dim and we heard a roaring, buzzing sound so loud we could not hear ourselves. We ran to the window and saw clouds and clouds of locusts in the sky, dipping and churning in a black mass so fearful we hid under our bed covers. We expected them to be all over us like the lice and stinging insects.

"But Yahweh had a different plan. He allowed the locusts to eat only the plants that had not been destroyed by the hail. After that not one green sprig was left in the whole land of Egypt, but the land of Goshen had been spared. Then Yahweh sent a strong wind from the west and blew away the locusts.

"How do I know all this? Asmath's father and brother walked over the land in all directions to see what damage had been done. Not one leaf had been harmed in Goshen.

"From then on I began to feel my master's hatred for me and Yahweh. But at the time I still did not know he planned to send me to the auction block."

Plague of Darkness

"Well now…

"Has it ever been so dark you could feel the darkness? Of course not. We have the pillar of fire to give us light at night. Yahweh provides manna for bread, water when we need it, and his pillar for light. You have never been outside of his light.

"Well, after Yahweh blew away the locusts on the west wind, Moses did not go see Pharaoh. The servants could not spread the word about things to come. Yahweh did what he did and that was that. Everyone was taken by surprise."

"What did he do, Nana? It was awful was it not?" asked Tirza.

"I am going to tell you. And yes, it was awful."

"Asmath and I woke up on our bed and it was so dark we thought it must still be night. The lamps had all gone out, even the shrine lamps, and the darkness was so thick, we could feel it, as if a blanket had been thrown over us. We were so afraid, we started crying out for her mother and father. Hopi woke up, and he was frightened too. He kept saying, 'What is happening? What is happening?'"

"Did they come quick?" asked Milcha.

"They came as fast as they could."

"Their lamps had gone out, too. Soon we heard their hands slapping the walls coming to the sound of our voices. Then Asaph felt along the walls and found his way to our room. Everyone gathered on our bed, including Hopi. Now he was a very large man so he had to squeeze on, but no one forbade him. Asmath's father felt around until he found the oil lamps, but he could not get them to light. We could hear the cook and her helpers calling from the kitchen, helloooo. Helloooo.

"There was no moon and no stars. It was as dark outside as it was inside. We could only find the window and the door by feeling. Even Pharaoh's palace was dark, and we could always see lights from there. The Nile could not be seen, for no moon or starlight reflected on it. In all the land there was not a glimmer of light. We were like blind people, and still, that horrible feeling that a blanket had been thrown over us.

"At first the family prayed quite loudly to their gods. When that did not work, Asmath's mother began to lament and say that we were all dead. She claimed Anubis, god of the dead, had come in the night and ferried us off to the underworld, a place where Osiris, king of the dead, ruled. She said we had crossed over to the underworld, a scary place which dead people must pass through on their journey to their final destination. For five years I had lived in a home where hundreds of gods ruled the people. So for a while it all seemed quite reasonable; maybe they had taken me with them.

"Then a little scrap of me began to think with reason. I knew the god, Sothis, did not make the Nile flood. I knew the god, Ra, did not make the sun come up, and I knew the goddess Nut did not bring on the night. From my early childhood, I had been taught about Yahweh, the God who created everything that exists. So I remembered Yahweh. Even Asmath's father admitted the God of the Hebrews had spared the Hebrew people from the other plagues. Had he not spared me from the insects and the boils? Surely he would not send me to the underworld where false gods live, would he?

"So I began to pray to Yahweh and it came into my mind what to say to my family. I told them that all the other plagues had a beginning and an end. This plague would have an end also. Then Asmath said, 'Is there an end to these scars on my face?' And for that I had no answer. They refused to be comforted.

"We could not move freely about the house. We had only the walls to guide us. Asmath's mother convinced the family that we were dead. They all began to mourn and cry. Then she began to scream. I found Hopi's arm in the darkness and pulled him into motion. Together we felt along the walls and fled down the stairs to the kitchen. We sat on the floor with our backs to the wall near the cook and her helpers. He put his arm around me, whether to comfort himself or me, I do not know.

"We did not know how many days passed. I later learned the darkness lasted three days. Hopi and I were sitting in the kitchen when the door and the window began to show light. The moon came out as if it had been behind a cloud and the stars—how beautiful they were. We walked out into the garden. All the plants were dead from the hail and the locusts, but the smothering cloak of darkness had lifted. The sun rose the next morning. Only then did we realize we had neither felt a breeze nor heard a bird all that time.

"I went up the stairs to see my family. My mistress had pulled out most of her hair. Clumps of black hair lay about the room. I thought she must have gone mad, but no, she was so glad not to be in the underworld, she wrapped a veil around her head and sat on the balcony with her face turned up to the sun. She spoke to me with her eyes closed, basking in the warmth. 'You were right, Rachel. We should have listened to you.' She asked Asmath to bring her jewelry box and the pouch with the mother of pearl disks. I left my mistresses—the young and the old—there on the porch and went back to the kitchen. On the day when Enoch came to get me, Asmath gave me the pouch. Grandpapa and I used the pearls and the gold objects it contained to buy all the things we needed."

Passover Plague

"Well now…

"This story is about the last plague Yahweh set upon the people of Egypt. This first part I did not learn about until later. Long ago I had twin brothers named Perez and Hazor. You have heard us speak of them—how beautiful they were and how joyful they were. When they were boys, they were sent to Pharaoh's palace and stood guard at the very door where Pharaoh sat upon his throne. So they heard everything that went on. They heard when Pharaoh's servants begged him to let the people go, and they witnessed the meetings between Moses and Pharaoh. They heard every word.

"After the plague of darkness, Moses went to the palace. This time Pharaoh said, 'Get away from me! Beware, do not see my face again, for in the day you see my face, you shall surely die!' And Moses answered Pharaoh and said, 'You are right; I shall never see your face again!'

"Then Moses told Pharaoh, on that very night all the first-born in the land of Egypt would die at the hand of Yahweh—from Pharaoh's first-born son, to the first-born of the slave, to the first-born of the livestock. Then Moses left the palace in hot anger.

"All this was told to me by my brothers who heard it all. That night Perez and Hazor slipped away from the palace and went to the land of Goshen. While they were escaping, Enoch was making his way to the vizier's house in the city of Ramses to rescue me—and just in time, too. That was the day the vizier was going to take me to the market. He was going to sell me! We all met in Goshen at the home where we were all born. I met Phinehas that day and married your Grandpapa that night. And Grandpapa found the first puppy named Morsel. There have been many black Morsels since.

"Nana, I hate that name." said Mahlah.

"Do you know what a morsel is? It's a tiny bite. A hawk was about to eat the puppy when Grandpapa found it lying on his shoe. He gave me the puppy that night. We kept him a long time."

"That night is called the first Passover for a very good reason. Moses told all the Hebrews to paint their door posts with lamb's blood as a sign Hebrews lived there. Just as Yahweh did not send the other plagues to the Hebrews, he did not want any of us to die when he set about to slay the first-borns in Egypt. So we ate a special meal called the Passover meal, and we shut ourselves in the house. When Yahweh saw the blood on the post, he *passed over* our house and all the houses of all the Hebrews.

"When we get to the Promised Land, every year on that night, we will eat a Passover meal to honor Yahweh for this blessing."

"Why do they call it the land of milking honey?" asked Mahlah.

"Oh, Joseph's bones!" said Hoglah.

"Because it is a very rich land. This wilderness will be behind us. We will have grass to feed the goats, and they will make lots of rich milk and there will be honey to eat."

"But when will we get there?" asked Milcha.

"We will get there in Yahweh's perfect time."

Ma'at Idol, Goddess of Peace &
Justice

Found 1953, near Kadesh-Barnea
(present day Nitzanei, Sinai –
western Negev desert, Israel)

Egyptian   Dynasty XVIII   c.1400 BC

Imperial Jade   W.2.5 cm x H.7.6 cm

(On permanent loan from the

Barmore Collection, San Diego, CA)